DIANNE CHRISTNER

Something NEW

THE PLAIN CITY BRIDESMAIDS

BOOK 2

BARBOUR PUBLISHING

DEDICATION

To Jim, my own Plain City sweetheart.
I hope this story honors your fond memories
of growing up on a farm.

PROLOGUE

Ten-year-old Lillian Mae Landis inched her toes to the edge of the tiny square platform fifty feet above the ground. She ran clammy hands down her glittery red costume and poised them. Her heart rose to her throat as she watched the trapeze swing through the air toward her. She counted one, two, three and then leaped forward.

Lil's stomach somersaulted, and she exulted when her hands clasped the swinging bar with perfect timing. The crowd gasped. Her body jerked, but she held fast and tightened her tummy and leg muscles as she brought her body into perfect form. The air rushed across her face. The music came to a crescendo. Every eye was riveted on her performance.

A second trapeze carrying the teenager Rollo—a handsome boy with flowing blond hair—made its descent. Rollo's knees gripped his trapeze bar. Keeping silent count, Lil let loose of her bar at just the correct moment, and Rollo's sure, strong hands caught her arms. The crowd roared in delight. She basked in their admiration.

"Ouch! Stop it!"

Lil blinked, torn from her fantasy. She pulled her face from the open van's window and looked sideways to where her cousin Jake Byler was pulling Katy Yoder's black ponytail. Lil tucked one foot under her homemade culottes and twisted so she could look him square in the eyes.

"What was your favorite part of the circus?" she asked. Their families had attended the Ringling Brothers and Barnum and Bailey Circus together when it had come to Columbus, Ohio, earlier that month.

"The tigers." Jake growled in her friend Katy's ear then sank back in his seat and started tussling with his buddy Chad Penner.

Lil rolled her gaze heavenward. Forgetting about Jake, she told Katy, "I liked the trapeze artists." She had already described the circus to her two best friends—Katy Yoder and Megan Weaver—repeatedly, but she didn't think they really understood how magical that experience had been for a girl whose normal day consisted of gathering brown eggs and snapping green beans. Lil lived on a farm.

Katy bit the inside of her cheek thoughtfully, and Lil let the conversation drop.

The van veered off the smooth interstate onto a rural road and rattled over a cattle guard. Lil could hardly contain her excitement. At last she was getting a break from her farm chores, a chance to have some real fun. "I heard Camp Victoria has a huge swing that goes right out over the river."

Katy's eyes widened. "Where'd you hear that? You think they'll make us do it?"

"It's true." Megan turned around, fingering a long, blond braid. "But I don't think they'll make us do it."

"I'll do it!" Lil replied.

"I hope you don't try any of those circus tricks," Katy replied, her dark eyes fretful.

"Look. There's the camp." Megan pointed ahead. Through the window, they saw a green-lettered sign on a rectangular log building.

Sure enough, the van turned into a gravel parking lot. As soon as the door slid open, the children piled out of the vehicle. Stretching, Lil quickly scanned the campsite. She didn't see any swings. She heard her cousin Jake's snickers, however, and glanced over because he was usually in the middle of any fun activity. But he and Chad Penner were only staring at some girls about her age. Instantly, she understood why.

Those girls wore shorts and brightly colored T-shirts. Their hair was cut, too. The other girls were observing their group's arrival. Lil felt a pang of envy, as she so often did, wishing she hadn't been born on a hog farm, of all things. Her family attended the Big Darby Conservative Mennonite Church in Plain City, Ohio. Now she wished she'd been born in a different Mennonite church like those girls so she didn't have to wear ugly, homemade culottes. She muttered to her friends, "I wish my mom let me wear shorts."

"I hope they're nice," Katy replied, ignoring Lil's comment and eyeing the girls in shorts.

As if a mind reader, one of the girls waved.

Lil grabbed Megan's arm. "Let's go." Heart skipping, she released Megan's arm and waved back.

A girl with brown bobbed hair and blue eyes said, "Hi, I'm Lisa."

Lil stared at the other girl in amazement. "I never met another Lil before."

Lisa smiled. "I think you misunderstood. It's Lisa."

"Oh, sorry."

"Hey, you're in our cabin. I saw your name. Come on. We'll show you where it is."

The girls got acquainted as they strolled down a freshly graded dirt road edged with white daisies. It led to a row of brown cabins with blue roofs. All the while, Lil kept sneaking peeks at Lisa's green shorts and suntanned legs, wondering how such a freedom would feel.

"This is it," Lisa announced, skipping up the steps to the cabin. Lil almost stumbled when she noticed Lisa's painted toenails glimmering through her sandals. The girl didn't know how lucky she was to have been born in a more lenient Mennonite family. Lil studied the names posted on the door of Cabin Colorado, relieved to see that she and Katy and Megan would all be bunking together. Inside the cabin, a friendly blond woman greeted them.

"I'm Mary, your counselor. Our group is complete now. Go ahead and choose a bed. Soon the tractor will come around with your bags. We're going to do an icebreaker in about a half hour, so stick close by."

Katy rushed to claim a vacant bed, and Megan took its top bunk. Lil asked Lisa where her bed was. She took the top bunk over Lisa's bed.

"I wish the tractor would lose my bag," Lil admitted to her new friend.

"Why?" Lisa asked with surprise.

"'Cause my clothes are ugly. I love your shorts."

"You can wear them if you want. I've got more, and my bag's right here." Clearly Lisa understood Lil's situation.

Pleasure shot through Lil, and her hand covered her heart. "Are you serious? You'd let me?"

"Sure. It's no big deal." Lisa unzipped her bag and riffled through, sizing up her new friend. "Actually, these might fit you better. Want to try them? Here's a tee that matches."

Lil didn't even get offended that Lisa had noticed she was a bit chubbier. She was out of her culottes in a flash, squeezing herself into the borrowed shorts. Red! Even better. And the T-shirt had ruffled feminine edging. She wasn't allowed to wear T-shirts at home because Conservative girls could not dress like men. She flung her culottes up onto her bunk, and they hung down over the edge like an ugly navy flag that waved "here's plain old Lil's bunk." She wished she could toss them on the campfire. Looking away, she embraced Lisa. "Thanks so much!" Then she rushed over to Katy and Megan's bunks.

Katy's naturally sulky lips parted. "Lillian Mae!" she scolded.

But Lil ignored her rebuke just like she always did and gracefully raised her arms—circus performer style—twirling to give them the 360-degree view.

Lil didn't miss that Megan placed a calming hand on Katy's shoulder and whispered something in her ear. Whatever it was, Katy continued to narrow her eyes in disapproval.

"Well I like them. Wish there was a mirror in here," Lil replied, flouncing away.

~

Lil propped an elbow on her bare knee, making sure she sat in a sunny patch so that she could tan her legs like Lisa's. She could tell that Katy was still mad at her, but she wasn't going to allow her friend to ruin her week of fun and freedom. She'd worry later about any consequences there might be when she got home. Megan was always good at getting her out of scrapes and patching up any spats between her and Katy. With that in mind she insisted, "I say, Three Bean Salad."

Their counselor had divided them into groups of three, and they were supposed to come up with a name for their group. She and Katy had been arguing about whether or not to call themselves "Three Bean Salad" which had been Lil's choice. The argument was really a battle of wills, and all three girls knew it. When Mary blew her pink whistle, Lil knew she'd won. She ran over to Katy, who was lounging under a tree, staring at a squirrel on a high branch with glistening leaves. She touched her friend's shoulder. "I'll let you choose the next time. I promise."

Megan intervened softly, "You can be the green bean, if you want, Katy."

"That's okay," Katy replied. "I'll be the dumb kidney bean."

Lil did a little shimmy with her shoulders and sing-songed, "Garban-zo, Gar-ban-zo," for the bean she had picked for herself. Soon she had Katy grinning. Camp was great, way better than shucking corn.

On the last night of camp, the three friends sat mesmerized by the campfire. Lil brushed her hands down her borrowed jeans. She was lucky to have such good friends. She knew they would never tattle on her, even if they didn't approve of her wearing shorts and jeans all week. Although Katy and Megan would always be her best friends, she had enjoyed her time with Lisa, too.

Not only that, but their counselor, Mary, had shown Lil some exercises she could continue to do when she got home. She envied Mary's flat tummy, but it was hard to stay slim when Lil's mom was such a great cook. They came from a family of wonderful cooks, and Lil enjoyed cooking, too. She already knew how to make piecrusts, and she also made a tasty meatloaf.

The young man who played guitar and led the singing each evening put away his instrument and dismissed the group to return to their cabins. Seated on a log next to Megan and Katy, Lil looped her arm through Megan's and watched the rest of the group disassemble. "Mary's still standing over there, talking. Let's stay here until she's finished."

"I can't believe tomorrow's our last day," Megan bemoaned.

Lil wasn't ready to go home, don her dark skirts, and get back to chores. She glanced desperately at the sparking campfire. "I never want this to end. It was the best week of my life. And that swing over the lake was the scariest thing I ever did."

"Better than the circus?" Katy asked.

"Just as good." Lil clenched her fists. "Let's make a vow tonight that when we're Mary's age, we'll all move in together. It'll be like camp. Only forever."

Katy furrowed her brow. "We'll probably get married."

"Just until we marry. And we'll be each other's bridesmaids, too! Oh, swear it!"

Katy frowned. "You know Mennonites don't swear or take oaths."

Lil dropped her head in her hands and stared at her jeans, feeling desperate enough to cry.

Megan, who was seated on the log between them, reached out and clasped each of their hands. "The Bible says where two or three agree on something, God honors it. We can agree, but we must never break a promise."

Lil felt rising hope. She leaned forward and sent Katy her most earnest gaze.

Katy bit her lip, then nodded. "Oh all right. I promise. And I already know who I'm going to marry. Jake Byler."

"Ew! Yuck!" Lil made a face because it was gross to think that Katy would want to marry her cousin. But from that day forth, Lil did everything in her power to make sure that their campfire dreams came true. Someday she would break free from her stifling, navy-blue chains. Someday she would own her own pink fingernail polish. She would move in with her two best friends. They would be each other's bridesmaids, and when she married, she would shine in a beautiful lacy gown.

CHAPTER 1

"**D**on't tell your mother."

Lil clutched her father's dirty breakfast plate and glanced down the hall to make sure Rose Landis was, indeed, still asleep. But then, why wouldn't she be? Her depression kept her abed most mornings.

"Oh Dad. Things will get better. They always do." She'd been hanging on to that hope for weeks now, ever since her own desires had been temporarily deferred.

Although Mom had been suffering from depression for months, she had temporarily rallied for Katy and Jake's wedding because Lil had asked her to help with Katy's wedding cake. Lil had even gotten Mom to take that cake decorating class with her, but the day after the wedding, Mom fell to her bed in exhaustion, and afterward, she reverted to her earlier depressed state, even more tired than before.

"This didn't happen overnight, girl." Dad broke into her thoughts. "And it's not getting any better. Only getting worse." He placed his elbows on the newly cleared table and clasped his unshaven face between his work-worn hands. "It wouldn't be so bad if it was just me, but the farm is the life of this family. All your brothers depend upon it for the livelihood of their families, too."

Lil had inherited her dad's grit, which was why it was unusual for him to cave in to despair. He'd always been the hundred-year-old girder truss that held the Landis family together. But he should have given his sons more leadership. They were grown men, and one old truss didn't have to hold an entire barn together by itself when other trusses were ready to share the load.

"You shouldn't shoulder this alone. You need to share your burden with the boys. Maybe one of them even has an idea."

The Landis men had farmed for generations. Willis Landis owned 140 acres, inherited from his father. The farm had two hog barns, and most of the acreage was used for corn and soybeans because the government made those crops more profitable and they fed the hogs.

Lil had detested those hogs since she was old enough to know that raising them carried a stigma, sometimes even among other farmers. Oh she didn't hate the animals themselves, just the chore of raising them. As a child, she'd even had a pet or two. Hogs were smart animals, and the piglets were cute in their fat-bellied, flat-snouted way, each with their individual personalities, but she would rather have been raised anywhere other than on a hog farm. Katy's dad had a respectable woodworking shop. Jake—Katy's husband and Lil's favorite cousin— was in construction. Megan's dad worked at an automotive shop and even restored Chevy Novas for extra income. But of all the possible scenarios, Lil had been born to a family who raised smelly, squealing hogs.

Picking up the aqua-colored canning jar that served as the centerpiece for the kitchen table, she unscrewed its silver lid and removed the candle. From habit, she swirled a green-checkered dish towel around the inside of the jar. Holding the candle in the palm of one hand, she stared at her dad; her heart broke over his humble and disappointing lot in life. Such a hard worker and doing the only job he'd ever known. She'd never seen him so worn as he had been this past year. The continual struggle against the raw elements of nature had sapped his strength. The recent stress of finances and Mom's depression had shaken his morale.

Lil replaced the candle and put the jar back in its distinctive place, her hands dusting the tea towel over a set of green Depression glass salt and pepper shakers. Just when Lil had been so close to fulfilling her own dreams, everything had been snatched away from her.

Last winter, she'd finally moved into the Millers' doddy house with Katy Yoder. The freedom to chase after her own dreams had long been coveted, along with the fun adventure of rooming with her closest friends. So when the house originally designed for a family's grandparents became available, the three friends had jumped at the chance to rent it. Megan Weaver had been set to join them in the fall after her mission trip. Once Megan helped pay the rent, Lil would have been able to start buying the other things she dreamed about, too, like a new car to replace the brown tin can she drove and referred to as Jezebel.

Mechanically, Lil twisted the tea towel and untwisted it again, considering how the three friends had taken such delight in renovating the doddy house with modern conveniences. Once Lil had graduated from culinary school and gotten her first restaurant job, everything had fallen into place. That is, until Mom had become depressed, and Dad had asked Lil to move back home and help take care of her.

Not knowing anything about depression, Lil thought the illness would only last for a couple of days or weeks at the most. But once she came home, she'd gotten stuck in a sinking routine, trying to keep up with all the chores her mom had once performed. There was cooking and cleaning and laundry and some farm chores, too. But one thing she refused to do was the garden.

Under those circumstances, once Katy and Jake had married, they took over the doddy house. The only fragment of Lil's dream that remained intact was her restaurant job. Low paying and rather dead-end, it didn't provide the career opportunity of moving up to head chef position, but it was still a respite from the farm and her family's troubles. Not only did the farm finances affect her dad and brothers, but this grave problem could be the final blow to her mother's emotional state and affect Lil's future, too.

Replacing the dish towel on a homemade wooden towel bar inside the pine cabinet beneath the sink, Lil quickly turned back to face Dad.

"Maybe you need to modernize."

He stared at her and tugged one of his large ears—which pitched up his hat's straw brim like soil to toadstools. "That's what Matt always says."

Lil's middle brother was the one most likely to challenge Dad. Matt had Lil's personality and was open to modern ways, changes that might keep them out of bankruptcy. Like her, he had often tested the church elders, too. "I know it's hard for you, but couldn't you ask Matt about some of his ideas? If all the other farms are utilizing new methods, well. . ." She shrugged.

Dad abruptly rose. "Got chores to do. Thanks for breakfast." He started toward the door and snatched his truck keys off the yellow peg shelf that had served the family for as long as Lil could recall. "So you won't tell your mom?"

With a heavy sigh, Lil glanced regrettably down the hall again. "No. I won't tell." She looked back toward the yellow shelf visible through the doorway that separated the kitchen from the mudroom. It had been there ever since she could remember. Five feet in width, it was firmly secured to the wall studs to bear the family's offerings. Its row of sturdy six-inch pegs provided a stopping off place for the family's odds and ends, mostly hats and coats and items of clothing the boys used to bring home for their mom to mend.

A basket containing gloves and garden tools perched in readiness for her mom's frequent trips to the garden. Of late, the basket had been neglected. Beside it was a folded set of clean overalls. The shelf harbored items both entering and departing the house. Beneath it was a matching bench where family members sat when tugging on their boots. Things on the farm didn't change much, and Lil had always hungered for change. She only hoped it wouldn't be change for the worse.

—⟲—

Lil replaced the gas nozzle into its receptacle and jerked open her car door, then lifted it so that it would latch. She was going to have to get those door hinges checked before the whole door fell off. She locked it for good measure and reprimanded herself for forgetting that Jezebel needed gas. Now she was going to be late to work again. She grabbed for the seat belt before she'd even slid onto the vinyl seat cover that protected her skirt from bare springs and stuffing, and was soon pulling back into traffic.

Nearing the four-o'clock rush hour, the traffic moved slower than she would have liked, especially when she needed to make up the ten minutes she'd lost at the gas station. But she came alive to the hustle and bustle of the Columbus streets that were so different than the rural Plain City roads.

Being a few minutes late wouldn't have been such a big deal if she weren't already on the manager's bad list. He'd had to rearrange the restaurant's work schedule several times lately to accommodate Lil's personal needs, which revolved around her mom's care. Doctor appointments and Mom's neglected household chores all bubbled together like a boiling pot that Lil barely managed to keep from overflowing. A smart cook either removed such a pot from the fire or turned down the heat, but she could do neither.

Yes, she was overworked, but she didn't want to let her job at Riccardo's slide; it was her door of escape. Sure, she wasn't using all her culinary skills, but at least she was working in her area of expertise and building a résumé. She shuddered to think how her dad would react to her use of *résumé*—such a worldly word. He would rebuke her for striving to become a famous chef. He thought her ambitions were foolish and unladylike. He thought she should be pursuing a life that included marriage, children, and homemaking. It wasn't that she didn't want those things, but she wasn't ready to settle down without pursuing her dream first.

At last Lil saw the Riccardo's sign and whipped Jezebel into the parking lot. She pulled next to head chef Beppe's expensive SUV then realized she was far too close. If he came out to the parking lot and saw her car, he would yell at her again because he claimed somebody was repeatedly dinging his car door. Quickly putting Jezebel in REVERSE, Lil backed up to adjust her car's alignment.

But with that action, her car unexpectedly jerked. Simultaneously, a loud crashing sound filled her ears. With it came the awful realization that she'd backed into another vehicle. She yanked her gearshift into PARK, finagled her car door open, and jumped out, not bothering to turn off the ignition of her sputtering engine.

"Move your car forward. I can't open my door," a curt male voice demanded.

One look at the shiny silver Lexus caused her heart to sink. Quickly, she hopped back inside Jezebel and pulled back into the parking spot, still remaining too close to the chef's car. She got out again, so flustered that her car door banged hard into Beppe's SUV.

"Do you always go around destroying cars?" Feeling the rise of indignation, she jostled her door shut and turned. Her lips tensed with an angry retort. The derogatory question had been asked by a strikingly handsome man who now stood glaring at her, waiting for an explanation.

"Of course not!" Unless she had been the one putting dings in Beppe's car. Her mind had been preoccupied lately with personal problems. Was she the one? She'd been so frustrated lately with her rickety door. For the first time, she entertained the possibility that she might be the culprit dinging Beppe's car door. Her voice carried her growing dismay. "At least not until my car door broke."

The blond stranger eyed her clunker, and pity softened his glittering brown eyes. Lil despised pity. Her pride always raised its hackles at any pity or scorn directed her way.

"Do you have insurance?"

"Yes. Just a minute." She opened her sagging car door again to get her insurance card out of the glove box, and his hand shot out and caught the edge of the door so it didn't bang against the chef's SUV again.

Drowning in embarrassment, she scooted across the vinyl seat cover and retrieved the card. When she moved back, he still hovered outside, holding the top edge of her car door. Eyeing his shirt, she thought, *He certainly is a tall one.* The way he towered over her and the manner in which he protected Beppe's car while assuming the worst of her, provoked her to fulfill his expectations with a shove of her door. It gouged into his body, and she heard his surprised grunt.

"Excuse me," she said, holding back a smile and easing out.

His gaze narrowed onto the card she waved. "I'll go get a pen," he said warily, starting toward his car.

She fumbled inside her purse. "No wait. I have one." She saw him stare at his creased car door with droopy shoulders. *At least his door has two working hinges.* She sighed. If she had a nice car like his, she'd be feeling pretty discouraged about now, too. Her fingers still groping every cranny of her purse, searching for that pen, she muttered beneath her breath, "Too bad he's such a cute guy."

"Too bad she's such a beauty."

She jerked her gaze over at him, wondering if she'd spoken her thoughts aloud. Was he referring to her or his car?

Whichever, his expression had softened, making him even more appealing. "You didn't get hurt, did you?"

"No. You?"

She watched him shake his head then glance back at his creased car door. With disappointment, she figured he must have been referring to his car.

She shoved the pen and paper at him. "You can use the roof of my car to write if you want."

Protective as he was about cars, he must have agreed that another scratch on her clunker wouldn't matter because he took her up on her offer.

"Another year or so, and I'll be driving a beauty like yours," she remarked.

He ran his gaze over her. "You work here?"

"Yes. You eat here?"

Handing back her insurance information, he gave her his first genuine smile. "This was going to be my first time."

She stared at the tiny dimples on either side of his mouth. "You'd better be nice to me if you're going to order pasta."

Surprise lit his brown eyes. "I ordered takeout. It's probably in there getting cold. You're a cook?"

"Line cook, soon to be head chef."

He chuckled. "I like that."

"Look, mister." Not having his name, she continued. "The least I can do is get you a free meal."

"Fletch Stauffer." He held out his hand to shake.

Something familiar tickled Lil's brain, but when she placed her hand in his palm, the pleasant firmness pushed the murky thought away.

He released her hand. "Here's my boss's insurance card. Better write down his information, too."

She pulled a face, about to ask him if he thought Jezebel really needed fixing, when she caught the *boss* part. She stared at the card, suddenly understanding his dismay.

"It's my boss's car," he explained unnecessarily.

With a penitent nod, she realized she wasn't getting Fletch Stauffer's personal information at all. She'd never have the nerve to call him anyway. And Jezebel certainly didn't need a new bumper. Today's scratch was just another wrinkle. Trying to cover up Jezebel's age with some shiny new chrome would be about as foolish as the bright red lipstick some elderly outsiders wore into the restaurant. In Lil's opinion, it would only make the car appear more ridiculous.

As if their minds were running along similar tracks, he said, "Let me add my phone number." He shrugged. "Just in case something comes up."

When she read his information, it finally hit her. "The name Stauffer sounds familiar. You're not a Mennonite, are you?"

His shoulders relaxed. "I am. I was wondering. Are you, too?"

She felt a moment of embarrassment that he must have noticed her plain clothing. "Yeah, I attend the Big Darby Conservative Church." She lowered her gaze and was surprised to see that he wore red tennis shoes. Nope. Nothing conservative about him.

"No kidding. Small worl—parking lot."

She laughed. "Exactly. Too small. If they just made these spaces a little wider, none of this would have happened." But she couldn't deny the pleasure she was feeling at his expense. She hoped his boss wasn't as ill-tempered as Beppe. "Where do you go to church?"

"Crossroads Mennonite."

Just as she had earlier surmised, he was an Ohio Conference Mennonite. Envy and disappointment rushed over her. It seemed the good things were always just out of her reach. She longed to attend a church with fewer restrictions on things like television and more modern clothing, but she didn't want to leave her family and friends or feel condemned by them.

Another car honked, and Fletcher looked over his shoulder. "Guess I better move my boss's car before somebody else hits it."

"Sure," she said, slapping at a pesky mosquito.

When she looked up, Fletch had already turned away. Maybe she'd get a chance to talk to him inside. *Inside*, where she should have been a half an hour earlier, or more. Beppe was going to be mad. Quickly she started toward Riccardo's, breaking into a run.

CHAPTER 2

You're late," Beppe, Lil's Italian boss, snapped, just as she'd known he would. Once again she'd managed to light his short fuse, and she wasn't sure how far his patience with her would last before he showed her the exit sign.

"I'm so sorry. I had an accident. . .with Jezebel. . .in the parking lot."

Beppe's eyes flared, and his voice barked, "You didn't hit my car did you?"

"No. Of course not." Well she hadn't had the accident with his car. She really needed to start avoiding his car altogether. But his choice spot was close to the restaurant, and none of the other employees had the nerve to park next to him so that spot was usually vacant. Since she was usually running late, it drew her like a moth to flame.

"That car of yours is an annoyance. Maybe you'll get a new one now?" His expression was hopeful.

"Didn't hurt Jezebel. But the car I hit, it was a Lexus."

Beppe cringed as if his own car had taken the blow.

Lil explained, "And it was the driver's first time at Riccardo's. Do you think we could give him a free meal?"

Beppe suddenly turned all business. "You paying?"

"If I could afford that, I wouldn't be driving Jezebel, now would I?" she quipped.

"How many are in his party?"

"I don't know. He has a take-out order."

"Yes. You hand deliver the bill, tell him it's covered, and be sure to smooth things over. And for the love of good food, be more careful."

Lil glanced anxiously toward the take-out counter but couldn't see Fletch. She needed to catch him before he paid. "Okay. Thanks. Sorry I was late."

"Again."

She cringed. Beppe was chalking up another offense for her on his mental blackboard.

"You're wearing my patience, Lil. You really are. Now go to your station."

"Yes, sir. Just as soon as I hand deliver that bill." Hurrying away from him before he changed his mind, past the stations to the hall, she rushed to the take-out counter, where Fletch was already thumbing through his billfold. She exchanged a few words with the clerk, scratched paid on his check, and slid it across the counter to him.

"I took care of your check."

He accepted the receipt and stuffed it in his billfold, which he jammed into his jeans pocket. His smile flashed more than appreciation; it possessed all the elements that could make Lil's toes curl inside her black oxfords.

"Thanks, Lily."

"I thought you should have my number, too, so I put it on the back of the bill."

"That's considerate."

Lil felt her face heat. "No problem. Well let me know if. . .you know. . .you need anything. For your boss's car, I mean."

"I will." Concern briefly clouded the sparkle in his toe-curling gaze, and she figured he was thinking about his boss's reaction, but honestly, she couldn't afford to offer to pay his deductible. She was saving up her meager paychecks to move back into the doddy house as soon as her mom got better.

"It was the least I could do. Well, better get back to my station. Sorry about everything."

Fletch motioned as if he was tipping the bill of an invisible hat, and Lil turned away while her feet could still carry her.

"It wasn't all bad."

She halted at the soft statement. Turned. When their gazes met, she recognized the look of male appreciation. "Thanks." She paused momentarily, but when he didn't say anything more, she smiled and clambered to the kitchen. Her heart peddled faster than her little nephew Scott on his new John Deere tractor trike. Would Fletch give her a call? How long had it been since a guy had shown interest in her?

The idea lingered. Even after a half hour bent over a steaming black pot, Lil was still dreaming about Fletch Stauffer. She brushed her sweaty forehead with the inside of her forearm, aggravated that the bangs she had impulsively cut had slipped out of their bobby-pin moorings to mercilessly tickle her face. They needed trimming, but she couldn't do that while she was living at home again, at least without getting a lecture.

The restaurant had been what Beppe called in-the-weeds busy with the pregame crowd at the nearby SportsOhio complex. Her stomach rumbled from working around the aromas of the Italian sauces she loved so much. Usually, she skipped dinner on the nights she came in early. It helped to keep her rebellious waistline trim, although it was never small enough to suit her. That was probably one of the reasons guys weren't interested in her. Why should they be?

She was a plain woman in every aspect. Born on a farm. Born into a Conservative Mennonite church where the women were forbidden to adorn themselves in the latest fashions or paint their flesh with cosmetics. And having come from a family of wonderful cooks, she'd had to battle her waistline all her life. Oh she had it under control now, but only because of a regimented exercise program and bouts of deprivation.

Clumping her black oxfords to the back room for another crate of tomatoes, she hoisted them with a grunt into her arms and placed them on a prep counter, all the while persuading herself that he wouldn't call.

She had plain brown hair and freckles to boot. No, a tall, blond, good-looking guy like Fletch Stauffer wouldn't be calling the likes of her. He was just being kind. She remembered how he'd looked down his nose at Jezebel and gazed with pity at her. Fletch certainly wouldn't be calling her. She leaned over the sink and washed her hands.

Glancing around the kitchen, she squared her shoulders and started washing tomatoes. She still carried high hopes of becoming head chef, and then her life would change. She would make her dreams happen. She blew a puff of air at her bangs, but one stubborn strand still obscured her vision. Oh, she knew she wouldn't be replacing Beppe at Riccardo's. For now she was biding her time, scrubbing vegetables and cooking plain pasta. Plain, plain, plain. But someday—

—᷏᷏

For a Conservative girl, Lillian Landis was anything but plain, Fletch thought as he strode out of Riccardo's and headed toward his boss's car. Her shiny brown hair was pulled up in a knot, but many cooks wore their hair secured. He'd noticed the restaurant's customary uniform was either black slacks or black miniskirts, but Lillian wore a modest-length skirt that teased her curves. Instead of a tight-fitting T-shirt beneath her apron, she wore a crisp white blouse. But the tell-tale sign that Lillian was Mennonite was in her voice, which carried the thick slur that came from the Pennsylvania Dutch accent of many of the Mennonite's older members. She must have family still from the old order.

He shook his mind from her cute image and relived the accident. He'd been so mad when her old brown clunker had backed into Vic's expensive car. Until he got a look at Lillian Landis.

She was average height, lots shorter than him—but then five foot four seemed short when a guy was six foot one—and such a curvy little thing with a waist tiny enough to encircle with his hands. Her modest clothing added to her feminine allure, following her movements and tightening in the right places for the briefest of moments and skimming over her curves as if draping an exquisite piece of art that was not on exhibit for public viewing.

Her eyes were multiple shades of blue that in their brief encounter had ranged from a soft sky blue to a sparkling glacier green. What a contradiction they were to her cute freckles and upturned nose. How refreshing to meet an honest, candid woman, startling him by admitting she was a car destroyer. In the next breath, her Dutch accent slayed him with the news that she found him attractive.

He reached Vic's car door and crouched to examine the damage, disbelief and regret rushing through him anew as he ran his hand along the whitish-green horizontal crease. Fletch had never owned a car this nice and hoped Vic's car insurance premium wouldn't skyrocket.

He slid into the driver's seat and started the engine. As the Lexus glided out of its doomed parking space, Lillian's face flashed in his mind again. What an intriguing woman. Mennonite woman, of all things. Was that some kind of God sign?

Fletch made it a habit to observe everything that happened around him, watching for God's direction. Could it only be coincidence that in the big city of Columbus, Ohio, he'd run into a Mennonite girl? Well, strictly speaking, she had run into him.

In church, he hadn't met any single women half as attractive as Lillian. He was tempted to call her just to listen to her cute Dutch accent again. Unconsciously, he raked a hand through his fine blond hair. Although he could make a pastime out of thinking about women, he shouldn't be doing so as busy as he was with his studies and trying to please Vic.

He had been placed at Vic's veterinarian clinic as part of an offsite selective experience, a senior requisite of the veterinary school at Ohio State University. As intense as these final requirements were, the last thing he needed to knock him off course was a romantic fling, especially with a Conservative girl. He didn't even know how their faith differed.

Fletch eased into Dublin's traffic and headed toward Plain City, where Vic's practice was located close to the farms that sprawled across acres of plowed fields and pasture lands. Fletch's cheap apartment was near the practice. Vic's brother owned the small apartment complex, and he allowed Fletch to live there rent-free as long as he worked for Vic. The veterinarian paid his utilities and gave him a small stipend for his other living expenses. Fletch was grateful for that, because all the veterinary students weren't so fortunate. Vic had his generous moments, which was why he had offered Fletch his car for the food run. He could only hope that Vic's attitude wouldn't change when he saw what had happened.

A siren's shriek tore Fletch's glance from the surrounding landscape to his rearview mirror. At the flashing lights bearing down upon him, he groaned with the realization he was speeding. Brooding over his unbelievably rotten luck, he pulled to the side of the road and lowered his window. He had removed Vic's registration from the glove box by the time the police officer stepped up to his door.

"May I see your registration and insurance information?"

Fletch handed the officer Vic's registration and insurance card, relieved for the second time that day that his boss kept his documents in his glove box.

"This is my boss's car." He pointed at the food bag. "I was getting his lunch."

The officer hardened his gaze. "I'll need to see your license."

Fletch removed his billfold from his pocket and nervously fumbled through his cards, which spilled onto the floorboards. He leaned forward.

"Stop right there. Step out of the car." The officer's voice was curt, nonnegotiable.

Fletch froze. The officer seemed suspicious that he might be going for a gun under the seat. "Sure." Fletch opened his dented car door. "I was just going after the cards that I dropped on the floorboards." Was the officer about to pat him down and throw him up against the car like he'd seen in the movies?

Instead, the officer quietly studied him, securing the information Fletch had given him to his clipboard. "Did you know you were going 55 in a 45 mile-per-hour speed zone?"

"No. I was a bit preoccupied. I was just involved in a minor accident." He pointed toward his car door. "I guess I was still thinking about how my boss will react. The accident wasn't my fault. A woman backed into me in the restaurant's parking lot." Too late, Fletch realized that admitting he'd just been in an accident probably hadn't been the brightest thing to do.

Eyeing the crease in the car door then looking back at Fletch, the officer's expression softened. "You a resident?"

"I'm attending OSU's veterinary school. I graduate in the spring."

"Have you signed a rental lease?"

"No."

"Own a car?"

"Yes, sir."

"Gainfully employed?"

"No, sir." He didn't think there was anything gainful about the housing stipend Vic provided.

"I'm giving you a warning." He finished scribbling, tore off a sheet of paper, and handed it to Fletch.

"Thanks, sir. I appreciate that."

The officer eyed him again, then smiled. "Figured you needed a break."

Fletch uttered another thanks. Of all the scenarios zipping through his mind—owing a hefty speeding ticket, having to register his car, applying for an Ohio license—he'd gotten off easy.

"Drive safely," the officer said, then strode back to his patrol car.

With a sigh, Fletch got back in the car. Dare he get back on the road? he wondered, leaning and sweeping his hand along the floorboards to retrieve the fallen cards. The restaurant receipt slipped out of his grasp and floated farther beneath the seat. He abandoned it for the sake of getting back to the practice before Vic's hunger added to his distress.

CHAPTER 3

Rose Landis had lost interest in life. Lil's mom kept her bedroom's heavy brocade drapes drawn and her antique German lamps snuffed. It took daily bouts of coaxing just to get her to rise and dress. And this morning, Lil had to get her inside the car, too.

"But Mom, we have an appointment with that nice counselor today."

"Don't be fooled. It's his job to be nice. That's all. He'll just have to fill in my appointment slot with some other lunatic. I'm not up to it today. And I didn't ask you to make that appointment, anyway."

Lil gazed at her mom. Until spewing out her objection, she had looked like a small lifeless lump in a big bed. Her long hair was plaited in one white-streaked brown braid. Her lips were pulled tight and thin. Lil softly reasoned, "You're not crazy, Mom. Everyone has times when life becomes unmanageable. That's why God made friends and family."

"To force their moms to go to counseling," Mom huffed back.

Lil knew that counseling was a bit out of the ordinary in their Conservative circles. In their church it carried a stigma of personal and spiritual failure because everybody knew that God was sufficient, and if a person couldn't cope—and it wasn't God's fault—putting two and two together added up to a faulty faith. Even for Lil, who had no clue where Mom's problem had begun, it was hard not to judge her in some way. But now she gave her a patient smile. "Just like you forced me to brush my teeth and learn my ABC's. It's not that you don't know what you should be doing. You just need a little nudging." Mom turned her unconvinced expression toward the wall.

"I'm going to turn the shower on now. Nice and hot like you like it. I wish I had a new massage showerhead like the one Dad installed for you. He sure does love you, catering to you like he does."

Rolling toward the edge of the bed, Mom muttered, "Hmmph. Cater, my eye. And making me feel guilty doesn't make it any better." Then she murmured so low that Lil almost didn't catch it, "It's too late for that man."

Lil wondered about the meaning of that snide remark. Were her mom and dad having marriage problems? She remembered telling Katy a while back that she was positive her mom's depression had nothing to do with their marriage. But love was a mighty force, and just by watching Katy and Jake's tumultuous relationship and how it had affected her friends, she could attest to its strange powers. Did she dare question her mom on the topic? Mom and Dad never talked about their relationship. It had always been a private thing without much public demonstration. Or should Lil encourage Mom to bring the topic up to the counselor?

Meanwhile Mom had placed her bare feet on the oval, braided rug beside the bed. Her shoulders slumped. "I don't know why I don't have any energy. I hate getting old. Don't know what your dad even sees in me. And I never asked for a new showerhead, even if the old one dripped for two-and-a-half years."

"Dad sees the same things we all do," Lil went on, without acknowledging her mom's complaint about the house's old and faulty plumbing. "You're a wonderful person. Of course your cooking has nothing to do with it," she teased, hoping to stir up some of her mom's old confidence. Mom's laughter used to fill the home, and her sense of humor had kept everyone on their toes. She had passed that gene along to Lil's brother Matt.

"I do miss baking. If only I had the gumption, I'd make us some cinnamon rolls with brown-sugar icing. Maybe tomorrow."

"I'll help if you like," Lil replied, staring at the starched head covering on her mom's nightstand, though she knew from experience that when tomorrow rolled around Mom wouldn't feel like baking. Something terrible was wrong, but nobody could pinpoint the problem. This was only their third session with the counselor, and Lil hoped he would get to the bottom of it soon. Mom had lost weight, too—judging by the way her waistband hung, probably at least twenty-five or thirty pounds.

Later that morning after the appointment concluded with the kind, but noncommittal counselor, Lil brought her mom home and settled her in the new rocker Dad had purchased for Mom's fiftieth birthday. Dad's tenderness toward Mom, of late, baffled Lil, too, because as her mom had earlier insinuated, Will Landis had never been the thoughtful, caring type. He'd always just been sturdy, hardworking, and dependable—the practical type.

Leaving her mom by the living room window so she could watch it rain, Lil hoped to get to town and back before the actual downpour hit. She used her purse for a makeshift umbrella and made a dash for Jezebel. On the road, her windshield wipers did little to clear her vision as she drove to the Plain City pharmacy to get the pills the therapist had prescribed for her mom. She wasn't sure if she could get her to take any, but maybe if Mom knew they were already purchased, she would comply with the psychiatrist's wishes.

The canopy in front of the pharmacy beckoned with its dry patch of sidewalk but traitorously startled Lil with a gush of water down the back of her neck. Inside, she agreed with the pharmacist that the farmers would be glad for the rain and paid the bill with her own money, not wanting to burden her dad after learning the farm was about to go bankrupt. Assuming pharmacists took oaths of privacy, she was glad that she didn't see anybody else she knew while she purchased a prescription of bottled happiness.

Outside, the awning baptized her again, and clutching her small white bag of hope, she made a run for Jezebel. Drenched, she finagled the warped door and tossed her purse and bag on the plastic slipcover.

A shiver tingled up and down her spine as she stuck her key in the ignition. Jezebel wouldn't start.

—⟨⟩—

On the same side of the cow as Vic, Fletch leaned his shoulder against the heifer and tightened his grip on the animal's green-and-black-striped lead rope. Water dripped off his red ball cap, and with one hand he flipped the hood of his slicker back up over it. Impatient, for it seemed to be taking the vet examining the cow far too long, he called, "Can you see anything?"

"The leg wound is infected. We're lucky she's still on her feet. But we're going to have to get her back to the barn before I can treat it, or the bandage will just get soaked."

Thinking of the truck's cab with desire, Fletch remarked, "Would have been nice if Johnson would have already had her confined."

"He probably wasn't expecting the rain. It's all part of the job. You might as well get used to bad weather and contrary animals. Believe me, if it's not the animals, it's their owners."

"I suppose so."

"Or are you going to take one of those cushy jobs taking care of pets?"

Fletch figured every job had its drawbacks. "In school, they warned us that house cats are as deadly as a mountain lion."

Vic scoffed. "Pure exaggeration. Well you've got the lead rope and I've got the truck keys. So I guess I'll see you and this heifer back at the barn in about an hour."

"More penance?" Fletch teased.

"Just exposing you to a wider range of experience," the thin, red-haired vet replied.

"Exposure, all right," Fletch muttered, stepping in front of the cow and gently pulling her forward. Ever since he'd returned to the veterinary practice with Vic's dented car—correction, Vic's wife's dented car, for Fletch had discovered that the couple had exchanged vehicles that day—the veterinarian had mustered up every conceivable dirty job for him to perform. Fletch didn't mind getting his hands dirty. After all, he was raised on the mission field and used to all kinds of adverse and unexpected conditions. But Vic was getting far too much pleasure out of watching him slosh around in manure and probe stool samples for parasites.

He guessed the honeymoon had worn off between them. For all Fletch knew, maybe Vic's ire stemmed from the fact that he was sleeping on the couch at home. Fletch hadn't been around Britt enough to determine her personality type. He didn't know if she was supportive or resentful of Vic's practice. Part of their schooling had prepared them for the hazards of choosing a career that demanded long, irregular hours.

Most of the students spent their summers involved in some sort of on-the-job experience, and Fletch had been fortunate to get on with the same veterinarian he was going to help once the fall term began. At least he had previously thought he was fortunate. Though they were barely getting started, he had to wonder what the next year would hold.

Fletch hunched his shoulders against the rain and urged the heifer toward the dirt tire tracks that crisscrossed green pasture, where he and Vic had earlier driven to reach the field where the animal had been last seen. Fletch's muckers sank deep in the muddy track, making his progress slower, and the animal must have felt the change of terrain, too, because it suddenly balked, practically jerking Fletch's arm from its shoulder socket. With several tugs, he got the animal moving again, but Fletch still couldn't see the barn. He spoke as softly as he could over the wind and rain to urge the animal forward, but a bolt of thunder changed the animal's will.

The cow reared back, and Fletch frantically strove to secure his grasp on the slippery lead. But the strong animal turned and dragged Fletch backward until the lead slid through his gloves. Moments after that, he found himself sprawled facedown in the muddy lane. He lay there, momentarily stunned, until a current of rain made its way onto his bare skin between the hem of his hiked-up slicker and his belt. Rising to his elbows, he sputtered between mud-caked teeth, "Stupid cow!"

Staggering to his feet, he glared through the rain at the animal that had stopped only a short distance away. The heifer stared him down with a frightened curiosity. The animal's injury had to be severe if she hadn't bolted away, Fletch thought, yanking his slicker back in place and starting toward the frightened animal. Regardless if Vic was dry and sipping coffee with Johnson or not, he needed to get the animal back to the barn as quickly as possible.

⟶◦

Later that week, Lil slid five pieces of pie onto her mom's Autumn Leaf dessert plates and placed four of them in front of the men seated around the kitchen table. She glanced nervously down the hall, assured that her mom was in her room. Mostly, she was nervous for her brother Matt's sake. Dad had called a family meeting to tell the brothers about the farm trouble. She just hoped he gave Matt a chance to express his ideas. Matt had recently started attending a more liberal-minded Mennonite church, and she knew there was still underlying friction between him and their dad.

Hank, the darkest and oldest of the Landis siblings, looked up at her from his seat at the table. "Thanks, Lily Mae. This looks good."

"You deserve it for coming to my rescue the other day. I don't know what I would have done without you."

"Anybody can replace spark plugs."

"Yes, but you got drenched doing it while I stayed dry in the car."

"That's what brothers are for, but I worry about you driving that piece of junk."

"It's my piece of junk, and usually it gets me around." Lil's face heated. "I'm sorry. That was rude."

"Mom still not cooking?" her youngest brother, Stephen, interrupted.

Stephen's waist size reflected his main interest in life was food—with a partiality toward his mom's cooking. All the sisters-in-law had an inferiority complex when it came to their cooking. They were good cooks, just not as good as the Landis women.

"No." Lil lowered her voice. "But she went to the counselor again and even took some medication this week."

"You think that's a good idea?" Hank frowned. Unless he shaved twice a day, her brother sported a dark shadow of a beard, which added to his formidable countenance. As the eldest, he was always looking out for everyone, appearing grumpy and overbearing at times.

Dad came to her defense. "It's more serious than you know. Lil's doing her best with your mom."

Hank nodded. Dark, serious, and traditional, he was clad in his usual short-sleeved, button-down shirt and a pair of jeans, his only fashion vice his penchant for the John Deere label. He could always be found in the classic green J. D. hat. He splurged on the more expensive J. D. farm boots, too, and loved to buy his sons J. D. pedal tractors and push toys.

Hank's wife, Sara, claimed he spoiled their children, Scott and Sammy. His feisty wife came from Kansas, and Hank's nickname for her was Sara Cyclone, taken from *The Wizard of Oz* book.

Lil took a small wedge of the peach pie for herself. "You care if I join you?"

Dad narrowed his eyes as if wanting to get the meeting going and dreading it at the same time.

"Go ahead and start your meeting. I won't interrupt," Lil urged. She figured after picking all the peaches—which was an itchy job—freezing them, and baking the pies, she had a right to sit and eat at the table with them. Anyway, she really wanted to hear what was going on with the farm's finances. She had to wonder if her mom knew about it and if it had anything to do with her depression.

Dad tugged gently on the lobe of his large ear, considering her request. "I guess we can talk in front of Lil." Then he thrust a warning finger at her. "But you have enough to worry about helping with your mom. Remember to leave the farm problems to us men."

Although his voice remained gentle and he meant his warning for her own good, she resented his male finger pointing and shutting her out just because she was a female. She had hoped he was changing his attitude when he'd confided in her the other morning. Now she realized he'd been sharing with her only because he didn't have his wife to vent to any longer. Will Landis didn't usually ask anyone for advice. He was the girder. He didn't expect her to help him find a solution to his financial woes. Probably didn't think she was capable of such things. She gave a small nod and dropped her gaze to her pie.

She intended to linger and listen even if she had to set a record on how slow a body could eat one piece of pie—the same piece for which she would have to add extra sit-ups to her nightly regimen. After eating her dessert, she could refill coffee cups, if need be.

"I missed my loan payment this month," Dad announced.

The brothers' gazes swam in confusion. Lil remembered how painful it had been to receive the bad news. Her brothers understood that Dad referred to the farm loan, which had accumulated with various farm needs from equipment to seeds. On a row of good years, it was temporary, enough to get by until harvest. On a row of bad years, it provided the payroll and carried the farm. But the confusion came because the boys hadn't known the farm was in trouble.

"Do you need some money to tide you over?" Hank asked. "The cyclone and I can spare a few thousand temporarily."

Dad gripped his coffee cup. "It's too late for tiding over."

Stephen pushed another heaping fork of pie into his mouth and chewed, his brows forming a frustrated *V* as if they might take wing and fly off his face.

Hank's forehead furrowed. "Let's sell off some hogs."

"We can do that, but it will only delay the inevitable. The last couple of years should have been good ones; instead, we're steadily sinking."

"Can I have a look at the books?" Hank asked, as eldest son.

Dad rose without comment and left the room.

In his absence, Hank muttered, "I should have taken over the books years ago." Lil knew he had taken accounting courses in college. Hank had gone to Hesston Mennonite College and returned one year later with his wife, Sara, but had never finished his bachelor's degree. Instead, at Dad's urging, he'd gone straight back to farming. But he had been a natural with numbers and spreadsheets.

"Shh! Here he comes!" Matt warned.

Dad pushed a ledger across the table. "Look all you want. It won't change a thing. But at least I won't have as much to explain."

Matt exchanged glances with Lil, and she knew exactly what he was thinking. Dad should have computerized his books by now. Matt had finished his degree at Hesston and was the most liberal of the brothers. Not that it would have magically corrected all their financial woes, Lil imagined. But surely every problem had a solution. Even multiple solutions. Hank had just turned thirty. It was high time that Dad let her brothers help shoulder the farm burdens besides doing the manual labor and receiving a paycheck.

The men bent their heads over the books while she refilled their coffee cups. Then they spent an hour probing at the situation from different angles. Finally, Matt spoke up. "Dad's right. Without a major change, we'll be bankrupt before harvest. Our only hope is to modernize."

All gazes fastened on Matt to see if he was joking, because their middle brother had a corny sense of humor. He liked to pull practical jokes on the others, and since he'd begun attending a different church, he'd started wearing T-shirts that bore messages like "Tractorologist" or "Farm fed and rural raised." But this time, Matt appeared to be dead serious.

Stephen motioned at Lil for more pie, clearly wishing to escape.

Hank set down his John Deere mug. "He's right."

Dad took a long swig of coffee, then set down his cup so hard it clattered and spilled brown liquid onto the plastic, lilac-flowered tablecloth. Lil jumped up and returned with a green-checkered tea towel. She pushed it toward her dad, but he ignored her efforts. "Guess it won't hurt to listen to your newfangled notions."

With relief, Lil sank back on her chair, the cloth dropping to her lap. Her eyes stung, knowing how much that statement had cost her dad. She barely breathed, hoping Matt really did have an idea. He didn't disappoint. He started talking about factory farming where more animals could be raised in tighter, modern pens. His ideas brought out some scoffs and raised some questions, yet most of it was taken to heart by the other men. Lil sat engrossed as they batted around possible scenarios and discussed what the church would allow and what might be forbidden. Suddenly, the room became quiet as a morgue.

Lil looked up. There stood Mom in her bathrobe, her disheveled head tilted to the side. "You having a party without me?"

Dad paled, quickly scooting back his chair and then easing Mom into it. With one meaningful look in Hank's direction, the books were snatched and hidden beneath the table.

"Peach pie, Mom," Lil said. "Would you like a piece?" She quickly wiped up the spill to protect her mom's ribbed, terry-cloth sleeve.

"I think so," Mom replied, oblivious to Lil's ministrations. "For some reason, I can't sleep tonight. Just restless, I guess."

Lil exchanged a look with her dad. Were the pills already causing a change and bringing her out of her stupor? Mom had not gotten out of bed on her own for weeks.

The business discussion was dropped on the spot, and all the attention was riveted on Mom. Even with the dark circles under her eyes, she was a pretty woman. Lil's sister, Michelle, looked like their mom, but Lil took after their dad. Mom's long braid was draped over the front of her mint-green robe, and she'd taken the effort to put on her covering. "What are you boys talking about? Sure sounded lively out here."

"Just farming," Hank explained.

Mom's expression fell in disappointment. "Oh?" She looked at the untouched wedge of pie before her. "I'm more worn out than I realized. Help me back to bed, Lil?"

Lil rushed forward. "Sure."

"Give those grandbabies kisses," Mom said flatly as she shuffled along the wood floor that, like her, had lost its luster, for Lil didn't buff it like her mom had always done. Mom's terry slippers had a piece of elastic hand sewn across the ankles. She used to do small things like that, paying attention to all the little details that make a family a home. Her appearance at the table now was not much in comparison, but it had been an unexpected effort.

It took Lil a while to get her mom settled.

"It was good to hear the boys talking about the farm," Mom said. "Will's finally allowing them a say?" she asked, hopefully.

"Yes, I believe he is."

She sighed deeply. "There was a time when he used to talk to me about the farm. Now he just clams up." Her voice took on a childlike hope. "Maybe if the boys do more, your dad won't be so busy."

Not if they lost the farm, Lil supposed, though she kept that opinion to herself.

"Get me one of those sleeping pills, will you?" Mom asked.

Lil touched her mom's forehead and unpinned her covering. "They aren't sleeping pills." Sometimes she gave her mom an over-the-counter painkiller. "And you already took your new pill."

Mom suddenly clutched Lil's arm. "What if I can't sleep anymore? I can't bear it if the days get any longer." She tightened her grip. "I just can't."

CHAPTER 4

At the rooster's untimely crowing and intrusion upon her wonderful dream, Lil awoke with an overwhelming desire for one particular chicken cooked with tender dumplings. Of course she shouldn't have been dreaming about Fletch anyways, because it only made each passing day that he didn't phone her more difficult to endure. Even though she knew he wouldn't call, she charged her phone's battery every night while she slept. Hopefully time would remove the sting of his rejection.

Wistfully, she dismissed him from her mind, dressed, and prepared breakfast for her dad. When she had placed the last hand-washed breakfast plate in the drying rack—for the farm kitchen didn't have the latest appliances—she went to see how Mom had slept and if she couldn't coax her out of bed and into making those cinnamon rolls she'd mentioned.

Lil padded into the dark room and frowned at the lump of empty bedcovers, for it was unusual for Mom to rise on her own. Once again, her thoughts turned hopeful that the new pills might be helping.

Light filtered beneath the bathroom door's threshold. With a rap, Lil softly called, "Mom. You in there?"

There was no answer so she knocked again, calling a little louder,

"Mom!" Still no reply. Lil twisted the knob and inched the door ajar, but it hit an obstacle that kept it from fully opening. Looking down, Lil gasped to see her mom's bare leg. Diving through the narrow opening, she quickly took in the scene and dropped to her knees beside Mom's rigid body.

"Mom!" She didn't respond. Her eyes were rolled back, and her body was contracting in some sort of seizure. "Oh, no. Oh, no." Trembling with fear, Lil scooped her mom's head under one arm and used her free hand to grab her cell phone from her apron pocket. "Matt! Get Dad. Quick! Something's wrong with Mom! We're in their bathroom."

Lil's gaze fell on the empty painkiller bottle. Helpless to know what to do, she held her mom's shuddering body. "Oh Mom, what did you do?"

By the time Dad arrived, Mom's body had gone limp, and she'd either fallen asleep or fainted. Dad quickly scooped Mom up into his arms and ran for his truck. On her way out, Lil snatched the generic painkiller bottle, Mom's covering from the nightstand, and her own purse from the mudroom.

Since they lived too far from the nearest emergency vehicle, they planned to drive Rose to the hospital themselves. Lil jumped in the cab of her dad's truck, clutching her mom's limp form and praying all the way to the Dublin Methodist Hospital. Matt had called ahead, and when they arrived, a gurney was waiting outside the emergency entrance. Hospital attendants promptly strapped Mom to the gurney and rushed her through a set of glass doors.

Dad went with Mom, and Lil was left with the admitting paperwork. Her hands trembled too violently to use the kiosk, even if she knew how, so she stepped up to a clerk. He motioned her into a chair where she clenched her hands on her lap to keep them from shaking. Still wearing her apron, she answered the questions as best she could, but the hospital clerk eyed her inquisitively. "Plain City?"

"Yes." She gave her address.

"You Amish farmers?"

The farmer part should have been obvious, the way her dad had whisked through the room in his overalls without even removing his straw hat. The clerk's probing glance and nosy questions made her feel like an oddity and served to ruffle her farm-girl feathers. Jutting her chin, she asked, "Is that a question on your admissions form?"

"No, just curious."

"We're Mennonites. We drive cars," she snapped, knowing from past experiences that would probably be his next question.

The young man quirked a brow, and after that he stuck to the questions needed to fill out the admittance forms. "Wait over there. I'll take this form back and have your dad sign it."

"Thanks."

She found an empty chair in the waiting room just as her brothers filed through the entrance. Several strangers in the room lifted their gazes to the newcomers. Lil motioned her siblings over and told them everything that had happened. After that, they all settled in to wait for word from Dad or the doctor.

Lil's heart throbbed with fear for her mom and family. Although she didn't want to think about such things, this hospital visit would add additional financial strain to an already serious situation. She brushed away the negative thought and prayed for her mother to pull through and come out of her coma.

About an hour passed before Dad finally stepped into the waiting room, looking quite lost. At once, Lil jumped to her feet and waved. "Over here."

When his gaze lit on her, he seemed relieved. With hat in hand and heavy steps, he crossed the room to his children.

"Is she okay?" Hank asked.

"Yes. She's sleeping." He explained how Mom had been treated using uncustomary words such as *activated charcoal* and *gastrointestinal tract*. "They started an IV."

"Does she need to be admitted?"

"Yes. They want to keep her at the hospital and give sodium bicarbonate until her urine reaches a specified pH level."

"But she will be all right?"

He gave a weary nod, and Lil heaved a huge sigh of relief, as did her brothers. To hear her dad use medical terms reminded her that he was an intelligent man, even though he usually didn't use big words. Actually, she corrected herself, he usually didn't talk much at all.

His worried brow caused Lil concern. "Can we see her?"

"Not yet." Dad shook his head wearily. "I'm going to stay with her. The rest of you best go home and take care of the farm."

Lil knew that the chores needed to be done, but she didn't want to go. "Me, too?"

He studied her and shook his head. "You've been taking her to the doctor visits. You'd better stay with us."

———෴———

Fletcher moved his hands over the steering wheel of his blue Ford Focus. The car was a gift from a donor who supported his parents' mission work and had been third-handed off to him. All his life, Fletch had survived on hand-me-downs. His missionary parents lived mainly on donations and a few odds-and-ends jobs—from working at the local discount stores to mixing pesticides for migrant workers—along with piecework his dad picked up when they took leave in the States. Frank Stauffer once hauled Amish people to Florida, returning with a load of citrus fruit to sell. The family had always been thankful to God for each job or donation.

Although Fletch's family never owned many valuable possessions—unless you counted various trinkets given to them from the natives—their real wealth was in their experiences. Fletch had received a good education, both from personal experience and the classes he took at Ohio State University. His college tuition was being covered by one of his parents' longest and most dedicated supporters, Marshall Lewis. Marshall was also Fletch's mentor and second father figure. This kind, generous man had guided Fletch in his career choice when it seemed that his own father was too busy to be bothered with such details.

Fletch pulled up to his apartment complex's mailboxes, shifted the Focus into PARK, and got out to check his mail. At present, his parents were in the Congo, trying to put their camp and ministry back together for the third time in a war-torn land. They were too occupied with the Bambuti, Congo Pygmies, to write. E-mail was sporadic.

Phone service random.

Fletch flipped through the usual junk mail and a utility bill he would pass along to Vic, who still harbored a grudge over the accident between Britt's car and Lillian's brown rattletrap. Her ugly vehicle was a reminder of some of his experiences with embarrassing clunkers. Recalling bits and pieces of their conversation, he had to admire Lillian's determination to acquire a prominent chef's position and own a nice car like Britt's. Given Lil's Conservative Mennonite background, her goals had been surprising to him.

His own goals were not so surprising. His vocational direction evolved out of his natural love for animals.

Although he was a Christian, he didn't feel driven to evangelize people, like his parents. In fact, he wanted to keep as far from the mission field as he could. His focus was on obtaining his degree, starting a veterinarian practice, and living a normal life. If anything, Fletch's dream was to be ordinary because he'd always been different than most people.

Entering his apartment with a whistle for his pet, he dropped his mail in the trash and tossed the utility bill on a small table. The room was sparse, containing only the barest of necessities, and he easily spied his companion bounding toward him from across the room. Fletch scratched the dog behind one droopy ear. He'd gotten the dog at veterinarian school, where the students were encouraged to adopt abandoned animals from their hospital. Fletch didn't regret his decision to adopt Buddy. The basset hound finished sniffing his leg and went to the front door.

"Wait a minute." Fletch snatched a package of frozen burgers out of the freezer and set it on the counter before he picked up Buddy's leash and an empty grocery bag. The dog wagged his tail, anticipating their customary walk. Once around the block, and Fletch was home again, tossing burgers on the grill that came with the apartment's eight-by-ten-foot walled-in patio. When he opened the slider to return inside the apartment, the basset's nose sniffed the smoky scent that had entered the room.

As Fletch ate his dinner, his thoughts returned to Lillian. All week long, he had squelched the urge to drive back to Riccardo's, but he didn't even know which days she worked. He would look pathetic hanging out at Riccardo's until their paths crossed again. But he was still entertaining the notion. Driving over there seemed the only way to reach her since her phone number was on the back of the take-out check that had floated under Britt's car seat.

His shoulders slumped with regret that he hadn't remembered to look for her phone number. At the time, he hadn't realized his mind would become obsessed over her. Considering the differences in their faith, he should just forget about her. That was his original intention, but his thoughts riveted on the image of Lillian Landis and the idea of pursuing her.

Calling Riccardo's could get her in trouble with her boss. Hadn't she mentioned something about him having a temper? He let out a long sigh. *Lord, could You just prompt Vic to send me to Riccardo's again? Either that, or please help me forget her?*

One thing he'd learned from the Bambuti: if you asked God for direction, He would send you a sign. The native group had signs and superstitions about everything. Only they didn't seek Fletch's God, they turned to nature for their answers, considering the forest their god. Fletch's personal theology had naturally evolved from his own experiences; if God created nature, He could certainly use it to speak to mankind. Fletch believed that God cared about details. If Vic sent him back to Riccardo's, Fletch would take that as a sign to pursue the object of his imagination.

―⌒―

Rose Landis clapped her hands to the sides of her head. "My ears are ringing. Sounds like a swarm of bees in the lilac bush. Only they are inside my head. I can't stand it."

"Just a hangover," Lil's dad joked, but nobody laughed. Lil didn't understand why her dad would jokingly allude to drinking alcohol when the church forbid it, unless it was his passive-aggressive reminder that the ringing was a direct result of ingesting too many pills.

"It will fade," Lil consoled her mom for the third time. But in actuality, the physician that was assigned to Mom's case hadn't guaranteed that the ringing would ever go away. The causes and cures of tinnitus weren't understood by the medical world. Lil could only hope Mom hadn't ruined her inner ears with the overdose.

Mom clawed at her bedcovers. "I want to go home. When can I go?"

Dad patted her arm. "As soon as they release you."

"Don't treat me like a child, Will. Do you know, or don't you? Why do you always try to keep things from me? You treat me as if I don't have a brain in my head. Of course I may not if these bees keep buzzing around in there."

He kept his voice calm. "Because you can't cope with stress these days."

Mom jerked the sheet up to her chin. "What do you know about anything?"

With a sigh, Lil snatched up her purse and retreated to the hallway. She wished she could call her friends and vent. But Katy was still on her honeymoon. Jake was on it with her. And Megan was on a summer mission trip. All her friends were busy, getting on with their lives. Frustrated, she dialed her sister, Michelle.

Her sister's voice sounded breathless, probably from chasing after her three children, all under the age of six. "How's Mom?"

"I think they'd release her now, but they've called for a psychoanalysis."

"Oh no." Michelle groaned. "What will Brother Troyer think? And the elders? Do you think they'll make her get up in front of the church and ask for forgiveness for trying to commit"—her voice broke—"you know?"

Lil sympathized with her sister's anguish. Suicide was almost nonexistent among the Mennonites because they believed that killing was a sin, and if a person committed sin without asking for forgiveness, he or she might not get to heaven. The few bereft families who did experience such a loss clung to the consolation that nobody could know for sure that the dying person hadn't asked for forgiveness on their way to the other life. Suicide was something that happened in the outsider's world, not in Lil's congregation.

Even though a nurse's station was ten feet to her right and a hospital hallway stretched out to her left, Lil found it hard to accept that Mom had tried to commit suicide. It hurt to think she was that miserable, that her family wasn't important enough for her to fight to survive.

With grief thickening her throat, Lil replied, "No. But Dad said Brother Troyer might make a house call. I think it'll be kept hushed. I'm hoping the staff here will call her psychiatrist and then discharge her."

"What can I do to help?"

Lil's gaze darted around the sterile hall. How could Michelle help with her active little ones who needed constant care? When her gaze rested on a clock, she gasped. "Oh no. I forgot to call Riccardo's. Beppe will be mad."

Michelle replied, "He has to allow for family emergencies. Do I need to bring Mom some clothes or anything?"

With irritation, Lil brushed back a fringe of bangs and repositioned her bobby pins. "I can't think right now. Beppe claims I've already had too many family emergencies. I've got to call the restaurant. I'll call you back later."

"Okay," Michelle's hesitant voice insinuated what they both knew— that nothing was okay. "Call me."

Lil ended their call and quickly punched in her speed dial.

"Riccardo's."

"Hi, Beppe. I'm sorry I'm late." She tucked her hair behind her left ear.

"You know there's a baseball game tonight. It's going to be busy."

"I had an emergency. My mom's in the hospital. She took an overdose of aspirin. I'm not going to be able to come in tonight."

There was a long pause on the other end. "I'm surprised to hear that. Didn't think your people—Look, I'm sorry about your mom. But this restaurant has to operate regardless of personal problems."

Lil glanced back at her mom's room. "Fine. I can be there in an hour. But I don't have my uniform."

Suddenly his tone became overly sympathetic. "Maybe you need a leave of absence. Just wait to come back until things settle, and meanwhile, I'll hire somebody else to fill in."

Panicking, Lil knew that once she was replaced, the door to Riccardo's would be forever closed to her. "No! I'll be there," she cried.

Ending the call and stuffing her phone in her purse, Lil ducked her head into her mom's hospital room and motioned for Dad to come to the hallway.

He stepped into the hall beside her, his brows creased in worry. "What is it? Did the doctor speak with you?"

"No, nothing like that. I have to go to work. I'm already late. Call me if Mom gets discharged. Otherwise, I'll come straight back here."

"But you can't go. You know all about her depression stuff. I don't know what to tell that shrink."

"I have to go, Dad. Otherwise I'm losing my job."

"You don't even have your car."

"I know. I need to borrow your truck."

Dad's eyes narrowed in anger. He glanced into the hospital room and back at Lil. "You can't be in two places at once. You cannot ride the fence any longer. It is time to quit your job and help your family. It is the right thing to do."

"You sent the boys home to work. I have work, too."

"Yes. To help with your mom."

Lil stilled. Her job was her last grasp for freedom. She loved both her parents, but she couldn't give up her job. She shook her head. "I'm sorry. I'll call someone then."

"Don't go. We need you."

"I know. It's just for a few hours." Lil had never truly accepted the path her parents had chosen for her life and had become accustomed to continually scrapping with them. They usually gave in pretty easily, as they weren't nearly as strict with her as they had been with Michelle or Hank. But with the recent turmoil that had entered her parents' lives, she found it painful to add to their burdens. She bit her tongue and turned her back to him.

Her dad remained silent.

Feeling sick to her stomach, she walked away before she changed her mind and somehow ended up forever trying to fill her mom's shoes at home—the very shoes that had led her mom into a bout of depression.

She started running. She punched the elevator button. It would take Michelle too long to come for her. Her brothers were busy, and her friends were out of town. Mustering every bit of courage to keep her job, she decided to ask one of the hospital clerks how to call a cab.

—⟨∽⟩—

After her shift, Lil took a cab back to the farm, eating up more than her night's wages. Beppe had been hard to please, and her emotions were frazzled. Bone-tired, she trudged toward Jezebel, intending to go straight to the hospital. Curiously, her dad's truck was parked in the driveway. Turning, she went into the house.

She hurried through the mudroom and kitchen to the hall. Her parents' bedroom door was closed. Not knowing if her mom had been released or if her dad had come home to sleep, Lil would have to wait until morning to unravel it all. She would rise early and make a good breakfast to appease her dad's anger for going against his wishes.

But the next morning, Lil's special waffles and raspberry syrup did not mollify him.

"I suppose hamburger gravy is too plain for you to make?"

Lil was taken aback. Her dad had never once complained about her cooking. Nobody had. He knew he was the luckiest man alive to have married into the matriarchal line of Mennonite potluck queens. Hurt, she swallowed. "I'll remember next time."

He shot her an angry glance and then looked back at his plate. "You'd better go through the medicine cabinet and make sure your mother won't find any more pills." The tips of his ears pinked, and Lil knew he was shamed that his wife would seek such a route of escape. He probably blamed himself for all the troubles at the Landis farm.

"Is she here? Did they discharge her?"

He looked up again. "Now why else would I be sitting here eating your fandangled waffles?"

"Maybe because you like them," she quipped, her eyes mirroring his. "Just maybe they're the best waffles you ever tasted." Lil tried one of her mom's tactics from before her depression. She had been an expert at making Dad laugh when times were tough.

"And maybe you need to get your nose out of the air. I never thought my own daughter would be too proud to wear her covering."

Stunned at his out-of-the blue dig, Lil steadied her hand against the countertop. "I didn't know it bothered you." The church had recently changed the ordinance allowing women to have the freedom of choice when it came to wearing the covering outside of worship services. She had quit wearing it when she lived at the doddy house. She had been living on her own at the time and hadn't thought to ask her parents' permission. They had never spoken of it.

He didn't reply, just finished eating.

Hurt, Lil tried to reason with him again. "I had to go to work. It's the only thing left of my—" She broke off. He would scoff at her dreams. Her dad seemed broken. How long would it be until she was broken, too? "We're a lot alike, you and me. Matt is like us, too."

"That's not much to brag about," he replied. "By the way, you might have to help with the chores come Saturday."

"Why?"

"Because Matt's dragging us to some farm seminar." He stuck a warning finger in the air. "I'm allowing him his chance. But if this doesn't work, well let's just say there might not be any chores for any of the Landis clan in the future."

"I'm glad you're open to new ideas, Dad. But sometimes one chance isn't enough. I imagine it will take plenty of hard work, too. You'll have to give it time. It's only fair."

He shook his head and rose from table, then stepped into the mudroom and plucked his straw hat from the yellow peg shelf. As she watched, he squared his shoulders. "You should know by now that one thing I never shirked was hard work."

His presence filled the small mudroom. She watched the broad shoulders of his plaid shirt slouch again beneath his worn overalls. One sleeve was rolled higher than the other, exposing a tan forearm and sun-freckled hand. It clasped the screen door, and he was gone.

She looked up at the ceiling and, falling into a Dutch accent, demanded, "Do You see what's happening here, God? Do You even care?"

CHAPTER 5

Fletch looked out the passenger window of Vic's white Chevy pick-up at the low, sleek facility with neatly trimmed hedges. Strong winds strewed lavender phlox across the rolling green lawns that made the property an appealing place for a farm seminar. A row of newly planted trees bent low to the onslaught. The country feel of the landscape would aid in setting the farmers at ease, allowing them to be more receptive to new ideas and equipment.

The concept of attending a farm seminar to drum up work was something he hadn't considered as part of his future job description. They pulled into the parking garage, and Fletch asked, "How many of these do you attend in a year?"

"Depends on how busy I am." They exchanged glances, and then Vic said almost grudgingly, "Three this year. The kids have to eat." Since the accident, Vic had remained in a sour mood.

"Did you get the car fixed yet?"

"It's in the shop. Britt's driving a rental. Has to take the boys to school and all their activities."

"I'm sorry for the inconvenience." It wasn't as if Fletch had been a careless driver, but Vic had made it plain that he regretted allowing

Fletch to drive his wife's car.

"I shouldn't have bought that car anyway."

Fletch felt it was better to let that comment alone and focus on the seminar.

Inside the entry, they followed signs to a room designated for the meetings. A brunette in a trim, chic suit handed him a packet of material and a name tag that he stuck to his button-down, short-sleeved shirt. Vic had warned him that the farmers didn't show up in suit coats or even long sleeves in summer, and they needed to fit in with the farmers, present themselves as people who could be trusted and even befriended. He pointed out that in a small community like Plain City, businesses treated their clients like family.

Several dividers had been opened to make one room large enough to display various types of farm equipment for differing livestock, such as mechanical devices to facilitate the feeding, reproduction, and nursing of hogs. The usual computerized units for temperature control, including sample misting equipment, also were being exhibited.

When Fletch looked at the equipment, most of which had been set up the day before, he wasn't thinking about profit and convenience; he was thinking about how it would affect animals' health and well-being.

Fletch helped Vic set up their booth, which consisted of one large banner representing the practice, a table, two folding chairs, some flyers, and a notepad to take down names and phone numbers. By the time they were finished, the farmers were trickling in for the workshops that would be starting within the hour. Fletch enjoyed observing the farmers.

"How long have you been practicing?"

Fletch turned left to see a man who looked faintly familiar. He had a sun-freckled face and the rough hands of a farmer. He wore a graphic T-shirt under a pale-blue, button-down shirt, and some bold lettering that Fletch couldn't quite read showed through the fabric. He tilted his head inquisitively.

"Vic's been practicing for almost twenty years. I'm his assistant."

"The vet we always used just retired. We'll be expanding soon and will be looking for somebody new."

"What kind of livestock do you have?"

"Hogs."

"Vic's really good with all animals. Why don't you take one of our flyers?" Remembering Vic's comment that clients were treated like family, he said, "By the way, my name's Fletch Stauffer."

"I think I've seen you at my church. That's another reason why I stopped at your booth. I haven't been going to Crossroads Mennonite that long."

"Me either. I've only been going there since I enrolled at OSU, and it took me a while to find a church."

"Matt L—" The young man's introduction was cut off as another man carrying an insulated John Deere mug stepped up to join them.

"There's a great buffet over there. Too bad Steve's not here. Dad's saving us some seats." The newcomer motioned to the far side of the room.

"This is my brother Hank."

Both men looked familiar, though Hank was darker than his brother, but Fletch didn't recall seeing either of them at his church.

Hank picked up one of Vic's brochures and placed it on top of a flyer he had on pressure washers.

Matt turned his attention back to Fletch. "What kind of classes are you taking?"

"Oh, didn't I say? I'm going to veterinary school." Fletch finally caught the wording barely visible through Matt's shirt: *hog heaven*. He bit back a smile.

Hank had been thumbing through his brochures. "You familiar with the slatted flooring? These pressure washers?"

"Yes. I understand they work best when the waste is flushed out of the building into a lagoon and later spread over the fields." Fletch was pleased to share the information he'd learned in one of his agricultural classes. The way this was going, he might be drumming up some new customers for his employer. "Vic's giving a workshop about antibiotics. It might be worth your while for one of you to attend, especially if you're expanding."

Matt tapped Fletch with his brochure. "Thanks for the tip. We're all taking different workshops. I've already decided I'm taking the one on contract growers and integrators. How about you, Hank?"

"All?" Fletch asked, curious now. "How many brothers do you have?"

"Just two. More than enough." He pointed to a farmer who was headed their way. "And that's my dad, Will Landis."

Landis? At the name, Fletch stared at the farmer who was now extending a hand toward him. Landis? His mind scrambled. As in Lillian Landis? No wonder Matt and Hank looked familiar. This was Lillian's family! He clasped the older farmer's hand. Gripped it solidly in hopes of making a good impression.

"Pleased to meet you, Mr. Landis." More than ever, he didn't want to lose this customer. Special customer. God hadn't prompted Vic to send Fletch for more Italian food, but to the One who made the universe, there was more than one way to answer a prayer.

"If you register with us today, Vic Fuller, the owner of the veterinary practice, will give you a discount on his services or even on vaccinations." When he saw interest in the farmer's eyes, he quickly grabbed the notepad off the table, supplying him with a pen as well.

As Mr. Landis scrawled his name, he said to his sons. "I found us some seats next to the coffeepot so Hank can stay awake."

Hank shrugged. "Coffee is my best friend most mornings."

"Wait until I tell Sara that," Matt teased.

"She already knows, blabbermouth."

Fletch watched the farmers leave his booth, almost dumbstruck that God had brought Lillian's family to him. A future encounter with her might happen naturally, not with him playing the part of a lovesick fool who stalked her at her place of work.

Even if the Landis men did not seek Vic's veterinary services, Fletch now had her address. This changed everything. Instead of spending his time daydreaming about how to contact her, he needed to embrace the likely possibility and consider the consequences of pursuing a Conservative girl. Matt Landis had left the Conservative Church. Would his sister be willing to do the same? Fletch had to have one more look at Lillian Landis.

—⸉⸊—

Lil literally blew into the mudroom. She swiped her hair out of her eyes and spit grit from her parched lips as she removed her barn shoes. It was the kind of dry wind that downed wheat and damaged fields. This time of year, wind could be real trouble for farmers.

Now midmorning, she'd already put in a full day's work. She'd risen early and rearranged her schedule to help with the chores since her dad and two of her brothers were at the farming seminar. But she was glad to do it if it helped them find a solution to the farm's financial woes.

Lil went to the kitchen to wash her hands and halted with surprise. "Mom? Hi."

"You got up early. What's going on?"

A pang of resentment shot through Lil that her dad remained so secretive with her mom these days. Intuition told her it was only adding to her mom's depression. "Dad had some farm business and asked me to do some extra chores."

Mom dipped her head. "I'm sorry everything falls on you. I wish the doctors could find out what's wrong with me. I'd like to do my share around here." Then she tilted her face and studied Lil curiously. "Why, you have your covering on. I didn't think you were wearing it anymore."

Lil shrugged, unwilling to make any commitments, and pulled out a chair across the table from her mom. She wondered if the medication had given Mom the desire to get out of bed. Aside from the overdose incident, she hadn't been complaining or sleeping as much anymore. Lil searched her mind for something enjoyable to occupy her mother's time. "I do have something you could do for me. Michelle's zucchini are starting."

Mom actually smiled. "And so the battle begins."

They both knew that keeping up with a zucchini crop took plenty of ingenuity. "Anyway, she lost her relish recipe. Maybe you could jot it down for her again, along with any other good zucchini recipes." Lil raced to the drawer that held their recipe cards and plunked a couple down in front of her mom. Stephen's wife, Lisa, had gifted Mom with some special-order cards that read ROSE'S YUMMY RECIPES.

Mom tapped a pencil on the table. "Yes, I believe I know it from memory." She started to write, glancing up at Lil. "And the men love your chocolate zucchini cake." She became totally absorbed in the zucchini project until the sudden chime at the front doorbell announced a potential visitor. She instantly paled. "Quick, Lil! Help me back to my room."

Lil placed a steadying hand on her mom's tense shoulder. "No need for that. You look fine. Let me just go see who it is." When she entered the living room, her heart sank to see Brother Troyer's car through the windowpane. Though it was partly hidden by blowing tree limbs, she knew in her heart it was him. The entire family had been anticipating and dreading his call. She wondered if he'd purposefully chosen a day when the men would be gone. She sped back to the kitchen. "It's Brother Troyer. Look busy so he'll think you're doing well."

"Oh no."

"It will be fine."

When she saw her mom relent, Lil patted the wrinkles out of her apron and hurried to the door. "Hello," she said as the screen door blew wide open and hit the outside wall. "Come in."

Brother Troyer pulled the door closed behind him and entered the front room with his hat in his hand. "Whew, hope that wind passes on through the county without doing any harm to the fields."

Lil nodded. "Yes, the recent rains shot the crops up, and now they are vulnerable."

He looked toward the back of the house and attempted a joke. "Well you know the old saying about what the wind blew in." He shrugged and his black collarless coat bunched around his thin shoulders. "Guess that's just me."

Lil gave an uncomfortable smile, hoping her mom hadn't slipped back to her bedroom. She didn't want to face the preacher's questions alone. "Yes. Here you are. How may I help you?"

He cleared his throat. "I hoped to have a chat with Rose."

"Of course. She's in the kitchen. Please follow me."

The older man followed Lil into the kitchen and smiled kindly at her mother. "Don't get up, Rose. I'll just join you at the table, if I may."

"Yes," Mom said, dipping her head.

Lil felt her mom's shame, felt her own face heat. "Would you like some iced tea or lemonade?"

"Iced tea would be nice. That wind parched my lips." Brother

Troyer settled into a chair and gazed at Mom. "Are you writing one of your splendid secret recipes, there?"

"Oh no. Just jotting down a few old faithfuls for Michelle. Her zucchini's in. Besides that, she's got her hands full with those little ones."

"Yes, she does." He studied her a moment. "Our hostess committee has their hands full, too, without you, Rose. You've been the hub of that committee ever since I can remember. We could use your help."

"I'm really tired these days. Why I even had a little hospital stay."

The glass in Lil's hand clinked as she set the preacher's iced drink before him. Listening to the conversation progress, she slipped into a chair at the table with them.

"I'm sorry to hear that. There's many ways to get weary. I remember a time about ten years after I'd entered the ministry when my soul got so weary. For me, I was trying to do too many things on my own and lost the will to keep up the battle. We can't do it on our own, you know."

"What happened?" Mom asked.

"Why there wasn't any one thing I did to snap out of it, but it was a journey, let me tell you. Learning to lean on God and not on my own strength."

"Oh."

Lil heard the disappointment in Mom's voice. She'd probably been hopeful that there was a simpler solution.

"Looking back now, I'm glad it happened. God walked me through it and taught me little things that altogether brought me out of my slump. The key was realizing I'd come to my end and really depending on God to help me out of it."

"Yeah?"

"Do you have the strength to pray?"

To Lil's surprise, Mom answered honestly with a negative shake of her head.

"I thought so. That's how I felt back then. But people prayed for me. And I'll pray for you. I'll pray that God will give you enough strength to pray for yourself. Promise me you'll just try. You have to ask to receive.

See if God doesn't provide. Remember, when Jesus healed the lame, they had to try to walk to find out if they could."

"I suppose."

Brother Troyer patted Mom's hand.

CHAPTER 6

Lil poured herself a glass of well water from the kitchen sink and peered out under the lilac-print window valance. Clothes gently flapped on the wash line just beyond the flower beds, where monarch and swallowtail butterflies flitted around Mom's scraggly perennials. The only flowers this year were the ones that had survived of their own accord.

The bird feeder remained empty, but she had noticed that occasionally a small flock of goldfinches came in to investigate. Over the years, Dad had grumbled that birdseed was a waste of money, and in a sense it was, because God provided plenty for the birds to eat. But she knew Mom used the feeder to draw the birds in close to the window where she had to while away so many hours washing dishes and preparing food. Conservative women didn't have televisions on their countertops for entertainment, and Lil's mom had few modern conveniences—like the dishwasher Lil and her friends had installed in the doddy house—so chores took plenty of time. She determined that if Mom ever got well enough to do kitchen chores, she would buy birdseed for that feeder whether Dad thought it was a waste of money or not.

Farther out, barn swallows swooped over the corn and soy fields to snatch insects. After the rain, the insects seemed to flourish. Earlier in the week, the wind had brought just enough moisture to raise the humidity and officially bring in the dog days of summer.

Lil's gaze followed the long circle drive that ran all the way to the barn. She leisurely scanned the hog pastures, wondering if Dad would be in late again. She had no way of telling, because she would already be at work. She was not going to be late. Beppe's insolent attitude had not improved.

Lil's thoughts returned to her dad, curious over his recent behavior. Since he and the boys had gone off to that farm seminar, he'd been silent. On the nights when she hadn't worked, she'd noticed that Dad and her brothers were having frequent meetings and lingering longer than usual after their chores.

When Lil didn't stay home for supper because of her work schedule, she always set the table for two, hoping Mom would join Dad for the meal. Usually Lil needed to be at work by four o'clock. Then she would scribble last-minute instructions about the meal for Dad.

With a sigh, she set down her glass and went to fetch the clothes off the line. Since the preacher's visit, Mom seemed more determined than ever not to lift a finger. It was as if her spirit had vacated her body, especially when Dad was in the room. But Lil had noticed something new. Mom often had her Bible open. At least she was taking Brother Troyer's advice.

Lil got the clothespin bag off the mudroom shelf and grabbed the clothes basket off the floor. At the clothesline, she spied Dad coming across the drive from the direction of the barn. When he got within earshot, she called out to him.

He waved and joined her at the clothesline. "Do you have enough food for the boys and their families?"

"What?" Lil sputtered, placing her hands on her skirted hips. "No. Did you invite the entire family?"

He stuck a thumb under his overall's suspender. "Yep."

"But Dad, I can't just whip up an entire meal. Usually it's just you and Mom."

He reached out and tussled her hair. "Sure you can, sweetheart. You can do anything with food. Just whip out those fandangled waffles and that fancy syrup of yours."

Lil straightened her head covering, wanting to scream. *But I don't have time. I can't be late to work again.* But it had been so long since her dad had ruffled her hair. So long since he'd even smiled. Since anybody had smiled. Including Beppe at work.

"I'll finish my chores, then come in and shower and get your mom up myself."

Lil gazed down the row of clothing as if an idea would pop off the clothesline. Amazingly, one did. "All right. I'll throw a big batch of chili together, and Michelle can finish it up when she gets here."

"Why Michelle? Where are you going?"

"Uh, Riccardo's?" The moment she'd said it, she realized her voice had sounded disrespectful.

"Oh." He waved his hand as if to dismiss her job as a mere inconvenience. "Well you're going to miss the big announcement then. When I told Matt to come, he asked if he could bring along the vet." He stopped speaking and eyed Lil speculatively. "Somebody we met at the farm seminar."

"He's bringing company, too?"

"Yep. A good-looking guy. Nice enough. But don't get your hopes up about him. He's a Mennonite, but not Conservative." Her dad twisted his mouth in an unpleasant grimace. "He goes to Matt's church."

While her subconscious probed the bits and pieces her dad had flung at her, trying to make sense of the information, she wondered what a good-looking stranger would think of chili in the middle of the summer. *Not a stranger,* her brain corrected. *Mennonite vet.* She breathed a sigh of relief that she wouldn't be there to witness a good-looking Mennonite vet's reaction to the meal. "Maybe you can just tell me the news, since I have to work."

Ignoring her last remark, Dad kept on talking about the invited guest. "His name's Fletch Stauffer. Did I mention he goes to Matt's church?"

She felt her face heat, momentarily forgetting all about the big announcement. "Did you say—" She choked off the words. No need to bring the minor car accident and object of her daydreams to her dad's attention. She tried to stay calm, to still her speeding heartbeat. "And you say he's a veterinarian?"

"Yep." Dad rocked back on his heels, then slapped his straw hat on his leg and placed it back on his head before he strode back toward the barn.

It had to be the same Fletch Stauffer. *Well!* Lil quickly unpinned the dry clothes, folding and dropping them into the clothes basket, all the while trying to digest what had just transpired. Dad was happy, almost boyish. And Fletch Stauffer, the handsome blond who never called her, was coming to dinner.

Emotions battled inside her, making her want to skip work to see Fletch again. Wanting to hear every little detail about the big news that would be discussed over supper. She especially wondered what had Dad seeing blue skies. Next he'd be singing and filling the bird feeder. Her heart raced with hope. He had promised to get Mom up for dinner, and with his new cheery attitude, Mom might come out of her shell.

But Lil had to go to the restaurant. She hadn't mustered up courage to call a cab when Mom was in the hospital just to lose her job now. With a disappointed sigh, she realized she could get Michelle's version of the big announcement later. And if Fletch was going to do veterinary work at the Landis farm, surely she'd get an opportunity to talk to him another time. Wouldn't' she?

But what if after tonight, Fletch didn't want anything to do with the Landis bunch? What then? She'd miss her one and only chance to connect with him.

With the basket propped on one hip, and her phone at her ear, she started toward the house. "Hi, Beppe," she said, passing through the mudroom. "Can I switch nights and come in at six tonight and four tomorrow night? If not, that's okay. Just checking."

She heard Beppe's irritated grunt. "I don't have to ask who this is."

"Oh sorry. Yeah, it's Lil."

"Hold on." She waited, never so hopeful over missing a few hours of work. Finally he returned. "You can be here by six?"

"Yes. Thanks."

"Don't be late," he warned.

She set the clothes basket on the washing machine and jerked open the freezer door. She grabbed some frozen ground pork and slapped it on a riveted thawing board. After that, she diced tomatoes, fresh from Michelle's garden. She could slice fresh corn off the cob, and she'd add some cilantro and maybe some summer savory. As she worked, temptation came to her. *Don't go to work. Stay home and see Fletcher. If you lose your job, you could work on a recipe book. Dad's been after you to quit, anyway.*

She shook aside the fantasy she sometimes had of writing a fabulous recipe book. If she lost her job, the farm would suck her in and sap the life right out of her. There'd be no time for recipes. *I love my job,* she argued.

It's a dead end, temptation beckoned.

No. If Fletch wants to ask me out, he has my phone number. And now he has my address, too.

Temptation warned, *Matt's bringing him. They go to the same church. He's coming as Matt's friend. Maybe he doesn't even know that Matt is your brother.*

Back and forth her thoughts went. Even as she slipped into her freshly ironed black skirt and white blouse uniform, she debated. Before she left the house for work, however, she gave the dining room a final once-over.

Mom's Autumn Leaf dishes were set on a pristine, white lace tablecloth. The chili concoction simmered in two slow cookers that the family used in the summer so they didn't heat up the kitchen. And strawberry cobbler would do for dessert. It was the best she could do on such short notice. An easy meal that could be served without the cook's presence, she determined.

With the decision made to fulfill her responsibilities at the restaurant, she took her purse off the peg shelf and bolted for the back door, confident that for once, she'd be right on time for work.

"Oophf!" she exclaimed, ramming into something solid. Splaying her hands on a firm, shirt-clad chest, Lil saw the familiar red tennis

61

shoes. Her face burned with embarrassment as she looked up into soft brown eyes. She quickly dropped her hands.

He shook his head. "Never saw a more accident-prone woman."

"You're early." She instantly regretted the slip of tongue that made him aware that she'd been expecting him. Didn't want him to judge her cooking when it had been so hurriedly tossed together. Didn't want him to think she was trying to avoid him. Beans! Just didn't want him to think she was thinking about him, period.

And she wasn't thinking, she was feeling. Tingling from her palms to her black-toed oxfords. She wet her lips, frozen to the spot. Frozen and tingling.

But he hadn't missed her declaration. His brows arched. She'd remembered he was good-looking, but she had forgotten about the interesting brown brows/blond hair combination. It intrigued her because the darker brows made a nice frame for his eyes. But intriguing as he was, she snapped her mouth closed, determined not to stick her foot back in it again.

He gave her a dimpled smile. "You aren't running away, are you?"

She tucked her errant bangs behind her ear, and her response came out in thicker Dutch than she would have liked. "I am on my way out. I'm off to work."

His expression fell. "Riccardo's?"

She nodded.

"I'm sorry. Ever since Matt gave me the invitation, I've been looking forward to seeing you again."

She stared at him, still unable to fathom his presence. Almost as if she was conjuring him up like her imaginary Rollo. But his comment reminded her of the disappointment she'd felt when he hadn't called. "If that's true, maybe you should have called."

"I wanted to. But I lost your number."

Lil frowned. It would be nice to believe him. Even though she didn't date much, she was able to recognize a flimsy excuse when she heard one. No matter how tingly he made her palms and heart and toes, she wouldn't tolerate feeble excuses. She narrowed her eyes. "A likely story."

He raised both hands in objection. "It's the truth. Our accident was just the beginning. After I left Riccardo's, I got stopped by a police officer for speeding. The dinner check with your phone number floated under my seat, and when I tried to get it, the officer thought I was going for a gun and made me step out of the car. Later, my boss had me so flustered, I forgot to look for it." He shrugged. "It turned out the car belonged to my boss's wife."

Lil's lips twitched, and it was hard not to smile and fall under Fletcher's dimpled charm. The story seemed too far-fetched to be fiction. "That's an interesting story."

That was when she noticed Matt, leaning against the wall with crossed arms.

"Hi, Matt."

"What's going on with you two?"

"Oh Fletch can explain. If I don't leave this instant, Beppe's going to give me an earful."

"You're afraid of a Beepie?" Fletch asked, refusing to step aside.

"Beppe," she corrected, with a grin. "Yes, because he's my boss. Maybe, I'll see you. . .sometime." Lil started toward the door, but it was too late. Michelle flounced in with her three little girls in tow—in birth order, Tate, Tammy, and Trish. Tammy reached up and wrapped her arms around Lil's waist. "Hi, Auntie Lily. Swing me?"

The nieces were dolly stepping stones all dressed alike in homemade dresses that were tinier versions of Michelle's own dress. Their little dresses hung well below their knees, but unlike their mommy, the girls wore no stockings. In spite of the heat, they looked pretty with their light brown hair freshly braided.

Lil swung Tammy in a circle like she always did. After that it was Tate's turn. And next, she took Trish from Michelle's arms to give her a row of cuddly kisses. Her nephews barreled in too, and after that, Lil couldn't have gone against the tide of incoming bodies even if her future position as head chef depended on it. But when she was able to get away, she slipped into the living room to call the restaurant manager.

"Guess what, Beppe?"

"Lillian, please don't start."

"Remember that guy with the Lexus, the one I ran into in the parking lot?"

A frustrated sigh came from Beppe. "Yes, what about him?"

"My dad invited him for supper tonight. I haven't had a date in a really long time, Beppe. Surely you don't want me to miss an opportunity like this?"

"Actually, I don't care about your personal life, Lillian, because you don't work here any longer."

"Come on, Beppe. You don't really mean that." But no reply was forthcoming. Only a click and silence. With a moan, Lil returned to the kitchen. Regardless of her best intentions, it seemed her fate had been decided for her.

CHAPTER 7

Stephen lifted the slow cooker lid and sniffed. "Wow, chili in summer? Now that's a crazy idea."

His red-haired, pregnant wife, Lisa, elbowed him.

"Summer chili," Lil corrected.

"Then you should have served it cold." Now why hadn't she thought of that? Because her brain had malfunctioned after learning that Fletcher was coming to supper. That's why. She'd have plenty of time to tweak recipes now. Plenty of unemployed time.

As usual, it was a major production to get the Landis clan all seated and situated. Everyone knew their places, for a natural pecking order had been established over the years. All the chairs around the extended dining room table would be filled, as well as the children's table, and a high chair for Trish beside Michelle and her husband, Tom.

Hank's wife, Sara Cyclone, made several trips to the kids' table before she was satisfied that Scott's ant farm was still intact and Sammy's shoes were securely tied. Seated next to Sara, Lisa rested her arms over a bulging belly, and her errant red curls bounced each time her gaze followed Sara's movements. Most likely, Lisa was observing and gathering future mothering skills in preparation for her own baby's arrival.

Lil's dad presided at one end. Sitting next to him, Mom wore a pasted but somewhat pleasant smile. Being single, Matt claimed a man-sized space which crowded into Lil's. Across from them, a chair had been squeezed in for Fletch, who watched all the commotion with mild amusement.

Although it seemed to be a typical family gathering, it was anything but normal to Lil, whose heart hammered from its proximity to the *good-looking Mennonite vet.* The very idea that she had the next half hour to scrutinize him and, if possible, impress him with her feminine charms was too good to be true. Now if only she could breathe.

"I'll ask the blessing," Dad announced, still uncharacteristically happy, even after what must have been a draining half hour of getting Mom out of bed and dressed for the occasion. The prayer was spoken in that reverent tone the Mennonite heads of house used, barely audible except for a recognizable phrase or two.

Afterward, Lil gestured toward the crocks of chili at each end of the table. "Sorry supper is informal. We'll just have to pass the chili and serve ourselves." If Fletch thought it strange that the youngest daughter was acting hostess, he didn't let on, but Lil still felt her face heat as Stephen lifted the ladle. Why had she kept things so casual? What would Fletch think of them? Better to underplay his presence, she finally concluded.

With Stephen's help, Lisa passed a large citrus-and-lettuce salad that she had contributed, and Lil passed the rolls. Sara had brought cucumber salad, and Michelle had contributed zucchini bread. Thankfully it all went together wonderfully even though nobody had called to ask what to bring.

Michelle opened her cloth napkin and sprang to her feet. "Matt! You scoundrel!"

Lil bit back a smile and craned her neck to see what had happened. You'd think Michelle would be more cautious since Matt loved to single her out for his practical jokes, probably because she screamed the loudest and was the most gullible. She shook out her napkin, and straw floated to the floor. Her daughters giggled.

Michelle reseated herself, jutted her chin, and speared Matt with a fake glare. "You can sweep the floor."

"Sure." He shrugged. "Think we live in a pigsty?"

"But we don't live here. Neither do you, Uncle Matt," four-year-old Tammy pointed out from her place at the children's table.

"No, sweetie. It's just an expression," Matt explained.

"Don't pay any attention to him, girls. Better start eating," Michelle warned with a smile.

When everyone had been served, Lil stole a glance at Fletch. His lean face, planed in masculine angles, sported a wide forehead and those dark expressive brows. She watched him taste the chili. His soft brown eyes lit with pleasure. He raised them and met her gaze with a slightly dimpled smile that made it hard to forget that there were more than a dozen other people in the room.

Stephen mumbled, "Delicious. Really good, Lil." There were several affirmative murmurs around the table.

"Thanks." She glanced at Fletch again. "Tell me about your work. Dad said you're a veterinarian?"

"Not really. I'm still in school at OSU. But I'm doing what the course calls an off-site selective experience, working with Vic at his clinic. It's a senior requirement."

She tried not to blush as she asked, "How long will you be helping there?"

"Until next spring when I graduate."

On learning that Fletch would be around for a significant length of time, she did a mental garbanzo bean dance, her personal way of celebrating ever since childhood camp days.

He leaned forward and said softly, "I'm glad you didn't go to work after all." His expression was seductively smug.

"I—I hadn't seen my nieces and nephews for a while. They're hard to resist. I guess when they came in, I had a change of heart."

"Yes. Very hard to resist."

The room grew stifling hot. What had she been thinking? Chili in summer?

"I met your family at the farm seminar where Vic was giving a workshop. Matt recognized me from church."

Fletch Stauffer in the flesh was a gorgeous contradiction. Flirting

67

one minute and in the next breath forewarning her that he was merely Matt's friend. Was his flirtatious behavior part of a natural charm and not meant to be taken personally? She needed to tread carefully. After all, he attended a Mennonite church that didn't hold to the same restrictions that her church maintained. She glanced warily at him. In the background, her dad cleared his throat. Fletch glanced down the table at him. The gesture reminded Lil that they had all gathered for a specific purpose. Hearing the big announcement.

Dad cleared his throat a second time. "I suppose you all wonder why we gathered you together on a weeknight?" It wouldn't have been unusual a year earlier when Mom was healthy, but of late, they'd mostly gotten together for birthdays and holidays.

Lil glanced around the table, observing her family's reaction. Sara's blush meant that Hank had already filled the Cyclone in on the big secret, but Michelle seemed surprised that Dad had an announcement to make. A general hush fell over the gathering, except for Stephen's nervous slurping. He wasn't much on table manners; even now he had his bare arms resting on the tablecloth. Lil figured he tried to cover up his growing pouch by displaying his muscular arms. Beads of perspiration dotted Lisa's pretty forehead.

Dad continued. "It's time for change." He explained about the farm's decline. "I don't know if I've told you lately, but I'm proud of all you kids." Lil noticed Mom's eyes get teary. "It's time I let you modernize. We're going to expand, put up one of those newfangled metal barns so we can handle more hogs. We're going to contract with one of them big integrator companies. And I just wanted to get everybody together and make it official."

Beside her, she felt Matt's shoulders swell with pride over his modern ideas. His green T-shirt—that no Conservative farmer would wear—said it all: PROUD TO BE A FARMER.

All around the table, conversation buzzed with excitement and questions, mostly from the wives. Lil gave Fletch a curious glance, wondering why Matt had invited him and what he thought of their family's modernizing plans. "How do you fit into this, Fletch?" she asked, softly.

He glanced at Matt with hesitation.

Matt shrugged. "Just thought it would be a good opportunity to get to know us better."

As a friend or professionally? she wondered.

"Actually," Fletch grinned, "I aim to do what I can to keep the Landis hogs happy."

Matt broke into laughter.

Lil felt her face redden for Fletch, but he seemed impervious to his gaffe. *Happy hogs?* She could just envision the sort of practical joke Matt would play on him because of that foolish remark.

When Matt stopped laughing, he started the rolls around again. "I ran into Ivan Penner at the farm implement store. He said that Katy and Jake have returned from their honeymoon."

The good news caused Lil to forget all about Fletch. She broke into a happy squeal and did a garbanzo-dance shoulder shimmy against Matt. "I can't wait to see them. Thanks."

She missed them so much and wanted to tell them all that had happened lately. As she thought about all the changes, she quickly sobered. Too many changes. It had hardly sunk in.

Beppe had fired her.

Across the table, their visitor grew quiet, perhaps overwhelmed by their large, talkative family. The conversation skittered in a million directions. Her brothers eagerly discussed a tentative meeting with the Plain City Bank.

Lil caught Mom's gaze. Her face had become stoic again. "What's for dessert, dear?"

"Strawberry shortcake."

Over at the children's table, Tate clapped her hands. "My favorite."

Everybody laughed, surprised the six-year-old had been following the adult conversation.

"She's been helping me in the strawberry patch." Michelle smiled at Mom. "You should come over and spend a day with us, Mom. The girls would love to show you the garden—wouldn't you, sweethearts?"

The tiny heads bobbed in agreement, and the children broke out in chatter which included a cute string of mispronunciations.

Mom let out a ragged gasp, her shoulders convulsing.

Dad scooted his chair back and draped an arm around her. "Honey?"

He looked over helplessly at Lil. She didn't know if she should help Mom back to her room or let her cry. Nobody else knew either, because they were all looking at her to do something.

—◦—

"None of us knew what to do," Lil told Katy. "I've never been so thankful for my nieces' spontaneity. When they saw Mom crying, they jumped up and crawled all over her, throwing their little arms around her neck. And it was so weird. Mom went straight from weeping to laughing. And when she started laughing, so did everybody else, including Fletch, even though I don't think he had a clue what was happening. Honestly, he must think we are the strangest family."

"Wait." Katy shook her brunette ponytail, pushing a glass of lemonade toward Lil. "Who's Fletch?"

"Oh, no. He can wait. You tell me about your honeymoon first." Lil examined the glass. "Where'd you get this?"

"Jake's mom. She adores sunflowers." Katy pointed to the window. "See the sunflower chime?"

Lil giggled. "What's it like to have a mother-in-law?"

"First I have to tell you what it's like to have a husband."

Widening her eyes, Lil hoped her friend wasn't going to go into details about her cousin.

"Jake is the greatest." Katy's dark eyes turned dreamy. "Marriage is better than I thought it would be."

Lil was relieved to see Katy so in love with the man who was like a brother to her, and probably even closer to her than Matt. "That chump?" she teased.

"We got sunburned on the beach, took a cruise that was so romantic." Katy quickly highlighted their trip from sunset strolls to a reunion with her old employer—a sweet elderly woman who had played a big part in deepening Katy's faith. Only a year earlier, she had been experiencing a personal winter. Lil couldn't be happier that Katy had found happiness, even if her own future seemed uncertain.

70

"And Jake's mom and I found some common ground." Katy suddenly tilted her head. "I noticed you're wearing your covering again."

Shrugging, Lil replied, "My dad said something to me about it."

"So it's just temporary?"

"I don't know."

Lil gazed wistfully around the doddy house, wondering if she would be able to move in, come September. So much had changed. The little farm table now sported Jake's computer. Sunflowers splashed bits of new color. Only six months earlier, she and Katy had moved into the tiny Amish guest house, renovating it together. Their other best friend, Megan, had helped them and had planned to move in with them as soon as she graduated from Rosedale Bible College. It had always been the friends' shared dream, but especially Lil's. She came up with the idea all those years ago at camp—to room together and be each other's bridesmaids.

But when Lil had moved home, Katy married Jake. The doddy house became their honeymoon cottage. Megan went on a mission trip as soon as she graduated. The new plan was for Katy and Jake to find another house. Megan and Lil planned to move in together in the autumn. September, to be exact. Lil was counting the days.

But now that she had lost her job, she would not be able to afford her part of the rent. And Mom was still struggling with depression. Moving back into the doddy house seemed impossible. How could she admit to her friends that she had been fired?

"Who's Fletch?" Katy asked, returning to the earlier question.

"You're never going to believe it." Lil started telling the basics of the story: how they met, the farm problems, the farm seminar, and how Matt had invited Fletch to a family supper. But some important adjectives like *good-looking, Mennonite,* and *veterinarian* found their way into the narrative. Then Lil caved altogether and crooned on and on about his dark brows and soft suede eyes.

Katy's mouth gaped. "How could so much happen in three short weeks?"

"Three weeks may seem short to somebody on their honeymoon," Lil teased, "but they've been an eternity for me. I've missed you so much."

"Well, it's good to be home."

"I'm glad you're happy." Lil hugged Katy.

When they drew apart, Katy brought the conversation back to Fletch. "But a cute guy delivered right to your back door. Now that's amazing."

Lil grinned, thinking that Katy made him sound like a brown UPS package. "He wasn't exactly wrapped and delivered to me. He's Matt's friend." And just in case Katy maintained the brown parcel image, she added, "Did I mention *good-looking* and *charming* friend?"

"I did catch that. *Mennonite veterinarian.* Got it. But just because he's Matt's friend doesn't mean he's not interested in you."

"Matt told me later that Fletch was drumming up work at the seminar. Matt plans to use their practice for our veterinary services. Fletch's interest in Matt might be work related."

"Their practice?"

"He works for Vic Fuller. Fletch is doing some sort of internship."

"Interesting. You never fell for a Mennonite guy before. This could be the one."

"But he's not Conservative Mennonite."

Katy bit her lip.

Lil saw her friend's hesitation and understood it. In their friendship pattern, Katy always tried to persuade Lil to be more conservative in her thinking and actions. In her black-and-white thinking, Katy closely adhered to all the church restrictions. But last year, her friend had learned forgiveness. She wasn't as judgmental against the outsiders anymore. But would she approve of Fletch and his red tennis shoes?

CHAPTER 8

Fletch patted Buddy on the head, deliberating over his dinner at the Landis farm. Lil's huge family was so different from his own. He and his sister had been raised on the mission field. Often it felt like his parents had been more involved with their ministry than concerned about their children. He and Erica had been close, but now she was married to a Canadian she had met in Africa. They lived in his country and were involved with Wycliffe Bible Translators. Erica and Fletch hardly talked anymore. Watching the Landis family interact had made him aware of his personal loneliness.

Sure, he was a friendly sort, and people were always around him, but that wasn't the same. Right now, his closest friend was his mentor, Marshall. The man who funded Fletch's tuition came from a wealthy family who had acquired money in Texas oil. He was a southern gentleman and a bit of an eccentric. Like Fletch's own dad, Marshall was passionate about life. Not only did he support his favorite causes, but he got involved in them.

Marshall had first discovered the Stauffers by visiting a Mennonite church to learn about their peace stance. That Sunday, the Stauffers were on furlough and reporting on their Congo mission work. Before

Marshall left the church foyer, he'd pledged his financial support to them.

Marshall was the Stauffer family's most consistent supporter. Over the years, he'd visited the mission field three times to see firsthand where his money was invested. On those visits, he'd noticed Fletch, especially his love for animals. Marshall shared this passion and had been influential in encouraging Fletch to chase his dreams and become a veterinarian. And now he was financing his schooling. Fletch owed Marshall. He missed him.

Acting on impulse and loneliness, Fletch pulled his cell phone from his jeans pocket.

Soon Marshall's southern voice drawled, "Ya can't throw in the hat now."

Fletch grinned. "Don't worry. I'm not calling for a pep talk. I just miss you."

"So this isn't one of them 'I'm out of money' calls?"

"Of course not. I'd call my dad if I needed money."

They both laughed over that irony. "So how's it going, working for Victor?"

"It was going great until I wrecked his wife's car."

"Oh Fletch, ya didn't?"

"Afraid so. But it wasn't my fault. A girl backed into me in a parking lot. But Vic's been acting like he's got a chip on his shoulder ever since."

"Hm. His recommendations were excellent."

"Don't get me wrong. He's a good guy. I like him, and I'm learning a lot."

"Has he taken ya to the farm shelter yet?"

The shelter was a farm that took in abused livestock. "No. I'd almost forgotten about it. That's one of your charities, isn't it?"

"It's more than a charity," Marshall drawled. "Marcus is running that place now."

"Give me the address. I'd like to go see him."

After the conversation ended, Fletch wondered why he hadn't been informed earlier that Marshall's son was in Plain City. The farm shelter was all his mentor had wanted to talk about. In their conversation,

Marshall insinuated that Vic was one of the shelter's volunteer vets, but Vic had never mentioned it to Fletch.

Buddy licked his arm, and Fletch ruffled the basset's head. "Wanna go for a walk?" Buddy responded by dancing in circles.

Fletch went for the dog's leash, remembering Marshall's positive reaction to his description of dinner with the Landis family. Marshall had thought it was hilarious that Lillian was the one who'd backed in-to Britt's car.

"Ya better ask her out before some pasta maker plucks her off to Italy."

For a rich world traveler, opportunities were endless. Marshall could make anything sound feasible.

But then, Lillian had skipped work after Fletch asked her to stay. She told him that her nieces and nephews had changed her mind, but he hoped it was his invitation. He'd like to believe that he would get one more look at her angelic, freckled face.

—☙—

Lil heard the door to the mudroom slam and quickly shoved the news-paper ad into the trash bin, while turning and pretending a calm de-meanor. Her guilty conscience ebbed when Dad stormed into the room.

Red-faced with anger, he stated, "Heaven is against us."

Lil's blood went cold. Her dad never said such blasphemous things. Well, at least not in her presence.

"Matt said the Plain City Bank won't even listen to him. They want to talk to me, or I have to give him legal authorization."

"Well that can be worked out," Lil soothed.

Her father slumped into a kitchen chair. "And the hogs are sick."

"Oh, no!" Lil paced to the sink and back. "Well, you can call the vet that Fletch works for, can't you?"

"Hank already called him." He pounded his fist on the table. "He should have been here by now."

Lil quickly went to the refrigerator and poured her dad a glass of lemonade, sliding it in front of him. She touched his arm. "You mustn't lose heart."

He chugged the drink and pushed the empty glass away, turning to Lil with a bitter expression. "Why not? I'm losing my wife, my farm, and now my hogs. What is left?"

"Your faith?" Lil reminded him, although she didn't feel as though she should be the one to talk about God to a person as devoted as her dad, when she was not that. . .well, just was not. She tried to remember the last time she'd prayed. It had been on the way to the hospital when she'd petitioned for Mom's life. God had spared her. She was about to remind her dad about that, but he spoke first.

"Well we might be losing that, too. We might even be kicked out of church."

"Why?" Lil demanded, hoping she hadn't done something to provoke the elders. Had Matt?

"The preacher called again. This time he talked to me. He said that gossip is going around the church about your mom about why she doesn't come to church anymore. He suggested it would be better for the unity of the believers if she comes before the congregation and publicly repents for trying to commit suicide."

Lil clutched the table.

"He says the congregation will gladly forgive her. That it will help her recover. He asked me how I thought she'd respond to the idea."

"What!" Lil cried. "She'll never do that. She's too weak. She'd be humiliated. Why, he never talked like that the day he visited Mom. He—"

"I know that. He claims the elders came up with it. He said they're not demanding it, just recommending it. They want to help her."

"Well! They can recommend it to the moon!" Lil replied. She wondered how Katy and Megan's dads, both elders in the church, could come up with something so hurtful for their friends. Tears burned her eyes. Surely that was what was riling her dad up, too.

The house phone rang, and Lil resented the interruption, but Dad, who didn't own a cell phone, jumped up to answer it. "Yah-low." He nodded. "Be right there."

"What is it?" Lil's hand flew to her heart fearfully, wondering what else might befall them. Perhaps the barn had collapsed, like in the book of Job. Surely her dad was right about heaven being against them.

"Vet's here." He turned and strode away, leaving Lil to bear the burden of her hurt alone.

She rushed to the window and saw a white Chevy pickup. The vet must have already gone inside the barn. Fletch drove a blue car. She wondered if he was out there, too. She watched her father's squared shoulders, the image of a man bracing himself for the worst. *Oh Lord,* she prayed, *I'm sorry I only pray in need. But there goes a man who's been faithful to You. Please, won't You help him? He's my dad.*

—꒰

Fletch felt his heart sink. Six piglets were coughing and two inside the creep, the portion of the pen that the sow couldn't get into, had already expired. Vic examined one of the sick piglets and asked Will Landis, "Is this the first sign of pneumonia?"

"Yep."

"Do you have a regular vaccination program?"

"We did. We were using antibiotic feed, too. But we've been strapped and let up a bit."

The fear in the older man's voice tore at Fletch, for they all knew that once something like Porcine Reproductive and Respiratory Syndrome got into a herd, it was a costly, lengthy process to rid the herd of the virus.

Vic placed the piglet back in the straw and made a nest around the baby animal then picked up another. "Introduced any new breeders into the herd?"

"Yep, last fall. Surely we would have seen signs before now if that was the cause?"

Vic's expression softened. "These are just routine questions. Could be parasites, could just be a sick sow. I'd like to get a blood sample from her and take the two dead corpses back to the lab. Either way, we should get you started back on a vaccine routine and feed precautions."

Will gave a frustrated nod.

Vic placed the piglet down and stood. "Fletch? Can I have a word with you?" They moved to a nearby corner, and the vet placed his hand on Fletch's shoulder. "I've seen this kind of thing sweep through a herd. It's hard to eradicate."

"The Landis farm is already in financial trouble," Fletch replied.

"I can give them a discount, but if you'd want to volunteer your time for the vaccinations and some ongoing blood draws, it would help me and the Landises, too. I know you've become friends with Matt. Would you be willing to do that?"

Fletch was eager to help Matt—and Lillian, too, for that matter. He didn't hesitate. "I'll do it."

Vic warned, "You'll be busy. I've agreed to volunteer at a local farm shelter, and Britt's already on my case about being away from home so much. This could turn into a big project here, and. . .well, I appreciate it."

"I'll do whatever it takes to help."

"Thanks." Vic turned away and strode back to the farrowing pen. "Fletch has agreed to volunteer his time to give vaccines and take blood draws, if that will help."

Matt grabbed Fletch's arm. "You'd do that?"

Fletch nodded. "Sure. I told you I'd do what I could to make the Landis hogs happy."

Will Landis gave a huge sigh, and Fletch wasn't sure if it was from relief or dread of what the future had to hold for all of them. "Guess you know about our struggles here. We thank you. And for the discount, too."

Fletch wished he could do more. As they continued to discuss the Landis hogs, he got an inkling of the emotional turmoil this job would entail. With clients treated like family, their pain was felt as one's own. Just the other night, he'd been feeling sorry for himself, engulfed in his personal loneliness. Getting close to people carried a price. Now he shared their fears.

After further examination of the sow and disinfecting again at the barn's entrance, Fletch and Vic took their leave.

"See you at church," Fletch called, while sneaking a peek toward the house. Lillian's car was there, but he hadn't caught a glimpse of her.

"You bet. Thanks again," Matt replied.

On their way back to the practice, they discussed the Landis hogs some more, and then fell quiet, content to watch the landscape of green cornfields and soybeans. When Fletch saw Vic's eyelids drooping heavily with sleep, he started up another conversation, hoping to keep them out of the ditch.

"What can you tell me about the shelter?"

Vic sent him a startled look. "I thought you knew all about it."

"Not really. Marshall mentioned it the last time we talked on the phone. I meant to ask you about it before."

The truck bounced over a pothole, causing Vic's hands to bounce off the steering wheel. He tightened his grip. "It's in rural Plain City. Just getting started, actually. It takes in abused or abandoned farm animals and lets them stay for the remainder of their lives. The place is operated solely on contributions and volunteers. They work with a multitude of institutions. For instance, their summer volunteers can earn credits towards certain degrees. Right now they have two other vets on call. I'm offering more of a routine rounds type of service. I think they'll take whatever they can get."

"What's their purpose or function besides animal rescue? Surely they can't afford to just keep accumulating animals?"

"I don't know that I can answer all your questions, but I think they get endorsements from certain vegetarian food companies and activist groups that want to introduce certain animal protection laws. Usually, activist groups don't deal with people like me who endorse vaccinations and antibiotics. But Marshall claims they need all the help they can get."

"His son Marcus is heading it up. He's a friend, but I haven't seen him in a long while."

Vic's eyes lit up. "Maybe I can pawn the routine stuff off on you. You can catch up on old times."

Fletch grinned.

⸺ ❧ ⸺

Thank the Lord, when the callers came, it was one of Mom's good days. Lil had set up the ironing board in the dining room so she could keep an eye on her mom and intervene if necessary. From her vantage point, she could hear the ensuing conversation between Marie Yoder, Anita Weaver, and Mom.

"We've missed you at church," Marie said.

"I haven't been feeling well." Mom used a diversion tactic with which Lil was altogether familiar. "How are the newlyweds?"

Mom was an expert at avoiding important matters by placing emphasis on the little things. Like the time that Lil asked her if she could get her driver's license, and Mom had shoved an envelope in her hand, telling her to run to the mailbox or they would miss the mailman. Or the time Matt wanted to purchase a high school lettermen's jacket, and her mom had marched him off with a spiel about making them proud by finding his pole and catching a stringer of trout for their supper.

Lil set down the hissing iron, wondering what Marie had to say about Katy and Jake.

"Doing well. In love and happy," Marie replied. "The wedding cake was so lovely. You did such a good job."

Aha. Marie was quick, directing the conversation back to her friend.

"Thanks, and Megan? Have you heard from her?" Mom asked.

"No, but she gets home this weekend. I'll be glad when she's back in the country," replied Anita Weaver.

The room grew quiet for a spell. Then Anita said, "Rose, we came with an ulterior motive today."

"Oh?"

"We need your help. The church is having a fund-raiser, and we need someone with experience to head up the food."

"What kind of event?" Mom asked.

Lil picked up a white blouse and smoothed out the yoke, wondering if her mom was considering helping or just being polite. Or maybe she just felt out of touch and was curious about the event.

"It's an auction. There will be food and quilts sold, and a few used items that folks donate. It's to go toward the cost of the new Sunday school rooms."

"I wish I was up to it. I owe it to the church."

"What do you mean?" Anita asked.

"You know that I'm the one who caused the fire. And now they need money to rebuild."

"You are not responsible for that!" Marie scolded. "It was a combination of things."

"But you weren't there. You were home sick with a cold that night. How would you know?" Mom demanded.

"Because Vernon is on the elders' committee."

"That's right," Anita vouched.

Lil set the iron upright and strained to catch every word. Had these women—who were as close to her as second mothers—come to persuade Mom to repent? The idea made Lil burn with resentment.

"It was old wiring. And then the punch bowl accident."

"And the paper towels fell against the coffeepot."

"Those contraptions catch on fire all the time. You are not to blame. Is that what this is all about, your quitting the hostess committee?"

"You don't understand."

"Help us to understand," Anita urged.

"That committee was my life. The one place I shined. And I failed. And now nothing else matters."

"Nonsense," Marie argued.

Although relieved they hadn't brought up the elders' notion of repentance, what had just been revealed to Lil pierced her heart. She now understood the reason behind her mom's depression. And she felt her mom's pain. Because it was the same for Lil.

Lil's life was ordinary except for her hopes of becoming head chef, becoming known for beautiful presentations and perfection of flavor. She dreamed of writing a bestselling recipe book. But she'd never known until now that her mom felt the same way about her job on the hostess committee. Lil wanted to cry. Her mom had failed at the one thing that brought her joy and purpose.

"That's just it," Marie argued. "The hostess committee *needs* you. Your church family misses you. We need you."

"But it doesn't matter anymore. It will never be the same for me. You know why. I'm sure everybody knows by now."

Lil held her breath. As far as she knew, her father had not told her mom about the preacher's second visit. She hoped it did not come up in the ongoing conversation.

"We are not here to judge you. We love you. How do you know until you try it again?"

Lil exhaled with relief.

"I just know," Mom replied.

"I don't suppose you'd want to try your hand at quilting?" Anita asked. "Those bring the most money."

Lil could feel the resignation in Mom's voice. "No. I'm too tired and too old to learn something new. I'm too tired to do the things I used to do."

"Over at Plain City Druggist, they sell some herbs that pep folks up. Why don't you give those a try?" Marie urged.

Lil determined then that, whether her mom was able to pull out of her depression or not, she wouldn't end up like her. Lil would accomplish her dreams. She would find that happiness if she had to claw her way to the top. Because if she didn't, she might end up just like her mom—passing her days doing dead-end chores on a hog farm.

CHAPTER 9

After Mrs. Yoder and Mrs. Weaver left, Lil struggled with anxiety and churning emotions for the remainder of the afternoon. She felt like she had swallowed Scott's entire ant farm. Her parents had problems that she couldn't resolve, but worse, their problems were keeping her from reaching her own happiness. She should be working more hours instead of getting fired. She needed to find another job.

When she couldn't stand the emotional upheaval any longer, she fled the house for her favorite spot of refuge. As a little girl, she'd spent hours in the back pasture's cottonwood, watching its fluffy wisps burst from their capsules and float up into the air. The robins would snatch the cottony substance midair and fly away to line their nests with it. When life was easier, she would stretch out on the grass and watch the triangular leaves sparkle as they fluttered in the slightest of breezes.

Her brothers had put up a swing the summer she turned ten, inspired by the circus and church camp. She used to pretend she was a circus performer. The old swing was still there, but she didn't fit into it nearly as well as she had as a child. She came less frequently now. She clutched the frazzled rope and looked over the grassy field.

It was overgrown. Her dad moved their hogs from pasture to

pasture, and this one had been vacant long enough for wildflowers to mature and bloom, creating a charming patch of nature at its wildest.

It had been months since she'd touched the splintery board seat. As soon as she rested on it, she felt as if she'd come home—to a place where truth resided, where God used to come to meet her and touch her soul. Here many dreams had been birthed and many sins had been confessed and forgiven. She felt a shudder rake over her shoulders, thinking about Mom's predicament. And when had she grown so far from God? Lil covered her face with her hands and allowed her sorrow to manifest itself before she sought divine intervention, before she even knew how to pray.

"Lillian?"

She jerked up her head with a gasp, Fletch's voice sending a tremor down her spine. Quickly swiping an arm across her face, she caused the swing to swivel awkwardly. She used her feet to stop its movement. "Hi." Her thoughts scattered. *Now he thinks I'm crazy. Just like Mom's performance at dinner the other night.* Of course Lil shouldn't have entertained any hopes for this man anyway. He wouldn't want a Conservative girl when he could date some cute girl in jeans and toenail polish.

Fletch removed his red ball cap and slapped it across his jeans. "Sorry to intrude."

"I didn't think anyone was around."

"I came here because Matt mentioned it might make a good place for the lagoon."

"You're kidding," she snapped. She didn't want to lose her paradise hideaway. "This is the prettiest place on the farm. Surely it's not going to be ruined?"

"I don't know. I had to come out to that pasture"—he pointed off to Lil's left—"to check on some hogs. While I was this close, I came to see what it's like. I didn't mean to barge in on a private moment."

Her shoulders slumped. "It's all right. I'm just dealing with a lot of stuff right now."

He sat on the ground and crossed his arms over his bent knees. "Want to talk about it?"

She looked at him. Really looked at him. His blond hair was neatly trimmed, but it was long and fine enough to waft in the breeze. He looked so different from her brown-haired brothers and cousins. More refined, like Megan with her silky hair. Even in his mucking boots, he looked city bred. But he wasn't; he'd been a missionary's kid. Why was she judging him when his eyes shone with kindness?

—⟳—

Fletch didn't know why he hadn't turned and hightailed it out of there when he saw Lil, especially when she was crying. But the tender scene had gripped his heart, and he found himself drawn to her instead. And now he'd asked her if she wanted to talk about it. Either fate or God was drawing them together, and he hoped it was the latter.

"Today I overheard my mom talking to her friends. I found out why she's depressed."

So that's what Mrs. Landis's odd dinner behavior had been all about—depression. Fletch nodded, not knowing what to say.

"Mom's a plain woman. Like me," Lillian explained.

He definitely had an opinion on that, and he blurted it out, "You're not plain at all."

She pulled an ugly face, as if he'd just said something disgusting. "Never mind. Someone like you in your red shoes and red hat would never understand, anyway."

How could such a captivating creature think that she was plain? Or was her plainness a badge of self-righteousness? He frowned. "That's hardly fair. Anyway, haven't you noticed I have my mucking boots on?"

"Yeah, well you're still a pretty boy. You wouldn't understand about the dreams of plain people."

He frowned, shocked and disgusted to be referred to as a pretty boy. "You have a low opinion of me." Maybe he didn't understand what it was like to be plain, whatever that meant, but he understood about being different. "Look, Lillian. My parents were missionaries. We survived on charity and hand-me-downs. Have you even noticed that the car I drive isn't that much newer than yours?"

Lil's jaw dropped. "I had no idea."

They stared at each other.

She must have changed her opinion of him on the spot because she began to explain, "Cooking is the one place we Landis women shine. For my mom, it was being the head of the hostess committee. I already told you my goal."

"To become head chef."

She nodded. "That and more. Anyway, one night during a baby shower, a fire started in the church fellowship hall. Mom blames herself for burning down the entire fellowship hall. It was humiliating for her. After that, she resigned, and then she fell into a depression. She even took an overdose of pills. She almost died. As you know, Mennonites don't commit suicide."

He wasn't sure that was true. He always figured that depression and suicidal inclinations could hit anybody going through hard times. He wasn't entirely familiar with how the Conservative Mennonites' beliefs differed from his own—and his own beliefs might even be a bit convoluted from the norm just because of his upbringing. But he didn't argue the point. "Wow. That's tough."

Lil went on to explain how she moved out of the doddy house that she and her friends had renovated to help her family, and Fletch was reminded again what had first attracted him to her. She was a woman with grit and conviction. Not only that, but she didn't shirk back from helping others. He liked that a lot. But he didn't like seeing her so dejected.

He jumped to his feet and brushed off his jeans. "I know just what you need."

She eyed him warily. "What?"

"Somebody to push you until your feet touch those branches up there." As he hoped, he caught her off guard. She smiled, and before she could protest, he hurried behind her. "Hang on."

She did. Her black oxfords reached for the sky, and her navy skirt billowed. He felt a fond tug for the petite girl in plain, Conservative clothing. He'd never known a Conservative girl before and would never have imagined one would have big-city dreams and man-sized grit.

"Enough! I feel silly," she cried.

He caught the rope and slowed her down. The swing careened, and the small black oxfords scuffed the grass. He reached for her hand to help her off, but the old weathered rope chose that moment to snap in two, propelling Lillian's seat out from under her. Her bottom hit the ground with a hard thump, and Fletch toppled helplessly on top of her.

"Ouch!" Lil exclaimed.

His heart sped when he realized they lay in each other's arms. He rolled slightly to the side but hadn't the will to leave her. He breathed, "Lillian? Are you all right?"

She whispered back, "My friends call me Lil."

He knew he needed to get up and would, just as soon as they finished their conversation. He stroked her face. "I heard your family calling you that. I think it's cute." At the moment, he was interested in more than friendship. Tentatively, he tilted her chin, closed his eyes, and tasted her sassy lips. The kiss was brief, and like he expected, her lips were naively eager. He pulled back.

Wonder brightened the blue of her eyes.

In that moment, she seemed so naive that it almost frightened him. He needed to slow down before he hurt her. His sister, Erica, had always called him a natural flirt, and he didn't want to mislead Lil. But if she was plain, it was plain irresistible.

"Always dreamed about kissing someone like you," she said breathlessly.

Definitely time to get up. He laughed nervously, rolled away, and got to his feet.

She jumped up and brushed off her clothing. A rosy blush covered her face. "I need to go back to the house and start supper."

He glanced toward the path that wound through a stand of tangled oak and maples and concealed them from the house and barn, suddenly remembering his purpose at the farm. He wasn't here to seduce the farmer's daughter. Of course he was. He had been after her all along. And now she was mad, misunderstanding his sudden withdrawal. She had no idea how hard it had been for him to be a gentleman and pull away. "I'll go with you."

"Suit yourself." She ran her hands down her skirt and started walking away from him.

Quickly moving to her side, he said, "I have an idea about your mom."

She glanced sideways, warily. "What's that?"

"It sounds like she's lost her purpose. While we were talking, an incident popped into my mind about one of my dad's friends who had to leave the mission field and come stateside because of health problems. He fell into depression, and my mom said it was because he lost his purpose. You need to find her a new one."

"Like what? Her friends tried to get her to quilt, but she refused."

"My mom always told me that even if you don't really want to do something helpful, afterward you're glad you did. She lives by the motto that service brings joy." *That and kissing the farmer's daughter.*

"I like that, a guy who listens to his mom." She grinned, warming up to him again. "So helping animals, is that your purpose? Does that give you joy?"

Had she read his mind? He gave a scoffing laugh, thinking of the past couple of weeks working with Vic and all the sleepless nights studying. "So far it's brought me a lot of hard work."

"Service usually does."

"I suppose so. Right now my main focus is getting a diploma." That sounded as ignoble as his earlier advice had probably sounded trite, especially for a guy who wanted to get as far away from his parents as possible. A guy who just wanted to live a normal life. He tried to explain, "There's this person in my life, in my family's life. . . . His name is Marshall. He's given a tremendous amount of financial support to my parents over the years. He became a family friend and saw my interest in animals and is paying for my tuition."

"So you don't want to disappoint him?" she concluded.

"He's my person. The one who is always there for me. I can't let him down."

"Do you think if you hadn't met him, you'd still feel drawn to work with animals? I always knew what I wanted to do. Just kept gravitating toward it."

Fletch couldn't resist asking, "And do you feel this same gravitation toward me?"

Her face reddened, swallowing up her freckles. "Surely you don't expect me to answer that?"

If her blush was any indication, she might be gravitating. They walked a little way in silence, and then the barn came into view. Lil glanced sadly toward it. "Tell me. Is the herd infected?"

"We don't know yet," he answered gravely.

CHAPTER 10

It was a happy occasion for Lil. Megan had just returned from her mission trip, and in celebration, Katy had rallied the friends together at the doddy house. Megan's enthusiastic stories had captivated Lil for well over an hour, before the conversation shifted its focus. Now Lil found herself in the spotlight, being grilled about Fletch.

For Megan's sake, she glowingly described his attributes. After that, she went on to share her reservations. "So he's telling me my mom needs purpose in her life, but then when I asked him about his choice to become a veterinarian, he seemed more concerned about pleasing the man who was paying his tuition." She shrugged. "I thought that was unusual."

"Guys have to be concerned about financial obligations," Jake pointed out.

Lil thought about her dad and knew her cousin made a valid point.

"You're falling for him," Megan observed, twisting a long strand of blond hair.

"He's amazing. But he wears red shoes and a red cap, and I never should have let him kiss me."

"What!" Katy squealed. "We need to meet him. Give him the once-over."

Lil glanced at the braided area rug and back up at Katy. "The point is, if I don't quit drooling over him, it's going to be too late for me to let him go. And I don't know if I can really commit to a guy who might take me away from my church."

Katy grinned.

"What?" Lil asked.

"It's not like you to worry about a guy. You always just drooled, even if he was an outsider. And usually you complain about the church."

"Which means she didn't really like those guys," Jake observed from the sofa with his arm draped over Katy's shoulders. They were a picture of happiness now, but Lil recalled how difficult it had been for them to finally get together. Jake had fallen away from the church and even pursued an outside girl for a brief time before he'd settled down with Katy. But he'd come back. He surely understood her dilemma.

Katy was still perplexed. "Don't you remember how you wore shorts and jeans at church camp? You registered for culinary school *before* you had your dad's permission?"

"Remember the toe ring at foot washing?" Megan interjected.

"So now you're concerned about church?" Katy asked, as if her jog down memory lane validated her point.

"Of course I am! It's one thing to wish and another to actually do something that will force me to step over the line of no return. I don't want to be forced. I want to do it when I'm ready. Katy, you're the conservative one. I'm shocked you're encouraging me to consider Fletch. I depend on you to reel me in when I drift away."

"I'm just trying to understand you."

"Women. I'm in the middle of too many women," Jake protested.

Megan's eyes lit up. "Know how they court in Bangladesh?"

On the back of Jake's taunt, Megan's serious yet out-of-nowhere question set them all into a fit of laughter.

Except for Megan, "No seriously, they have a lot of rituals." She pushed her shimmering blond hair off her shoulder, and it fell into a straight line across the middle of her back.

Sweet, naive Megan, Lil mused. Always lovely, gentle, and graceful. The exact opposite of Katy, with her dark smoldering beauty and feisty personality. At times, Lil envied them both. She worked hard to maintain a trim figure. She had plain brown hair and freckles. But it was always a mild envy. Her sin, not theirs. No matter what, Lil experienced a fierce love and devotion toward them. How she'd missed them.

Megan ended her explanation with a flourish of one slender finger. "So you see, it involves various gods, touching their elders' feet, and bathing in pond water."

This raised Lil's hackles. After her church elders' request for Mom to repent in front of the entire congregation, Lil would not touch their feet. But even in her anger, she was not ready to confide in Megan and Katy about her problem with their elder-dads. She frowned, having missed some of the story. "You mean like the foot-washing service at church?"

"Kinda," Megan's perplexed expression revealed she had never connected the two events.

Lil grew contemplative, too. What kind of rituals had Fletch been exposed to as the son of missionaries? Working through her thoughts, she said, "I don't know if I could touch the elders' feet and swim in pond water for Fletch, but I did lose my job over him."

"What!" Megan exclaimed, scooting to the edge of the sofa.

Lil explained everything, trying to keep her voice upbeat. "Looks like we'll both be looking for a job if we hope to boot Katy and Jake out of their honeymoon shack."

Megan sneezed into a tissue. "Dad suggested I try Salvation Army or Red Cross." She rolled her gaze toward the ceiling. "Mom mentioned Mennonite Disaster Service."

"Your allergies bothering you?" Lil asked.

"Yes, and it was the strangest thing. I wasn't bothered at all in Bangladesh."

"Maybe you're allergic to job hunting," Jake teased.

Katy elbowed him. "Before you boot us out, we need to find another house."

They were a sorry lot. Lil sank back into the armchair her mom had donated to the doddy house. To replace it, Dad had bought Mom a small rocking recliner for her birthday, hoping it would cheer her out of her gloom. That was before they had discovered the truth—nothing would cheer her. "My mom said that, after the church fire, she felt like she'd lost her purpose in life."

"Yeah?" Katy urged, gently biting her lip.

Lil's heart sped. Could she expose the fears that had been plaguing her ever since she overheard her mom's confession? She lowered her voice to a near whisper. "What if I don't find another job? What then? Will I be just like my mom?"

Megan shook her blond mane fiercely. "You're not your mom. If anything, you're like your dad."

Lil objected, "No. I'm like her, too."

"It's a good thing that you can relate to her." Katy pushed up from the sofa. "Because that will help you to find a way to help her. You're always helping people. You're good at that. And Megan's right. You have your dad's determination. That and God will get you through. I know you don't like me to preach, but Lil Landis, enough gloom and doom."

Katy went to a drawer and pulled out some Rook cards. "I don't mean to minimize what you're going through, Lil, but God is faithful." Katy handed the cards to Jake. "You deal, and I'll go cut the strawberry pie."

"I'll help." Megan jumped up as though she wanted to get as far away from the talk of job hunting as she could.

Lil blinked the mist from her eyes as she watched her friends leave the room, pondering Katy's remarks. She had gone through a rough patch. And she probably did understand what Lil was going through in the romance department. She was right about needing to enjoy the evening. She and her friends had been apart too long, and they couldn't possibly solve all of their problems in one evening anyway.

Jake hadn't moved to do his wife's bidding yet. Lil grinned at him. "So does Katy get on you about picking up after yourself?" She remembered how Katy was always the neat one when they'd lived together. It worked out to her advantage, however, because while Lil had cooked, Katy had cleaned. At the farm these days, Lil was doing it all.

He tilted his face, and a shock of wavy black hair fell over his eye. He brushed it back, looking sheepish. "Yeah. Sometimes she's a little bossy, too, but I wouldn't change her much."

Lil could only wish she was at that place in life. "Can I ask you a guy question?"

"Sure. You helped me win Katy."

"No kidding, chump." She wet her lips, thinking how to phrase it, and opted for bluntness. "It's about Fletch's kiss."

"You've come to the right person. I'm an expert in this category."

Ignoring his boast, she explained, "Afterward, he couldn't get away from me fast enough."

"Hm. Either he didn't like it, or he liked it too much."

"What do you mean by too much?"

"He didn't trust himself to be a gentleman without pulling away."

"Oh." She sighed with confusion.

"If he likes you enough, he won't be able to stay away long."

Megan popped her head back into the room. "Pie's ready."

Lil smiled at Jake. "Thanks. I've missed you." At the table, she was impressed with Katy's pie-baking ability. "This is absolutely mountainous. Heaping with strawberries."

"Scrumptious, just how I like it." Jake winked at Katy.

Megan poised her fork in the air. "Hey, Lil. What about that cookbook you always wanted to write? Maybe we could do something creative with that instead of getting a real job."

Once again, everybody burst out laughing.

"What did I say?" Megan raised her palms in frustration.

"You come up with a lucrative way to do that, and I'll supply the recipes." Lil looked at her cards. "Now come on, green bean, we've got to make a good team. These two are hard to beat."

"That's what I mean," Megan countered. "We'd make a great team."

A tug of sympathy dismayed Lil. Megan was terrified to go job hunting. The interviews didn't frighten Lil as much as the commitment she would need to actually keep her next job. "Say, if you decide to apply at those places your parents mentioned, I can help you fill out your applications."

"That's not what's bothering me," Megan argued, slapping down a card. "Actually, I don't know what's bothering me. Just settling back into everyday life, I guess."

Lil nodded, understanding how hard it must be for her friend. She smacked her trump card on top of Jake's suit king and winked. "Got them this round!"

—◦—

Gawking at the countryside, Fletch's tire hit a pothole that shook his car so violently that it resonated throughout his entire body. Belatedly, he hit the brakes and drove at a slower speed. Only five miles lay between the Landis farm, where he'd been doing some more blood draws, and Marshall's Plain City Farm Shelter.

He was supposed to meet Vic at the shelter. He turned the steering wheel and entered the long gravel lane, glancing over the pasture. There was even a pond for waterfowl. An old barn appeared to have been remodeled. When he hit the brakes, a small cloud of dust rose over the hood of his car. When it settled, he saw the welcome sight of his mentor's son striding toward him.

Fletch jumped out of the car and waved at the muscle-clad bodybuilder. "Marcus!"

"Hey, man. I recognized your car." The two men embraced and then stepped apart. "How's it going Fletch?"

"Good. I lost track of you. I had no idea we were living right next to each other. Until I spoke with your dad."

"I was on my way to the barn. Walk with me?" They fell into step as Marcus explained, "All along, Dad intended to head this project up himself. He wanted to surprise ya with it. But he's been having some health issues, and his doctor set him up for some testing. He sent me out instead."

"Marshall didn't mention any of that. I hope it's nothing serious."

"I doubt it. Probably just an old malaria flare-up or something. He's still as forceful as ever."

Fletch knew that Marcus often resented his dad's take-charge attitude, but mostly they got along. He and Marcus often joked about their domineering dads. Amazingly, there had never been any jealousy or animosity between the two of them. Rather, they'd gotten along like brothers, estranged by location rather than choice, always happy to get reacquainted after long periods of separation. Of course, they were as different as night and day. Marcus came from a family of money and opportunity.

Fletch was happy to spend some time with Marcus on this new project. He was sure his benefactor had been delighted to put his two favorite people together. They entered the barn, and Fletch halted at the sight of a tall blond woman kneeling over a shivering lamb.

Marcus didn't seem to notice his hesitation and introduced her as Ashley. The blond stood and dusted off her low-slung jeans.

"Nice to meet ya, Fletch."

Marcus ran a hand over his shiny, shaved head. "Hey, man, Ashley's going to be our other staff person."

Fletch arched an inquisitive brow. "Other?"

"Well you're coming on board, aren't you?"

"Didn't Marshall tell you why I'm in Ohio?"

"Yeah, working for Vic's veterinary clinic."

Fletch felt an unfamiliar bristling that Marshall and Marcus both took his involvement for granted. His schooling and work were both difficult and time consuming. "Actually, I'm meeting Vic here I'm on his timecard these days."

As if Ashley had read his mind, she smiled and went for the throat of the matter. "That's just a technicality. Everybody is overworked. That's life, right?"

A voice from the open barn door interrupted their conversation. "I guess I'm at the right place?" Grateful for Vic's timely appearance, Fletch made the introductions. Vic's attention instantly riveted onto the lamb. "What have we got here?"

Marcus replied. "A couple out for a country drive found the little guy discarded on a pile of dead carcasses. They saw the lamb move."

Ashley handed Vic a clipboard containing documentation of the treatment the lamb had already received.

"When was its last feeding?" Vic asked.

"It's recorded there," Ashley pointed out. "It's time now."

"Good. Fletch, let's increase the formula. You get the pleasure this time."

Fletch mixed up the formula according to Vic's instructions. He twisted the bottle's screw cap and dropped to his knees. Taking the lamb in his lap, he felt himself melt when it started sucking the large rubber nipple.

As Fletch fed the animal, Vic explained, "Lambs need gentle treatment because even trauma can lead to pneumonia. Most likely, though, it was just inadequate colostrum in the ewe's milk. Makes the babies more susceptible to pneumonia. Could also be lungworm. The lamb's on the same medication I would have prescribed." He scribbled some notes on the clipboard. "I see nobody's done a blood draw, but you should keep the lamb isolated, anyways." While Fletch continued to feed the baby, Vic examined its hindquarters for fly-strike, but explained that all looked good on that account.

"Will the lamb pull through?" Ashley asked.

"It's too soon to tell," Vic replied.

When he was finished, Fletch nestled the baby into some straw and went with Vic to complete their rounds. There weren't many animals yet. Only two needed treatment: an old horse that a farmer had brought in to live out the remainder of its life and a cow that had managed to escape on its way to the slaughterhouse.

As they worked, Marcus talked about the farm shelter. "That cow brought us newspaper publicity."

Fletch discovered that Marshall had purchased the sixty-acre farm, donating it to the animal shelter. The farm included a white, two-story house that was getting some updated wiring to satisfy the inspector's code. The house had several bedrooms that had been turned into dorms to house their volunteers. Ashley was in charge of donations, and she'd gotten the farm connected with a university's agricultural program that supplied them with volunteers and grants.

"You've already done an amazing job with this place," Fletch said, holding the steer's lead so that Vic could examine its mouth.

"Yeah, man, the barn has been totally reinforced. Ashley got some contractors to donate new siding, paint, and roofing."

"Do you put the animals up for adoption?"

"Yeah, but not to get butchered. So keep your eyes and ears open." Marcus chuckled. "It's kinda like getting religion. These animals got saved, and now they receive life."

Fletch frowned, thinking it was a blasphemous analogy, but he got the point. "I'll let you know if anything turns up."

"Great. Can I take ya out to dinner when you're done here?"

Fletch glanced over at Vic.

Vic nodded. "Sure, I'm headed home after this. Come straight to the clinic in the morning."

Fletch agreed, glad to catch up with Marcus but hoping his mentor's son didn't exert more pressure on him to help out at the farm shelter.

—⊙—

"Calm down," Lil told her sister over the phone. "Where are you now?"

"At the hospital."

Lil couldn't believe a family member was in the hospital again. "I'll be right there."

"No. That's not necessary. Tom is taking care of everything. The neighbor girl's sitting the kids. It's just that the x-rays show that my ankle's broken, and I don't know how I'm going to manage."

Lil anxiously thought about the six weeks or longer that her sister would be laid up with a cast on her ankle. Michelle's garden was in full swing. It was her sister's pride and joy. As Lil's mind scurried for some scrap of assurance to give Michelle, she saw herself adding her sister's work to her already heavy load. It was impossible. Unless. . .a plan began to formulate.

"Look, sis. I know it seems bleak, and you're probably in a lot of pain right now, but I think we can make this work for the good."

"How is a broken ankle good?" her sister bemoaned.

"It might be the motive Mom needs to get out of bed."

"You're thinking if you help me, she'll get up and do her work? But she wasn't doing anything before you moved home. I don't think that will change."

"But I'm not coming to help you. I'm dropping her off at your place."

"What! You're going to make me deal with her depression, too? You don't understand. I don't know how I'm going to manage as it is." Thinking with resolve about Fletch's advice that her mom needed a purpose, Lil didn't back down from her newly formed plan. "I'll do whatever it takes to get her in the car. Then I'm dropping her off at your place and driving away. And you're not getting out of your bed until she helps."

"But Lil. . . I called for reassurance, not more complications."

"I really think it will work. She can't resist her grandchildren. She won't let them go hungry or run around looking like those ragdolls we used to have. Remember those?"

"Yeah." Michelle still seemed leery. "The girls do miss her. I do, too."

"Meanwhile, you pamper yourself. Haven't you always wished for some time for yourself?"

"That part sounds good. But I don't know if I can turn a blind eye to what's going on in the house. What if Mom just sits on the couch and stares out the window? What then?"

"She chipped in when I needed her to help me with Katy's wedding cake."

Michelle's voice heartened. "Maybe."

"It will work. You sure you don't want me to come to the hospital or go sit with the girls?"

"No. I just needed to vent. We're fine here. I can't believe I fell down the porch steps. What a klutz."

"Everything's going to be fine, sis. I'll go tell Mom about your accident. Give her some time to stew about it. Who knows? She might even offer."

"She won't."

"You're right. But I'll be over tomorrow morning with Mom in tow."

"Ouch! Oh! Careful! Ow! Gotta go."

Lil flinched at the sound of her sister's pain. In the background, she had heard a stranger's voice, no doubt a physician or nurse who had come into the room to examine her injury. She wondered if she'd asked too much of Michelle. It would probably take both Mom and herself to adequately fill in for Michelle, because honestly, if anybody was the family cyclone, it was her sister. But they would make do. They always did. And just maybe, if Fletch was right, her plan would work.

For an instant her thoughts went back to the last time she'd schemed. She had teamed up with her cousin Jake, working as a matchmaker, to help him win Katy's love. When Katy discovered her interference, she'd been furious. Mom would get mad, too. Lil hoped this didn't backfire on her.

CHAPTER 11

Fletch squinted at the blinding glare of the sun rising over the horizon. Beside him, Buddy squirmed on the car seat. As he drove, Fletch processed the conversation he'd had with Marcus the previous evening over dinner.

"Ya do realize that Dad strategically placed you in Plain City? He thought you'd be thrilled to help him." Marcus had given him a look that translated to *after all he's done for you and your family.*

"Fourth-year selective internships are hard, and anything below C minus is failing. The last thing I want is to disappoint your dad with failing grades and the cost of an extra semester. Anyway, everything I do has to go through Vic. He's covering my cost of living, you know. But he'll probably let me provide a lot of the shelter's animal care. Maybe that's what Marshall had in mind all along?"

"Ya can stay at the shelter."

"No." Fletch shook his head. "I have to follow the school's protocol—what's already been set up—and Vic is paying for all my living expenses. But I have a dog that would love to spend some time out there. A basset that's either stuck at my apartment or in the tiny fenced yard at the clinic."

"Sure, bring him over."

"Thanks."

"Tell me about your work. About the farms you visit."

Fletch had talked about the Landis family after that and had even shared about his attraction to Lil. Marcus showed interest in the discussion. Finally, his friend had relented. "I can see ya don't have time to run down donations, but Dad mentioned something specific ya can do for him."

"He did?"

"He wanted ya to take some video footage of sick animals."

Shocked and repulsed, Fletch asked, "Why?"

"We're putting together a documentary-type film to use at fund-raisers. It would just be a little filler, ya know, to play on crowd sympathy."

"Why can't you use the animals here at the shelter?"

"Oh we are. But we don't have many animals. It's one of those 'which comes first, the chicken or the egg' things. We need the fund-raising events to buy feed for the animals, but first we need animals for the fund-raising film. You're around sick animals all the time, and it won't hurt anything. It will help us."

Fletch understood but wasn't eager to film sick animals. Who would view the film? What would the narrative contain? How might it affect the farmers where the animals were filmed? Thankfully, after Marcus had presented the details and stressed Marshall's wishes, he'd let the issue drop. Fletch had to wonder if next Marshall would call him.

They pulled into the farm shelter, and Fletch ruffled Buddy's fur. "You're going to love this place. Even ducks. I know how you love to chase birds." He leashed Buddy, and after seeing nobody outside, walked him to the farmhouse. The front door was propped open with a paint can, and Fletch let himself in. Paint fumes drifted from the dining room, which was situated off to his left, and he followed his nose, stopping short in the entry.

His gaze involuntarily caught the backside of Ashley, who was kneeling on the floor and stroking some unfinished pine cabinetry with a paint brush. She was clad in rolled-up jeans and a yellow T-shirt splattered with white paint. He couldn't help but notice she was an attractive woman, from her white tennis shoes to her hair that was swept up in a perky ponytail that didn't even reach her neck. He must have released some kind of unintentional sigh, because she suddenly looked over her shoulder. When their gazes met, her eyes lit up.

"Hey, Fletch. You here to help?"

He gazed around at several pieces of unfinished cabinetry. "What is all this?"

"Our new office furniture."

Buddy let out a yip, and Ashley smiled. "Who's that?"

"Didn't Marcus tell you?"

She shook her head, and her ponytail swung from side to side.

"My dog. Ashley meet Buddy." He released his end of the leash, and the dog sidled over to the girl, wagging his whole backside.

Ashley laughed. "You're adorable. I love your saggy eyes. And you're so plump and cute." She placed her paintbrush down and bent to pet the dog.

"Marcus said I can drop him off sometimes."

"Oh good. I need a break anyway."

"At seven a.m.?"

"Coffee break, silly. Don't you drink coffee?"

"Yes, I have a mug in the car. Which reminds me, I've got about twenty minutes to get over to the clinic. Vic wanted me to be there when it opens this morning."

Ashley looked a little disappointed but offered, "I'll show Buddy around and keep an eye out for him."

"Can you keep him inside until I've driven away? So he doesn't chase me?"

"Sure. Wait a minute." She strode to her desk and opened a drawer. When she came back, she thrust a palm-sized video camera at him.

"What's this?" Fletch asked, warily.

"Marcus asked me to give it to you next time I saw you."

"I didn't. . ." Fletch wet his lips, trying to figure out how to turn her down without offending her or Marcus.

She snatched his hand and pressed it into his palm. "Just keep it. You'll know when to use it. That's all. And I'll take care of Buddy."

Fletch stuck the camera in his jeans pocket, thinking he might not be dropping Buddy off that often, after all, if doing so brought ultimatums.

"Thanks." He bent and gave the dog a pat. "Stay." Buddy studied him with soulful eyes, and Fletch almost regretted leaving him.

As he headed toward the car, he heard, *Woof!* Next he heard Ashley's soft feminine voice. He could see why Marshall had hired her to get donations, why he'd asked her to give him the video camera. If anything, the incident opened his eyes to the power of an attractive female. Ashley wasn't his type. He saw how she used her looks to get what she wanted. She wasn't at all like Lil, who was honest and forthright.

He shook his head. Too many distractions. He needed a cool head. He needed to get his diploma and—

His thoughts came to a dead end, startling him. He'd been so set on getting that diploma and making Marshall proud that he hadn't thought much beyond that one event. Oh, he had a vague idea of his options. He would probably take an internship and try to work himself into an existing practice. He'd never have the funds to start up his own place. Probably not the experience, either.

Sometimes it was easier to probe an issue from the opposite direction. He knew what he didn't want to do with his life. He didn't want to follow his parents' footsteps. He didn't want to make his children feel unwanted. When he settled down, he wanted to provide the sort of home where kids had an ordinary life.

With a mother like Lil? With a sinking heart, he realized that dating wasn't even included in his limited budget.

—⌒—

Mom fastened her seat belt. "It's a pity you have to drive such an undependable, ugly car."

Lil glanced at her with a glint in her eyes. "Now, Mom, don't go putting ideas of rebellion in Jezebel's head."

"I'm so tired of all these sessions and appointments. If you really loved me, you wouldn't drag me through all this. Nothing helps anyway."

Her heart picking up a speed to match Jezebel's engine, Lil replied,

"We don't have an appointment."

Mom snapped a panicked gaze in Lil's direction. "Then where are we going? You're not taking me to the church. I told you I didn't want to help with that fund-raiser."

"We're going to Michelle's."

"Oh Lil. I'm not up to that. I know she needs help, but surely you can't expect me to—" Mom cut off midsentence, probably because she realized how selfish her remark was going to sound.

In silence, they passed a few farms where colorful combine harvesters moved through the golden wheat fields, kicking up a swirl of dust and chaff. When they pulled into Michelle's driveway, Lil pulled as close to the house as she could. "Let's just go see how she's doing."

Mom shook her head. "I know it sounds awful, but I can't go in there because I know she needs me, and I don't have anything to offer her. I'm sure you can't understand. I don't even understand it. But I feel paralyzed. Useless. We didn't even bring any food. We should have brought a casserole or something."

"We're here now. Michelle has plenty of food stocked up and ready for use. I'm sure you want to see the grandchildren?"

"You know I love them," Mom snapped.

"Let's go inside. You can tell them."

"No." She turned her face away, toward Michelle's huge vegetable and flower garden.

It was a reminder to Lil that not only was she trying to help her mom, but Michelle really needed them. Lil was ready to roll up her sleeves, but she had to try her plan first. "Mom." Lil hardened her voice. "We are sitting in this car until you go inside. I'm not backing down."

Mom put her hand on the door handle. "Then I'll just walk home."

"Good idea. And when one of the neighbors stops to pick you up and asks how your daughter's ankle is doing, you can explain that you don't know because you're out for a leisurely stroll."

When Mom flinched, Lil felt her pain. And Mom was correct; Lil didn't understand it all completely, how a woman could turn her back on her family. But she saw the pain involved and thought she understood the root of the problem. Lil's thoughts went to Fletch, and in her mind's eye she told him, *You better be right about this.* But Fletch seemed world-wise with his multicultural upbringing. She trusted his judgment, happy to have somebody help her through unchartered waters.

Lil's thoughts snapped back to her mom when she heard the car door open. "Fine, but let's not stay long. Maybe we can take some laundry home or bring the children back to the house for you to watch," Mom suggested.

Lil grinned inwardly. Mom was already focusing on the problem. Sure, she was figuring on Lil doing the actual work, but then she didn't know about Lil's plan.

Over an hour later, Lil pulled Jezebel into the Landises' large circle drive and slipped into her usual parking place near the house. It would seem strange going into the empty house. As she headed toward the mudroom, she realized she should have told Dad about her idea before she toted Mom off to Michelle's. But it was too late for—her thoughts broke off when she spotted a red dot peeking over the other side of the azalea bush. She scurried over and stopped in amazement.

The tomatoes had reseeded themselves in a place that was out of the way and hidden by the house-hugging shrubbery. That is until they had gotten leggy and scrambled over the azalea bush. Amazingly, the tomatoes were doing great without any human help. She yanked out a weed, tossed it in the yard, and brushed her hands against her brown skirt.

Normally, Mom kept a garden, but she also kept a couple of tomato plants near the house for quick use. These were experiments, too, using different hybrids and species. But this plant had survived without any human help. Lil cupped the ripest orb in the palm of her hand, thinking about her mom and wondering how she was doing. With a sigh, she stepped back and went to get a watering hose. When Mom returned, she'd have tomatoes to tend. Even if there wouldn't be enough to can, it might give her mom a little joy.

Lil unwound the hose and dragged it toward the bush until it caught on something. Retracing her steps to see what hindered the hose, she stopped short. A blue Ford Focus was driving onto their property, moving along the far side of the drive.

It stopped, and Lil's heart did a little flip to see Fletch step out of the car. With her free hand, she waved.

"Hi, Lil." He gave his red cap a nudge so it didn't block his vision or his gorgeous brown eyes. "I come bearing good news."

"About the hogs?"

"Yes. It's not the PRRS virus."

Lil gave a relieved sigh. She knew that the threat of Porcine Reproductive and Respiratory Syndrome was a dreaded threat to any hog farm. "I'm so relieved. You have no idea."

"I think I do."

He stepped nearer, causing her mind and body to act all befuddled. He hadn't put on his mucking boots yet, and there was something intimidating about those red sneakers. Her mind picked up the warning, but his smile charmed her traitorous heart, as if it had never learned anything about men. His eyes sent dual messages. When flirtatious, she was defenseless. When sincere and caring. . . . Wait! She was defenseless then, too. Had the Africans he'd grown up with been as confused about the blond-haired boy? She swallowed uncomfortably.

And he stepped nearer. "The vaccinations are done, but I'll still need to take some random blood draws."

She nodded, grateful to see him again. No. She shouldn't fall for him or his red sneakers. He didn't fit on this farm, wearing his clean white T-shirt and standing more than a head taller than any of the Landis men. He was different. Even if he was a Mennonite. He reminded her of her imaginary Rollo. Why had she made her imaginary circus performer tall and blond?

The closer Fletch came, the more she worried that he might try to kiss her again. That she might let him. Right here in the yard, where her dad or any one of her brothers might observe them. She turned away and yanked on the hose, freeing it from its obstacle. Her voice came out thick with her family's Dutch accent, as it usually did when she was emotional about something. "I was taking your advice, just now."

Keeping her back to the wonderful intruder, she dragged the hose toward the tomato bed, her pulse speeding when she heard the soft sound of red sneakers following.

"I don't remember giving any advice on watering tomatoes, but I can tell you that you need to turn the faucet on."

Biting back a smile, she tossed the end of the hose to the ground at the edge of the tomato plants and started back toward the faucet, tossing over her shoulder, "I just got back from Michelle's." When she turned, she noticed his intriguing dark brows formed a sharp *V*.

"Matt told me about her ankle. That's too bad. How's she doing?"

"She's in pain because she doesn't believe in taking medicine unless it's a last resort."

"I'm sorry to hear about her accident. Who's taking care of your nieces?"

She watched the water gush into the dry soil surrounding the tomato plants and adjusted the flow. "My mom. I hope. I tricked her into getting into the car and then convinced her to go into Michelle's house. Then after visiting a few minutes, I snuck out the side door. I left her there," she admitted. Her eyes widening over the gravity of her deed, she glanced over at Fletch.

His left cheek twitched. He glanced at the barn and back. "Are they in on the scheme?"

"No. I acted on impulse. So if this backfires, it'll be my fault. But I think Dad will go along." She shrugged. "Nothing else is working."

Fletch arched his brow. "Will Landis does not seem very flexible."

Lil glanced toward the barn, wanting to disagree. Actually, her dad was compromising a lot these days. She admired him for it, too. But when she saw the teasing light in Fletch's eyes, she let his comment slide. "If you're scared of him, you'd better not let him see you loafing like this. Anyway, I just wanted to tell you that I'm testing your theory about Mom needing a purpose."

"From what I saw that night at supper, the grandchildren will lift her spirits. There's general need, and then there's family needs. And family trumps everything else."

"You play Rook?"

"Poker."

Lil's mouth dropped open. But before she could reply, he laughed. "You'd be surprised at some of the games I've played. But even across continents, most games are similar."

She nodded, intrigued by the mysteries of his background and understanding what he meant about family. "Michelle will call if my plan backfires."

Fletch touched her arm. "Let me know how it turns out. You're right, though. I need to get to work. To give your dad the good news." After another reluctant gaze toward the barn, he turned away. But he'd only taken a few steps in that direction when he turned back to her.

Embarrassed that he'd caught her watching him, she quickly dropped her gaze to the ground.

"Lil? Would you like to go out with me sometime?"

She raised her gaze. "Yes!" Instantly regretting her eagerness, she qualified, "But I shouldn't."

He tilted his face with confusion. "Why not?"

"Because we don't go to the same church."

"But we both attend a Mennonite church."

She arched an eyebrow at him. "You know what I mean."

"Could we just talk about it? Maybe it's not the big obstacle we think it is. Look, I'm still in school, and I don't have much money. But what if we went on a picnic?"

Lil glanced toward the barn, saw her dad striding toward them, and wondered what he would have to say about the matter. She wanted to settle her internal conflict over Fletch once and for all. Would a date do that? She didn't have much time until her dad would be able to hear their conversation. "All right."

Fletch grinned. "Great! How about Sunday after church?" He explained that Vic gave him time off to attend church, so it shouldn't be too hard get the extra time off for a picnic.

"Yes. That will work." She whispered, "I'll provide the food."

"Great!" he repeated. "I'll see you then." He turned and ran smack into Lil's dad, who let out a surprised grunt. "Oh! Sorry, sir," Fletch quickly apologized. "I was just. . . ."

Dad shoved his straw hat back and frowned. "Was what?"

Lil tried not to smile at Fletch's reddening neck. She really should have warned him.

"Just coming to give you the good news."

They started toward the barn together, and she hurried inside, doing the garbanzo dance all of the way through the mudroom.

CHAPTER 12

Most mornings, the clinic was open for drop-in clients, but Vic didn't set regular appointments because his loyalties were with the local farms, and he wanted to be available for emergencies. Fletch was glad that Vic often trusted him to work unsupervised. He had just finished muzzling and treating a house cat for infected animal bites. When the waiting room had finally emptied, he felt Vic clutch his shoulder. "You've been a great help. I wish I could afford to hire somebody full-time."

Glowing under the praise, Fletch turned. "Well you have me full-time for a while yet."

Vic gave him a halfhearted smile. "About the time I get you trained, your term will be over."

"Maybe you'll get a quicker student next year."

"Huh?"

Fletch saw the momentary confusion in Vic's eyes. "You thinking of quitting the program with the school?"

Vic turned and washed his hands in the basin, talking over his shoulder. "This is the first time I've ever had a student. I wouldn't have even thought about joining the program if Marshall hadn't approached

111

me with his offer."

"What offer?" Fletch probed, grabbing a bottle of bleach and water mixture.

Vic dried his hands and stared at Fletch. "You didn't know that Marshall set us up together?"

"He only told me he knew you, highly recommended you, and that he'd gotten the school's approval. He thought it would be ideal because it was close to OSU."

Vic gave a sardonic laugh. "Probably bribed the school with donations just like he did me."

Fletch didn't understand Vic's insinuations. "It's true that Marshall is a generous man. What is it you have against him?"

"I don't like being coerced."

Fletch spritzed a table and wiped it down with paper towels, trying to tamp down a rising premonition. "So he gave you money to join the off-site program?"

"Don't you get it? It's all about the farm shelter. I didn't get it at first either. I thought I was just taking his gift and returning a favor, but now that I've been out to the shelter, I see there's strings attached."

Fletch swallowed, feeling a bit coerced himself when it came to the farm shelter. He put the bottle back in the cupboard. "Do you mind telling me the entire story?"

"This stays between us?"

Fletch quickly considered. "Yes."

Vic grabbed the broom, his strokes matching his frustration as he explained. "Somehow Marshall found out that I was in financial trouble. It was my own fault. I took too much money personally. But Britt was always nagging me, wanting this and that. Anyway, he bought me some equipment I needed and paid off a debt I had. In return, I was to apply at the college for the off-site experience. He led me to believe that I was supporting the veterinary school. Like that was his main objective. To me, it seemed like a win-win situation. For me, the school, the student—you."

"But now you believe that he handpicked you because you were close to the shelter, and he wanted me to get involved there?"

Vic stopped sweeping and studied Fletch a moment. "He recently called me and requested that I volunteer at the shelter. Britt was already upset because I work so many hours. A lot of the work there is routine, so naturally, I can turn that over to you."

Fletch swallowed, hating to blacken Marshall's character without knowing the full truth, but also feeling like he owed Vic some loyalty. "I think Marshall wanted me to help at the shelter. Marcus wants me to video sick animals for a documentary they're doing."

Vic ran his hands through his hair. "So that's it. You understand they'll use it against the farmers? The shelter is probably connected with organizations that hope to abolish animal abuse by establishing laws that make it harder for the farmers to make a living."

"I don't like abuse. You don't either."

"Of course not. And I'd do something about it if I came across it. But my clients are good people. I don't want to get in the middle of an issue, right or wrong, that could ruin my practice. I'm not going to that shelter any more than I have to until our agreement is over. I'll send you in my stead, like Marshall wants. But I want you to be discreet about this. And don't be taking any videos. Marshall may have me by the throat, but just remember that you need my recommendations to get a passing grade. Until the new term starts, I can still back out of the program."

Fletch wondered. Surely he'd signed a contract, but he didn't know that for sure. "Yes, sir." But he determined to call Marshall that very evening. He didn't like being caught in the middle.

⎯⎯ Ꮗ ⎯⎯

The next day, Lil punched the speed dial and waited for her sister's voice. "How's it going over there?"

"You checking on me or Mom?" Michelle asked.

"Both. It's hard not knowing what's happening at your house. I feel like I should be there."

"Let's just say that I smell fresh zucchini cake, and I hear giggles coming from the kitchen."

"Whew!" Lil blew out a sigh of relief. She twisted a lock of her hair.

"It's too soon to come and get her. If I bring her home tonight, most likely she'll take to her bed tomorrow to recuperate."

"She thinks you're coming back to get her. Last night she slept in our attic bedroom. Does Dad care if she's here?"

"He's skeptical, but he's all right with it."

"Ouch!"

"What?"

"Oh I just bumped my foot."

"You're not out of bed?" Lil demanded.

"No. Tammy just left some toys on the bed. But I can't stay in bed forever."

"How quickly you change your tune. I thought you were always complaining that you needed rest."

"I know. But now I'm rested."

"Are you in much pain?"

"It's bearable. But I need some magazines or something."

"What about hand sewing?"

By the time Lil finished her conversation, she felt confident she was doing the right thing for her mom and Michelle. And even though Michelle was already growing restless, she could use some pampering.

—❦—

On Friday, Lil joined Megan for lunch at a restaurant near the company where Megan was interviewing for a job. Although Megan claimed she didn't need the moral support, she'd allowed Lil to come along. Right across the street was the Italian restaurant that Beppe had always raved about. It was his model for running Riccardo's. Lil wanted to scope the place out to see if it might be a place where she could apply for a job.

Megan parked her dad's restored dark-blue Chevy Nova at the far edge of the parking lot to avoid paint dings. Even so, a few heads turned at the car's rumble and watched the two Conservative Mennonite girls step out of the classic car. Megan seemed used to it, but Lil always enjoyed the attention. Megan locked the Nova with her key, and they started toward the restaurant.

Lil's excitement mounted over dining at Beppe's favorite restaurant.

114

"They have valet parking here in the evenings."

At the entrance, a hostess greeted them. They passed stone pillars that imitated ancient Roman architecture. Lil saw that the eating facility was upscale and received a lot of corporate clientele. She understood Beppe's obsession.

They ordered soft drinks, and a menu was placed in front of each of them, but Lil resisted the temptation to open it because once she did she would be absorbed with it. Instead, she leaned forward on her elbows. "So tell me all about your interview."

Megan's eyes lit up. "I think it went well. It sounds like a dream job. Char Air is a charter service that has achieved a superb reputation for the service they give their customers. They are looking for individuals to build relationships with a portfolio of clients who regularly need to charter commercial jets all over the world."

"Wow. I never pictured you in a place like that."

"Sometimes they charter sports teams and private corporations, but they do a lot with humanitarian workers and relief organizations. The name Char stands for charter and charity. Clever, huh?"

"Aha." Lil leaned back as the waiter came to their table and asked if they needed more time to select their food. "Yes, sorry."

"No problem. Take your time." He dipped his head and backed away.

"I want to hear more, but we'd better order." Lil scanned the entrées, her eyes passing over the lasagna and penne, but she took her time reading the descriptions of the items that many Italian restaurants didn't carry.

When the waiter returned, Lil ordered the gnocchi that Beppe always raved about. They had never served gnocchi at Riccardo's. Megan went with an antipasto salad. When the waiter left, Lil confided, "I should order salad, too, but since I'm checking this place out, I wanted to order one of the entrées."

"A nice place like this, you have to try the food. I'm just too excited and nervous over the interview. I don't think I'll be able to enjoy my meal."

"Of course you are. Anyway, if you get the job, you'll have plenty of chances to eat here."

"Or if you get a job here."

They grinned at each other, thrilled over the possibilities. Then Lil came back to earth. "I'm just checking it out; I didn't bring a résumé. I need to make sure Mom's doing okay before I botch up another job."

"So how's it going with her over at Michelle's?"

Plucking a roll from a bread basket and swirling a small chunk in herbed olive oil, Lil smiled. "She's working hard, and Michelle said she seems happy. Like her old self again. I'm bringing her home on Monday. That will be the real test. I'm hoping she'll want to continue going over to help Michelle with her garden. Or at least do more at home, so I can help Michelle."

"How long will Michelle be in a cast?"

"She'll probably get it off in six weeks, but I doubt it will stop her once she's feeling better."

Megan nodded somberly.

Lil thanked the waiter for bringing their meals. "Back to the interview. Would it be strictly office work or would there be travel?"

"Both. I love the airport location. I always had a fascination with planes. As you saw, it's right by one of their hangars. The view from the office is amazing."

Lil took a bite of the creamy, peach-colored sauce. Delicious. Beppe was right. "I didn't know you were interested in planes."

"But I am! Especially since Bangladesh. I saw some charter planes bringing in supplies, landing on makeshift runways. It was thrilling."

"You think this company lands on runways like that?"

"Maybe not. But listen to this. If I got the job, I might get to go on some foreign trips. He said that the last girl who worked there went to Haiti and India, free of charge by the company who chartered the plane."

Lil couldn't deny the spark of excitement in Megan's blues. "What happened to her?"

"She had a baby and decided not to return."

Lil took another bite of pasta, noting its perfection, and glanced up. "He probably liked that you were single?"

Megan nodded. "I think so. But he says he's got a couple of more interviews. He'll call next week. I hope I get it. There's nothing else out there in my field. Well there was a payment coordinator. How dull does that sound? I guess they deal with money for relief projects."

"Maybe that sort of job would have the same travel opportunities."

Megan shrugged. "It sounded like dull paperwork. Anyway, there was a news position with a local Christian television station. Can you imagine how that would go over at church? Television?"

Lil rolled her gaze. "I don't think it would suit you."

"I had no idea, but so many of the jobs I am interested in are military or government organizations, and the church wouldn't be happy about those either."

Lil nodded her understanding. Because of the commandment "Thou shalt not kill," the Conservative Mennonite Church took a stance against war or anything supporting war. That ruled out members' participation in the military and law enforcement and most government positions, too.

It wasn't that the Conservatives weren't appreciative of their freedoms, but they gave their thanks to God, who they believed used outsiders to move in areas that their people would never consider, such as the military. Lil had grown up being taught that Conservative Mennonites were not of the world, only passing through it, and that God was their provider.

The war-and-peace issue had never been that important to Lil because it hadn't touched her life in a personal way, but Megan was very involved in causes related to world peace. She would like nothing better than to work for an organization that would help bring world peace.

"I suppose you've checked out all the Mennonite organizations like Mennonite Mutual Aid or Mennonite Disaster Service? What's that organization that deals with world peace?"

"Mennonite Central Committee. It has a few positions but nothing local. I'd have to move. Many humanitarian jobs are headquartered in another city. There're plenty of volunteer positions in Columbus. Oh"—she reached across the table and touched Lil's hand—"I found a job opportunity for head of missions in Sudan, with no education required."

Lil gripped Megan's hand. "Oh please. Don't consider that. You have to get *this* job. I've never seen you so excited over a job before." She released Megan's hand and relaxed back in the booth again. "I want you here. I want us to move into the doddy house together."

"Of course! That's why I'm job hunting instead of volunteering someplace."

Lil urged, "I'm really hoping that by September, things will fall in place for us." Unlike Megan, who was insecure about finding a job, Lil hoped to find something quickly. If her present scheme, her mom helping at Michelle's, didn't work. . . It would work. It had to.

"I need to work," Megan admitted. "I'm starting to get bored. Antsy."

"I know that feeling. But I know I won't be bored on Sunday."

Megan tilted her head. "Why not on Sunday?"

"Because I have a date with Fletch."

"And you're just now telling me that?" Megan reprimanded. "I can't wait to meet him."

"He's taking me on a picnic. After church."

"How romantic!"

"Yeah, but you know what? I'm scared."

"Those red sneakers, huh?"

"No. It's definitely the guy who wears them."

CHAPTER 13

Fletch was uncharacteristically nervous. He felt more like he was facing an important exam than going on a date. But he was also excited to see Lil again and certainly didn't regret asking her out, at least that's what he told Buddy on the way to the Landis farm. But Buddy didn't seem interested in romance if the basset's droopy eyes and saggy jowls were any indication. He seemed more interested in the passing scenery.

"Yeah, that's how you feel now. But once you see her, you'll change your tune."

And Buddy did. He literally drooled when he gazed into Lil's eyes. And when she knelt down to pet him, he licked her face. When she stood up, he whined. So she got down again, and he licked her face again.

Seeing that somebody was going to have to break the cycle and intervene, Fletch took Lil's arm and helped her back to her feet, whispering, "I think Buddy's in love. I don't blame him. But this is my date." He whisked her toward the car, but she kept glancing back at the pooch, who panted at her heels. Fletch was pleased to see Buddy capturing Lil's heart, too. If he was lucky, he'd at least get the leftover scraps of affection.

Glancing to the backseat, Lil laughed. "I didn't know it was going to be a trio or I would have packed an extra sandwich." Staring at Buddy, she added, "He's irresistible. In fact, if you're not careful, Fletch, I might just give Buddy your portion of my special avocado BLT's."

"Have I mentioned how happy I am to be dating a cook?"

"I'm not sure we're dating. More like having a picnic to talk about dating," she corrected.

"I stand corrected but not dissuaded. Regarding Buddy, I had no intention of having a pet while going through school until I saw this dog."

"Kind of like us," Lil said, straightening in her seat and blushing. "I mean the 'no intentions' part."

"I guess so. But that doesn't sound very romantic."

Lil sighed, "Intriguing though."

Fletch grinned. "My thoughts exactly."

When the river became visible in the passing scenery, Lil remarked, "I've never been to Antrim Park."

"It's close to the university. Buddy loves it. That's why I didn't have the heart to leave him at home."

The Olentangy River park was divided in to two portions. The west side of the park had tennis courts, a basketball court, several baseball diamonds, and soccer fields. It included a parking lot, where they unloaded. Fletch gave Lil Buddy's leash, in exchange for the blanket and picnic basket.

"This is a real picnic basket. I expected a cooler."

"It's old. Handed down in the family. Could probably tell us some tales."

"Like your parents dating?"

"And my grandparents."

"Then I'm glad I asked you on a picnic for our first date." He figured he must be wearing her down, because she didn't protest about it not being a date this time. Of course that could have been because Buddy had discovered where they were and was straining and pulling on the leash.

"If you wrap the leash a couple of times around your hand and pull him in closer, he'll be easier to control."

"I don't want to hurt him."

"You won't."

"Funny, I don't think I've ever walked a dog before."

That struck Fletch as painfully sad. "Ever wanted to?" he asked.

"I do now," she replied. "It's fun."

Her answer satisfied him. Placing his hand at the tiny waist he'd been itching to touch, he asked, "How does this spot look?"

"Perfect!"

While Buddy sniffed the grass, they spread out the mouth-watering picnic of Lil's special sandwiches, fruit, and homemade cookies. Fletch whistled, and the dog came and laid beside the tattered quilt, panting and gazing steadily into Lil's face.

"Obedient," Lil noted.

But Fletch was more interested in the food and the girl than in Buddy's manners. "You told me you always knew that you wanted to be a cook, but it's hard for me to imagine you as a baby, babbling, 'Sauté it, Mommy.'"

Lil giggled. "I'm glad you know a little about cooking."

"I live alone. Have to fend for myself."

"How long have you lived alone?" she asked.

"Nope. We're talking about you first. I don't know that much about Conservative Mennonites, but I have a hunch that most of the women aren't career-minded. Tell me more about your journey to become head cook." He took a bite of his sandwich and muttered, "Wait. First tell me what's on this sandwich. This is awesome."

Lil grinned as if he'd just given her the moon. "That's my special avocado spread, and it's a secret this early in a relationship."

He loved the challenge but played along. "That's cruel."

Her expression became serious, even serene. "I think the cooking thing is a Mennonite gene that my mom's family inherited. My sister has it, too, only she's busy raising a family and really enjoys the gardening part of it. I always had to help Mom, and I loved both cooking and baking."

"But that doesn't explain your dream to take it beyond cooking for your family."

Her blue eyes lit up. "At an early age, I received praise. Heard Mom's friends telling her I was talented. It was probably the attention, and then my imagination just fueled it."

He was utterly intrigued. "What do you mean?"

"I always had a strong imagination. . . . I remember the time we went to the circus. It was one of those rare outings where I got a glimpse of life beyond the farm. We went with my cousin Jake's family. We went to a real sit-down restaurant, which was unusual with all us kids. I was mesmerized by the whole thing. After that, my life came down to the fact that I had two choices: I could join the circus or I could become a famous chef. The latter seemed the better choice."

Fletch burst out laughing. "I'm sorry. It's just I wasn't expecting that."

She blushed.

Fletch eased close and touched her arm. "You're such a delight. So fascinating. Did your parents encourage you to pursue your dreams?"

"Not exactly. They let me go to culinary school because it was a talent I could use once I got married. But Dad thinks my goals are foolish and unwomanly." She squirmed. "You don't really know me. Growing up, I was a bit of a trial to my parents. I've always been a little rebellious."

He thought she would probably still be a handful for a man.

"As you know, the family's under a lot of other strain right now, so I'm really trying to cooperate. But I can't wait to leave the farm." She sighed. "Well, it's my turn to eat. You talk."

"What was it you wanted to know again?"

Her expression softened. "How long have you lived alone?"

"My folks sent us to a school where a lot of the missionary kids went. I wasn't always alone, but I was always lonely for family. I hated being sent away. My sister and I were close, but then she married a man she met in Africa. He's Canadian, and they live in his country now."

"I'm sorry. My friend Megan is an only child. Sometimes I see the sadness of it in her eyes. Then again, sometimes I'm envious of all the attention she gets from her parents."

"Well I didn't get much attention. We moved around a lot, too. I had to make new friends. At the university, I lived in the dorms or shared apartments just to be around people. Usually, I lived off donations. Marshall's helped me because my dad wasn't financially able. Right now I'm living in an apartment furnished by Vic, in a complex owned by his brother." Fletch shrugged. "Maybe I haven't always lived alone. But I mostly fend for myself. I look forward to the day when I can pay my own way, too. Settle in some place for real. Quit moving around. That's one reason I'm dreaming of that diploma. One more milestone."

He quit speaking and glanced at Lil to see how she was receiving the information. She smiled and passed him a cookie. He took a bite and thought he'd gone to heaven. He started talking with his mouth full. "Mm. I can't tell you the last time I had a homemade cookie. And never one as delicious as this."

"Do you compliment all the girls? How many girls have you dated?" she asked.

He almost choked from her blunt question. He swallowed. "My sister says I'm a flirt. But I really mean it when I say this cookie is delicious. As to the other question, I've dated a few women, the usual school functions. Not so much lately. What about you?" Trying to play down his past experience with girls, he nibbled on his cookie. But as he waited for her reply, he felt as if the question was the most important one he'd ever asked anyone. He wanted her all to himself.

She grinned. "My friends tell me I'm a flirt, too."

That hit him painfully, but he remembered thinking that about her the day she backed into Britt's car. "Are you?"

She laughed. "I don't know. I've always liked guys. I think I'm just honest and friendly."

"Go on." *How many guys?*

Lil shrugged. "I've had a few dates, but like you, nothing serious. Never a real boyfriend."

No serious boyfriend. Fletch felt as if the weight of the world had just been lifted off his shoulders, and if he wasn't careful, he was going to float up off the old quilt. Now if he could just get her to turn all that friendliness his way. Only his way.

⟶❀

Lil felt cherished, the way Fletch held her hand in his. After taking their picnic supplies to the car, they started along a gravel path that encircled the lake. With Fletch's free hand, he threw a stick for the basset.

"What happens if it goes in the lake?" she asked, wondering if she'd have a wet dog panting down her neck on the ride home. Buddy was a sweetheart, but she needed to know what to expect.

"He doesn't like the water. He'll just shuffle back and expect me to find a new object."

"Smart dog."

She was trying to think of a question that would get them on the topic of their religious beliefs, but Fletch beat her to it.

"When you mentioned you were a little rebellious, what exactly did you mean by that?"

Lil figured the easiest way to explain was to show him. She removed her bobby pins and slipped them into a pocket. When Fletch saw her bangs fall down and sweep across her eyes, his mouth opened in surprise.

"Wow. So you still feel this rebellion? I noticed you're wearing your covering, but you weren't the day we met. Does that mean anything?"

"The church recently voted to change the ruling on the covering. We only have to wear it to worship. I had stopped wearing it other places, but when I moved back home, my dad seemed so disappointed in me that I started wearing it again. Look. I was the girl who borrowed shorts at church camp and wore them until I had to return home. I once wore a toe ring to foot washing."

Fletch burst out laughing. "Now in the church I attend, that wouldn't be a big deal, but I can only guess what happened to you."

"My friend Katy took it off and hid it before anybody saw it. I loved to get her flustered. She always covered for me and always tried to boss me around. It was like having a second mother. I figured Katy would keep me straight. But I think she's quit doing that now."

"I don't understand. Are you saying that you wouldn't have a problem going to a church like mine? It sounds like you might even welcome it."

"Once I thought I might change churches. I always wished I'd been born in a different church."

"You're a Christian, right?"

"Yes, but that's what I'm trying to tell you. Since I moved home, I'm seeing things differently. That's why I'm pinning back my bangs and wearing my covering. I'm not so sure that I can leave the Conservative Church, after all. I saw the way it hurt my parents when Matt left. And all the people I love are in that church. They are wonderful people." With that she blushed. "You know what I mean. And my conscience has been bothering me lately. I've been praying more. Seeking God, and I don't know yet what that's going to mean for me."

"I understand how you don't want to hurt your parents, but faith is a personal thing. I have to be honest; I can't picture myself attending your church. This is all very revealing. I think we are going to need another date to figure out the puzzle."

Lil stopped walking. Removed her hand from Fletch's and faced him. "I thought that was what today was all about."

"This is going to take time. I don't want to give up on us though." He pulled her close and whispered, "Do you?"

She knew that her friends wanted to meet him. If anybody could help her work through her concerns, it was Katy, Jake, and Megan. On one hand, it wasn't fair that her allies were all of the Conservative faith. But an evening with her friends might help them come to a solution. Maybe Fletch would see that living the Conservative lifestyle could be fun, too.

"Yes, but we can't skirt around the issue either. One of us might get hurt." *Probably me.*

"If you won't see me again, then that somebody is me," he insisted.

"Would you like to meet my best friends? Spend an evening playing Rook with them at the doddy house?"

"Yes," he said. "And if we don't get any time alone, we might have to go on a third date to talk about this again."

"Don't count your chickens before they are hatched," she warned, pulling away before he could kiss her. But then she let him hold her hand all the way back to the parking lot.

―◦―

When Lil returned from her date, her dad met her in the kitchen. "So you are dating the vet," he said.

"I thought you knew. That you heard him ask me the other day."

"Lillian, I don't understand you. I have tried to teach you the difference between right and wrong. But you are like your mother. You have your own ideas." He pressed his lips together and stared at her.

Her heart pounded, wondering if he was going to say more about her mother. Things she wasn't ready to hear. "But I thought you liked Fletch."

"I do. That's not the point. If you insist on dating him, then at least bring him to church. Maybe then Matt will come to his senses, too."

"He might not want to come to our church."

"Be real careful, Lil. Don't be like your mother and live with regrets."

Lil was relieved he hadn't forbidden her to see Fletch again. That was something.

"You need to start making good choices. Dating a Conservative man would be a better choice. Choosing to follow the Lord."

"I understand your concern."

He narrowed his eyes and said gruffly, "I think it's time to bring your mother home. It's time that she makes her choice, too."

"What do you mean?"

"We can't make her do anything. She has to choose to live."

Lil nodded. "I'll go get her. Unless you want to?" she asked hopefully.

"It was your idea. You get her," he said. "I have enough to worry about around here."

"The hogs?"

"The Plain City Bank turned down your brother, even after I signed all the paperwork. After all these years. They said the loan was too high. But it's what we need."

"There are other banks," Lil suggested hopefully.

"You sound so much like Matt. I'm going to go read my farm magazine."

All Lil had wanted was some time to reflect on her date with Fletch. That had just been stolen from her, like everything else she wanted. But she wasn't the only one in the household who was disappointed or had problems.

She snatched up her purse and headed for the door.

Later on the drive back home, Lil's mom seemed miffed, too. As soon as she arrived at the house, she announced she was going to her room to rest. From the miracle Lil had witnessed firsthand at Michelle's earlier—the pretty rows of canned tomato sauce, the delicious aroma coming from the slow cooker, and the way she handled her granddaughters with a cheerful ease—Lil was sorely disappointed. She'd hoped that Mom would walk into her own home, see the details that had been neglected, and just carry on. She had envisioned Mom bustling about as though she'd returned from a trip and had never sunk into her earlier depression.

Instead, the moment Mom had gotten into Jezebel, she'd stiffened her shoulders. When they got home, she had started toward the house as if she was heading for her execution. Lil couldn't figure out what had caused the change between Michelle's house and the Landis farm, unless it was coming home to reality.

Surely Mom wouldn't hold a grudge against her?

When Rose had been sleeping or hiding in her room for at least two hours, Lil slipped into an apron. Swiping at the tears that welled up in her eyes, she opened the fridge door. She needed to make supper for her father, who was presently napping off his bad mood.

"What time is it? I slept like a rock."

Lil whirled around, astonished to see her mom's hair combed and her head covering on crisp and straight.

"Oh."

If Mom noticed the condition of Lil's red eyes, she didn't comment. Her gaze went to the rooster clock in the kitchen. "Six already? The clock in the bedroom said eleven. I knew that couldn't be right."

Coming to her senses, Lil said, "It must need batteries. You look rested." Afterward, she feared she'd said the wrong thing again. Usually any positive remark incited a negative response or reaction, with her mom refusing to be drawn out of her gloom.

"I am. I don't know how Michelle does it. Those little girls are so active. But why are you standing with the refrigerator door open?"

"Oh." Lil released the door with a grin. "I was figuring out what to make for supper."

Mom grabbed the refrigerator handle. "Let's take a look and see what you've got in there. I'm starved."

Stunned, Lil found it hard to step aside or move at all. She watched Mom pull out remnants of a ham, which had always been a Landis staple. "Grab that lettuce. Do we have any cheese? We'll make a chef's salad for supper."

"Okay!" Lil said, breaking free from her stupor and jumping to do whatever Mom bid.

Mom donned an apron from the yellow peg shelf, and they began chopping and dicing. She snacked on bits of ham and told a cute story about Trish and a garden frog. Then as the reminiscence ended, her gaze rose to Lil's. "I was furious at you. But you did the right thing. Taking me to Michelle's. I didn't realize how much I'd missed my grandchildren."

"Thanks, Mom. In the car I thought you were holding a grudge against me."

Mom straightened her shoulders. "I was exhausted, is all. You should know by now that Mennonites do not hold grudges."

Her transformation was surreal, and Lil could only hope it was permanent. She hadn't taken on a mother's role for such a long time, it almost seemed foreign for Lil to receive instruction and not be the one giving it.

Suddenly Rose laid down her knife, her eyes panicky. "I'm afraid, Lil. I don't want to slip back into the darkness again."

Lil slipped her arms around her mom's waist and whispered, "I won't let you."

After the embrace, Rose wiped her hands on her apron. "Well! I guess we're done here. I'll put plastic wrap over the bowl and chill it till supper."

"I think Dad fell asleep with his farm magazine, but he'll be hungry as soon as he wakes up. I've got something to show you first. Get your shoes."

Mom glanced at the bowl of freshly cut vegetables with uncertainty. "It'll just take a moment."

She shrugged and went to the mudroom's yellow rocker that she had once painted to match the shelf. Mom loved the colors of yellow and lilac. When she was finished putting on her shoes, she followed Lil outside.

Lil noticed a sad pallor fall across her mom's face when she glanced toward the barns. "This way," she said quickly.

They stepped onto the grass and went around the corner of the house. "What?" her mom squealed. She looked at Lil skeptically. "You planted tomatoes?"

"No. They're yours. They reseeded themselves."

"But they're doing well," she observed, touching the twisted vines that bent to the ground, laden with ripening tomatoes. Rose plucked one and turned it over in her hands. Suddenly she started laughing.

"What?" Lil asked.

"I'm so sick of tomatoes right now, canning all that tomato sauce at Michelle's. And yet this bush excites me."

Lil laughed, too. "Sorry about that. But I thought this would make the perfect addition to our chef's salad."

"It makes the perfect addition to my homecoming," Mom said cheerily as though she'd been gone for months. In a real way, she had.

CHAPTER 14

Fletch came out of one of the Landis barns to notice Lil standing by the back door of the farmhouse. That was odd. She usually bustled around like a hummingbird. Yet there she stood, absolutely motionless.

He watched her staring at some shrubbery, and his curiosity escalated. Then his phone jangled. He pulled it out of his jeans pocket, and it was an unidentified caller. Since he'd been getting weird calls all day, he stuck his phone back in his pocket and kept his gaze riveted on Lil. The caller could leave a message.

As he drew nearer, he called out so that he didn't startle her. "Hi, Lil."

She raised her finger to her lips, warning him to proceed quietly, and motioned him forward. More curious than ever, he quietly joined her, surprised when she gripped his hand.

"It worked," she whispered.

He didn't know what had worked, but surely his heart wasn't working given the way it was flopping insanely inside his chest. Her unexpected touch had sent his entire body reacting as if they were back at the lake, hand in hand. Following her silent gestures of instruction, he leaned forward and peered through the bushes, even more startled to see Lil's normally glum dad kissing Lil's mom. Dismayed, he jerked his gaze away. "Didn't anybody ever tell you it's not nice to spy?"

"As the youngest kid, I spied on all my siblings. Anyway, in this case, I can't help it," she whispered. "My mom is happy again. I can't see enough of that." She tugged his hand. "Come with me."

He allowed her to lead him around the opposite corner of the house, which faced the road and front porch. "I'm glad," he said, knowing his words weren't nearly strong enough to match Lil's elation. He took her free hand, drawing her close to face him. His voice low, he said, "I mean, it's a miracle, isn't it?"

"I probably shouldn't be telling you this, but I was beginning to think there was something wrong between Mom and Dad. But they seemed okay, didn't they?"

"I'm not a great one to judge relationships, but it seemed to me like they were getting along fine."

Lil didn't seem to catch his humor. "And I have you to thank. I don't think I would have had the brains or the courage to dump Mom off at Michelle's if you hadn't told me that she needed to get involved again."

"I'm happy for all of you," he said, wishing he didn't have to tell her or her dad what he'd just told Matt out in the barn. Besides that, Rose's improvement could be just the beginning of a long process of healing. "Is she still going to help out at Michelle's?"

"I'm not sure what she'll do." He felt Lil's grip tighten on his hands, as if she was experiencing a moment of panic.

"I've been praying for her. For you." He didn't add that he'd been praying about their relationship as well.

She looked up at him with misty blue eyes. "Thanks." She released one of his hands and touched his cheek. "That means a lot. I've been praying, too."

Standing so close to her, taking in her sweetness, he felt himself pulling her close. He bent his head and whispered, "It's natural. You're special to me."

Her eyes widened then filled with longing.

She melted into his embrace, and he cupped the back of her head, forgetting all about the fact that they were standing in broad daylight in the Landis front yard. He'd given her a brief kiss after their date, but this one was the most meaningful. It gave him a warm feeling, the "I've come home" feeling for which he'd always longed. Afterward, he could only marvel and wonder over its meaning. Lil was precious, and he had to treat her with care so that he didn't harm her or lose her. He couldn't bear that. "Very special," he repeated, giving her a winsome smile. Lil smiled then, and his world brightened like when the sun came out on a cloudy day. "Sunshine," he said, feeling instantly foolish.

"What?"

"You're like sunshine." Then he clamped his mouth shut before he blurted out, *I can actually feel you on my skin.* Foolish or not to admit, it was exactly how she affected him, making him all warm and tingly.

"That's the nicest thing to say." From around the back of the house, they heard a door close. Lil's gaze lowered to the ground and swept up again. "So I guess I'll see you on Saturday? To meet my friends?"

Her question momentarily caught him off guard. He was still thinking about sunshine. "I'm looking forward to it. I just need to get off work."

"Oh? Do you think that'll be a problem?"

"I'll be persuasive." At her worried expression, he added, "And persistent."

━━━◦

"Hello," Fletch snapped, interrupting the caller midsentence. "No, my car is not for sale. You have the wrong number." The call was one of a dozen he'd received that week asking if his car was for sale. At first he'd thought that it was merely the matter of an ad gone awry, his number getting posted by mistake. But every time someone called, they described his exact car.

Puzzling over the situation that was getting increasingly inconvenient and aggravating, he strode toward the Landis barn.

"What's that all about?" Vic asked.

Fletch explained the situation to Vic, adding, "I guess I'm just on edge. I hated to hear that there's more sick hogs."

Inside the barn, Matt led them to a batch of sick piglets and a couple of other hogs they had isolated. After a thorough examination, Vic explained, "See the sow's ears—the blue tint? I'm afraid this is the beginning of PRRS, after all. As you know, we found it in one of our most recent blood draws, too."

Just then Will entered the barn. "Saw your truck." He stopped when he saw their glum expressions. His shoulders sagged.

Vic explained, "This is nothing to be overly alarmed about. Although we've found evidence of PRRS in the last batch of blood draws and this sow has the blue ears, I think we've caught it early on. The fact that it was in the blood before we saw sick hogs means it could be a mild strain. There's over twenty strains, and some are mild and don't cause major loss. They can even help to bring immunities into the herd."

"So the other piglets were infected, after all? We need to isolate that sow?"

"No. They were all negative. Just a coincidence. But lucky for you, it brought us in to start vaccinations and be here from the start of your first real outbreak."

"Maybe not luck. Maybe God?" Fletch suggested.

Matt gave him a sadly wistful smile.

"So what now?" Will asked.

"Early weaning of pigs at fourteen days. Clean and disinfect the nursery and allow it to rest for two to three weeks. We can give antibiotics to infected hogs. We can sacrifice one to come up with a custom-made vaccination, or you can use a commercial one that works for various strains."

"You know we're strapped for money," Will reminded the vet.

"I think a commercial one will work for you since it's my gut feeling that this is a milder strain.

"Back to treatment," Vic continued, "Practice a sixty-day isolation for new breeding stock. We've already done the vaccinating, but we need to keep vaccinating the weaned pigs. Those need to be tested at sixteen weeks and again at twenty-four weeks, and if they are negative, they can be entered into the herd."

Will lifted his straw hat and ran a hand through his hair. "I don't know where we're going to get the room to isolate all these hogs. We need another barn, but we just got turned down at the bank. You know that whenever we fill out paperwork, they ask about the health of the herd. And now this." He shook his head and replaced his hat.

Vic replied, "Fill out the paperwork as soon as possible. I can give you a letter that gives the small percentage of infected hogs. Really, it's a rare farm that doesn't have some infection."

"Then I guess we've been fortunate until now. We never should have let up on the vaccinations."

"We can only go forward," Fletch said. "But disappointing as this must be, remember that Vic brought up a lot of positive factors."

Fletch followed Vic to his truck.

Vic jumped in his cab and cracked his window. "Meet you back at the clinic after your next appointment."

They exchanged knowing looks, for Fletch's next appointment was the farm shelter, but Vic had been discreet not to mention it in front of Matt. "Right. I'll see you in an hour or two," Fletch replied.

Matt placed his palm on the hood of Fletch's car. "You know, this is a real nice car. You wouldn't be willing to sell it would you?" The tone of Matt's voice clicked in Fletch's mind. Of course. The practical joker had been at work. Fletch shook his head at his own thickness. "You had to have put a really cheap price on it. I must have gotten a dozen or more calls today."

Matt grinned. "I don't know what you're talking about."

Fletch reached into his car to the passenger's seat and withdrew a shopping bag. "Well, here's your payback." He thrust the bag at Matt. "You wear this, and I'll call it even."

With a surprised expression, Matt cautiously accepted the gift. He held the T-shirt up in front of him and started laughing. The T-shirt featured pictures of a wolf and three little pigs and bore the message "Big Bad Wolf."

"Never saw this one. Where'd you get it?"

"I noticed it at the feed store when I was buying my muckers. Then when you showed up every day wearing a funny shirt, I couldn't resist it the next time I had to go in there for Vic." He didn't add that it had been marked down 60 percent, which might be indicative of Matt's poor taste. Fletch patted his car, acting as if he'd known what Matt had been up to all day. "Trying to blow my house down."

Still examining the shirt, Matt admitted, "I like it. But I hope it doesn't scare the girls away."

It probably will, along with all your other T-shirts.

Fletch grew serious. "You know I've been thinking about what your dad said in there about the loan for the new barn and equipment. I remember hearing about a thing called hoop barns, tent-like structures that are cheaper than the metal barns most factory farms use. It might be a way for you to start your expansion."

"Thanks. But all I need is a good contract with an integrator company. I'm going to work on that next."

"You think? Maybe Vic had a point about getting his letter now before more of the herd is infected."

"I guess there's more than one way to go about it. But the integrator companies require the same documentation a bank does. And I want to be better prepared the next time I go face a bank officer. It's demeaning to get turned down cold."

"I'll see if I can scrounge up some information on the hoop barns. At least look at it, won't you?"

At Matt's frown, Fletch realized he'd just stepped on the other guy's testosterone. "I hope I wasn't out of line, just now." He shrugged. "It's just another angle."

Matt still frowned, and Fletch figured he'd better just shut up before he dug himself in deeper.

"You have a thing for Lil?"

The question hit him like a sledgehammer, forceful and unanticipated. Matt could be as blunt as his sister, and the disapproving tone of his voice made Fletch squirm. Had Matt seen them kissing in the front yard? "Well. . ."

Matt tossed the shirt over his shoulder and narrowed his eyes.

Fletch took off his ball cap and tapped it against his jeans. "I guess I do."

"I haven't figured out if Lil's unhappy because she doesn't want you chasing her or if it's because she thinks you're toying with her. It better not be the latter." He took the shirt down and opened it up again. "Big bad wolf, huh? I hope that's not a theme with you."

Fletch felt his face heat. If it had been, that was long before he'd met Lil. "Of course not!" But then he remembered their kisses.

Matt's expression softened a bit.

"The thing that's troubling both of us is that we go to different churches."

"Dad wasn't happy about me leaving the Conservative Church. I can't blame Lil if she wants to do the same thing, only the timing is tricky." Matt tossed his shirt over his shoulder again. "I don't like to see Lily get down in the dumps." He glanced at the house. "This family's got enough of that already. I don't want it to rub off on her."

"I'll back off if she wants me to." Fletch swallowed, wondering if he could or would really do that.

Matt nodded. "Fair enough. Thanks for the shirt." He started to walk away.

What a strange character, Fletch thought. *Most practical jokers aren't hotheads.* "So how long is the ad going to run?" Fletch called.

Matt looked back with a triumphant grin. "I have no idea what you're talking about."

Getting in his car and starting the engine, Fletch grimaced. That hadn't gone well at all. First delivering the bad news of the infected herd then getting called out for dating Lil. And now having to head over to the farm shelter.

—⟲⟲—

Fletch had never felt so powerless. "I understand, Marshall, but if I do that, it could place Vic in a precarious situation, and I still have an entire term to finish with him. He can make it so that I fail the class."

"Oh I think that's an exaggeration. It's such a simple thing. More simple than the last thing I asked ya. Let me see, help me here, do ya remember the last thing I asked of ya?"

Fletch switched the phone to his other ear. "I don't believe you ever asked me to do anything," he admitted, feeling lower than a worm.

"No kidding? This is the first thing?" Marshall drawled in his southern accent. "Well that surprises me. And we've known each other for years."

Fletch squirmed like a spider under a giant thumb, pacing to the sliding glass door of his apartment. "Will I be able to see the film before it's available for public use?"

"Well sure, Fletch. We can arrange that. Your commitment and integrity is commendable. That's why I. . .well, why I like you so much."

Fletch felt his face burn with humiliation. Marshall had never manipulated him like this that he could remember. But how could he object to one request, even if it wasn't quite on the up-and-up? Buddy sidled up to him and stared out the sliding glass door. Fletch heard himself relenting, "If I can see the film and hear the narration, I guess I could raise any objections later."

"Just trust me, Fletch. I won't do anything to harm ya."

"I wouldn't want to harm Vic's practice. Actually, he warned me not to do any video taping."

"Maybe ya should be more discreet. Just so there won't be any misunderstandings."

"I suppose," Fletch whispered.

As if in tune with his master's feelings, Buddy lifted his nose and gave a mournful howl.

—◦◦—

Exhausted from spending the day at Michelle's, Lil entered the Landis kitchen and stopped short. She didn't know if she'd ever take such a sight for granted again. Mom stood over the sink, paring potatoes. Her apron was tied in a perfect bow that rested just below her newly slim waist. Lil swallowed, hoping her mom's first day alone had gone as well as it appeared.

"I'm home."

Mom dropped her peeler and turned, wiping her hands on her apron. "You look awful."

Lil smiled, thinking how their places had taken such a reversal. "Thanks."

"Seriously, I know how exhausting it is over there."

"Yeah, and it's not going to get any easier for Michelle."

With concern, Mom asked, "What do you mean?"

Lil hung her purse on a peg and wiped her hand across her sweaty brow, knocking her covering askew. "She thinks she's pregnant."

"What!" Mom exclaimed. Then she put her hand to her mouth and started laughing.

Lil couldn't help but catch the joy in the situation, too, for they all loved babies, despite the work they created. "I know. Well, it's not for sure. She's making Tom pick up a pregnancy test at the store on his way home from work."

Mom shook her head. "Such modern conveniences. Won't be necessary. A woman knows such things. If she thinks she is, then it's probably so."

"I suppose. What can I do to help?"

"You can wash the broccoli. I'm making a broccoli salad."

Lil headed to the refrigerator to get the broccoli that her mom had brought back from Michelle's garden. "Are these from the second growth?" Lil asked, staring at the small, tender shoots.

"Yes. So tell me about Fletch."

Lil jerked her gaze up to her mom's, surprised because their date was before her mom had come home from Michelle's. That meant that her dad must have told her about it. She guessed it must not be troubling him too much if he'd discussed it with Mom. He usually tried to keep things like that from her. "You heard about our picnic?"

"So that is why the picnic basket was moved? No, I've seen how you look at each other."

Lil didn't know when her mom had seen them together, but that hardly mattered. "I really like him."

"And he goes to Matt's church?" She had learned that when Matt brought him to supper.

"Yes."

"Are you seeing him again?"

"Yes."

"I don't suppose you'll look to me for advice, the kind of mother I've been to you lately."

"That's not true, Mom. I always welcome your advice." *But I have to make up my own mind.*

Mom placed the potatoes in water and dumped the peelings into the trash. "Hand me the potato pot?"

Lil reached in the cupboard beside her for a medium-sized pot and handed it to her mom.

"All I know is I want you to be happy. But then there is also duty to consider. I only wish happiness were not so elusive."

Lil was grateful that her mom had remained philosophical, because if Mom forbid her from seeing Fletch or even cautioned her not to see him, she would have become defensive, like she had with her dad. "Thanks, Mom," she said. "But I already invited him to go with me to Katy's on Saturday night. Maybe we can talk more about it after that?"

Instead of a worried expression crossing her face, Mom's eyes brightened. Lil figured it had something to do with the promise to confide in her again.

CHAPTER 15

Fletch opened the passenger door for Lil and placed the dessert she had made in the backseat.

"You sure you don't want to take Jezebel?" she teased.

"Maybe next time. That is, as long as you don't mind riding in a car that's up for sale and could get sold right out from under our noses."

He watched his petite date slide into the seat. He walked around the front of the car and wiped his clammy hands on his jeans. In the car, he turned on the air conditioner to combat the hot, sultry evening. The soothing breeze which came from the vents played with the fringes of Lil's hair. He splayed the steering wheel and gave her a smile. The fiery highlights in her hair made it a color that needed an exotic name description other than brown, like he'd described to Marcus. It was shiny and beautiful. His heart swelled with joy to be alone with her again.

Lil smiled back at him. "So what's this about putting your car up for sale?"

"Maybe you ought to ask your brother about that."

"Okay. Which one?"

"How about Matt, the prankster?"

"Uh-oh." Her blue eyes twinkled. "He pulled that on my cousin Jake when he first bought his truck."

Fletch's mind flashed to a red Dodge he'd seen on a vacant corner he'd passed on his way to the farm shelter. Someday he would own a truck like that. First he had to get his diploma and a real job. "What kind? He still have it? 'Cause the offers are wearing me down."

"You can ask him yourself. Tonight."

"Common ground. That always helps. So, are your friends going to give me a hard time?"

Lil tilted up her cute freckled nose. "Maybe if we keep sitting here and show up late."

With a grin, Fletch put the car in gear and brought it around the circle drive. "I wouldn't want to disappoint you and get on everybody's bad side."

She smiled. "Thanks."

He nosed onto the road. "Which way?"

"Turn right. The doddy house isn't far."

"Doddy house?" He remembered she'd told him about it before, but it had only sparked his curiosity.

Over the next several miles of narrow country roads edged with deep weedy ditches, Lil told him all about the doddy house. She talked about her childhood vow and her few months living there with Katy. As she talked, he tried to imagine three Conservative Mennonite, ten-year-old girls huddled around a campfire.

When she finished, she gave him a sideways glance. "You think that's dumb?"

"Are you kidding? I think it's sweet."

He was about to add *like you,* only her arm flew out. "Turn! Turn!" she cried, pointing at the lane directly in front of them on the right.

He whipped the wheel and slammed on the brakes, veering off the drive and clipping the ditch with a bump, before they stopped.

"Sorry about that." Her Dutch was thick and apologetic. "Wasn't paying attention."

"We're okay," he said, feeling like she really must have a penchant for destroying cars.

"Just pull around back. That's it." She pointed proudly.

A small, white-sided house with a blue roof and a cute porch that ran the entire length of the front sat at the end of the lane. "Looks like a dollhouse," he commented. Then his eyes swept over the rest of the farm. It was nice. Something about the country drew him. He spotted Jake's black truck and let out a low whistle. Involuntarily, he turned off the ignition, startled to notice Lil reaching for the car door. He tore his thoughts from the truck and caught her left hand.

"Wait."

"What?"

For some reason, his dad's Pygmies came to mind, and the ceremony they performed for luck before they went hunting. He knew that being in God's plan wasn't about luck at all, and he wasn't sure why the memory had struck him, but since it had, he decided to have some fun with it.

"What?" she repeated.

He nodded toward the house. "These are your best friends, right?"

Lil nodded. "Yes, best in the world."

"Then I think this calls for a good-luck kiss."

Her eyes lit up with surprise. "I never heard of those."

"What? But it's our tradition."

Lil pointed at herself, then Fletch, then back at herself. She shook her head. "We don't have any traditions. This is only our second date."

"Exactly. But it won't be our last, so let's start the tradition."

She tapped her chin, as if trying to decide. "What will this good-luck kiss be like?"

He turned sideways in his seat, resting his left arm on the steering wheel. Considering that he'd just seen a couple of females peek out a window with a green roller shade, he figured it would be pretty chaste. "Oh they're very short. Nothing like the ones we had before." His heart tripped when she blushed. He liked how the rosy glow swallowed up her freckles. He really liked that he was the one who caused it. He stared at her mouth. "Just a mere brush of the lips." He curled his finger, inviting her closer.

Breathless, Lil unfastened her seat belt and inched closer. He leaned forward, closing the distance between them. Good for his word, only moments later, he drew back again. Even though it was a brief encounter, she looked breathless. Her freckles returned.

"Good luck, then," she said, pulling away.

But Fletch grabbed her hand. "Wait. That was for your luck."

She grinned. "And why do I need luck?"

"You need the most because they're your friends."

She laughed. "On one hand you are so right. But on the other hand, that doesn't even make sense."

Rather than argue, he brushed her lips, which stilled against his touch. Then he released her.

"See. It worked."

"How do you know?" she asked.

He beamed. "Because now I don't feel like I need any luck." It was true. A little assurance went a long way. Not that he was shy about meeting people. It was more about winning Lil over—not botching his chance with her.

He jumped out of the car, and the hot, humid air struck him like a wall. He stuck his head back inside. "Don't move." He liked that she allowed him to open the door for her. He didn't want to miss a second of their time alone or an opportunity to touch her soft little hand again.

When he opened the door, he reached for her. "Let's go, before it wears off."

She glanced at their hands. "You sure a hand squeeze couldn't have done the same thing?"

"Probably, but it wouldn't have been as much fun. Don't you think?"

She wrinkled her nose. "You're right. I haven't had that much fun since I accidently put salt on my cinnamon toast."

Sassy-soft. That's what she was. He'd never known anyone like her. She was the most intriguing little thing. But his thoughts shifted when a man about his own age opened the door. He offered Fletch a friendly smile and firm handshake.

Lil gave Jake a hug and made the introductions.

During this interval, Fletch didn't miss the look that passed between Lil and Jake. He remembered that she once referred to Jake as a friend who was as close as a brother. Oddly, it gave him a twinge of jealousy. He wondered if Jake felt it, too, or some brotherly protective emotion. Was the friendly demeanor only on the surface? She seemed to be giving Jake the eye, warning him to behave. As if Fletch needed Lil's protection. He saw the moment that Jake acquiesced.

"My wife, Katy, is in the living room, talking to Megan. Come on. They're anxious to meet you."

Lil rolled her gaze to the ceiling. "Chump and blabbermouth," she muttered.

Fletch glanced at her with amusement, pleased that she'd been talking about him to her friends. Pleased to see Lil squirm with embarrassment. Surely that was a good sign.

As soon as they entered the living room, Megan and Katy quit talking and shot to their feet. Jake's wife was beautiful with a black ponytail and exotic features. Megan was just as pretty, only she was the exact opposite with long blond hair and a sweet face. No three women could be more different in appearance, yet more striking.

As they were introduced, Katy touched his arm. Megan cupped his hand in both of hers. Their warm welcome was family-like, and he could see that their friendliness was genuine.

"While we're up, let's move to the table." Katy played the perfect newlywed hostess and led them to a country-style kitchen. He tried to imagine Lil living here with Katy, as she had related to him on their ride over. He imagined curvy little Lil in an apron, cooking up her fancy dishes in the plain but refurbished Amish kitchen. Quaint. He loved the image.

"This is new," Lil said, fingering the table's centerpiece.

Jake entered the room, carrying an extra chair, and Fletch moved some of the other chairs to the side so it would fit at the table. It didn't match the other four chairs, and he hoped that wasn't some sort of sign that he would never fit in.

"It was a wedding present," Katy said, eyeing the rose-patterned teapot sporting a blooming African violet. "From Mrs. Beverly." Her eyes softened. "It's not really my style. Too fancy and delicate. See the gold edging? Since I moved the plant here, it's thriving. It deserves to live since we dragged it all over on our honeymoon. Anyway, seeing it every day is a good reminder for me."

"Reminder?" Fletch asked, not wanting to be the mismatched chair when everyone else knew exactly what Katy meant.

"There was a time I was pretty judgmental regarding outsiders."

"Outsiders?" Lil teased.

"Well, most people," Katy corrected, touching her covering. He'd seen her do that earlier, as if it served as a security blanket. He remembered Lil telling him how Katy liked to adhere to rules. Recalled the face Lil made when talking about it. From the little he'd seen of Lil, he knew she didn't like them. She was this beautiful creature trying to break free from her chains. Sometimes it almost hurt to see her trapped at the farm. But his thoughts returned to Katy. Would she accept him? By Katy's blush, Fletch wondered if he shouldn't have pried.

Lil warned, "A year ago, you would have been discarded or at least labeled forbidden for your red shoes."

As if on cue, everyone stared at his shoes. Thankfully, he was wearing dressier ones. He shrugged, wondering if Lil even liked his shoes. She mentioned them a lot, but he wasn't sure if she liked them.

He considered Lil's dreams of a new car and a head job at a restaurant with a fancy signature dish, her complaining about being plain. He knew she didn't like the plainness associated with the Conservative Mennonites.

"So you two are pretty opposite then?" he asked.

"Wow, you know Lil pretty well," Megan said, clutching his arm. "All my life, I've been refereeing those two. They're like cats and dogs. Black and white."

"No we're not!" Katy and Lil denied in unison.

Lil wouldn't let the comment go without rectification. "When was the last time you had to do that?"

Megan tilted her face and tapped her chin. Then her eyes widened, and her hand fell away from his arm. "It's been months. Of course I was gone for a while."

"Anyway, Mrs. Beverly was Katy's employer," Lil told Fletch. "But she retired and moved to Florida, where they honeymooned."

"I misjudged her and didn't think she was a Christian, but she sent me a letter explaining things about her faith that opened my eyes. So I think you're safe to wear the red shoes around me."

He wasn't sure he'd followed the entire story, especially with so many pretty mouths sharing in the telling. "Thanks."

Lil turned back to Katy. "The plant must be hardy. Look at all those blooms."

Katy looked at her husband with admiration. "Jake has the green thumb."

Lil made a face. "You guys are too mushy. Even when you aren't being mushy, you're mushy."

"Lil!" Megan flipped her hair to the side. "Be thankful they finally get along."

Lil blushed, and Fletch wondered if she was thinking of their budding relationship and the good-luck kisses they had shared in the car. When she glanced over at him, he quirked an eyebrow, delighted to make her freckles disappear.

"Fletch, I hear you traveled a lot, growing up," Katy said.

Megan instantly came alive, peppering Fletch with questions. He was used to it. Missionary life intrigued most people. He found that his experiences usually made interesting conversation, and he was a skilled storyteller. He fed on Megan's enraptured expression and explained to her how the Bambuti Pygmies climbed more than one hundred feet to the tops of the trees to collect honey, stunning the bees with smoke from burning wood clubs.

Then she told him about her trip to Bangladesh. He could relate to her experience. With Megan it was more than fascination over an unusual topic. She had missionary-fever in her eyes. She reminded him a lot of his mom, what she must have been like in the early years of her marriage. In moments, he could tell that Megan was destined for the missionary lifestyle.

At a nudge against his arm, he remembered his date. He glanced up, surprised to see that her expression had cooled. Her face was paler, and her freckles danced boldly.

"I need your keys. I left my dessert in the car."

He feared he was responsible for the change he saw in Lil and knew that it was not a good change. "I'll go with you."

As they started to the door, Jake taunted, "Talk about mushy, Lil."

"He's just being protective," Lil snapped.

"Am I?" Fletch asked, shooting Jake a grin.

"Just give me your keys."

"Nope," he dangled them and started toward the door.

Lil faltered and he could see she was struggling with something. Finally she relented. "I suppose there could be a rabid squirrel out there."

"Or a vicious fox!" Megan teased.

"An angry deer."

"Or a bear!"

"All right!" Lil exclaimed. "Let's go."

Although there was no real reason to protect Lil in the short traipse to the car, having his date clutch his arm was a good thing. "What was that?" he whispered. "Did you hear that crackle?"

"Yeah. It's good the car is so close." She played along, but her voice had lost its zest.

At the car, he swung her around. "Hey, what's wrong?"

She shook her head too quickly. "Nothing."

"It's something."

She sighed. "I was just thinking that maybe the reason we met. . ." She paused then started again. "Was so you could meet Megan."

"What? I was just trying to be friendly in there. Because she's your friend."

"But you have the same interests. She's really into missions."

He lifted her chin until their gazes met. "But I'm not into missions at all. My folks are. Not me."

She studied him carefully. Her voice was unusually timid. "You seem alike. You're pretty. She's pretty. And if you two want to date, I'm okay with that."

"I'm pretty?" He moved on to his next objection. "How can you ditch me? That really hurts."

"Okay, I'm not exactly okay with it, but—"

"Let me explain something. I was minding my own business, going to school. I was never out there looking for girls until you captured my attention. Lily, you're every bit as beautiful as Megan. But it's more than physical attraction with me. It's everything about you. The attraction is there," he quickly added, when he saw her expression fall. "You just strike a chord with me." He pointed to his chest. "In here. Remember? You're my sunshine." He knew that their relationship would have plenty of obstacles in store, but Megan certainly wasn't one of them.

"Thanks, Fletch."

"You're not going to be one of those jealous girls, are you?"

"I hope not."

He had to smile at her honesty. "Great. Now you keep a lookout for the squirrels while I duck in and get your cake."

"And foxes. Don't forget about the foxes, and careful you don't tip it and let the icing hit the sides," she warned.

He scooped out the cake and did a fake juggle act with it.

"Why do I adore ornery guys?" she asked.

"I thought I was your only boyfriend."

"I was thinking of Jake and my brothers, silly."

When they reached the house again, he paused. "That didn't go so well first time around. I might need a little more luck."

"Forget it, buster," she said, opening the door.

Fletch hurried after her and placed the cake in the kitchen, and then they joined the others waiting at the table for them.

Before the meal, Jake prayed. Afterward, he passed the chicken dumpling casserole and said, "Katy and I have an important announcement."

Fletch watched Lil's eyes widen.

CHAPTER 16

Lil's gaze sought Katy's, wondering what Jake's announcement would be. Was he going to announce a baby was on the way? Whatever it was, Jake's expression was both joyful and proud, and Katy's was that of adoration, like usual. *Total mush,* Lil thought, glancing over at Fletch.

"We made an offer on a house."

Lil's gaze returned to Katy, allowing the information to sink in. Her stomach twisted, yet her heart rejoiced. She wanted to do the garbanzo dance. She wanted to weep. This was all part of the plan—her door to freedom, but she was unprepared to make the move. She had no job. If she missed this opportunity, the doddy house might go to someone else. Her doddy house. Dollhouse, Fletch had called it. Her dream. She took a deep breath. "When will you move?"

"A lot has to happen first, but if everything goes according to plans, we will close the end of August and this place will be yours in September."

"So soon?" Megan asked, exchanging a worried look with Lil.

Katy's expression turned puzzled. "What's wrong? I thought you were so eager to boot us out."

"It's great news," Lil said. "Tell us about your house."

"Jake got a contract with a local land developer, and one of the original model homes became available. They're giving it to us at a great price."

"Which development?"

"The Pines. And it's near the Columbus outer belt. I won't have to live in the middle of the city someplace," Katy explained. "It's perfect." Her expression fell. "For us. But what's wrong? Is it your mom?"

"It's just that. . ."

Across the table from her, Katy bit her lip, waiting.

Lil's mind mulled over her circumstances, and she thought out loud. "Mom *is* doing better. By September, Michelle should be back on her feet. I guess the only obstacle is I need to get a job." Her voice turned uncertain. "That shouldn't be too hard."

"I didn't get the job at Char Airlines either," Megan said, nervously twisting a shank of shiny blond hair.

"Oh no," Lil exclaimed. "You wanted it so badly."

Fletch leaned forward. "Wait! Did you say Char Airlines? I might be able to pull some strings for you there."

All eyes turned to him, expectantly. Lil studied him and then saw Megan's awestruck gaze. They were doing it again, connecting.

"What do you mean?" Lil asked. She wanted to move into the doddy house. Megan needed that job. But she didn't need Megan staring at her date that way, ready to melt into a puddle on the doddy house kitchen floor.

"My mentor, Marshall. The man who contributed to my education," he explained. "He has a connection with them, uses them."

"Really? I can't believe it. This is my dream job," Megan gushed.

"Dream job?" Jake taunted. "Since when do you have a dream job?"

Everyone except Fletch knew that Megan had always floundered when it came to jobs, and Katy and Jake had been left out of the loop altogether regarding her most recent interview.

"This one was different. It came with opportunities to travel to various mission sites. It seemed perfect."

"And it's really close to my dream job," Lil added. "I plan to apply at Volo Italiano."

Katy frowned, obviously frustrated over the turn of conversation. "We don't get together often enough anymore." She thrust out her sulky lower lip. "Why am I just hearing about these jobs?"

Ignoring Katy's remark, Lil turned to Fletch. "Do you really think your friend could get her the job?"

His coloring deepened a bit, and Lil was sorry that she had made him self-conscious around Megan. Fletch wasn't normally the blushing type. He was the resourceful type.

"He's pretty influential. It's worth a try."

Megan shot out of her seat and flew to Fletch's side, tossed her arms around him. "Thank you so much."

Lil saw his neck redden deeper. When Megan withdrew, he shrugged. "Sure. No problem." Then he grabbed Lil's hand and squeezed.

She looked into his gaze, appreciating his reassurance. She wanted to believe that their relationship was intact and moving forward. She needed to shake off her ridiculous jealousy. It was a new emotion for her. She never would have thought she was the jealous type. But if she didn't relax, she was going to ruin their date. She would drive Fletch away. Now she understood how awful Katy must have felt when Jake was dating a girl from college.

Lil squeezed his hand back and forced a smile. "Happy endings all around. Just the way we like it."

Just as Megan was the peacemaker for the three friends, Lil realized she was the tone setter. She was the lively and cheerful one, the schemer who kept things interesting and fun. Up to that moment, the tension had expanded into a giant balloon over the dinner table, but her decision to put on a cheerful front was the pin that pricked that balloon and successfully drained the tension from the room. Everyone seemed grateful.

Afterward on the ride home, Lil realized she had overreacted to the connection between Megan and Fletch. Megan had given Fletch her family's phone number, but Megan didn't have a betraying bone in her.

"It's amazing that you have a connection with Megan's dream job," she remarked.

"God's the amazing One."

She studied him thoughtfully. "Do you think He cares about our dreams?"

"I think He plants them in our souls. Possibly in our DNA, too."

Lil gave him the awestruck smile that Katy reserved for Jake. She couldn't help it. When they pulled into her drive, he turned off the ignition. "Don't want to wake up the house," he teased.

"It's kind of weird moving out, then coming home again. September won't come around fast enough for me."

"But I'll miss seeing you here. I'll miss stealing kisses behind the azalea bush."

She remembered their first kiss, when the swing broke and they fell onto the ground together. She felt her cheeks heat.

He touched her hand. "Can we go out again?"

Her dad's advice came to mind. She shrugged it off. She remembered how the first time Fletch had asked her out, she'd hoped a date might clarify her feelings for him. But it hadn't. They had only scratched the surface in getting to really know each other. Before their relationship went much further, though, they needed to discuss their beliefs and talk about church.

"I'd like that."

"It's my turn to think of something to do. Unless you have something in mind?"

She shook her head.

"I should be by this week. Maybe I'll see you. Otherwise, I'll call."

"Great!" She opened the door, jumped out, and gave him a little wave.

He lurched out of the car and called after her, "Wait! Lil?"

She blew him a kiss, almost giggling at his astonished face. He probably had more kisses in mind, but she figured it was time to play a little hard to get.

—◌—

A crowing rooster did its best to awaken the humans on the Landis farm, but it didn't irritate Lil like it did some mornings.

Wrapped in a towel, she stared at the clothing she'd tossed onto the colorful pinwheel quilt. Even the plain garb—calf-length jean skirt; faded, tiny-flowered, yellow blouse; and white tennis shoes—didn't seem so drab today because of her date with Fletch.

Correction. Two dates, and another one lined up. She yawned. A smile replaced her yawn as she donned her clothing and pinned on her head covering. Her smile remained when she hung up her towel in the little bathroom at the end of the hall, and it was still in place when she went downstairs to start breakfast.

But when she stepped into the kitchen, her smile vanished, replaced by astonishment. Syrup, butter, and steaming sausage links graced the table, and her mom was already flipping pancakes on the griddle. "Mom?"

"Hi, honey. Hope you're hungry."

Lil scratched her head. Was she still dreaming? Surely all these wonderful miracles weren't happening to her. First a Mennonite guy appeared in her life, God-planted right under her nose. And now her mom was making breakfast again? This was, indeed, a morning of hope.

If God meant to bless her now, she'd better go job hunting, too.

"Lillian!" Her mom laughed.

Coming out of her reverie, Lil stepped into the room. "Sorry, I was daydreaming."

"I saw. That young man has you befuddled."

She opened her mouth to protest, but the rebellious smile came back. She figured it was best not to deny it. "I'll set the table."

"Use the Autumn Leaf set. We're celebrating."

"Okay. What are we celebrating?"

"Life, Lil. Just life." Mom studied her, then added with a half smile, "And perhaps love?"

"I'm all for life, Mom. You don't know how happy it makes me to see you feeling good." Even with her mom in such a glorious mood, the old fear lingered that one wrong word would send her back into depression. "Let's celebrate life. But if by love you're referring to my date, then I think that's a bit premature."

"Where's the Lily I know? You've always chased after the boys."

Chased them away, Lil thought, wondering why her mom was

promoting Fletch. "Yeah, I tried to keep up with my brothers and Jake, but—"

Mom plunked the platter of steaming pancakes on the table and removed her apron. "Well that must have been good practice, because I think you've finally caught one." She winked. "Okay, I'll humor you. We'll just celebrate life."

Lil hugged her, happy to see her zest for life returning. "This is a good day." Over her mom's shoulder, her gaze went to the window, and she stepped back. "Are we early, or are the men late?"

"They're late. I hope the pancakes don't get cold."

Lil swallowed. Her mom seemed better. This might be the only time that she would be receptive to Lil's plans. "Mom, I need to tell you something. Jake and Katy found a house."

"How nice," she said with uncertainty.

Pushing aside the light tension, Lil went on. "I would like to move back in with Megan the first of September."

Mom sank into the nearest chair. "But today is the fifth of August. That's less than a month away. Anyway, how can you afford it?"

Lil pulled out the chair next to her mom. "That's plenty of time for me to find a job. In fact, I thought I'd go looking today."

Staring at the sausage, Mom shook her head. "You are forgetting that Michelle needs our help." She looked over at Lil with hurt-filled eyes. "Or was that all some farce to get me out of bed?"

"Mom! Of course not. I just figured that by the time I actually started working, you'd be able to handle chores here. That you would want to do the things you love doing. I can put in all my spare time at Michelle's. Her cast will be off by September."

"Love doing?" Mom said mockingly. She sighed. "Look. I'm trying Lil, but I'm not ready for this. It was so lonely here the last time you left."

Fear gripped Lil as she watched her mom's fragile expression flit from emotion to emotion. She remembered that day at the doddy house when Katy had suggested that Mom's depression might have something to do with an empty-nest syndrome. Panic cupped Lil's heart, and she tried to reassure Mom. "This time I'll drop in all the time, and you can come to the doddy house, too. We'll do stuff together. You can help me start an herb garden."

"You know I don't drive," Mom snapped.

Lil scratched her damp, freshly showered hair. "But one of the boys can drop you off. It's not far. It will be different this time. You'll see." *I won't be so selfish.*

Mom tipped her chin upwards. "I see you will have it no other way. I hate when you act like your father."

The hope Lil had felt when she'd caught Mom and Dad kissing dissipated. Her mom had a myriad of problems. But Lil couldn't miss the especially bitter tone she directed at Dad. Was it resentment over her lot in life? Did that come from some distant "outsider's gene" that got handed down to Lil, too?

Only moments earlier, her mom had announced they were celebrating life. Now Lil regretted bringing up the doddy house. She should have gone job hunting without mentioning it. Her mom was too delicate. A setback now would be disastrous for all of them.

She touched her mom's tensed fist. "Let's not fret about this, Mom. This morning we are celebrating life. Remember? Let's—"

Mom stood. "You celebrate life, Lil. You are young. Yes, you go and fetch your dreams." She started across the kitchen.

"Mom!" Lil called out with panic.

But her mother slumped her shoulders and left the room.

Lil followed as far as the hallway, watching her mother turn into her bedroom and slam the door. From behind, she heard her father and brothers entering the mudroom. Needing to escape, too, she ran the other direction, through the living room. She turned the deadbolt and ran outside, shutting the door behind her. Her back against the door, she looked around. She needed to escape! To get away from this madhouse before it pulled her down and sucked away her life.

Her heart beating wildly, she hurried around the side of the house, unconsciously starting toward the cottonwood at the back of the farm. But she came to a halt at the sight of the blue Ford Focus. That meant Fletch had come without Vic. With the men inside eating breakfast, Fletch would be alone in one of the barns. She glanced at the woods, then at the barns, envisioning his strong open arms.

She wanted to feel his tight embrace. To pour out what had just happened and tell him about her mom's downturn. She longed for words of affirmation, telling her it was all right to go job hunting. She needed somebody who would understand.

Lil slowed her steps as she neared the first barn. When she reached it, she tried to calm her rapid heartbeat by going through a rote routine that everybody used before they entered. She squirted disinfectant on her hands. Next, she pulled on a pair of men's muckers over her white sneakers. They were one of her brother's extras, several sizes too big, and made her walk like a duck, but she'd done this a million times, even if never in front of a boyfriend.

She shuffled past pens filled with routing, snorting hogs devouring their breakfast. She needed Fletch. He understood her like nobody else and wasn't concerned with her appearance. He'd told her that on their date.

Once she would have run to Jake. Those days were gone. She missed him. And some of that need had been transposed onto Fletch. He was more resourceful than Jake had ever been. And with Fletch, there was more. There was the physical attraction, the need and desire. She hurried deeper into the barn, her eyes gradually adjusting to the darkness.

Then she saw him. But she froze in puzzlement at his peculiar behavior.

Fletch moved slowly about the stalls, slightly crouched. He peered through a palm-sized camera aimed at the sick piglets, pushing various buttons. Next he leaned over a short wall and aimed the lens at the sow. He slowly backed away and turned.

When the camera caught Lil, he jerked it away from his face.

He stared at Lil as if she were someone horridly intrusive and shoved the video camera into his jeans pocket. The alarm on his face was all she needed to know that she'd caught him doing something wrong. Even though she didn't understand what, her heart sank.

"What are you doing?"

"I'm working," he said defensively.

"Why were you taking pictures of our hogs?"

Fletch turned more pale than when she'd first caught him. "It's not what it looks like."

She tried to think. What did it look like? What did he mean? She strode forward with growing distress, forgetting momentarily her huge waders, and stepped out of her boot. Angrily, she stopped to replace it, then marched forward. She placed her hands on her hips. "Perhaps not, but I'm waiting to hear the reason. Why are you filming our sick hogs?"

She hoped for a reasonable explanation, perhaps some protocol that Vic demanded since Fletch was a student and Vic hadn't accompanied him to the farm. But in her heart she knew that there was no reasonable explanation. Something was terribly wrong.

Fletch acted increasingly uncomfortable. Finally, he sighed and started toward her. "You've heard me talk about Marshall?"

She could tell this wasn't going anywhere pleasant. "Yes."

"He has a farm shelter."

"What's that?"

"It's a place where they take in abused farm animals."

She narrowed her eyes in confusion, feeling pangs of betrayal. "Go on."

"Vic and I volunteer there. Marshall asked me to take some videos of sick animals. That's what I was doing."

"Why?"

"The shelter is doing a documentary that they'll use for fundraising."

"I can't believe this. You're going to put our farm on a documentary for abused animals?"

"No. The name of your farm won't be mentioned."

"Are you doing this behind Vic's back?" Lil's hands flew to her temples, holding her head, which throbbed with betrayal and disillusion.

"You don't understand. Marshall paid for my tuition. He's never asked me for any favors before this. I had no choice."

"You betrayed us, acting like you were Matt's friend, and my—" *Boyfriend?* She clenched her jaw. When she could speak, she said, "I'm getting the men." Her trust in him crumbled like chaff.

"Wait!"

She paused, turned around. "You are unbelievable! I never want to see you again!" Her eyes burning, she started to run, but her feet came out of her boots. For fear that he would catch up to her if she stopped, she left them behind. She ran through the muck, the squishy sound of her white tennies adding to her hopelessness.

She broke into the morning light and ran down the lane, scattering a group of squawking chickens. In a blind flash, she passed the clothesline, Jezebel, and the azalea bush. She hit the house screaming at the top of her lungs. "Da-a-ad!" She didn't care about tracking up her mom's house, but ran straight through the mudroom into her father's solid arms.

He towered over her, so strong and comforting in his worn overalls. "What? What's wrong?"

Two of her brothers stood behind him, their eyes wide and frightened.

Her chest heaving, she spat out, "He betrayed us!"

"Who?" Dad asked, looking fearfully over her shoulder.

"Fletch. He's filming our sick hogs."

"What?" Matt demanded, his eyes darkening in anger.

Lil wept and gasped, "He's doing a documentary on animal cruelty. He's. . . He's. . ." She couldn't finish.

Dad pulled her into his arms, but her brothers rushed past them. She heard the screen door slam. But she couldn't be consoled. She tore out of her father's arms and pushed him. "Go. See for yourself." She placed her fist to her mouth to keep her sobs at bay and ran down the hall. She hesitated outside Mom's closed bedroom door. Removing her fist from her lips, she opened it and stepped into its dark interior. Kicking off her ruined shoes, she climbed into bed with her mom and let the anguish spill.

Mom's arms clutched her, pulled her close. "What's wrong?"

Lil hiccupped, "I didn't catch one after all, Mom. Fletch is a big disappointment."

"Oh, honey."

Lil broke into inconsolable sobs.

CHAPTER 17

Fletch followed Lil out of the barn and watched her run toward the house, his own heart breaking for her. She thought he had betrayed her and her family, which was so far from the truth. At least his intentions. Part of him wanted to run after her, but he knew that given the state she was in, she wouldn't listen. Her eyes had become green frigid glaciers when she shouted that she never wanted to see him again.

He hoped he would get the chance to explain things again once she calmed down. Maybe he had done the wrong thing, but if he hadn't gotten caught, the video would have pacified Marshall without hurting anybody. Nobody would have known the hogs came from the Landis farm. He would have made sure of that.

When Fletch had asked Marshall about Char Air, the other man had used it for negotiating power. He would get Megan another interview if Fletch got him the requested footage. Fletch had wanted to refuse, but he couldn't dismiss Megan's enthusiastic face.

Fletch knew that once Lil reached the house, the Landis men would come after him. Feeling like the traitor he was, he hid the camera in his car until he could decide what to do with it. His survival instinct told him to drive away and never look back, but of course he couldn't do that. He needed to finish this. It wouldn't end at the Landis farm either. He would need to deal with Vic next. The vet would be furious if he lost the Landis account.

Fletch had only taken a few steps back toward the barn when he saw the men barreling out of the house like a herd of angry boars.

"Stop!" Hank shouted.

Fletch clenched his jaw and set his feet.

Hank screeched to a halt just a few feet from him. But Matt pushed past Hank and grabbed Fletch's arm. "Is it true? Are you filming our farm for a documentary on animal cruelty?"

Fletch jerked his arm away. "Not exactly."

Infuriated, Matt brought his arm back as if to hit him. Fletch's arm automatically went up to block the blow, but it never came. Will had caught up with his sons and snatched Matt's arm in midair.

"Don't lower yourself to his level."

Matt shook off his father's hand.

"I know you don't abuse animals," Fletch explained in his own defense.

"Of course we don't! So why are you filming our hogs?" Matt demanded.

"The man who is footing my college tuition owns a farm shelter and wanted me to film some sick animals to use in his fund-raising documentary. But it was just to stir up some sympathy. The footage would remain anonymous and not indict your name or farm in any way."

"That's pathetic," Matt sneered. "And I thought you were a friend. If you needed pictures, you should have come to us first."

Fletch said wryly, "As if anybody would let me film their sick animals." In truth, he would have asked Matt the last time they were together if Matt hadn't been in such a foul mood.

Will accused, "We are just trying to survive, yet you perch here like a vulture, waiting for us to do something wrong so you could film it? Is this the kind of stuff they teach you at your church?"

Matt cringed. "This has nothing to do with church."

"Doesn't it?" Will demanded. "Is Vic a part of this?"

"No," Fletch replied.

Will thrust a finger toward Fletch. "You tell him we want to see him. He has some explaining to do. And I want *you* to stay off our property."

"And stay away from our sister," Hank added.

"I'm going. But regarding Lil—"

Hank grabbed Fletch by the shirtfront. "You sleazeball. Don't even say her name."

"Let him go. Violence is not our way." The older man looked Fletch in the eyes. "She doesn't want you, anyway. You betrayed her."

"Stay away from Lily," Hank warned in a low, deadly voice.

Fletch's own anger flared at the way the others were attacking him and had so readily turned on him. If Hank didn't let go of his shirt soon, he was going to find himself sitting on his John Deere pockets. Just when Fletch thought he couldn't contain himself any longer, Hank released his shirt. Fletch jerked it down into place, gritting his teeth.

Glaring at the lot of them, he restrained himself. It wouldn't serve any purpose to say another word to this clan of blockheads. They were not receptive to any reasoning, especially regarding Lil. Words were finished.

Fletch turned away. Strode toward his car. Once he reached it, he started the ignition and backed down the lane, understanding why his dad had preached so many times about having to turn the other cheek—the Mennonite's practice of nonresistance. He imagined all of them had been tempted to break that stance today. Lil's brothers had wanted a piece of him as badly as he'd wanted to knock sense into them. The adrenaline continued to course through him. He didn't look back but peeled out of the lane.

⌒

When he arrived at the clinic, Buddy heard Fletch's car and was at the door waiting for him. He knelt down, scratching the basset's head. "It's over. I got what I needed on film, but I lost the girl, and I detest myself." The anger was gone. He should have refused Marshall. What he'd done was unethical.

Even if Marshall had withdrawn his support, he could have applied for a college loan. It might have added an extra year to his education, but it would have been better than this mess he'd gotten himself into. He should have let Megan find her own job. Buddy licked his hand, but it did little to lessen the hard lump in the pit of Fletch's stomach.

"How's it going at the Landis farm?" Vic asked. "Any more sick hogs?"

"No, but there's a problem."

Vic turned from the notes he'd been writing, giving Fletch his full attention. "What kind of problem?"

"They caught me filming their hogs."

Vic closed his eyes and pinched the bridge of his nose. "So you did it anyway? Well congratulations. In this small town, word will get around. By this time tomorrow night, not a farmer in town will trust me with their animals."

Fletch grew even more glum.

"I don't suppose we could get somebody from the shelter to apologize?"

Fletch shook his head. "Not a chance."

"You cover here. I'm going to the Landis farm and see if I can get them to listen to reason. Maybe they'll understand Marshall's hand in this if I explain it."

"You don't have to mention your part in this," Fletch said. "I don't want to be responsible for taking your company down. Just blame it all on me."

"Yes. That was my intention."

Fletch realized that if he couldn't set foot on any of the farms, his time with Vic was finished, and just when the fall term was starting. He probably wouldn't be able to get another vet to work with. He didn't think he could muster a passing grade if Vic let him go.

"If nobody wants me on their farm, how are you going to fulfill your obligation to Marshall?" Fletch asked.

"You're going to get him off my back."

That wouldn't likely happen. "What if the farms won't let me help you?"

Vic sighed. "Let's just take this one step at a time."

Fletch nodded, but the moment the vet was out the door, he sank to his knees in prayer.

—♋—

Lil clasped her teacup, glancing up at her friends. "I'm so humiliated. To think that the first guy I fell for was only using us for some farm footage."

"He seemed so down-to-earth, so honest," Katy replied.

"I thought he had a good heart, being a missionary and everything," Megan bemoaned.

"He's not a missionary!" Lil corrected, still a bit miffed that to Megan anybody associated with mission work was more than holy. "His parents are. There's a big difference. He's just a student who will do anything to get his degree."

"Well sure, I knew it was his parents, but I still thought he had a good heart."

"I'm sorry." Lil gazed out the doddy house window. When she looked back, she said, "I guess he fooled us all."

"I know how you must feel," Katy replied. "Jake betrayed my trust, too, when we were dating."

Lil pinched the bridge of her nose and tried to focus on her friend's analogy. "But he repented."

"Maybe Fletch will, too," Megan said hopefully.

"These things take time to work themselves out," Katy advised. "You might have to talk to him again before you can move on."

Lil stared at the African violet in the center of the table.

"Jake and I started reading the Bible together, and I came across a verse that I wanted to give you. I know you don't like me getting preachy, but this really is meant for your mother. It's an encouraging verse. I copied it on a recipe card for you. Would you like it?"

Lil wasn't sure why Katy was changing the subject, for she didn't feel as if she had finished ranting about Fletch. But then would she ever be? "Of course."

Katy got up and moved to a small side table in the living room. "Let me see. Here it is."

"Thanks." Lil gave it a quick glance and put it in her purse. "It has been a rough couple of months. I can use any encouragement." She blinked back her tears. "But I'm not letting you both down because of him. I have a job interview on Thursday."

"You do?" Megan's expression remained sad. "That's wonderful."

Lil touched Megan's hand because her friend didn't sound like it was wonderful to her, probably thinking of how Fletch had betrayed her hopes at Char Air. "Somehow this will still work out for us."

"We must believe," Katy added.

Megan placed a hand to her temple. "I better get out there again. If you can do it, then I can, too."

"That a girl," Lil replied.

She saw Katy glance up at the clock.

"Time for the chump to come home?"

"Yes, but you don't have to rush off. Stay for dinner."

"Thanks. Maybe another time. I'm not up to it."

Lil's despondency continued on the drive home as she rehashed their conversation. She grasped at the only thread of hope she'd received from her chat with Katy and Megan. If her interview went well on Thursday, she could land the job and go forward with her plans for the doddy house.

At home, she stepped into the mudroom and placed her purse on the shelf until she remembered Katy's verse. She pulled out the recipe card, brushed off a piece of purse lint, and read:

> *Then they cried unto the LORD in their trouble, and he saved them out of their distresses. He brought them out of darkness and the shadow of death, and brake their bands in sunder. Oh that men would praise the LORD for his goodness, and for his wonderful works to the children of men!—Psalm 107:13–15*

Usually Katy's habit of acting like Lil's personal Holy Spirit was intolerable, but this time, the words touched her soul. Lil brought the card up to her mouth to shield the sob that erupted from her throat.

These words weren't just for Mom. They were as personal as if God was speaking directly to her. Lil hurried to her room, shut the door, and fell to her knees, crying to the Lord to save her from her distress.

―⟨⟩

Fletch crouched in the lamb's stall and wished he could crawl under the straw and hibernate for a couple hundred years. He was alone in the world, like the lamb. No place to really call home, nobody waiting for him at his sparse apartment. Nobody to ask him how his day had gone. Now that his budding relationship with Lil had been prematurely ended, he felt bereft. Bereft and alone. He put his back to the wall and cradled the lamb.

"*I am the Lamb.*"

Fletch flinched. Where had that thought come from? His heart raced to think that the Lord was speaking to him. Comforting him. He replied, *Lord, I guess You know what will happen next, but things seem pretty bleak right now.*

He knew what he'd done was unethical, but nobody cared enough to listen to his reasons for caving to Marshall's request. He supposed that he shouldn't expect more out of Vic than his shifting of blame, because if Vic had been a strong man, he wouldn't have accepted Marshall's monetary help in the first place.

Vic had talked his way out of the trouble with Lil's family. He'd put all the blame on Fletch. He'd let on as if Fletch's actions had been a bewildering shock to him, as well. Now Fletch lived under the cloud of dread, that when he least expected it, some farmer would demand that he not be allowed to treat their animals.

If the whole thing didn't blow over quickly, his chances at starting any kind of practice or finding an internship around Columbus were doomed. And if his college instructor found out what he'd done, he might even be kicked out of the program. Why hadn't he thought of all that before he took the video?

The lamb stirred, gave a small bleat. Fletch felt a stirring in his heart. *Thank You, Lord, for reminding me that I'm never alone.*

"Isn't this a pretty picture? I saw your car," Ashley explained, for she wasn't usually in the barn much.

Fletch jerked his gaze toward Ashley. "You caught me loafing, enjoying the little guy."

"Hey, you're a volunteer. You can loaf a few minutes."

"Except Vic always has work lined up for me."

"Cottonball is enjoying this as much as you. It's good for him."

"You name them?"

"Yes, but their files have case numbers, too." Fletch rose to finish his rounds, but Ashley stopped him. "I have something for you."

"Yeah?"

She handed him a yellow sticky note with a date and time written on it.

"What's this?"

"An interview for your friend."

"For Megan?" he asked, staring at the note and wondering why Marshall had set that up before Fletch had even turned in the video.

"I thought you'd be happier about it than that. What's wrong?"

He let out a sigh. "I got busted taking video at the Landis farm."

Ashley's eyes widened. "Oh no. What happened?"

Fletch briefly sketched the fateful events.

"I'm sorry it was the Landis farm."

He wondered how she knew that farm was special to him. Fingering the sticky note, he said, "Megan probably won't accept this from me now."

"Maybe she will. It might help you win your girl back."

With a start, Fletch asked, "How did you know about her?"

"I'm here twelve hours a day. I have eyes and ears." Then she blushed. "Okay, so Marcus and I are pretty close. He told me."

Fletch fought the lump that came to his throat. "Her name's Lil."

"I know."

"She hates me."

"Understandable. But that can change if she loves you."

Love? The word cut his heart like a knife, because it carried some truth. In their brief acquaintance, he had come to love many things about her. But surely it wasn't *the* love. The kind poems were written about. Was it? He blew a puff of exasperation, staring at the little sticky note. "You think?"

Ashley touched his hand. "Yes. Look if there's anything I can do to help, I'm here for you."

Marcus stepped into the barn just then and stopped short when he saw them together in the stall. Ashley jerked her hand away. "What are ya doing here?" Marcus asked in a harsh tone.

"I work here," she replied.

"You know what I mean."

"I was giving him a note from Marshall. He got busted," Ashley explained.

"Oh, man. I'm sorry. Ya still have the camera?"

Fletch had the camera. It was still on the carpet, where he'd flung it. And his heart was urging him to go to it. To delete the footage he'd taken.

CHAPTER 18

At Volo Italiano, Lil sat across the black tablecloth from Giovanni and handed the head waiter her résumé.

Her interviewer was a light-haired Italian with a thick accent that missed many of the English vowel sounds. "The school is a good one. Everything seems in order, but. . .eh. . .I will have to check with your last employer."

"Beppe didn't like me, but I can explain. First of all, he thought I was putting dings in his car. Then there was a family illness, something unexpected, and I had to help my parents. I had to switch my hours several times, and finally I had to give up my job altogether. But all that is over now. I'm able to give one hundred percent. I don't think Beppe can complain about my cooking."

"You ding cars, no?"

"No. He was a fanatic." *Well maybe just that once after I backed into Fletch's.* Lil jerked her mind from that errant path and shook her head emphatically. "No."

"And how do I know that when another family problem pops up. . .eh. . .you won't have to help out again?"

"Because I have a rent payment. And I've determined to meet my goals."

"Is it too personal to ask about these goals?"

Lil squirmed. *To get your job.* But she knew that admitting she was eventually after a head-cook position like his wouldn't help the interview. She supposed it wasn't even very Christian-like to imagine it, but it was the truth. Instead, she replied, "To pursue my cooking career. I've been miserable these past months. Cooking is what I live for. It's in the genes. I come from a line of potluck queens."

He twisted his mouth with disdain, "Eh. . .potluck?"

"It's a church thing." She saw his gaze go up to her covering and back down to her face, seeming more puzzled than ever, and she knew she was botching her interview big-time. "I'm tired of driving a clunker. I'm putting my needs first this time."

Now he tilted his head. "Above your family's, no?"

"Yes. I will be the best employee you've ever had."

He pinched his Roman nose and frowned. "You sound bitter. My experience is that bitterness spreads and infects." He shook his head. "Eh. . .I do not like to be around bitter people." Then under his breath, she thought she heard, "I have enough of that at home."

"I love my family. But my mom has been experiencing depression. She's much better, but if she slips back into it, now I know that there's nothing I can do. Believe me I tried, but I didn't think you'd be interested in personal details."

"Thank you for sharing this. . .eh. . .which gives the better insight."

"And if I sounded bitter, that was because I just broke up with my boyfriend. But I'm naturally a very upbeat person." She shrugged. "My friends say I light up a room." She couldn't believe she'd just told him such personal details and even boasted about herself. She should have waited a few days until—

He touched her arm. "I understand."

She glanced at him, and he removed his long thin fingers and folded them together, studying her with smoky eyes. Now they brooded, but she had a hunch that this man could be as explosive as Beppe and that Giovanni's eyes could storm with the best of them. Only they bore a hint of sadness and a tremendous depth as if he would be the type of man to experience everything with intensity.

He blinked, and she asked, "You do?"

"Yes, my wife has these bouts with. . .eh. . .the gloom. But hers stems from bitterness because she cannot have babies."

Lil glanced from the Saltillo tile to the live potted plants that sent trailing tendrils around their adjacent pillars. "My mom is bitter, too," Lil admitted.

"Now I see that you are the victim, like me. Maybe we can support each other in this, no?"

His last sentence drifted away, as if he was talking to himself. Feeling awkward, Lil gave a hesitant nod.

"When can you start?"

The abrupt question nearly brought tears of joy to her eyes. "How about right now?"

"Good. I like that. Let's go find a uniform. Eh. . . There's a box of tissues in the stockroom, too." He pointed at her. "But no. Not today. You start tomorrow."

In spite of her general sadness over losing Fletch, it was hard to resist the garbanzo dance. Her new boss understood her situation. She nodded. "Thank you so much. I won't disappoint you."

His brown gaze settled on her, and before he opened the door to the stockroom, he said, "Eh. . . One more thing. In your case, I believe we will give you assigned parking." He pointed, "It will be way out at the end of the parking lot. Eh. . . We will even put your name on it. Just until you have proven you do not ding the head chef's car."

"Thanks a lot," she said sarcastically, wondering if he was teasing or serious. Well she didn't intend to be late to work anymore. This was a new start.

—⟲—

Fletch stared at the video camera in the corner of the room. It still lay on its landing spot, drawing Buddy to an occasional sniff. He slouched down in his chair. He'd acted unethically by going against client privacy. Lil never wanted to see him again. He would have to face Matt at church on Sunday. Matt might tell other people in the congregation. The Landis family might tell other farmers. Vic might tell his instructor.

Feeling trapped in a corner with no way out, he flung his red ball cap. It sailed across the room and landed near the camera.

If he deleted the film, Marshall might abandon him. He remembered the Lord's nudging back in the barn. He was not alone, he reminded himself. But his situation remained grave. The entire semester might be wasted. Fletch might have to pick himself up and find a new school. He hoped his credits would transfer, that he wouldn't be blackballed from the veterinary program. He was just a student. Weren't student's allowed to make mistakes?

He snatched up his phone and pulled up Marshall's name from his contacts. "Hi Marshall. How's it going?"

"Hi, Fletch. Actually, I'm talking from a hospital bed."

"I heard you were taking some tests." Fletch overheard bits of conversation in the background. "Marshall, you still there?"

"Can we talk later? I have to go."

"Sure. I. . .wish you the best."

"Maybe send up a prayer or two?"

"Of course I will. I'm sure you'll be fine."

Fletch dropped his phone in his lap. Was there something serious going on with Marshall? He'd never asked Fletch to pray before. The longer Fletch dwelled on the matter, the more he wondered about Marshall's faith. Growing up, he'd just assumed that Marshall was a Christian because he contributed so generously to his parents' mission work. It hit Fletch hard that maybe Marshall was trying to earn his way to heaven and had never heard about God's gift of forgiveness.

Fletch had heard fear in Marshall's voice. He racked his brain for a time when he had discussed Jesus with Marshall. Did his mentor know that Jesus had died on the cross for his sins? Had his father ever shared his faith with Marshall? Or had they all assumed?

He dipped his head and prayed for Marshall. While he was at it, he prayed for Marcus, and ended up by praying for his present situation. Time passed, and Fletch heard Buddy's whine. He looked across the room. The dog was sniffing his hat. The video camera was still there to mock him, but he no longer felt hopeless.

"Wanna go for a walk?"

Buddy jumped to his feet, and his rear parts wiggled. "Go fetch it."

The dog snapped up Fletch's hat and brought it to him. Buddy was smart. He was a good companion. Fletch's life might be a disaster, but he definitely wasn't alone.

By the time they had returned from their walk, Fletch had a new perspective on his situation. He felt that he needed to let matters with Marshall and the video rest. He was going to concentrate on mending his relationship with Lil and Matt.

—ᘓ—

On Sunday, Fletch held his head up as his heart and the rest of his body slunk into his usual church pew. He didn't expect Matt to sit next to him, but he was surprised to see that he chose the seat directly across the aisle. Inhaling a breath of courage, Fletch turned and gave Matt a contrite smile. He saw Matt's cheek muscle twitch, but Matt gave him a frosty glare.

Fletch would have welcomed a sermon on forgiveness or even some practical advice about frostbite, but it was the middle of summer, and the usually captivating preacher droned on and on about the Israelites' march through the wilderness. Fletch tried to listen, but the message wasn't getting through to him.

He found himself absently counting the stained-glass sections of the nearest window. He counted it from the top down and from the bottom up until he was completely satisfied it was exactly fifty-five sections. He was about to count them in individual colors, too, but the excruciating sermon came to a conclusion.

Fletch waited while Matt spoke to a pretty girl who had been sharing his pew. She was the reason they always sat on the tenth row up from the back. Matt was interested in her. Fletch felt conspicuous standing and waiting alone. It didn't help when the girl glanced over at Fletch as if they were discussing him. A chill ran up his back, but he wasn't going to turn coward. He took her glance as an invitation and crossed the aisle to face Mr. Frost.

"Hi, guys."

"Hi, Fletch." The girl squirmed and shot a quick glance at Matt.

"I gotta go." She squeezed past Fletch and whispered, "Hope you guys work out your differences."

"Thanks a lot, Stauffer, for chasing her away."

Fletch wanted to reply, *Thanks, Landis, for squealing on me.* "I came to apologize. I need to make things right with you. Can we go to lunch?"

"You pack us a picnic?" Matt asked sarcastically.

Ignoring the remark, he gave a half smile. "No, but I can afford fast food."

Matt looked at the exit and then back at Fletch. "Looking at you makes me lose my appetite, but I won't stop you from walking me to my car." With that Matt started down the nearly vacant aisle.

Fletch fell into stride, one hand slipping into his pocket and rubbing the few bills and change he'd scraped up in case Matt had taken him up on his offer. As they walked, Fletch spilled out his story, giving the bare facts, which in his own mind justified his motives though not his actions. "I thought we were friends, and that you'd help me out." He bit back his tongue from saying, *I was volunteering a lot of hours at your farm so you could afford treatment for your animals.* "I was going to talk to you about the filming the day you jumped me about Lil. I was going to ask your permission."

As they reached Matt's pickup, he replied, "You told me that day that if Lil didn't want you bothering her, you'd back off. Well she doesn't. So are you going to keep your word now?"

"I can give you my word that I'm not giving up until I win back your friendship. And your family's trust. I'm hoping that Lil will at least hear me out, too. I made a mistake. Can you forgive me? Give me another chance?"

"Look, I know it takes guts to ask that. I can forgive you. But what are you going to do about this mistake? Are you going to destroy that video? You said you wanted to make things right."

"Yes. I will. I was going to do that last week. I called Marshall to tell him, to face the music even if it meant losing my tuition and dropping out of school. But when I called, he was in the hospital. He was scared about some tests he's undergoing. He asked me to pray for him. It didn't seem the right time to approach the subject. But I'm going to tell him.

I just need time."

"I guess time will tell then. I hope it all works out for you." Matt turned and hopped up in his cab, obviously still angry even though he'd said he forgave Fletch.

Fletch stepped back and watched Matt drive away.

—⁂—

Sunday afternoon, Fletch grew weary of waiting for time to tell. Since Lil wasn't answering any of his phone calls, he decided to try Ashley's advice. He pulled the yellow sticky note off the screen of his laptop and headed for the house that Lil had once pointed out as Megan's.

Walking up the steps to Megan's front porch, he patted his shirt pocket to make sure he still had his admission ticket. He rang the doorbell, hoping his plan would work. Thankfully, Megan came to the door, leaving it ajar behind her.

"Fletch?" Uncertainty clouded her face. "Hi."

"Hi, Megan. I brought you something." He pulled the yellow sticky note from his pocket and handed it to her. "It's another interview with Char Air."

"No kidding? That's wonderful. I don't know how to. . .wow." Her tone of voice descended, losing its excitement. "I don't know. This makes me feel like I'm in cahoots with the enemy."

"I hoped to talk to you about that. Lil's not taking any of my phone calls."

"I'm afraid I can't accept this." She tried to give him back the yellow note.

He quickly stuffed his hands in to his jeans pockets. "Please, keep it."

Her face reddened. "I can't. Not after what you did."

"It's true I made a mistake taking that film at the Landis farm."

He saw her face softening.

"It was unethical. But it was a personal request from the man who financed my schooling. He also donated lots of money to the mission field, supplied a lot of personal needs over the years for me and my parents. And it was the first thing he'd ever asked me to do for him. Just take some pictures of some sick animals."

Megan's face contorted. "Why?"

"He's starting a shelter for abused farm animals. It was for a movie they would show at fund-raisers. He promised nobody would know whose farm was filmed, that I could see the film when it was finished. Honestly, it had nothing to do with Lil. The Landis farm is the only farm where I could take the pictures, because it's the only one I go to without Vic." He toed the porch flooring with his red sneaker. "If I hadn't got caught, nobody would have gotten hurt."

Megan closed the front door behind her and turned back to him with an arched brow. "Do you read the Bible?"

"Of course."

"Does this sound familiar? 'Your deeds will be brought to light.'"

Fletch cringed under her rebuff but knew she was right. "Yes, but it was a situation where no matter what I did, somebody could get hurt. I did what I thought was best at the time."

She twisted a shank of blond hair and said sympathetically, "We all make mistakes."

"You think Lil will forgive me?"

"I doubt it."

Fletch cringed.

"She's really upset. Feels betrayed. She thinks you used her. And you were the first guy she really liked."

He dipped his head. "Her family hates me now, too." He lifted his gaze to meet Megan's again. "But I'm not giving up on her. I can't. I don't want to give up on Matt either, but he's stubborn."

"This is all very interesting Fletch, but. . ." She shook her head.

Out on the road, a car stirred up dust and a flock of blackbirds from a neighboring field. He nervously jangled the coins in his pocket. "Will you help me if I try to win her back?"

Megan sighed. "I'm not going to betray Lil. Why should we trust you?"

He didn't miss the *we*, which meant she wanted to trust him. "Because that's the only way to fix this mess. And because all I was trying to do was repay a debt."

She leaned her shoulder against a porch post, crossing her arms and

175

studying him. "Do you have a plan?"

"My plan is to talk to Lil."

"And you want me to convince her to meet with you or pick up the phone or what?"

"You could tell her about the interview? Ask her to give me just a few minutes on the phone. Think she'd help you out?"

Megan straightened, her face paling with anger. "No! Lil doesn't need somebody who's scheming and using other people again. You're disgusting me right now, Fletch. I won't be a party to anything like this. I think Lil was right about you."

She reached out, and for an instant, Fletch thought she was going to strike him, but instead she slapped the sticky note on his chest. "I don't want your interview." She wheeled and opened the door.

"Wait! Please!"

She paused, turned, and looked at him as if he was lower than dirt.

"It was a stupid idea." He took the note off his shirt and held it out toward her. "Please keep this. No matter what. I want you to get that job."

Megan crossed her arms. "Under the circumstances, I can't go on that interview."

He licked his lips. He hadn't expected it to go this poorly. Megan was supposed to be the peacemaker. "Look, I have an idea."

She rolled her gaze toward the porch ceiling impatiently, and he knew that any second she was going to leave him standing alone on the stoop.

"Come to the farm shelter. Meet the people and see what it's all about. I need an advocate, Megan. Please?"

Her hands flew up in a gesture of refusal. "Absolutely not. If Lil finds out—"

He touched her arm, and it stilled.

"She told me how she tried to help her friend Katy. If it was you, Lil would try to help. I thought you were a peacemaker."

Gently, Megan pulled her arm away. "And that backfired on her."

His eyes pleaded. "At first. But Katy did end up with Jake."

Megan pinched her eyes closed. Her hand went to her temple. Her voice was barely audible. "I want Lil to be happy. Tell me more about your shelter."

"It's not my shelter. It's not my cause. See that's the whole point. But it's not really a bad cause either."

"Fletch." Her tone warned him she was losing patience.

"Okay. Marshall bought a farm and donated it to be used as a rescue farm. They operate on donations, volunteers, and grants. They need donations to operate. The film is to garner sympathy at fund-raisers."

"You work there?"

"Vic volunteers our veterinary services."

Again there was a moment of silence. "Okay, Fletch. I'll help you, but I'm going to be honest with Lil about everything."

"You won't regret it. I'll call you the next time I'm going over. Probably tomorrow afternoon." Fletch stuck the yellow sticky note on the nearest post and sprang off the porch, afraid if he lingered she'd change her mind. "Thanks!"

CHAPTER 19

Lil turned Jezebel into Michelle's lane and hopped out of the car while it was still sputtering.

She opened her sister's screen door and yelled, "Hello! Michelle?"

"In the kitchen. Come in."

The moment Lil stepped into the sunny room, little Tammy clamped her by the leg. Without missing a beat, Lil knelt down and scooped the girl up, cuddling her as she went. Michelle sat at a rectangular farm table, snapping green beans with her casted leg stretched out. "Next year, I had planned to do a vegetable stand. But now that, you know. . ." She glanced at Tammy, "I guess that will have to wait."

Lil heard the wistful note in her sister's voice and knew that when Michelle had the baby, she would be far too busy for a vegetable stand. "I imagine by next summer, Tate will be a good helper."

"Yes, she will. Tammy, go tell your sisters that auntie is here."

Lil let her niece down. "Are you feeling morning sickness?"

"No, I never have."

"That's good news. I have news, too. I got the job! Got the job!" Lil did a little garbanzo shoulder-shimmy dance around the table.

Laughing at her antics, Michelle reached out and snatched a handful of Lil's skirt.

Lil took Michelle's hand and slipped into the chair next to her.

Michelle squeezed her hand. "I'm so glad for you, sis. Glad everything's turning out good." Then sadness touched her eyes. "I mean with Mom and the new job."

Lil determined not to allow Fletch's betrayal to steal her joy. "Me, too. But I need to get to work here. I'll get my apron while we talk."

On the way to the pantry, she gave Tate a hug and spun her in the air until she squealed. When she set her down, Tammy jumped up and down. "I want to show you what Mommy did with her *gassed* on!"

Both girls scampered out of the room. Lil understood they were talking about Michelle's *cast*.

"Don't wake your sister," Michelle warned. "They want to show you the doll clothes I made."

With a chuckle, Lil returned to the table.

"When do you start?"

Lil began snapping beans. "Tomorrow."

"Does Mom know you had the interview?"

"Yes. At first she was angry." Lil remembered how her mom had comforted her after Fletch's betrayal. "Now I think she understands. But Dad is another story. He thinks it's foolish for me to work outside the home. He said that once the farm got on its feet again, he'd pay me to help around there, like he does the boys. And he's dead set against the doddy house and can't understand why I want to move in with Megan. Claims I should have 'that folly' out of my system. Honestly, he can be so—"

"Pigheaded," they said in unison. It was an ongoing joke Mom had started because he always had hogs on the brain and he was stubborn, too.

"He's not going to budge."

"Will you go against his wishes?"

Lil's nieces bounded into the room, holding out their dolls and new doll clothes. They wore miniature outfits that matched the girls' own look-alike Conservative-style clothing. Lil oohed and aahed, and then the youngsters skipped off to the quilt in the corner of the room, which was designated as a play area.

"So will you go against Dad's wishes?" Michelle repeated.

"Yes," Lil nodded. "I don't want it to be that way. But I don't belong on the farm. I never have. . . . I've been praying about things. I'm asking for God's help. I hope God will work things out between me and Dad. Funny, I used to think of Dad mainly as an authority figure. But lately I see him as a person." Her glimpses of his pain had changed her attitude toward him.

"That's a strange thing to say."

"The only thing is—" Lil stopped, choked up.

"What?"

"I don't want Mom and Dad to get in a fight over it. I don't think they get along that well behind closed doors. It would have been better for me if I'd never moved back home."

Michelle nodded. "This gives me a better understanding of how to pray. I'm so thankful for you. For the way you've helped Mom. For your help here. You can't imagine how hard it is for me to wear this cast."

Lil smiled. "You mean your *gassed?*"

—⁓—

Megan followed Fletch into the two-story farmhouse, pausing inside the front door. He motioned her to a side room that had been fixed into an office, where he introduced a woman named Ashley. Megan vaguely remembered his mentioning her, and she wondered how this woman played into everything.

Ashley jumped to her feet and offered Megan a handshake. In one sweep, Megan saw that Ashley was beautiful in typical outsider style, dressed in snug jeans and a bright tank top and sporting a stylish bob.

"Have a seat," Ashley offered. She flashed Fletch a dazzling, teeth-brightened smile. "Why don't you leave us alone for a few minutes?" She waved her manicured hand. "I'll bring Megan out to the barn when we're done chatting."

Fletch hesitated.

"It's okay," Megan urged, her curiosity mounting over Ashley. Once Fletch had gone, she looked at the other woman expectantly. "I don't really know what I'm doing here."

"You came because you have a kind heart. I see it in your eyes."

"That's a nice thing to say. What is your job?"

"I get donations from suppliers and companies that help us stay afloat. I guess I'm kind of a receptionist, too. There aren't that many volunteers yet, so I have to juggle quite a few jobs right now. Marcus, Marshall's son, is the person who heads everything up. Fletch comes a couple of times a week to give care to the animals. Most need veterinary care when they arrive. I can answer any questions you have about the shelter, but it's Fletch I wanted to talk to you about. You know, girl to girl."

Megan felt her face heat. "You know I'm not his girlfriend, right?"

"I know about Lil and the interview with Char Air."

Following Ashley's lead, Megan decided to be forthright and set the other woman straight. "I'm not going on that interview. But I'm willing to hear more about Fletch, for Lil's sake. Right now she despises him."

"Most of what I know comes from Marcus. We're dating." She sighed. "When we have time." She waved her hand in a feminine gesture. "Sorry. Off track. Marcus told me that Fletch got tossed around as a kid. He told me about the time that he and his dad flew to Africa to see firsthand what the Landis mission work entailed."

Megan was hooked. "Go on."

"They hired somebody in a Jeep to take them into the field, to Fletch's family. It was a shack with limited resources. Out in the boonies. But the natives would come to them from every direction and at every hour of the day. They brought all sorts of needs. Fletch's mom had medical training, and his dad was resourceful and also taught them about God."

Megan could picture it in her mind. "That's a beautiful story."

"There's more. Fletch's sister followed his mom around, but Marshall noticed that Fletch seemed rather lost. Marcus was allowed to play with him. When Marcus asked him about his friends, Fletch told Marcus the animals were his friends because they looked at him when he spoke, and they were the only ones that ever listened to him."

Megan felt a lump in her throat. "That's so sad." She remembered Fletch's pleading expression when he told her on Sunday that he needed to talk to Lil. To make her listen. "And you think that's why he went to veterinary school?"

"Marcus told me that Marshall felt sorry for Fletch. That Marshall knew Fletch's dad was a powerful man and expected his son to be the same way. But Fletch is different, real tenderhearted. Marshall saw that Frank was too hard on his son, being gentler with the daughter." Ashley leaned close as if to share a confidence. "Now from what I hear, Marshall is a bit overbearing sometimes, too. But Marcus loves him in spite of it." She relaxed again. "Anyway, Marshall loves animals, too. He's a great philanthropist, and it was only natural that he wanted to help Fletch with his career."

"I see." And Megan did. Fletch had been torn between refusing his longtime mentor or taking advantage of his new friends. She still had questions, but she wanted to save them for Fletch.

Ashley fiddled with a pencil. "Fletch is a caring person. Perhaps what we did was unethical, but it was to help his friends and a lot of abused animals. I don't know how some people can be so cruel."

Megan could see how his friends had helped him rationalize his actions. "Thank you for sharing."

"You're welcome. Now let's go to the barn. You'll fall in love with Cottonball. Everybody does."

Megan allowed Ashley to lead her toward the barn, feeling torn about Fletch. She could only imagine how he felt. She didn't know if she should drag Lil back into Fletch's world, where he was obviously still finding his way, or tell her to run as fast as she could in the other direction.

⁓෴

Monday night, Lil had just finished helping her mom with the supper dishes when the doorbell rang. "I'll get it." Her heart sped hopefully. She'd just been thinking that if Fletch really cared about her, he'd quit calling and present himself on her doorstep. Taking a deep breath, she opened the door.

"Megan?" With fleeting disappointment and growing concern, Lil pulled her friend inside. Untying her apron, she drew Megan to the couch. "Everything all right?"

"Kind of. We need to talk."

Megan's nervous manner worried her. Was she going to back out of the doddy house?

She knew she would have to wait to find out when Mom stepped into the room. "I thought I heard your voice."

"Hi, Mrs. Landis."

"Hi, sweetie." She touched Megan's shoulder. "Talking about the doddy house plans?"

"Sorta."

Mom confided, "I'm trying to wear Lil's dad down."

Megan looked surprised. "That's great. Thanks."

Mom sat down and made a little small talk, but apparently sensing the girls' unease, she stood again. "I need to make sure I turned off the stove."

"Okay, we'll be up in my bedroom."

Megan furrowed her brow. "What's that all about? You have to get permission all over again?"

Lil snatched Megan's hand and led her toward the stairway. "Dad's just worried about Mom. I'm moving out no matter what. Unless. . .are you here to talk about the doddy house?"

"No. It's about Fletch."

Lil almost missed her footing. She was glad that Megan was following her up the stairway so she couldn't see her shock. Had they seen each other? She didn't know what the man was capable of when it came to destroying her heart. Now that she knew Fletch was deceitful, it seemed possible that he could have been attracted to Megan all along. Why wouldn't he be? Megan was way prettier. And ever since Megan had arrived, she'd sported a guilty expression.

Lil closed her bedroom door behind them. "So don't keep me in suspense. What about him?"

Megan sat uneasily on the edge of the bed. "He came to see me."

Lil wanted to scratch the man's eyes out. Instead, she snatched up a white eyelet pillow and hugged it to herself. "Oh?"

"He tried to make me his ally."

She lowered the pillow to her lap. "What do you mean?"

"Fletch asked me to help him win you back."

Lil tossed the pillow aside. "What?" It was exactly what she'd hoped for, but it was still unbelievable. "But—"

Megan moved to the middle of the bed and crossed her legs. "Why is that such a shock? He really likes you. He always has."

Although it was a relief that Fletch hadn't asked Megan out, Lil was wary about his intentions. She propped her back against the headboard. "So he's winning you over? I have to warn you, he's persuasive. You can't be naive around him, Megan."

"There's more." Megan fleetingly touched her arm. "This is hard for me, so please, just listen while I try to explain."

Lil nodded. Even though she'd just warned Megan not to trust Fletch, her rebellious heart grasped for a ray of hope, willing Megan to say something that could mend their broken relationship. "Okay. You talk. I'll listen."

"He and Vic both volunteer at a farm shelter for abused farm animals. It's just getting started, but his mentor has other ones already operating. He's the man who helped Fletch get his education."

"Marshall. I know all about him."

Megan frowned.

Lil's hand went up to muffle her mouth. "Sorry. I'll be quiet. Go on."

"He asked me to go with him to the shelter to meet the people there."

"You didn't!"

Megan nodded. "I met a girl there named Ashley. She told me a story about Fletch. Do you want to hear it? Because it might help you understand him."

"You know you can't bait me like that. Yes, I want to hear the story she told you."

Lil listened, and the story meshed with what Fletch had already told her about himself. Megan helped her see that Fletch had been backed into a hopeless corner.

"But if he liked me, why did he take pictures at our farm? Didn't Matt's friendship account for anything?"

"Because he only has a few farms where Vic leaves him alone. He hasn't had that many opportunities. And he thought since you were his friends you'd understand."

"He should have asked for permission. Why didn't he take pictures of the animals at the shelter?"

"They don't have very many animals yet. You should ask him these questions."

"I don't know." Lil shook her head. "I'm afraid to talk to him. I like him so much, and he's so persuasive."

Megan twisted her hair. "There's more. Now keep in mind that the only reason I listened to Fletch was for your happiness. If there was a way for you two to make amends I. . ." She shrugged.

"I know how you like to see things get resolved. I understand."

"I hope so, because I never asked him to, but he set up that interview with Char Air."

Lil's mouth fell open in disbelief. He'd won over Megan by dangling her dream job. Lil fought back the tears. "He bribed you. Surely, you see that."

"I do. It was a rotten thing for him to do, and I told him so. I also told him I wouldn't go to the interview. And I won't. But he was desperate to win you back. And that's why I went to the farm."

Lil sighed. "If you get the job, would you be working with Fletch?"

"No. Of course not. Marshall uses their company. But it doesn't matter. I'm not going on the interview. This isn't about that. I just came to convince you that I wasn't trying to betray you. My intentions are pure."

"I can't believe you guys talked about me behind my back. That you went to the shelter."

"Fletch told me you'd understand because you had intervened in Katy and Jake's relationship. That's why I went. I thought it was what you would have done for me if our situations were reversed."

Lil narrowed her eyes. She wanted to object, but it was similar to the situation with Katy. She had even tricked Katy into seeing Jake. She guessed it was true that she reaped what she sowed. Now she knew how humiliating and infuriating it felt to be on the recipient's end of a matchmaking scheme. She should apologize to Katy again. Only Katy was in love, living the happily ever after. "I don't know what to say."

Megan nodded. "You have a lot to think about. I don't know if Fletch is right for you, but if you want him, the next time he calls, you should pick up the phone. Now that you've both had time to think about everything, just listen to what he has to say." Megan released her hair and gave her head a little shake so that it fell down her back again. "I need to go, but can you forgive me for interfering?"

"It hurts, but you're right. I did the same thing to Katy. And I feel bad for Fletch that nobody listens to him."

Megan moved off the bed. "Sleep on it. We'll talk tomorrow."

Lil stood. She resented her friend's interference, but Megan's intentions were too sincere to rebuke. She remembered how happy Megan had been to hear about her successful interview. She felt terribly guilty that she had landed her dream job while Megan was sacrificing hers. Whether Fletch was trustworthy or not, she couldn't stand in the way of Megan's second chance. She clutched her friend's arm. "You have to go on that interview."

Megan's eyes lit up, and Lil saw how badly she wanted the job. But her friend shook her head. "I can't. That's not why I met with Fletch. I didn't come here because of that."

"I know. But let's do it for the doddy house."

"I don't know. We better pray about it."

Shrugging, Lil replied, "Okay. But I promise I won't hold it against you. I want you to get that job." She followed Megan downstairs to the door and gave her a forgiving hug before letting her go.

When she returned to her room, Lil considered Megan's petition. If what Megan said was true, Fletch still wanted to date Lil. He wanted her to give him another chance. Like Megan suggested, she prayed, but she still didn't have an answer. Contemplatively, she stretched out on an heirloom rug and started her sit-up routine. "One. Two. Three. Four," she counted, getting warmed up.

Then her mind fell into a chant. "Five. I'll answer the phone." She sucked in her abs. "Six. I won't. Seven. He deserves a chance." She took a deep breath. "Eight. He's a deceiver. Nine. He loves me." She puffed, "Ten. He loves me not."

CHAPTER 20

Y ou have the natural instinct. . .eh. . .take this pan a moment. I'll be right back."

Volo Italiano was not a typical restaurant because Giovanni was not a typical chef. He didn't go by the books. Lil quickly discovered that her boss was temperamental and acted on his whims.

Lil stirred the sautéing ingredients and watched Giovanni push open the door to the cooler. She had flourished under a week of the chef's praise and instruction. To her utter amazement, he'd personally taken her under his wing, allowing her to do jobs that were normally reserved for the cooks with more seniority. She'd gotten to do more than polish the stainless and stir the sauce. Giovanni was a hands-on boss. He ran an orderly kitchen, and nobody complained because he was a likeable man who had earned their respect. Most likely, he'd given them all breaks at one time or another.

Volo Italiano was nothing like Riccardo's, where everybody had been on edge and out to get one another. The politics of her old workplace had not been a new experience for her because she had experienced the same type of rivalry at culinary school. She had thought it was just the way of the outsiders. But Volo Italiano had a friendly, family-like atmosphere, where everyone had welcomed her, not even questioning her about her plain clothing or head covering.

At Riccardo's, she had opted to quit wearing her head covering even before the church elders lifted the restriction. She'd never appreciated the little piece of organdy like her friend Katy, who thought it represented her faith.

With Lil, it was just a necessary contrivance, even an embarrassing one, that made her an object of curiosity to the outsiders. How she envied the Mennonite girls in progressive churches who never wore theirs, even to church.

When their congregation had taken a fresh look at the ordinance last year and then voted to change it, Lil had rejoiced that she only needed to wear it to church meetings.

She thought sadly of her dad's recent disapproval, how she'd donned it again to make life at the farm easier. She considered it a temporary nuisance. Yet she had found herself wearing it to Volo Italiano's. But she would make some changes when she moved into the doddy house. The first thing she would do was get her hair trimmed.

Giovanni returned to her side. "Now! Remove. Now!"

She jerked the pan from the gas burner and looked up in confusion, for even though she'd been daydreaming, she had been watching, and the vegetables were only half cooked.

"Most cooks leave it too long. I remove it before the celery and onions are clear. They will keep cooking after you remove them from. . ." His hands made a circular, churning gesture as if she would fill in the words for him. "Eh. . .the fire."

"Yes, sir." Another little secret to store in her mind's recipe box. She set the pan on a heat-safe surface for him to add in his tomato mixture. She felt the vibration of her cell phone in her apron pocket and turned slightly to peek at its screen. Her heart drummed beneath her white blouse and bib apron. Fletch again. She hadn't quit with ninety-nine sit-ups instead of her usual one hundred for nothing.

Turning her back to her boss, she pressed the send button and without any small talk said in a breathless voice, "I can't talk. I'm at work."

"I'll call back."

Her thumb pressed the red button, and she dropped the little heart-stopping rectangle back into her apron pocket. Her hand shaky, she moved back to the chopping board to resume the dicing she had been doing before Giovanni had taken her aside for special instruction.

"Grab some new gloves," Giovanni said, more snippy than usual as he passed behind her.

Embarrassed that he'd caught her phone conversation, she snapped off her little white gloves, tossed them in the garbage, and wriggled into a fresh set. She quickly apologized. "I'm sorry. I had to get that call."

"Your old boyfriend?"

"Yes."

"I hope that was wise, no?" Then he turned away. "Elaine, take over. . .eh. . .I have my ordering to do."

Lil felt crushed under Giovanni's sudden change of attitude. She peeled an onion and chopped and diced until her eyes watered.

⁓

In the clinic's side yard, where Buddy often lounged and chased birds, Fletch pumped his arm in the air. Although Lil's voice had been curt, she had finally answered her phone. That was a good sign. He hoped Megan had convinced Lil to accept his apology. He watched a cone-necked collie sniff around the yard's perimeter.

Vic was treating Fletch better now, as if he wasn't that kid who had been plunked into his life just to make it miserable. And he wasn't. He wanted to take some of the strain off Vic's shoulders, if he could. He was grateful that Vic had allowed him to do the surgery on the collie. The tumor had been successfully removed. The dog moved slowly, not chasing birds like Buddy, but his teeth dazzled whiter than Buddy's. Fletch didn't like putting an animal under unnecessarily, especially his own companion, but Buddy would need his teeth cleaned one of these days.

Vic stuck his head out the door. "Got an emergency call. Take over here?"

"Sure."

The vet's head disappeared just as Fletch's phone rang. When he saw the name on the screen, his heart leaped. Stuffing one hand into his jeans pocket, he answered it with an enthusiastic, "Lil!"

"I just wanted to ask if you'd please stop calling me."

His hand flew out of his pocket, and he switched the phone to his other ear. "I don't think I can do that until I have a chance to explain some things."

"I have a new job, and I don't want to lose it."

Whatever that meant. All she needed to do was set her phone on vibrate. But she was opening the door to him, even if it was only enough to get one toe inside. He tried to remember what he'd planned on saying, only his mind froze. All he could think to say was, "I can't quit calling. I'm falling in love with you."

"What?"

Not the response he had hoped for. "Look. Can I meet you after work?"

"No. You're not listening to me. I don't want you to know where I work."

"Okay. Then let's meet someplace else. Any place. You name it. I have to see you."

"How about my living room?"

He could tell by her tone of voice it was a challenge. "I don't think your family would let me remain there long enough to properly beg your forgiveness. Matt forgave me. On Sunday."

"He told you that? Wait. It doesn't matter. You don't have to beg for my forgiveness. I forgive you, too. Just quit calling, all right?"

Fletch could tell she hadn't forgiven him at all, but her contrivance might be a small start. "I'll meet you at your swing at. . ." He didn't know what time she got off work, so he made it late. "At midnight."

There was a brief silence. "Don't bother coming," she said. "I won't be there. You're wasting your time." Then his phone went dead.

He took off his cap, slapped his knee with it, and put it back on. He didn't believe her. Lily would be there.

⁓

Lil stood in front of her bedroom mirror. She ran a brush through her hair, then replaced her head covering and pinched her cheeks. *I'm falling in love with you.* It had been all she could think about. She heard the downstairs grandfather clock chime on the quarter hour. *I'm falling in love with you.* She wouldn't go until one minute after midnight. That would make her at least ten minutes late and give Fletch time to change his mind. She didn't wish to appear eager. She moved to the edge of her bed and prayed. *Lord, help me to know if I can trust him. Please reveal the truth to me. Help me let him go again, if he's not the one You've chosen.*

Grandfather Landis's clock chimed again, and she counted its bongs. One, two. . .and finally the twelfth bong. One more minute, and then she'd go. *I'm falling in love with you.* She watched the face of her cell phone with anticipation until the time finally changed. Her heart thumping louder than the clock's bongs, she crept down the stairway and made her way stealthily to the mudroom.

She opened a utility drawer and stuck her hand in, groping for a round handle. When she clutched the flashlight, she tucked it into a fold of her skirt and cast a glance over her shoulder and down the hall to her parents' bedroom. Thankfully, nobody stirred.

Lil flicked the deadbolt and slipped through the door, quietly closing it behind her. She stepped into the night. Overhead, a million crystals sparkled. All around her was the hum of nature's nighttime. The moon was full, and although she didn't need it, she turned on the flashlight, making zigzags across the tall grass so she didn't surprise any snakes or other night creatures.

I'm falling in love with you. Me, too, she breathed. Her heart drummed wildly for she felt as though she was Juliet sneaking out to meet her Romeo. She felt guilty because the family didn't like him. He was a traitor, after all. But she couldn't resist the urge to let him have his say. Even if she didn't fully trust him, it would be thrilling to hear words of love from the man who resembled the Rollo of her daydreams.

She hadn't told anybody about that because she didn't want to provoke snickers, but one morning she had awakened after a night of restless dreams, remembering that Fletch was the exact image of Rollo.

He was the boy she had always imagined in her childhood daydreams. Without the long flowing hair, of course. That coincidence, along with everything else that had culminated since she smashed into Fletch's car, made this rendezvous seem all the more fated. Traipsing through the darkness, she had the eerie sensation that Fletch was supposed to be a major part of her destiny. If only she could trust him.

A sudden hoot from an owl brought her hand over her heart. She paused, momentarily, thinking there would soon be one less mouse to keep out of the mudroom, then picked up her pace. By the time she neared the swing, the intensifying night sounds had her running.

"Over here."

Now breathless, she shined the light. She saw Fletch standing with both hands in his pockets. It tugged her heart, for she'd often seen Jake do that when he was troubled. But she tried to remain strong. "I almost didn't come. I shouldn't have. I felt sorry for you out here alone with the foxes."

He smiled. "I'm grateful you came."

She cast a backward glance. "I don't think I've ever been out here this time of night. Alone, anyways."

"You aren't alone." He stepped toward her.

One of her hands flew up to ward him off. If he touched her, she would lose all her good intentions to think rationally and block out his words: *I'm falling in love with you.* She hoped he didn't say that again. She prayed he did.

She warned, "Don't come any closer. You can talk from over there."

Fletch raised his palms in a gesture of truce and began talking as if he understood his time allotment was ticking away.

"When Marshall asked me to take pictures of sick animals for his fund-raiser film, I knew it was wrong. It made me sick to my stomach to betray a farmer's trust and right of privacy. But Marshall is special to me, my best friend ever. It was the only thing he'd ever asked from me."

"I understand that. But why our farm? Didn't we mean anything to you?" She realized one farm wasn't worse than another, but going behind a friend's back seemed worse.

"Because Vic let me come to your farm alone. It was the only place I could take the video. I was going to ask Matt's permission, but that day we got into a little spat. It was about you, and I never got the chance. If I could turn back time, believe me, I would tell Marshall no."

Lil saw the yearning in his expression. She remembered the story Megan told her about the little boy who had to talk to animals because nobody listened to him, and her heart melted.

He went on. "It's true I hid that from you, but I didn't lie about my attraction to you. That's real. You must remember that our meeting was purely accidental."

"Very funny."

He gave a dimpled, playful smile, and in Lil's opinion, an adorable and endearing shrug. Then his moonlit features grew serious. "I couldn't deny the instant attraction."

"To Jezebel, you mean?" *Don't tell me you love me. Please say it,* her conflicted heart begged.

He gave a nervous laugh.

"Attraction isn't the most important thing in a relationship," she pointed out, mimicking what he'd once told her and forcing herself to remember his shortcomings before she threw herself in his arms.

"I'm just saying I didn't go after you intentionally to use you or trick you. I wish there was a way that we could start over."

Lil's eyes brimmed with unshed tears. His explanation was reasonable. What he'd done didn't seem nearly as unforgivable as it had appeared that day in the barn when she caught him filming. "My brothers are stubborn. And now my entire family is set against you. I don't think they trust you anymore."

"I promised Matt I'd destroy the video. I want to talk to your dad and your other brothers, but Vic ordered me to stay away from the farm. I've got myself in a tight spot."

"I can see that. Matt's right. Destroying the video would be a start."

"I need to tell you what I already told Matt."

She listened to his explanation about Marshall being in the hospital. She thought he might not go through with it. The thought leaped into her mind that he might be trying to make amends only to restore his good name with the farmers and with Vic. Confused, she needed time to think and pray. She swiped her arm across her cheeks. "Thanks for the explanation. I have to go now." She turned and started toward the house. But the flashlight slipped out of her hands. She knelt, groping the ground under a patch of tall, brittle weeds.

"Ouch!" She drew back her hand, now filled with fine stickers.

"Here." Fletch moved into her vision and found the flashlight. "At least let me walk you back to the house."

She took it from him and flashed it across her pathway, walking silently.

"I don't want to make you mad, but there's something I have to tell you."

"I'm listening."

"I thought you were the sunshine in my life, but when I said that, I was thinking of the way you made me feel, all tingly. But tonight, in the moonlight. You're. . ."

She looked at his face, so serene, and felt her breath catch. When he hesitated, she pressed. "What?"

"Don't you know?"

He touched her cheek, and she gasped.

"Your light goes deeper than skin. You touch my heart."

"How can you say such things," she blurted out in a Dutchy accent. "We don't even go to the same church!" The house was looming ahead. "I have to go." She sprinted for the house, never looking back.

CHAPTER 21

On the drive home from his midnight rendezvous with Lil, Fletch's mind was determined. The very first thing he was going to do when he reached his apartment was to erase the video. Regardless of the consequences. He was going to act like a man and do the right thing. No matter how much he wanted to please Marshall or pay him back for his years of support, he had to do the right thing before God and the people in this community. Surely, Marshall would understand his decision.

He kept to the deserted country road, automatically watching for deer that might leap across the dark road, and remembered a game he used to play with his sister. It was their version of Pick Up Sticks they'd seen in the States. They would collect straight twigs, dump them in a tight pile, and take turns trying to remove one stick without moving any of the others. But sometimes the entire stack tumbled down.

Fletch knew that his next move would bring the stack down, and he would have to pick up the pieces of his life, but as much as he loved Marshall, he couldn't hurt the Landis family. He needed to make this right. He needed to erase the video he had taken even if it caused his veterinary career to come crashing down. He couldn't disappoint Lil and Matt one more day. One more hour. With his decision came relief.

He turned into a parking space, turned off the ignition, and locked the car. Walking briskly, he started toward his apartment. But a dark shadow moved on his door stoop, causing him to slow warily. The black silhouette moved. A man larger than himself blocked his door. He was sitting, hunched over, and Fletch couldn't see his face. He wondered if it was a homeless man. Unless he planned to spend the night in his car, he would have to find out. Swallowing, Fletch ventured closer. "Hello, there?"

The man looked up.

"Marcus?" Fear clutched him. "What on earth are you doing?"

"I'm sorry, man. I know it's late. I just need to talk."

Dread crept up Fletch's spine. "Let's go inside." Marcus stood and stepped aside, swiping his arm across his face. Fletch couldn't remember ever seeing his friend break down before, even as kids. He worked the key in his lock. "Come in."

Inside, they went to the small table, and Fletch moved his laptop out of the way. "Want some coffee?"

"No. You can make some for yourself."

Fletch thought better of it and took the chair across from Marcus. "Is this about your dad?" he asked.

Marcus nodded and broke down again. Fletch waited while the other man fought for control of his voice. "He's been diagnosed with lung cancer."

Fletch closed his eyes in despair. "Oh no. Are they sure? I mean. . ."

"Yeah, man. He's sure."

Fletch didn't know much about cancer, but it sounded serious.

"It's deadly. Probably those stupid cigars," Marcus bemoaned. "He always thought going to the gym would make up for it."

Fletch felt stricken. "Is he in pain?"

"He has a lot of coughing and chest pain."

"Is there a treatment?"

Marcus stared at his folded hands. "It's his call. Without chemo, the doctors claim he won't last more than four months."

The prognosis hit Fletch like a blow. "And with it?"

"Probably not any longer than five years."

"Well then he needs to do it."

"That's why I need to go home. That's why I need your help."

~⊙~

It was the early hours of the morning before Lil could finally sleep. Her Romeo and Juliet rendezvous with Fletch was paramount in her waking mind. The things that man could say, calling her sunshine and moonbeam. No wait, a light that goes deeper than skin and touches his heart. She wished there were no obstacles to overcome, only blissful romance. But that wasn't the truth of the matter. Like the fictional Romeo and Juliet, they had their problems.

She'd already forgiven Fletch. She did that the night Megan told her his story. But everything was befuddled. If Lil jumped into the fray with him and all his unsolved issues, her heart might become the real victim. Yet she was drawn to him, like basil to tomato sauce. Even her job and doddy house plans were trifles compared to her feelings for him. The words he'd confessed were the feelings in her own heart. He was her sunshine. His light touched her heart. She was falling in love with him.

And so the day lagged on, tamping down longings and rehashing his explanations. It lagged through the ironing and her trip to the grocery store, and by three o'clock, she was desperate to break the cycle. "I'm off to work, Mom," she called, snatching her purse in the mudroom and heading outdoors.

In the circle lane, however, she saw Fletch's Focus parked near the barns, where he used to park when he came to care for the animals. Her heart tripped with anxiety as she hurried past Jezebel—all thoughts of work gone—moving purposefully toward the first barn. At the open door, familiar voices made her hesitate.

Lil placed her back to the barn and prepared to eavesdrop.

"I can't do this to him now. He's been diagnosed with terminal cancer."

"I'm sorry. I know what he means to you."

Lil couldn't figure out who had cancer. Marshall? Why hadn't Fletch

197

mentioned it to her?

"Look, this is very sad news. But the video still needs to be destroyed."

"I know. I'll do whatever it takes to make things right with your family and Lil."

"Lil? You agreed to back off."

"I can't."

"It's wrong to pursue my sister when you don't even know if you have a job. You need to get things straightened out. I don't want her hurt any more than she already is."

Their voices stilled, and Lil's heart ached for Fletch. Would he do what Matt asked and pull away from her? She swallowed a thick lump in her throat.

"What about the farm? Have you isolated the hogs?"

"We started to, but we've run out of room."

"Hoop farming, Matt. It's cheaper. Maybe the Plain City Bank, the one that already knows your family, will finance a couple hoop barns."

"How do you know so much about this?"

"We studied it under our agricultural section. On the metal barns, the slatted floors are uncomfortable and dangerous for the animals. It prohibits them from following their natural instincts of rooting and nesting. The animals injure themselves on the metal stalls because when they are confined they bite the walls and attack each other. The slats allow the waste to collect. If for nothing else, your family would someday regret the slatted floor for the smell. But with hoop barns, you could isolate the animals. When you get your contract, you could expand without really changing your present methods."

"Why are you, just now, telling me all this?"

"Matt, I tried. You wouldn't listen before."

Lil's insides twisted. Poor Fletch.

"And you think those integrator companies would go for hoop farming?"

"It's cutting edge, but I think you should at least check into it. I've got to meet Vic just down the road. He's probably already there. . . ."

Not wanting to get caught at her eavesdropping, Lil took off for her car. A thunderclap sounded, and a small flock of frightened chickens ran in front of her. With a shriek, she threw up her hands. The chickens scattered, but the rooster went after her ankle. "Oh no, you don't, you irritating alarm clock." She swung her purse at him, and he flew off after his hens.

Dark clouds churned over the farm. Lil jumped into Jezebel and shimmied her door closed. If it stormed, the freeway would be congested. While she had been eavesdropping, she had lost track of time. She was going to be late to work even without a storm. As quickly as possible, she coaxed her rattletrap out of the lane and set the dust to flying.

—☙—

Fletch met Vic at the dairy farm, one of the vet's biggest accounts. He had accompanied him on several of the routine herd checks, and this one wasn't much different. Fletch followed Vic along the row of bovine backsides, while the herdsman walked along the cow's heads. He pointed out the ones who hadn't come into heat and needed pregnancy checks.

As they worked, Vic explained some things about udder health and how to check for food consumption, and then they switched places with the herdsman and checked eyes and ears. There wasn't an opportunity for any personal discussion until they headed back to the vehicles.

"Late night?" Vic asked.

Fletch quickly covered his yawn. "Marcus came to my apartment last night. Marshall has lung cancer."

Various emotions flitted across Vic's face before he ventured a reply. "I only met him once. He took me to dinner. Afterward he smoked a cigar in the parking lot." He sighed. "I wouldn't be a vet if I enjoyed suffering. I'm sorry."

Vic's behavior was a mystery to Fletch. At times, the vet was easily provoked to anger. Other times, he displayed compassion. Fletch was appreciative for Vic's show of sympathy. "Marcus is going home to try to convince Marshall to take chemo. Marcus asked me for a favor. But I don't want to make any more mistakes."

Vic took off his hat and swatted at flies. "What does he want?"

"He asked me to stay at the shelter while he's gone, just in case something comes up. They have a couple of volunteers there and Ashley."

"Thanks for running it by me. I don't blame you for everything that's happened, but this is a sticky situation. It reminds me of the Menno Coblentz farm. It has a shallow pond that's more of a mudhole than anything. In the heat, it lures the livestock in, and the animals get stuck, like they're in quicksand."

"Why don't they fence it off?"

"They do. That's not the point. That shelter is your quicksand."

Fletch saw truth in the statement and nodded.

"Did he say how long?"

"Three or four days."

"As far as I'm concerned, we didn't have this conversation. I'm not responsible for where you sleep nights. But if this all comes crashing down on my reputation and practice, you won't be getting a passing grade. And you won't be practicing in this county."

"I understand." Fletch grinned. "Kind of like the CIA."

Vic rolled his gaze toward the sky. "I wouldn't know about that."

"I'll be discreet as I can. And I'll try not to get my boots muddy either. Thanks."

Vic waved his hat in front of his face. "Pesky flies. Let's head back to the clinic. Then go together to the Miller farm."

Fletch started to nod, but it turned into another yawn.

CHAPTER 22

The storm had passed. Its minty-musty smell seeped through Jezebel's open window. Giovanni had reacted to Lil's lateness with silence and a steely gaze. Someone had whispered that he was having trouble at home, but Lil knew he was watching her, expecting her to fall into her old habits. It hurt that she had disappointed him. But as she started home, the landscape was peaceful and soothing to her weary soul. She breathed it in and tried to shake off her stress.

She watched her headlights illuminate the road's dotted white lines, her mind drifting until it latched on to the conversation she'd overheard in the barn. She sympathized with Fletch and wanted to fan the indomitable flame of romantic hope that should have been snuffed out long before now.

If her family accepted Fletch's apology for the filming, would they be able to accept him as a possible son-in-law? That's where Lil's mind was headed. If she dated Fletch again, it would be with permanent intentions, at least on her part.

If they married, they would have to choose a church to attend. Did she want to raise her children within the restrictions of the Conservative Mennonite Church? If she didn't, she would stir up a heap of trouble at the Landis house. Once such trouble wouldn't have bothered her. Lately she was more cautious.

Or did she want to raise her children in a progressive Mennonite church like the one that Fletch attended? Such a church would allow more freedom for their members to recognize sin by their hearts' own interpretations of the Bible. At least that's how she imagined it would be. Lil thought she could trust her own heart, but could she risk giving such freedom to her children?

If she extinguished the flame of romantic hope, she wouldn't have to make that decision now. But her life would be cold and painful. She was so tired of the pain.

Lord, she prayed, *Fletch told me my dreams come from You. I want to believe that You formed me in my mom's belly like the prophet Jeremiah wrote about in the Bible. That my personality is not a mistake. I see the fields and woods all around me, so diverse and interesting. I find it hard to believe that You would want me to walk a boring restricted path when creation beckons me to come and explore life.*

I'm not an outsider; I don't want to be one either. I agree with the beliefs that set the Mennonites apart from other denominations. I want to walk the life You created for me. Not my mom's or my dad's. Or the elders'. Just mine. Help me make the right choices. I don't want to be disrespectful and disobedient. I believe Your Spirit lives in me and is molding me to be a better person.

She turned onto a road that no longer had the hypnotic white ribbon. Lingering clouds made the night pitch-black. She blinked back tears. *Don't let me fall away from You again. Please don't lose me.*

You can see into my heart. I can't deny it to You. I want Fletch, Lord. I think he wants me, too. You put his face in my mind's eye many years ago. I called him Rollo. Fletch is part of my dream. If You love me, please help us. And, please, don't lose me.

Lil felt God's peace so strongly that she pulled over to the side of the road to bask in His presence. It was a rare moment for her. One in which she would willingly give up all her dreams, if He asked. She wasn't foolish enough to believe that she lived in this serene, almost holy place. But in this moment, her soul cried out for God's truth. She trusted the God of grace as the Father of her spirit.

She sat in the inky silence, longing for God and longing for Fletch. The desire melded together. It seemed so right. The peace and the sweet longing.

Thanks, Lord. Lil groped the black interior of her purse and pulled out her phone. It was late, but if she was right, Fletch wouldn't care.

⎯⎯☙⎯⎯

"Hello," Fletch said drowsily, not having the sensibility to look at his phone before he answered. Over the years he had become used to receiving calls at odd hours because his parents often lived in different time zones and made use of phones whenever it served their purposes.

But the feminine voice that hesitantly pronounced his name wasn't his mom's. Its sweet quiver brought him wide awake.

"Lil? Is everything okay?"

"Sorry it's late. I was driving home from work. Thinking about you. Everything you said."

His heart thudded. "That's great to know."

"I overheard you talking to Matt in the barn. Thanks for doing that."

He rolled over on one elbow. "Aha. Eavesdropping again?"

"Yes. Thanks for trying to help Matt."

"He's my friend." The line grew quiet. Fletch savored the moment as if they were actually together. He drank in her presence. "It's so good to hear your voice."

"Yours, too. I'm sitting beside the road in Jezebel."

"What! Now, I'm torn. I'd like to imagine you sitting there in the moonlight. But that's dangerous, Lil. I don't like it. Why don't you go on home and call me back?"

"This from the guy who asked me to meet him in the pasture at midnight?"

"On your property, with me to protect you," he reminded.

She laughed. "Not tonight. But you can call me sometime."

"Does this mean. . .you'll see me again?"

"I suppose that depends on your persuasion and persistence."

He knew exactly where he wanted to take her. "Would a mystery date entice you?"

She sighed. "You know it would."

"Then hang up. I'll call you right back. Only, don't answer. I'll leave details that you can check when you're safe at home. I can't wait to see you again."

"Sweet dreams, Fletch."

—⟲—

"Where are you going?"

Lil halted her steps before she reached the mudroom and turned. Her mom looked pretty in her long, night-tousled hair and snug slippers with the home-sewn elastic around the heels. "Hi, Mom."

Rose padded across the kitchen's hardwood. "Off to Michelle's so early?"

The day that Lil had rushed into her mom's bedroom, bearing the fresh wound of Fletcher's deception, her mom had become her advocate. It had been the turning point where Mom regained her ability to plant her slippers in the real world again. Otherwise, Lil might have bitten her tongue instead of revealing her plans.

"Fletch invited me to meet him. He claims he's falling in love with me."

The scoop in Mom's hand trembled, scattering coffee grounds across the counter and onto the floor. Grabbing a dishrag, she asked, "When did you and Fletch start talking again?"

Lil got the broom and cleaned up the floor. "Just yesterday. It's something I need to do."

Mom poured water into the coffeemaker then turned to face Lil, taking the broom from her hand. "I understand. You're at that age where a girl has choices to make that will set her life's course. Some decisions cannot be reversed. Tread carefully, daughter."

"I am. That's why I must see him. If he's the one and I let him get away, I may regret it the rest of my life."

Mom turned thoughtful. "On the other hand, I married my true love, but even so, life is not what I imagined it would be."

"There is still time," Lil urged. "Tell me what you imagined, so that

I can help you find your dreams, too."

Laughing softly, almost bitterly, Mom shooed Lil away. "Nonsense. Dreams are for young women. Women my age are meant to get the work done." Her voice faded. "So that when I'm feeble, I will have something to show for all my years. Now go."

"Thanks, Mom."

Lil knew their mystery date location was a rural address. She was familiar with the general location but didn't know the exact property. Perhaps Fletch was going to let her go on a job with him or maybe another picnic. Fishing? The day at the park they'd watched some kids fishing and talked about doing it sometime. Lil's mind was occupied trying to outguess her persuasive and persistent suitor.

When she got close, she matched the number from her paper to a mailbox and steered Jezebel into a farm drive. Fletch's eager face popped out of a barn. He was dressed in jeans and work boots. She jiggled her car door open and jumped out, shimmying it closed again.

"Isn't this the old Stutzman place?"

"I wouldn't know about that." His eyes sparkled with enthusiasm, and his mouth tilted into a winsome smile. "But I heard you a mile away. Why don't you just marry me, and we'll haul Jezebel to the auto graveyard?"

Lil put her hands on her hips. "Is that supposed to be persuasive? Cause it sounds a lot like bribery."

"Just dreaming."

She grinned at him.

"Come and let me show you the nursery first. I can't get anything done; I just keep ending up in there. This place grows on you. The animals seem more like pets than livestock."

Of course! This was the shelter. Clasping his offered hand, she allowed him to lead her into the barn. It was nothing like their smelly hog barn. This one carried the scent of fresh straw and pungent hay.

"Over here."

The sound of their voices provoked a little bleat from behind a stall's enclosure. Fletch pulled the gate open and drew Lil inside. Still adjusting to the dark interior, she let her gaze follow the soft bleating and rustling of straw to the little fellow standing on shaky legs. Instantly, she dropped to the floor. "Oh! You're adorable."

"He's something, isn't he?"

She petted his wrinkled fleece, and he cupped his nose into her hand.

"Name's Cottonball. But there's a baby next door that still needs a name. When Ashley heard you were coming, she suggested you name the other lamb."

Lil took a sharp intake of breath. "Ashley?"

"Yes." Fletch knelt beside her. "I have some things to tell you." She listened to his explanation of all that had occurred since the last time they were together. "Since I'm staying here for a couple of days, I thought I could show you Marshall's farm, that it might help you understand some things about me."

"I'm so sorry about Marshall."

She sympathized with his grief over Marshall's cancer, understood his need to help Marcus. Regarding the video, she believed Fletch intended to eventually destroy it. But until it was done, it remained a threat to their relationship and to her family. So many things hinged on that silver hunk of technology that most people in her church didn't even know how to operate. Their innocence made them all vulnerable to situations like the one that had happened at the Landis farm. The Conservative people would not place lawsuits. Was that why Marshall had sent Fletch into their community? To take advantage of them?

Fletch interrupted her thoughts. "I sent my dad an e-mail this morning, telling him about. . .everything. About you, too. I can't contact him by phone right now, but he checks his e-mail every time he gets into Goma."

"You asked him for advice?"

"I guess."

The real-live man beside her was not an imaginary Rollo, and life was no circus. Fletch had gotten himself into a fix, and she wondered how it would all end. How it would affect her.

The lamb nudged her again. The skinny little creature melted her heart. "How can the lamb we are to name be any tinier than this sweetie?"

"Come see for yourself."

She hated to put the lamb down.

"We'll come back in a minute. I'll let you feed Cottonball his bottle."

"Really?"

The newborn was tinier, but fortunately it had a mother. "Oh my," she murmured. Fletch didn't take her inside the stall because the ewe was still recovering.

"It's a male."

"How about Flannel? And when he grows up, he can be Sir Flannel." Fletch grinned approval. "I love it."

"I just want to take you home," she purred through the slatted gate.

"I'm all yours," Fletch replied.

After Lil returned to Cottonball and gave him his bottle, Fletch finally managed to pull her away for an outside tour of the farm, explaining the renovations that had taken place and about the many donors Ashley had found for supplies. He told her about the volunteers who lived and worked at the shelter.

"Honestly, a month ago, I didn't even know there was such a place as this. I never thought there would be a need."

"Let's head for the house, and I'll introduce you to Ashley."

Lil stumbled to a halt. "Wait a minute. You're staying here with a girl?"

"She's Marcus's girlfriend. There are other volunteers here, too. Mostly guys. A couple of girls. But you're the only girl for me." He gently touched her chin, tilting her face up. "Remember? You're my sunshine."

And don't forget moonbeam. The light in your heart. Her insides went as soft and warm as marmalade pudding, and she might not have been able to resist if he'd tried to kiss her in the barnyard under the sun he raved about. Only Buddy chose that moment to come bounding across the yard. His ears nearly swept the ground, his droopy eyes fastened on Lil.

She crouched down, and he licked her face and then nuzzled into her touch. She felt Fletch's smile. The basset, the lambs, and his work all reflected his love for animals. She loved both the passion and gentleness he demonstrated.

Buddy wagged his tail, and his whole behind did a little jig.

Lil giggled. "He's doing the garbanzo dance. Only with the wrong end."

Grinning, Fletch said, "What's that?"

The basset was as soft as the lamb. How, when she lived on a farm, had she missed the wonder of the animal kingdom? She had tried to make pets of the baby pigs, but her parents had warned her away from such affection and cautioned her that hogs were dangerous animals. Eventually, she'd grown indifferent toward them and most animals. It felt amazing to feel the stirring of awareness now.

She answered his question about the garbanzo dance as they walked to the farmhouse. He stared at her as if he'd just tasted her best-ever entrée.

When they went inside, Ashley was a wonderful surprise. Lil wasn't sure what kind of woman she'd been expecting, but surely nobody as classy yet friendly as the blond woman who greeted them.

"There's a job for a cook here. Doesn't pay much, though," Ashley admitted. "Except room and board. But it's fun working here."

The offer did not appeal to Lil, except the part about being near Fletch. But she understood that was only a temporary arrangement. "Actually, I'm already set at a great restaurant."

"But as head chef?" Ashley probed.

Lil gave Fletch a hurt glance, wondering if he'd shared her personal dream with Ashley. Had he even made sport of her? He quickly threw his hands up. "I never said a word. Ashley's perceptive. That's how we manage to survive around here."

Giving a skeptical nod, Lil told Ashley, "Thanks for the offer, but like I said, I have a great job with opportunity for advancement." Not head chef, but Lil figured if she wanted to cook on a farm, she could continue to live with her parents. That wasn't her idea of a good job.

"Okay, well while you're here, how about you stuff some flyers?"

Lil laughed at the other woman's ingenuity and doggedness. "Can I see them?"

As she eyed Ashley, the blond waved at Fletch. "Scat. Go brush a horse or something."

Something New

"I get no respect around here," he joked. But it wasn't a joke to Lil because she saw the setup for what it was: a time to ask Ashley some questions about the man who claimed he was falling in love with her. Only she wasn't about to stuff any of her propaganda. She did look it over, making sure there weren't any Landis hogs inside. Thankfully, there weren't.

SOMETHING NEW

Later that day, as Lil set her mom's table for lunch—her dad and brothers were all coming inside for a special treat of mush and eggs—Lil relived the thrill of being with Fletch. Their mystery date had only lasted a couple of hours because he had to go in to work, but it had been long enough to leave her with many unanswered questions.

Fletch was a lot like Jake, responding to life from the inside, rather than judging himself against what the church allowed or didn't. Even the mistakes he had made came from the loyalties he felt toward Marshall, something on the inside. Fletch was funny, gentle, and compassionate. Smart, too, and he was falling in love with her. She was his sunshine. The light in his heart. He. . .

"Here. Be careful—it's hot," her mom warned.

"Mmm. Smells good," Stephen said, washing his hands at the sink.

"You should do that in the sink outside," Mom scolded.

"Too crowded."

Lil figured the smell had lured him in. If anything, Stephen was predictable. Soon the others could be heard removing their shoes in the mudroom.

It blessed Lil to watch Mom scurry about the table, making sure there was ample tomato gravy for those who liked that better than syrup. Once the men were served, Lil and her mom sat down to join them.

About midway through the meal, Matt told his brothers, "I took a new proposal to the Plain City Bank."

"I thought you were going to try some banks in Columbus?"

"Dad and I talked about it, and we think this might work better. We need the new barn quick, to isolate the hogs. Hoop barns are cheaper, and we think the bank might go for it."

Hank's fork clinked against his plate. "Have you been talking to that Stauffer spy?"

Lil didn't even feign an appetite any longer, but folded her hands on the lap of her skirt. "He's not a spy."

Hank frowned at her. "Why have you changed your tune? Are you talking to him?"

Lil wished she'd had the discipline to remain quiet. She raised her chin. "I am a grown woman, and I will make my own decisions about who I talk to. Anyway, this isn't about me."

"You won't be dating him," her dad interjected. He placed his fist heavily on the table. "And that's final."

"I don't believe it is final," Mom disagreed.

Every gaze swiveled to fasten on her.

Stephen's face showed stark horror.

"What do you mean?" Dad asked, with a gravelly voice.

Mom's eyes glittered with anger. "I mean Lil should make up her own mind who she wants to date."

Dad stood up and slapped his napkin down on the table. "She needs to date a Conservative man!" He marched into the mudroom.

Mom's face turned beet red.

Matt told the others, "Fletch just made a mistake. He isn't a bad guy."

Hank's expression hardened. "Don't be leading our sister down the wrong path."

"What does that mean?"

"It's one thing for you to leave the church, but she is a woman.

Chasing after Fletch would be leaving the protection of her father and family. This is dangerous ground."

"I did not leave the church. I only moved to a different one," Matt protested.

"I will back your idea about the hoop farm, but don't get too big for your britches, little brother."

Matt pushed back his chair and stood, seething with anger.

Lil stood up, too. "Stop it. Please."

Hank turned to Lil, softening his voice but still clearly angered. "You don't know anything about making a farm prosperous. You just stick to cooking, little sister, and stay away from Stauffer, because one way or another, he's going to hurt you. That's all. It's for your own good." He seemed to have something more to say, but after a glance at their mother, he grew quiet.

Stephen wiped his mouth with his napkin, the last to stand. He asked Hank, "Think we need to pay Stauffer a visit?"

"Don't you dare," Lil objected.

"We're just worried about you, Lil."

"I know. But this time, you're all wrong."

"Thanks for the mush, Mom," Stephen said, following Hank out of the kitchen.

Matt stepped up to Lil. "You didn't make things any easier for me just now."

Her mouth flew open in disbelief. "I—"

"I like Fletch, too. But the others are probably right about you and him."

"I can't believe you're saying this. He's your friend. He's helped you, and you even told him you forgave him."

"I see you've been talking to him. Be careful. Like the others said, I don't want to cause you to stumble."

Hearing the tender catch in his throat, Lil could only nod.

"Sorry, Mom," Matt said, before he left them.

Once the men had all gone, Mom put trembling hands on her hips.

"Well that was about as bad as a fox in a henhouse," Lil observed.

"It was the roosters causing the trouble."

"I guess!" But even with her mom's attempt at humor, Lil could see that the whole incident had shaken her. "Thanks for sticking up for me."

Mom's hands slipped off her hips; her head sadly dipped. "More than one of us is being a bad example for you."

Lil wished they all didn't make such a cackle about protecting her. Couldn't they see she was a grown woman?

"I don't make it a practice of going against your dad's wishes, because I believe a woman is to be submissive to her man, but sometimes I just can't keep quiet." She grabbed Lil's sleeve. "But child, a woman must pick her battles. You do realize I'll have to apologize to him later? But maybe in the meantime, what I said will sink in a little bit."

Lil wanted to roll her gaze heavenward. What kind of twisted theology was that? She started to clear the plates, scraping the leftovers into the trash.

Mom sighed. "A shame to waste that much food. Especially when frying it takes so much time."

"I'm sorry, Mom. It was a lot of work." Reasoning with men was tricky business, especially stubborn Mennonite men. Lil had always fantasized about taking five minutes at Brother Troyer's pulpit. She would politely ask the congregation if they thought taking away worldly goods such as fashionable clothing and flashy cars really made people less prideful? It had never worked for her. And from her observations, it hadn't stifled the male egos coming and going in their household either.

— ᴄ⟩

On Sunday Lil did not take over Brother Troyer's pulpit. The sermon was about sowing and reaping, and she wasn't about to argue with that. Afterward in the foyer and sprinkled throughout the churchyard, she was relieved to see family members mingling as if yesterday's argument had never happened. The only family member missing was Mom. She still hadn't returned to church. But Lil knew her mom was struggling with the issue.

As far as Lil knew, nobody had told her mom about the elders' recommendation. But Sunday morning was the only time she didn't get out of bed, and the guilt of it was becoming too much for Mom to bear. Each Sunday, Lil expected her mom to join them and was sorely disappointed when she didn't muster up the courage. Lil knew that her first time would be hard but that her mom had friends who would surround her with love.

Standing under the shade of a huge elm, Lil took in the clusters of dark-suited men and modestly dressed women in starched white coverings. Inside the plainness were hardworking saints and sinners of varying personalities—some gentle and some spirited. But one thing they all had in common was that they cared about each other. That's what made the thought of leaving her church family so hard for Lil. These godly people loved her in spite of herself. Maybe that assurance, that broader sense of a caring family was the reason she hadn't been afraid to push the boundaries. Even her brothers meant well.

"Lil."

Megan squeezed under the shade beside Lil and the other parishioners who sought to escape the heat. She whispered, "I got the job!"

Lil squealed and did the garbanzo shimmy.

Megan giggled. "People are staring."

"Well my heart's dancing," Lil exclaimed. "So when are we moving into the doddy house?"

Megan snapped opened her purse. "I have a calendar. Just a moment." They both peered into the small datebook. Megan's slender finger slid over the numbers. "This is the second Sunday of August. Katy and Jake are moving out the last Saturday in August. We could take our stuff over on Sunday, if you don't think that's working on Sunday. Do you?"

"I only have clothes to move so I don't have a problem with it."

"I can get my dad to take my stuff over on Saturday. My mom's donating some more furniture. I'm sure Katy won't mind."

"This is going to be the longest two weeks of my life," Lil moaned.

"I suppose learning my new job will make the time fly for me." Megan's enthusiasm over her new job was undeniable.

Smiling dreamily, Lil replied, "And I've got a date with Fletch tonight."

"Oh, Lil." Megan clasped her by both arms. "I couldn't be happier for you."

"Well at least somebody sees it my way."

"Your family doesn't?"

"Dad and my brothers are all warning me away. Dad ordered me to date a Conservative man. Stephen claims he'll pay Fletch a visit. Matt even warned me to be careful."

"Oh no."

"But things are looking up for us. They must be."

—⟋⟍—

"You're going to love this place," Fletch said, juggling two fishing poles in one arm and carrying a small tackle box in the other. "Amos Miller owns this land."

Lil carried her grandma's hand-me-down quilt, the same one they'd taken to their picnic. "I thought his farm was just down the road."

"He told me I could come use his fishing hole any time I wanted. He even let me borrow his poles. And being the cheapskate that I am, I thought it might make a fun thing for us to do together."

"You're not a cheapskate." Lil stepped over a log that lay across the narrow footpath. "After I got my first job, I made a list in my journal of all the things I wanted to buy. Kind of selfish, wasn't it?"

"Only natural. I didn't know you kept a journal."

"A recipe journal. I'd like to publish a recipe book someday."

"So this journal's kind of a wish list?"

"Maybe it is." She glanced over at him.

"I hope you've written my name in it."

"Yes. Right under: Need a man who'll turn my world upside down."

"What a sweet thing to say."

"And that was next to: Need a man who'll misconstrue everything I say."

"The important part is that you need a man. And I'm a man."

Lil gave him a slow, intentional once-over, taking in the way he towered over her and how the river's breeze pleasantly tousled his hair. His eyes danced with mischief and charm. His shoulders were broad and his waist trim. And then there were those long slim legs and, of course, red tennis shoes. "Yes. I noticed that."

In the animal kingdom, the male species was the most striking. In humans, women were lovely. But in their case, she thought Fletch outshined her. *Even if her light did shine in his heart.* She just couldn't figure out why he was attracted to a plain Conservative girl and even more specifically to her. She hoped to find out today.

"Be careful what you say, or I might have to kiss you."

Lil made the gesture of buttoning her lips and turned her gaze back to the path.

Tucking the tackle box under his arm, he reached for her hand. "Let me help you down the embankment."

"Fletch. I think I can manage. I am a farm girl." But she found she really couldn't. The moment the boast was out of her lips, one foot slid ahead of the other. Her arms flew out awkwardly. The quilt fell to the ground. Thankfully, she caught her balance without falling and making a complete spectacle of herself.

Fletch chuckled.

She swept up the quilt, gave it a little shake, and straightened her shoulders, keeping her gaze forward and not giving him the satisfaction of a backward glance.

When she reached the bottom, she looked out over the Little Darby. Behind her, she heard him settling his tackle then felt his hands settle atop her shoulders. They slid down her arms, and he whispered in her right ear, "I noticed you, too. The day you backed into Britt's car. I thought you were the prettiest little thing I'd ever seen."

Before she could respond, he drew away. He took the quilt, making them a pallet to sit upon, and easily prepared both their poles.

"Where'd you learn to do that?" she asked.

"My dad taught me."

Lil had gleaned from their earlier conversations that he had a chip on his shoulder when it came to his dad. "That's nice."

"It was," he admitted.

They cast their lines in the water and enjoyed their natural surroundings. She noticed the way the water swirled around some rocks farther down the river, but the stream's current grew calm where they were fishing. "This is better than any place you could have taken me."

"I'm glad you like it. Glad Amos Miller called us to take care of his sick cow."

She ventured, "Yes, he's a nice man. Today in church I looked around me. The people in the congregation are like family to me. It was hard to think about leaving them."

"Do you really want me to give up my sneakers?" he teased. "Are the restrictions of your church important to you? Or can you be a Christian without them?"

"That's a good question. I've discussed these things with Matt and Jake, too. He left the church for a while. His conscience wouldn't bother him if he went to a more progressive Mennonite church, but it would Katy's, so he chose to stay Conservative. Like me, his friends were in the church. But he says that the restrictions are just there to make it easier for us not to sin. Take television, for example. I believe the television, itself, is not sinful. It's just a chunk of metal."

"Metal?" he questioned.

"Fine. I don't know what televisions are made of, but you know what I mean. It's what you choose to watch that dulls your conscience against sinful behavior. So if you don't have a television, you don't have to deal with those temptations."

"But if the church forbids the television, and you have one, then it's sinful?"

"Going against the ordinances set by the elders is an attitude of rebellion. If you are a member of the church, that kind of rebellion is sinful."

After that, they spent another hour discussing their personal beliefs. Finally Fletch asked, "Could you go to my church if you dressed the same, wore your covering, and I agreed not to bring anything into our home that you found offensive? Could you do that with a clear conscience?"

So he was thinking about marriage, too, and not just joking about it. "Yes. I think as long as my heart was at peace with God and my husband."

"Lil," he whispered, gratefully.

She raised a palm, quickly clarifying, "But I don't know if I want to leave my church. I don't believe it's the only way to heaven. But it's still hard to change."

His voice saddened. "I think I understand."

"Could you be happy to go to my church and abide by all the restrictions? Like Jake does?" she asked, hopefully.

"I've tried to imagine that. But it feels hypocritical because I don't feel the need to follow those particular rules."

"You don't even know what they all are," she argued.

"You're right."

Her shoulders sagged. "My family had a huge argument the day I met you at the shelter. It was about you."

He picked up a pebble and threw it off to his right. It thudded into a thick patch of weeds. "I'm afraid to ask about it."

"Everyone but my mom and Matt warned me away from you. Stephen even threatened to pay you a visit. Dad told me I had to date a Conservative man."

"And what did you do?"

"I told them that I would date whomever I wanted. But it hurt to see my family arguing. And they accused Matt of leading me astray."

"Away from the church?"

"Yes. So I need to think carefully about it. Leaving the Conservative Church will cause more family trouble."

"And your family has had their share of trouble. I understand that. I will just have to wait and see what you and God decide. But I have to warn you, I'm very persuasive—"

"And persistent. Which is why you just caught a fish. Fletch! Reel it in!"

CHAPTER 24

Lil carried an armload of skirts into the doddy house, passing Jake and Fletch, who were carrying a blue sofa in the other direction. Katy had insisted that the girls move in on Saturday, and they'd make it one big "moving-in/moving-out" party. If the boxes hadn't been clearly marked JAKE's or DODDY HOUSE with large black markers, it might have been chaos. While the others moved boxes and furniture in and out, Katy furiously cleaned every vacant inch of refurbished wood flooring and the empty cabinetry.

"You're working harder than any of us," Lil fretted, placing a hand on Katy's wilted sleeve.

"I'm thinking it may never get cleaned again." Katy gave a teasing grin.

"You're probably right. But you can clean whenever you come to visit."

"Oh no. That's called abusing your friends."

"No, it isn't. You love cleaning."

Katy swiped her arm across her damp brow. "Not the cleaning part, Lil, just the results. But go"—she waved—"I'm fine here."

"Okay, then I'll invite you for supper soon."

"I'm happy that you'll have your own kitchen again. Happy for both of us."

"I know. Me, too."

Lil hung her skirts next to some clothes she had left in the closet when she moved back to the farm. It looked as though Jake had just shoved them aside. Megan would fill Katy's part of the closet.

On her way to the car for another load, she met Fletch. By the silly expression he'd sported most of the day, he was as happy as Lil about the move, especially since he'd lost his welcome at the Landis farm.

"I think your little dollhouse needs a kitten to keep you company. That is, when I'm not here."

"I don't think a barn cat would feel at home in a doddy house," she retorted.

"I think Slinky would think he was in heaven. I know I would."

Given the kitten was named, she thought it must be from the farm shelter. "He sounds sneaky."

"No, he just does this stretching thing then curls up like a slinky toy. You won't be sorry. You'll love the little guy and his antics."

Falling into her Dutchy accent, she protested, "Oh, but I won't love it, because I didn't say yes."

They had reached the car, and Fletch put his arm on the roof, blocking her from her belongings. "It's only temporary until we get married. Then I'll take over Slinky's care. I'd take him now, but he's still so tiny, and I don't trust Buddy around him."

Lil widened her eyes. "Is this your way of warning me. . . ?" She faltered. It seemed silly to keep joking about marriage when they weren't that far along in their relationship. "Warning me that you come along with a whole entourage of animals?"

"Is that so bad? You explicitly warned me that you're a farm girl. Of course that was right before you fell down the river bank like a city girl."

She tapped his chest, emphasizing each word. "I did not fall down." Her hand dropped. "Anyway, I don't really want to be a farm girl. You're not planning to live on a farm, are you?"

"Not really. But I love pets."

"Won't you be tired of taking care of them all day?"

"Do you get tired of cooking? If you do, do you quit eating?"

She frowned, unable to follow the correlation.

"What do you hate about the farm?"

Lil stared, not really seeing Ivan Miller's house but only the country road that stretched off in the distance like her thoughts. What did she hate? "I hate the rooster that wakes me up so early."

"Surely a good cook could think of a way to solve that problem."

Without the rooster, there wouldn't be any cute chicks. But she wasn't telling him that. "I hate the chores."

"Who doesn't?"

Actually, she liked her mom's cheery kitchen and the picturesque window that looked out over the farm. She thought about the past couple of months. As much as she complained to herself and others, she had enjoyed rattling her Grandma Landis's pots and pans and ironing the heirloom tablecloths. She loved rubbing her finger over the golden rim of her mom's Autumn Leaf dishes when she set the table.

"I hate the smell of hogs, but not the scent of lilacs or the grass after rain."

"You hate the hogs?"

"No." Her eyes widened in the realization that she didn't hate the farm as much as she just wanted her own place. "Fine. I don't hate the farm. But I'm ready for something different."

"Me, too."

She smiled seductively. "You have a way of twisting everything I say to suit your intentions, don't you?"

"I confess when it comes to you my brain is only wired one way."

"Mu-shy!" Jake called, shaking his head.

"Busted."

"Now if you will kindly move to the side."

"All right. You don't have to commit to Slinky just yet. I'll bring him along next time for you to meet."

"Oh no you don't. That's not fair."

"Exactly." He opened the car door and pulled out a box of cookbooks. "You don't have to commit to me yet either. But I'm hoping if Slinky and I remain on our best behavior we'll wear down your resistance." He

221

grunted. "What do you have in here? Bricks?"

He headed back toward the house, and Lil paused to watch him. He was definitely wearing down her resistance. She wondered if her mom had ever felt that way about her dad.

Later after everyone was gone except Megan and Lil, they were in the kitchen, unpacking some dishes that Mrs. Weaver had donated.

"I don't mean to dampen your spirits, but I have to ask if your dad ever gave us his blessing," Megan said.

Lil threw a wad of crumpled newspaper into an empty box. "He told me that if Mom slipped back into depression it was all my fault. That he expected me to get this nonsense out of my head quickly and get back home where I belonged. He said I wasn't behaving like a Conservative woman with my worldly ideas of living on my own and wanting to be my own boss."

"Yikes."

Lil rested her hand on the counter. "My family's divided over Fletch, too."

"One day, you'll make the perfect couple. The best things don't always come easily."

Although they didn't talk about it after that, the next time Lil went to her sister's home to help out, Michelle had plenty to say on the matter. Her sister joked that Lil should be glad they were not Amish, because if they were, the family would have shunned her by now. Their father was angry because Lil was supposed to be under his authority until she married. Michelle had heard him call Lil a rebellious child who didn't care about her family. Michelle claimed their mom had responded to his comment by slapping the mashed potatoes on his plate and muttering something about choking. Hank and Stephen were scheming revenge on Fletch, even threatening to pay the shelter a night visit to free the animals. At that, little Flannel and Cottonball popped into Lil's mind, and she felt ill. She wondered if she should warn Fletch.

Thankfully, Michelle had ended their conversation on a positive note. Her cast had been removed, and she no longer required Lil's help. The way Michelle rushed Lil out the door, she had to wonder if she wasn't being shunned, after all.

Work was the one place that Lil forgot her family problems. Giovanni took her under his wing again. He hovered and flitted like a mama bird and left her in charge while he took a personal phone call.

When he had shouted out the order, Lil was embarrassed that he chose her over others with more seniority. That was a mere technicality. Everybody knew what to do. Giovanni wasn't an ordinary manager. His employees did not expect him to stick to procedures. Anyway, Lil didn't actually take charge of anything. If a problem cropped up that she could not handle, she would delegate it to somebody with more expertise. Nobody would criticize her.

Still, Giovanni's gesture set her deepest core into a secret garbanzo dance. For five whole minutes, she took charge of the kitchen that mean old Beppe had always envied.

In the sixth and seventh minute, her happiness fizzled. Giovanni hung up the phone with a face the color of a mozzarella cheese ball.

"Is something wrong?" she whispered.

"Eh, it is my wife." He gripped the countertop then looked up at her with wide eyes. "She's pregnant."

The kitchen became as quiet as if Giovanni was taking a bite from a new recipe. Lil sensed his fear, knew his emotions were at war with the news he had just received. On one hand, he was happy for his wife's joy, and for his own. He loved children. That was evident when he made napkin airplanes for the little ones as he mingled with customers. But on the other hand, he had taken this path before. It had led to disappointment over his wife's miscarriages and her ensuing bouts of depression.

"I will pray," Lil replied. "God is able."

"Is He?" Giovanni asked.

Lil flinched. But Giovanni whispered, "I am the reason this restaurant has been successful, no?"

"Of course you are," she replied, wondering why he was going down that track.

He whispered, "I see myself in you."

Lil nodded with confusion. "Thank you."

CHAPTER 25

The following Saturday, Lil stirred pasta sauce, shaking some basil into her palm and brushing it off into the contents of a cast-iron pot. "I hate using dried herbs. I want to start an herb garden in the windowsill." She stared dreamily out the window, "And a bird feeder would be nice, too."

"Those are great ideas." Megan pushed aside the study material for a children's Sunday school class she taught. "I don't know if I can stand the aroma if this simmers all afternoon. I'm going to get fat living with you. How do you keep such a tiny waist?"

Lil stared at her naive friend. She'd always been envious of Megan's thin figure and beauty. "You do realize I skipped dinner last night and did one hundred sit-ups before bed?"

Megan rose and stretched. "Yes, but I've always told you that you shouldn't skip meals like that."

"It doesn't hurt to skip meals as long as you eat healthy."

"Maybe you're right. We sent food boxes to Mexico last week. I'm sure the recipients of those boxes didn't stand around having this discussion. We are so fortunate."

Lil bit back a smile. Living with Megan was almost like living with

Katy. Only the sermons Megan gave took a different spin. While Katy hoped to narrow Lil's perspective, Megan tried to widen her worldview. Megan was all about saving the world.

But her friends' personalities differed so that Lil needed to take care that she didn't prick Megan's tender heart. Katy made a competent sparring partner with her black smoldering eyes and sulky lips, but Megan delighted in dismantling arguments. So Lil didn't dispute with Megan if she could avoid it. Instead, she used her mom's trick of changing the topic. "Your job is perfect for you. Have you met any cute guys?"

"Actually, my boss is probably the handsomest man I've ever met." Megan clamped her hand across her mouth, and her blue eyes widened in horror. "I can't believe I just said that."

Lil slapped her wooden spoon on the counter, forgetting all about her sauce. "What? Why haven't I heard about him before?"

Megan's eyes grew softly regretful. "Because. I think he's divorced. You know that makes him off limits." Her gaze fell to the braided oval rug Lil's grandma had made. She shrugged her shoulders. "I don't even know why I mentioned him."

"Oh no." Lil knew that if Megan made that comment about her boss, she had already fallen for him. The elders in the church would never honor a second marriage.

Megan glanced up again and tried to explain, "When I started working there, he was wearing a wedding ring. Now he isn't. He hasn't told me what happened, but I've heard rumors that his wife left him."

Lil's hands went to her apron's waistband. "So he's not pursuing you?"

"No! Of course not!"

"But you're attracted?"

Megan shook her head. "No."

"But you said. . ."

"Okay, I noticed him. He's a nice man. I feel sorry for him."

Lil's hands left her hips and rose to the air making a helpless gesture. "His wife must have had a reason for leaving him."

"It might not be his fault," Megan defended. Then she said, "If

I'm attracted, I'll get over it. I have to. I don't want to leave Char Air because of some silly crush. How childish would that be? I love this job. I'm really careful around him so that he doesn't see my admiration."

This news unsettled Lil. Megan, the butterfly, had never lit—romantically speaking. She'd never fallen in love. Why did this have to happen just when Megan had found her niche? Why couldn't she have fallen for some clean-cut Rosedale College student? "Be careful, green bean. Love is a sneaky thing."

Megan slowly nodded, then ran long fingers through her fine hair, pushing it behind her shoulder. "You're talking about Fletch?"

"Yes. Yesterday I stopped in to see my mom, and Matt pulled me in the barn to lecture me about causing problems between Mom and Dad." She placed a lid on the slightly simmering pot and stepped away. "He said I was going to ruin the family. Naturally, we ended up in a disagreement about Fletch." Turning her back to Megan, she went to the big, farm-style sink to scrub some utensils. Blinking, she whispered, "I hate what's become of our family. Matt and I used to be close."

"I'm sorry. Here, let me do that." Megan nudged Lil aside just as she was squeezing liquid detergent, and a billow of tiny bubbles rose above them.

"Oops." Megan waved her hand through the airborne bubbles and stared aghast into the bubbly sink. "That's wasting resources."

"It's just one squirt of detergent."

"Lil," Megan said with a soft but reprimanding tone. "My mom says that if everyone wasted a squirt, it would soon become an ocean."

⟿

Fletch watched Vic's scalpel move with expertise as he performed a necropsy. Animal autopsies were invaluable to Fletch's hands-on education, and he found the internal workings of the horse fascinating. But when his phone rang, the caller's identity was equally amazing.

"Vic, can I take this call? It's from my dad in Africa."

"Sure. Go on."

Fletch snapped his phone open and stuck it in the crook of his neck so he could wash his hands in the clinic basin. "Dad. It's good to hear your voice."

"Yours, too. It's been a long time."

"How's Mom?"

"She's great. She's out purchasing some medical supplies. I got your e-mail. I was sorry to hear about Marshall. He's been a friend to us over the years. A generous man."

"Yes." Fletch moved out of doors. "The news is hard."

"I know. So is your predicament. Do you want to talk about it?"

Fletch sat on the ground, and Buddy rubbed against his hand. He touched the dog absentmindedly, telling his dad about Marshall's request and how it had affected the Landis family and his position as Vic's assistant. "So the camera is untouched, but I have to do something."

"Yes, you do. If we aren't moving forward, we are losing ground."

His dad always peppered his conversation with frustrating maxims. Fletch pressed, "What would you do?"

"Without hindsight, I probably would be standing in your shoes about now. Tell me who deserves your loyalty."

"I knew Marshall first."

"If he's the one you serve, you shouldn't be feeling regret."

Fletch caught his dad's meaning. "You know I serve the Lord first."

"Exactly."

"So you're not going to tell me what to do?"

"You prayed about it?"

Fletch yanked a clump of grass from the lawn, and Buddy moved away. "Of course."

"Then trust God and follow your heart. The circumstance won't heal itself or go away on its own."

He let the grass filter through his fingers. "And you won't be upset if Marshall withdraws his support from your ministry, too?"

"I appreciate all Marshall's done for us, but the Lord is our provider. Anyway, we might not be needing his support. I was calling to tell you that we decided it's time to come home."

With surprise, Fletch sputtered, "You mean. . .the States? A furlough?"

"We think it will be for good this time."

DIANNE CHRISTNER

Fletch felt his adrenaline spike from the shocking news. He worked to keep his voice calm. "Well, Ohio is a nice place." He couldn't imagine having Dad back in his life—didn't need more disappointments along that line.

"Your mother and I were hoping for an invitation. You'll be there another year or so, right?"

"As far as I know, but once I destroy that video, anything could happen."

"That's what makes life such an adventure!" Even though his dad's voice came from across a continent and an entire ocean, it contained the power that swallowed lesser men. If he had not lost his fervor, Fletch wondered what was motivating Dad to leave the mission field. "We're looking forward to seeing you. Maybe we can get your sister to come to Ohio for a visit, too."

"I haven't seen her since she got married." The line got quiet. "When will you come?"

"Nothing's definite yet. I'll e-mail you when we know more."

Aha. There was the catch. As usual, Fletch didn't have to wait long for Dad to dash his hopes. As far as he knew, the move to Ohio was all bluster. He took off his cap, ruffled his hair. "Sure. That will be fine. Thanks for the advice."

Dad chuckled. "You already knew what to do."

Fletch felt resentful that Dad found the situation amusing.

"Give Mom my love."

The call was bittersweet, but it helped Fletch move ahead and delete the footage. That night as he pushed levers on the small video camera, he explained to Buddy, "A touch of the button and it's gone. But the consequences, not so easily."

Buddy raised his flabby jowls and howled.

"Well let's hope it's not that bad." Fletch placed the camera on top of the refrigerator, where it would remain until he returned it to Marcus. His friend had returned to Plain City, but Fletch hadn't gotten a chance to ask about his trip yet, and now more than ever dreaded their next encounter.

CHAPTER 26

Fletch drove around a curve just before the farm shelter came into sight and noticed one of the shelter's horses trotting down the center of the road. *What on earth?* He pulled the car over onto the embankment and hopped out. He tried to get the horse to come to him, but it was jittery. Without a halter, it was useless. Fletch hopped back in his car and swept his phone from his pocket. "Marcus! Come quick! One of your horses is out."

Fletch pulled into the farm and met Marcus, and they both ran for the barn. But ten yards from the door, they halted. The door wasn't left open like Fletch expected. It was demolished. Shredded and mutilated.

"Vandals!" Marcus cried bitterly.

Fletch ran into the vacated barn and located the halter and lead and jumped back in his car while Marcus stayed behind to round up the other straying animals.

It was hours before they had all the livestock located and secured again. The horse, Taffy, had reinjured his bad leg, and Fletch couldn't be sure if the recovery would be as swift or as complete as it might have been before the incident.

Weary and dejected, Fletch joined Marcus and Ashley in the office.

"Do you think the vandals will be back?" she asked.

"It depends if they have an issue with the shelter or if it was just a random kid's prank," Marcus replied with a grim countenance.

"What if they harm the animals the next time?"

"They injured Taffy. With the sprain the horse already had, frightening him added to the damage. I administered a cold press. Now he needs total rest. I'll make sure Vic stops in to take a look at him."

Marcus nodded. "I don't suppose the police will do much. This is a tight-knit community. They'll be backing the farmers, some of whom consider us the enemy." He placed his head in his hands and muttered, "With all that's going on with Dad, I almost wish we hadn't started the shelter."

"You must not say that." Ashley rushed over and placed a hand on his taut shoulder. "We're helping a lot of animals. You're just overwhelmed right now."

Fletch wondered if something worse was troubling his friend. "Did Marshall agree to take chemo?"

"He's leaning that way."

"Thank goodness." Fletch was relieved about Marshall but didn't have the heart to hand over the empty video camera now. Not when Marcus seemed so despondent.

—ॐ

Later that night on the way home from the shelter, Fletch swung by the doddy house in hopes of catching Lil at home. She was at the kitchen table with her recipe journal and a scattering of recipe cards. Megan lounged on the nearby couch with her pretty nose in a book.

Fletch picked up one of the recipe cards. "Gnocchi?"

Lil snapped it out of his hand. "This is top-secret stuff."

He grinned, harboring his own secrets of the heart variation.

The doddy house was quiet without the hum of television or computer, reminding him how different Lil's life was from his own. His apartment, though sparsely furnished, had both technologies.

"You guys always this quiet?"

"You caught her in a rare moment," Megan called from the adjoining living room.

Lil shrugged. "You look tired."

"A little discouraged."

Lil swept her recipe cards aside and aligned them into a neat stack. "Sit here?"

He pulled out a chair and joined her. "My dad called."

"That's good, right?"

"I guess. He might be quitting his missionary work. Might be moving here."

"Really? It would probably be good for you to spend some time together."

"Maybe. I'm not getting my hopes up."

She nodded, her gaze filling with concern.

"He didn't seem troubled about the possibility of losing Marshall's support."

"I imagine he was sad to hear about his cancer."

"Yes. Anyway, he didn't give me any advice, but after talking to him, I erased the video."

Lil jumped up and threw her arms around his neck. "Oh thank you!"

Her welcome rush of gratitude was a joyful relief, and he pulled her into his lap, holding her tight and stroking her hair. "I'm just sorry for what I did." He touched her cheek.

"I'm still in the room over here," Megan reminded them. "And in case you never noticed, my fair skin blushes easily."

"Oops. Sorry." Lil jumped up, embarrassed.

"Anyway, I went to the shelter to return the camera to Marcus. But I couldn't do it." He saw Lil's expression sag, and quickly explained. "He was still upset about his dad. Besides that, someone vandalized the barn. When I got there, the animals were out. I helped him round them up. Had to treat one of the horses."

Lil's eyes widened with fear. "What about the lambs?"

"They're fine." He smiled. "They didn't get very far."

Lil gave a sigh of relief. "Do you think it was one of my brothers? They made some threats against you."

Fletch rubbed his temples and briefly closed his eyes, hoping that was not the case. When he opened them, he saw Lil's distress mirrored his own.

─◦

The next day, Fletch and Vic returned to the dairy farm. Vic allowed Fletch to treat a white-faced cow with a cancerous growth by the eye. The cow had already lost the other eye, but they were able to save the second eye by numbing the area and then freezing the cancerous spot with liquid nitrogen.

"The cow will recover. Even after removing the first eye a couple of years ago, its milk production increased, which is a sign of improving health," Vic explained, returning his instruments to his satchel.

"Thanks for letting me do the surgery."

"You're here to learn."

"I know. But I feel like you're giving me a second chance. I appreciate it. And I wanted you to know I deleted that video footage." Thinking of Marcus's condition the last time he'd seen him, Fletch said, "I haven't returned the camera yet, but I will as soon as the Lewises have a break from their string of bad luck."

"The fallout I expected never happened. I guess it's a tribute to the Landis family's integrity that they didn't spread a bunch of gossip about us."

Fletch gave the cow a couple of pats then released the animal. "They're good people." Vic was right. After sleeping on it, Fletch was giving them the benefit of the doubt, assuming they hadn't vandalized the shelter.

"But they still don't want you taking care of their animals."

"How is their herd?"

"They're not isolating the hogs like they should. Until they do, they'll never get the disease under control."

Fletch frowned, wondering if Matt had taken his advice about the hoop barns.

They walked down the row of cattle, doing their routine checks. The herdsman had left them to take a customer on a farm tour, so they were able to discuss private matters.

"This whole thing with Marshall and you has forced me to take a hard look at my life. I shared some things with Britt, and we got in a big fight about finances. I told her we needed to cut back. She pointed out that I was the one driving the newest vehicle."

So Fletch's hunch was right—the vet had been under stress at home. He knew that the vet's truck barely had the dealership's sticker off its windshield, but Britt's car wasn't much older. From everything Vic had previously told him, he didn't think Britt was being very fair about their financial situation.

"I didn't tell her yet, but I'm thinking about trading my truck back in, getting into something older."

_____ ☙ _____

One week later, Fletch drove to Ivan Miller's farm, fiddling with Vic's used-truck accessories. When he pulled up next to the doddy house, Lil stepped out onto the porch.

Her eyes widening, she hurried down the steps and strode to the front of the truck. She turned sideways and bent to examine the emblem on the grill. The white bow tied at the back of her curvy waist made his mouth go dry. With a silent intake of breath, he hopped out of the cab, stifling the urge to clasp his hands around that captivating waist.

She said almost accusingly, "I know what this red contraption is. It's a Dodge Ram." Then she turned and faced him, her hands back on her apron-clad hips. "Is this yours?"

He smiled. "I wish. It's Vic's. He traded down."

"And he's letting you drive it?"

"He was in one of his better moods."

She gave him an impish smile. "The color suits you."

He reached for her hand. "Hop in."

When she grabbed the handrest attached to the truck's ceiling, he assisted her into the cab. He nearly melted when his hands completely swallowed her waist.

Lil settled into the leather seat and gazed down at him adoringly, with her feminine hands gripping the man-sized steering wheel. "You gonna let me drive?"

"Nope," he nearly squeaked, not having actually prepared himself for that idea. He thought she would scoot over to the passenger side, as it had a bench seat, and let him drive. She was, after all, a wrecker of cars.

But she was already fiddling with the gearshift. "It's an automatic? Great!"

He cleared his throat, scrambled up, and tapped her hip. "Move over."

She giggled but hardly budged, obviously intending to drive Vic's truck. But Fletch had other ideas. He squished into the seat beside her and closed the door. Thankfully, he had the keys in his pocket. He was still in control. He started the engine, and a seat belt warning chimed.

"That sounds prettier than most," she remarked. "Jezebel doesn't have one."

"Pretty like you." They sat so close that he took the driver's seat belt and wrapped it around them both. She gave him a saucy grin. He placed his arm around her and put the vehicle in gear.

"We can't go far. I have sauce on the stove."

"Okay. But I kind of like this." If it was any indication of what it was like to blend two lives into one, he could get used to it.

She wiggled her elbow between them, probably to remind him she wasn't easy—as if he hadn't already figured that out—and they merged onto the road. He gunned the engine, and she gave a joyful shriek. The air coming through the vent lifted her hair enough that he caught its tropical scent.

They drove past freshly harvested fields, and for lack of rain, a trail of dust billowed behind them, making a private curtain for them in their red leather cocoon. Fletch could have driven on for miles, for days, but suddenly Lil straightened.

"What was that squeak?"

Being so caught up in the Ram and Lil, he'd forgotten they weren't altogether alone in the cab. He steered the truck to the side of the road. When the dust settled, he unbuckled and jumped out of the cab, ordering, "Stay right there."

She tilted her button-cute, freckled face and studied him curiously while he reached behind the seat into a box on the floorboards. His hand engulfing a tiny fur ball, he laid the mewing kitten on Lil's blue skirt like a love offering. Lil took a sudden intake of breath, but her resistance quickly vanished, as he had hoped it would. He placed his elbows on the seat beside her, watching to see how quickly she'd fall in love with Slinky. Who was he kidding? He hoped she'd fall in love with him.

She brought the tiny kitten up to her face, nuzzling him against her cheek, and Fletch held his breath. Fortunately, Slinky didn't bat or scratch, too busy licking Lil's cheek.

"His tongue is scratchy and tiny," she giggled. Then she turned and gave him an arched look. "Oh, Fletch. What have you done? How will I find time to take care of him?"

That was all he needed to hear. He climbed back up and nestled next to Lil and her kitten. When he closed the door, the interior of the cab seemed cozy, like one happy little family. Only Buddy was missing. "Kittens aren't much trouble. They use a litter box and mostly sleep when their owners are gone. They hunt mice, too."

But this kitten had other ideas. He evidently didn't realize he was on trial and double-crossed Fletch by creating a wet spot on Lil's apron. Her eyes widened and her lips pursed. She made a disgusted face. Fletch waited for the inevitable. He knew the fury that could spew out of his girlfriend's mouth.

Lil clutched her apron with her left hand and stared at the kitten. "Let's go home. Slinky has a lot to learn." But the way she slowly emphasized *has a lot to learn* with a sharp glance Fletch's way, he understood that she was making a valid point about him.

He didn't care. He was content that she hadn't flung the miscreant at him with a quick change of heart. Yes, that was a very good sign. But sadly, Fletch's good fortune lasted only about five minutes longer. For when they pulled into the Millers' driveway, Matt Landis's pickup truck was parked next to the doddy house.

CHAPTER 27

Lil cringed to see her brother's blue truck. As soon as Fletch cut his engine, Matt jumped out of his vehicle. Sporting a ridiculous "Not by the hair of my chinny-chin-chin" T-shirt, her brother planted his feet and slapped his hands on his hips to wait for them.

Beans! She felt her face heat at the humiliation of being caught all cuddled up next to Fletch and even belted in the same seat belt with him. As if Fletch felt the same, he quickly unfastened it and jumped out of the cab.

Lil scrambled after him, accepting his assistance to lift her and the kitten down. Her long skirt caught the truck's seat lever, showing too much leg, which only added to her shame. With her free hand she yanked it loose, though not without a consequent ripping sound.

As soon as her white sneakers hit the gravel drive, however, Matt speared her with a condemning gaze. "Isn't this cozy?"

Lil felt more wounded than angry over her favorite brother's disapproval. It certainly wasn't like it probably appeared to him. She hadn't done anything wrong with Fletch. She took a deep breath and softened her voice. "Did you come to criticize me, or do you want to come inside and discuss this over a plate of pasta?"

She felt Fletch's reassuring touch at her arm.

"No, I don't want pasta," Matt said angrily. "I came to tell you that because of you two, our dad is sleeping in the barn. Without you, Mom has gone completely over the edge."

The news cut deep. Lil feared what her mother might do again. Anything was possible. Once, Lil would never have dreamed her own mother would overdose herself. Mom had never claimed it was an accident. Would her parents be the first and only members in their church to separate or get a divorce, too? Though she felt that she had contributed to the general family upheaval, and her heart clenched with guilt, Lil still couldn't allow Matt to dump all the blame on her. Out of her own pain, she lashed back. "Has she? Or has she finally stood up for what she believes?"

"You know that women are supposed to be submissive. Actually, you don't understand that concept at all." Matt shifted his gaze to glare at Fletch. He thrust his finger, poking it in Fletch's direction. "I did forgive you, but you attract trouble like hogs attract flies."

Fletch touched Lil's waist protectively and jutted his chin. "I don't care if you blame me, but I don't like the tone and insinuations you're using with Lil."

Matt gave a scoffing laugh that turned out more like a snort.

The men's angry expressions ignited the atmosphere with tension. Lil thought they might fly into each other at any moment. She tried to reason. "Matt, you of all my brothers should understand that the old ways aren't necessarily the better ways."

Her logic fell on deaf ears. Matt turned suddenly and stomped back to his truck. He jumped in and slammed the door.

The noise startled Slinky, and the kitten leaped, clawing, from Lil's arms. "Oh no!" she gasped, looking down to see if the poor thing had broken its neck. But it jumped up and darted beneath the doddy house porch.

Behind her, Matt's tires spewed gravel. Fighting back tears of desperation, Lil knelt down to look between the gray step and the porch.

She felt a touch on her shoulder. "Let me."

"I hope Slinky's not injured," she choked out.

"Not on my shift. And certainly not by the hair of my chinny-chin-chin," Fletch joked, his hand probing in the dark crevices as far as he could reach.

Lil let out a nervous giggle even though she knew they shouldn't be taking her brother's angry display so lightly.

"Got him. Ouch!"

The kitten came out batting and struggling in Fletch's hand. Nevertheless, he drew Slinky tenderly up before his face. Turned him this way and that. "I think all he needs is a small bowl of milk and some time back in his box."

Nodding, Lil touched Fletch's arm. "Thanks."

"I'll get his box." He looked at Lil hopefully. "Maybe we can have some of that pasta."

"Sure." She watched him stride to the truck.

He spoke to the kitten, and she knew it was for her benefit. He wanted to take away her pain. "Look, Mr. Slinky, you're not doing a great job of impressing your new mommy. You'd better. . ."

His words drifted off, but Lil was very aware of his presence as she watched him and wondered how she had gotten so attached to somebody who had caused so much havoc in her family. Then looking down at her potty-stained apron and ripped skirt, she made a dash for the doddy house.

A few hours later, Lil stood at the window and gazed under the plain green roller shade to watch Fletch drive away in the flashy red truck. Her blond Rollo and that red truck—even though it went against the prideful image that the Conservative Mennonite Church tried to shun—they both made her heart zip with pleasure.

If her family was already upset with her, maybe it was time to try Fletch's church. She imagined how it would be. Would his congregation take her in as one of their own? Would she be able to release the church restrictions that sometimes felt like a tightening noose around her neck? Or would she still adhere to them? Could she really step over the chasm that separated the Mennonites who didn't wear ties from the ones who did? Once, she thought she could. Now she realized it wasn't an easy thing to do.

She felt God drawing her to trust Him, but she felt impatient, wanting to know what her future held. The lyrics of an old hymn ran through her mind: *"I know whom I have believed and am persuaded that he is able to keep that which I have committed to him against that day."*

She sincerely hoped so. She drew Slinky to her cheek, finding comfort in nestling the kitten that Fletch had gifted her.

~&~

"Hello, Mom?" Lil went through the Landises' mudroom and entered the kitchen, which smelled of cooked cabbage and sausage. Mom turned away from the stove and quickly crossed the room to her.

"I miss you. Where have you been?"

"Just getting settled. Working."

"Dating that Stauffer boy?"

Lil nodded.

"I figured."

"I missed you, too. Cabbage from Michelle's garden?" Lil lifted the skillet lid and took the fork her mom had just abandoned to taste it. "Delicious. I wonder if you could switch Dijon mustard for German?"

"Always telling your mother how to cook."

"Sorry. It might make it too sweet, anyway."

Mom urged, "Sit down, and I'll make us a pot of tea."

Lil unconsciously fiddled with the canning jar centerpiece and watched her mom, looking for clues as to her frame of mind.

Mom returned to the table with the tea and some homemade oatmeal cookies. "I suppose you came because you heard your dad was sleeping in the barn."

With shock, Lil worked to keep her composure. "I hope it's not because of me."

"It's about you and everything else that has infuriated me over the last thirty years."

Lil's eyes widened fearfully. "Oh?"

Mom sipped her tea and jutted her chin. "I told your dad that if he'd treated me better I probably wouldn't have gotten so depressed."

Lil's appetite fled. Her dad had enough problems with the farm's failing finances and sick hogs. How could Mom blame her depression on him?

"Then he wanted to know what he'd done. So I told him."

Lil was terrified to ask what Dad had done to ruin Mom's life.

"I told him plenty. That he treated me like a child, never discussing farm business. That all he wanted me around for was to cook and clean and see to his needs. I told him I had a brain, and a heart, too."

Lil imagined herself in Mom's situation. Everything she said held truth, but Lil had never known that her mom hoped for anything more.

"Well! I tell you. Your father went off in a huff. Slept in the barn for two nights. And I felt miserable. Lower than a dirty old rug. So the next night when he was preparing to go out after I had fixed him his supper, I asked him to stay. Told him I was sorry."

Many images passed through Lil's mind. Her mom had still fixed his supper for him while he was sleeping in the barn? She folded her hands, tapped them against her chin, both enraptured and sickened in the details of her parents' big fight. "What happened?"

"He took me in his arms and cried."

Lil felt her own eyes mist. "Dad?"

Mom nodded. "He said some real nice things about us, and since then, he's been talking to me. Really talking. We're not good at it, but it makes me feel better about a lot of things. It could have been different for us if he'd always talked to me like this."

Lil released a loud sigh, grateful they had worked things out between them. "Maybe it can still be different. The way you hoped."

Mom nodded. "Maybe so." She took a sip of her tea. "When Will finds out you came today, he's going to ask me if you're seeing Fletch. And now that we're talking, I can't keep any secrets from him."

"All right. Tell him that Fletch deleted the video footage. That I believe he's sorry about what he did."

"Do you love him?"

"I wish it were that simple."

"Nothing's simple about love. That's for sure. Life either."

"Megan says that the most worthwhile things aren't the easiest." Lil sighed. "Mom, please don't fight with Dad about this."

"It's a touchy subject for your dad. He feels responsible for bringing Fletch to the farm."

"But he didn't really. Bring Fletch. It was Matt who invited him to supper."

"Good news! Matt got his loan from the Plain City Bank! He's ordered some hoop barns."

"That is good news." Lil touched Mom's hand. The hoop barns had been Fletch's idea. She hoped Matt remembered that and dropped his grudge against Fletch.

CHAPTER 28

F letch was working on a research paper for school, entitled "Obstacles in Obtaining Medical Attention." Across the room in Fletch's apartment, Buddy gnawed on a rawhide bone. Fletch tapped his finger impatiently against his space bar, and Buddy cocked one ear.

"Am I disturbing you?" Fletch asked. The dog lifted his head and panted in his direction.

It was eating away at him that he hadn't talked to Marshall since he'd been diagnosed with cancer. Since he'd deleted the footage. Fletch dreaded hearing the frail voice from the last time they talked, when Marshall had been in the hospital running tests. But he wouldn't be able to move forward, like his dad suggested, until he made the call. Finally, he picked up his phone.

"Hello."

"Hi, Marshall. It's Fletch."

"I may be terminal, but I'm not ignorant," the southerner drawled. "Ya are on my contact list."

Fletch grinned inwardly. "Genius would be more appropriate."

"That's my boy. Ya always know how to compliment me when I'm fishing for one."

"Speaking of fishing. There's a little river here called the Darby. I think you'd enjoy it as much as I do. Wish you were here and could throw in a line. I think you'd like Plain City."

"Actually, I've been thinking of driving over."

"No kidding? I mean, you'd be able to do that?"

"After the chemo is finished. I think Marcus needs my support."

"I'm relieved you're taking the chemo." Fletch swallowed. It sounded as if Marshall wanted to tie up loose ends. "The last time we talked, you asked me to pray for you. I've been doing that."

"Thanks, kid. Marcus tells me you're in the middle of a romance." Fletch didn't miss how Marshall quickly changed the topic away from God. "The little Conservative girl we talked about before? He told me that ya got caught filming at her farm and it caused a big ruckus."

Relieved that Marshall opened the topic he most wanted to talk about, Fletch quickly replied, "That's true. That's one of the reasons I deleted the film."

"What? Marcus didn't mention that!"

"I haven't told him yet."

"Look, the sooner we get what we need, the sooner this shelter can support itself. I'd like to see that happen yet, before I go."

Fletch pressed his eyes closed in pain. When he opened them again, he said, "I don't like to think about that, Marshall. I believe you'll recover or at least go into remission. And I don't mean to be disrespectful, but while we're on the subject, I need to let you know that I don't plan to do any more filming."

"Well I don't know what that is if it's not disrespect. I'm real disappointed in ya, boy."

"I sympathize with your cause. But I'm already in a bind with the farmers, with Vic, and possibly my grades. Client confidentiality is a big thing in a small town like Plain City."

"Ya can twist this around however ya want, but I was counting on ya. Ya let me down. It feels even worse because I'm laid up here."

"I'm sorry, sir. Real sorry about your illness."

"Sounds like it. Sounds more like that little girl has ya wrapped around her fingers."

Fletch felt hurt and confused. Hadn't Marshall urged him to pursue Lil?

"Let me remind ya that your dad depends on my support. I'll tell ya what I'm going to do. I'm going to let ya redeem yourself. I promised one of our big suppliers that we'd do some local veal boycotting. You head that up, and I'll forget about the video. Surely, that's not problematic? Not too much to ask."

Fletch tipped his chair back and stared at the ceiling in disbelief.

"Marcus will set you up."

After the call, Fletch stared numbly at the phone. It felt like he was losing Marshall in more ways than one. The man he had just talked to sounded like a complete stranger.

─ˢ

As soon as Lil stepped into Volo Italiano, Giovanni motioned her over. He was talking to the owner of the restaurant, an older Italian woman. Although Giovanni ran the place, Camila Battelli was the real heart of the establishment, often chatting with the restaurant's customers. Mrs. Battelli stepped forward in her tight pencil skirt and clingy sweater—both too young for a woman of her age and curves.

"Hello, Lillian." Her accent was thick.

"Mrs. Battelli."

"Call me Camila."

Lil glanced at Giovanni and saw the proud look in his eyes, like her father had looked when his children were old enough to sit on a tractor. "Thank you."

"Let's sit at one of the booths. My feet hurt today," the widow said.

Lil settled into the booth, thinking that the woman should give up wearing heels. When she glanced back at Camila, the older woman was curiously studying her. "So what do you think of my restaurant?"

"Why, I love working here."

"And we love having you here. Every day, Giovanni fills up my head with good things to say about your work."

Lil felt slightly embarrassed and very much aware that something good was happening, perhaps even a raise or a promotion. "I want to succeed."

"And you shall, little one. Giovanni has recommended you as his replacement."

"I wanted to tell you myself." Giovanni shrugged. "Eh. . .but Miss Camila, she has her own ideas."

"I don't understand," Lil fumbled, her heart beating so loudly she felt they must surely hear it. "Why are you leaving?"

"Because as you know, my wife she is pregnant. Eh. . . We can't stand to lose us another baby."

"But I don't understand."

"I am taking my sweetheart back to Italy to be happy with her family. She always wanted me to go into the family business." He shrugged. "Eh. . . I wanted to work here in America. But going home, this brings her much joy. I think it is what she needs to make a healthy baby. And even if it is not, well then, she will need her family, no?"

"But this is a great sacrifice for you," Lil argued, not wanting to lose her boss, even though it was an advancement for her own career. She couldn't understand how going to Italy could help the woman carry the baby to term, but then she knew this wasn't the time to argue the fact.

"Eh. . . It is what I want."

Lil swallowed and looked back at Camila. "But I am not the next in line. Surely you're not serious about me taking Giovanni's place?"

"The others, they do not work for the sheer joy of cooking. They work to feed their families and to pay their house bills."

"But I told you that I needed this job to buy a new car. That is why people work."

Giovanni argued. "You have the dream of a new car. Yes. But you also have the dream of becoming head chef. Eh? Don't deny it. You have the special flair. The potluck genes."

"Well. . ."

"The others, they do not realize they are working at the best restaurant"—Camila snapped her fingers to emphasize—"in Columbus. Do you want this job, or are you afraid, little one?"

Lil drew back her shoulders. "I am not afraid. Giovanni is right. I do covet his job. But I respect him, and I would never have wanted to take it from him."

"Oh, you are too kind," Giovanni exclaimed. "But I see right through you. And I see that you are just like me, no? And I"—he thumped his chest—"have made this place a success, no?" He looked at Camila, and she shrugged. "And you will, too. I give you my blessing."

Lil shot out of her seat and hugged Giovanni around the neck. "Thank you. I will not let you down." He patted her back, then gently drew her away. Lil turned to Camila. "You, either."

"Don't cry." Camila shook her head. "We have plans." She motioned at Giovanni. "Open up the restaurant while Lillian and I chat."

With sadness, Lil watched Giovanni leave them. She knew no matter how much he denied it that it had cost him a great deal to leave his position.

"This is for good business. You need a signature dish." Camila gestured with her ring-clad hands. "We will advertise it in all the right places. It will draw in the new customers and remind the old ones. They come to see what all the hoopla is about." She rubbed her hands together. "I've been thinking all this weekend. I think the perfect dish will be veal. It is something different, and we are known for special entrées. Do you have a specialty with the veal?"

—☙

At the doddy house, Lil bent over the meat grinder, pressing through a chunk of meat and tossing in premeasured amounts of onion and garlic. "Then Marshall asked Fletch to head up a veal boycott."

"Veal?" Megan's eyes widened from the other side of the counter. "Did you invite Fletch to dinner? I hope this isn't how you're going to tell him that veal is going to be your signature dish?"

"I'm not an idiot," Lil replied. "There, that's finished. Next, I. . ." She dumped the contents into a frying pan with sizzling butter and began to stir. "The recipe is up to me, and for Fletch's sake, I thought a veal-and-spinach ravioli was better than a dish where the plate was smothered in veal."

"But Lil, it's still veal. No matter how much you conceal it. It will still be listed on the menu. Fletch doesn't have a personal problem with veal, right?"

Lil turned away from the stove and faced Megan. "No, and I don't think he has any intention of heading up a boycott. But he didn't exactly come out and say that, and I didn't have the heart to ask him. This whole thing with Marshall is a touchy topic."

Megan's slanted brow gave away her displeasure.

"I didn't have any choice. Camila had already decided that the new menu item was going to be veal."

"I think you need to tell Fletch."

Lil blushed, feeling guilty that she hadn't already told him.

"Does he know about your promotion?"

Lil turned back to the skillet and dumped the ground meat mixture into a container that she put into the refrigerator to cool. "No, not yet." She meant to tell him. The last time they were together, he had already been upset over his conversation with Marshall. The timing hadn't been right. Especially since it was a veal dish. But she planned to tell him. She didn't want to keep secrets that strained their relationship. "Camila is nothing like Giovanni. She's pompous and stubborn, and frankly, she scares me a little bit."

"And do you want to work for somebody so scary?"

Turning away from the refrigerator, Lil shot back, "And do you want to work for somebody so charming and handsome?"

Megan colored. "Yes, I'm afraid I do. I like my job."

Lil softened her expression. "Then we're both doomed."

"But I know where I'm going to draw the line," Megan clarified.

"Oh?" Lil replied, pulling a bottle of dry white wine out from a bottom cupboard. "Where?"

But Megan's gaze was riveted on the wine bottle. "Where did you get that?" she gasped.

"From work. I have another bottle under there, too."

Megan shook her head, and her hair fell to the front of her shoulders, shimmering in the afternoon sunlight coming through the doddy house window. "I hope nobody from church sees it. That would not be good."

Lil smiled. "It's good for cooking, not drinking. I have to use it for this dish when I make it at work, but once I get the recipe perfected, I'll experiment with some substitutes for us."

"You must never let Katy find out you brought that into the doddy house. She'll probably disown us."

Lil grabbed the veal mixture out of the fridge and returned it to the skillet, adding the wine and beef broth. "You're right. It probably wasn't the best choice. Have you talked to her lately? I miss them."

"No, they just seem to be in their own little world. Happy just to be together."

Lil and Megan exchanged an envious glance. Then Lil repeated, "Where exactly are you going to draw that line you mentioned?"

"Don't worry. I won't end up like the last girl."

"What do you mean?"

Megan blushed. "Remember she was pregnant? I think they might have had an affair. I believe that's why his wife left him."

"What?" In shock, Lil placed her palms on the counter to think. Things like this weren't supposed to happen to them. Her first impulse was to demand that Megan quit her job. To protect her. But she knew that wouldn't work. She needed to remain calm. "Megan, you must be careful. Please don't go on any of those mission trips with him."

Megan's expression fell. "I hadn't thought about that. You know I wouldn't want to miss an opportunity."

Lil couldn't believe Megan could be so naive. "It might start out businesslike, but once he got you in another country, he might take advantage of the situation. Especially if you spent a lot of time together. Do you spend a lot of time together?"

Megan arched a blond brow. "What are you going to do if Fletch finds out about the veal before you have a chance to tell him? That's more likely to happen than your make-believe scenario about my boss. Who, by the way, has not done anything out of the way toward me."

"I'm going to tell him the truth the next time I see him. He's taking me to the Shekinah Festival on Saturday. Oh, no!" she cried, quickly pulling the skillet off the burner. "Ugh! Now I've got to start all over."

Megan sighed. "Will that be wasted?"

Lil turned away from her roommate, facing the stove and fighting back the tears that burned her eyes. "No. We can eat it. But I have to get it right before I introduce it at the restaurant."

"I'm sorry." Megan moved toward the sink. "Let me clean up for you, at least."

Lil nodded and went to the fridge for another chunk of veal. "I guess Fletch and I got started on the wrong foot from the beginning, but our relationship is moving forward. I just need my dad's approval. You know?" Lil turned the grinder's old-style crank. "Megan? Do you think any of my brothers would vandalize the shelter?"

"No. And I don't think you'd better ask them either."

"I don't intend to." And then Lil realized that Megan had just duped her, using her own tactics of changing the subject when she didn't want to talk about her boss.

CHAPTER 29

Fletch took Lil's hand and started through the parking-lot maze. "This is not your typical festival, is it?"

"The Shekinah Festival is huge. It's been going on for over thirty years. Some day I'm going to go up in one of those hot-air contraptions." Lil's eyes lit up with excitement as she turned her gaze toward the brilliant balloons, all in various stages of flight. "Look at the sky. It's full of giant teardrops turned upside down and made happy."

"What a nice thought." The observation was typical of Lil's general outlook on life. Overhead, the balloons floated in a parade of color, brightening the sky, just as Lil lit up a room and set the tone. She was a born helper who didn't hesitate to take risks if it could turn someone's teardrops upside down and make them happy, too.

"Megan went to the concert last night, held in the big tent over there." She pointed. "It featured a hometown boy who made it big—is actually performing with the big names in the Christian music industry."

As they made their way toward the activity, she took him on a shortcut across the tree-clad lawns. A cluster of teenage girls in plain dress and coverings approached, coming from the other direction. One waved.

"Hi, Anna." Lil waved back. After the greeting, the girls lowered their gazes until they were past. "Anna's mom heads up the quilt part of the auction."

"They seemed shy."

"Because of you. Probably your red shoes," she teased. "Conservative girls don't mix with the world much until they get a job. So seeing us together probably made them feel uneasy. They don't know how to act around a guy like you."

Lil's comment hurt. *Guy like you?* It brought a general concern to his mind. "Do the people at your church know we're dating?"

Lil nodded.

"And is this already causing a problem for you?"

"It's a small community. After today, it will be confirmed. My family is under a microscope right now, anyway. My mom went to church for the first time in months. After the sermon, she stood up and asked for the congregation's forgiveness for not attending church and for disvaluing God's gift of life."

Fletch tried to hide his surprise because he could tell that it was a painful admission for Lil. "She's doing better, then?"

"Yes. She even joined the hostess committee again. And something special happened. Ever since she took the overdose, her ears had been ringing. It bothered her a lot and reminded her of her mistake. She told me that when she confessed on Sunday, her ears quit ringing. She believes it is an affirmation that God forgave her."

"That's amazing." He knew that God was at work in all their lives, but that they needed to settle their church issue soon, before it drove a wedge between Lil and her congregation. "I have an idea. Why don't you come to church with me tomorrow? The next Sunday, I'll go to your church. We can take turns, switching back and forth. It might help us decide where we'll go when. . .you know, help us make some choices."

"And what if my dad and brothers run you off the church property?"

"If we tell them that we're giving both churches an equal chance, won't they want to welcome us, convince us to come to their church?"

"Well, they would if they weren't still mad at you."

"And what kind of forgiveness is that? Maybe we need to help them along. And I have an idea how to do that." He'd been tossing the idea around in his mind, but he didn't want to tell Lil more about it now. He didn't want her worrying that his plan would backfire.

⸺ↄ

"What's your idea?" Lil asked.

Fletch grinned. "It's a surprise."

What kind of surprise would help her family forgive him? Surely he wasn't thinking of proposing, of forcing them to make the choice to accept him or reject him? "Please, tell me what you're up to."

He touched the tip of her nose. "Nosy. My nose smells food. Come, on."

They came to a line of booths selling many tempting delights: apple dumplings, popcorn, funnel cakes, and ice cream. But Lil's senses were only partly engaged, for she couldn't get past Fletch's near slip of the tongue. When he had brought up the question of which church they would attend, he'd almost said *after we get married*. She was sure of it. It still amazed her that Fletch had fallen in love with her—plain Lillian Mae Landis. That he wanted to take her to his church.

"About going to your church. Maybe not tomorrow. But I'll think about your suggestion."

"All right."

She saw his expression sadden and quickly said, "You have to try the homemade ice cream. Roger Headings and his wife, Crystal, always have a booth at local events. And before we leave, you should buy some trail bologna and cheese to take back to your apartment." He chose chocolate, and she ate strawberry.

Since the festival was a school fund-raiser, it featured lots of events for the children, from a petting zoo to a pony ride. "The pedal event is hilarious," Lil told Fletch. "I believe it's getting ready to start."

They found a seat and watched some adults trying to get the little ones lined up and ready to go. It provided the interval she needed to tell him about her promotion and her new signature dish. She had made a vow with herself that she would tell him sometime during the festival. She wanted to get it over with and off her mind so that she could enjoy the rest of the day.

"Fletch? Something happened at work."

He chuckled at a little boy who got out of his car and sat on the ground. Then he turned to give her his full attention. "What?"

"I got a promotion. A big promotion."

"Why that's great."

"To head chef."

"What?" Fletch jumped to his feet. He grabbed her up and hugged her. "That's wonderful! I can't believe it. You just started working there."

She smiled up at him. "I know. Giovanni is moving back to Italy, and he recommended me to the restaurant's owner."

"Sit down!" Somebody from behind them yelled. "The race is starting."

"Not until she does the garbanzo dance!" Fletch yelled back.

Lil laughed, did one little shimmy, then promptly seated herself, pulling Fletch down by the sleeve. He turned and stared at her, still beaming at her accomplishment.

"I'm glad you understand how important this is to me."

"I'm proud of you. I'm speechless."

"Thanks."

Applause sounded as the event began. "Cute," Fletch said. The youngsters peddled every way but straight ahead. He glanced over at Lil. "But I can't believe you didn't call me right away with the big news."

"I had some things to think through first." And it seemed she still did. She had planned to tell him about the veal dish, but now she wasn't so sure. Things were going so great between them. He had destroyed the video for her and her family. And he had a surprise in store for her. Something that would help her family forgive him. Could she ask him not to boycott veal, too? When he gave her another side hug, she knew she couldn't. There would have to be another way. She would try to change her boss's mind instead.

───⟡───

In spite of the fact that Plain City was in the middle of a dry spell, harvest was starting earlier than usual. It stirred up clouds of dust in the corn and soybean fields on either side of the road so that Fletch kept his windows closed. Buddy panted against the glass, seeming to know where they were headed. It was Fletch's night to volunteer at the shelter.

He pulled into the drive, and once he'd parked, he released Buddy for some exercise. He knew the basset's routine of sniffing along the fence row and the strip of bushes on the east side of the drive. It ended by whining or howling at the front door of the farmhouse until Ashley fussed over him. He was smitten with all females.

A sudden noise similar to a creaking branch sent Fletch glancing up into a nearby pine. Curious, he brought his gaze down and extended it out toward the barn. The sun's glare was blinding so he gave his cap a tug to shade his vision. He heard another noise and saw two elongated shadows zip around the far corner of the barn.

Fletch hastened his steps until he broke into a run, chasing after the shadows. When he came around the barn, he saw two men preparing to hurdle the fence to the neighboring pasture. One of them was carrying a small animal.

His heart somersaulted. "Stop!" Not even wanting to think about their intentions for the animal, he sped after the thieves. They had stopped by the fence when one of them got his shirt caught. But by the time Fletch reached the fence, they had both taken off again. The bleating animal was one of the shelter's lambs. Fletch thought he could outrun them if his lungs didn't cave in first.

He hurdled the fence. "Stop!"

The men kept running.

Fletch chased after them. Panting hard, he got within several yards and decided to go after the guy with the lamb. He dove for his legs. The runner stumbled, smacked the ground, and rolled. Meanwhile, the lamb jumped clear. Fletch easily pinned down the intruder.

The guy he'd tackled was only a kid, about high school age. Fletch had the boy's arm pinned, and his knee was on the small of the boy's back. "What's your name?"

The boy grunted. "You're hurting me."

About that time, Marcus ran up to them. Probably given the bodybuilder's enormous physique, the lad was too frightened to try to escape, and he even blurted out his name. But when Fletch looked out over the pasture, he saw the accomplice had gotten away.

The police arrived soon after that. They had picked up the other boy farther down the road. When they saw him dash behind a tree, they hauled him in on suspicion. Both boys were handcuffed and placed in the back of the police car while the officers took Fletch's statement.

When they questioned Marcus about the shelter, Fletch told the officers he needed to get the lamb back to safety and to examine the other animals.

"We'll drive up to the barn before we go to get your report on the other animals."

At the barn, Fletch was relieved to learn that all the animals were unharmed, including Cottonball. He must have startled the intruders before they did damage to the barn again.

Later Marcus was able to explain to Fletch that the vandals were farm boys acting on dares. They claimed they'd gotten the idea listening to their dads speak negatively about the shelter. "Thanks, man, for stopping them."

"No problem, but you showed up at just the right moment. I was still trying to figure out how to call you and keep my hold on the kid."

"Ashley had gone to the door to let Buddy in and saw ya take off around the barn like your pants were on fire. She alerted me. I was pretty much right behind ya, only I couldn't keep up with ya."

Fletch shook his head. "I still have a stitch in my side. I can't remember when I ran that fast. I knew I could catch them as long as I didn't collapse first."

Marcus chuckled. "I owe ya. Thanks for your help, man."

"No problem." Fletch could hardly believe that Marcus thought he owed him, but it made a good opportunity to give him back the camera. He took it from his pocket, hoping he hadn't broken it in the scuffle. After a quick examination, it seemed fine. "I guess your dad told you I deleted that film?"

Marcus accepted the camera with a sigh. "Yeah. He was pretty upset about it. But man, with this arrest, what those boys did, we could get some free publicity. I think I'm going to call the newspaper."

"What if it's not good publicity?"

"They admitted they were the ones who vandalized us before. They injured a horse and stole a lamb. How can that be bad publicity for us? Even if it is, it will still promote awareness." Marcus ran a hand over the top of his shaved head.

"I'm glad the horse is recovering."

"I know. Funny how those kids confessed to everything. I wonder if more kids were involved? The ones who dared them?"

"I suppose the officers will get the entire story out of them."

"Who knows? There might have been other incidents."

"That's true."

Marcus looked at the camera he held. "I guess Dad gave you an ultimatum?"

"The veal boycotting? I won't be doing that either."

"Oh man. Ya sure ya can't humor him?"

Hard as it was to see Marcus's pain, Fletch held firm. "Sorry. Not this time. How's his chemo going?"

"We don't know yet. But at least he's willing to give it a try."

Fletch nodded. "I'm praying for remission."

"Thanks."

"Well, I'm done here. Cottonball's fine. But if this had happened a few weeks earlier, or if they'd taken Flannel, it would have been traumatic, probably life threatening. Anyway, I'm finished with my rounds. Guess I'll go find Buddy and be on my way."

On the drive home, Fletch found it hard to release his anger at the kids' disregard of animal life. He didn't know what their intentions had been with the lamb, but he knew if they'd swiped or hurt Buddy, he'd have had a hard time getting over it.

$\sim$

The next morning at the clinic, Vic greeted Fletch with the *Plain City Advocate*. "Looks like you had some action last night. You made the local news."

"I'll bet it's going to be in the *Columbus Dispatch*, too."

"I don't like your name being listed, being involved with the shelter."

Fletch quickly scanned the article to see what had been written about him:

> *Fletch Stauffer is a veterinary student interning under Vic's Veterinary Clinic. The Plain City Farm Shelter operates mostly with volunteer help, and Stauffer is one of many who donate their time to help abused animals.*

Fletch groaned and continued reading:

> *He was getting ready to do a routine check when he saw two shadows sneaking around the barn.*

"I can't believe you gave them all that information. My name!"

Fletch slapped the paper back down on the waiting room coffee table. "I didn't. Marcus must have."

"Well, let's hope this doesn't cause us to lose any clients."

"You would have done the same thing, if it had been you. The kids were stealing an animal."

"I know. I know. I'll be glad when we don't have to go out there anymore." Vic picked up the newspaper and threw it in the trash. "Don't want anybody seeing that."

But that evening when Fletch had returned to his apartment, he snapped open the newspaper that he had retrieved from the trash on his way out of the clinic. He read the article more thoroughly, considering all the implications for himself, Vic, and the shelter. As his mind worked through the matter, he found himself flipping through the rest of the newspaper.

In the restaurant section, where he usually found some fast-food coupons, something caught his attention. He pulled the paper closer, studying it carefully. Volo Italiano? That was Lil's restaurant. The article was about her! His face broke into a beaming smile. She was making her dream come true. He was so proud of her. So glad he'd dug the paper out of the trash. He continued reading:

Volo Italiano is proud to announce its new chef, Lillian Landis. She brings delicious new entrées to the menu. Look for her signature dish, Lily's Veal Ravioli. The first twenty-five customers who order her special entrée will be given a 10 percent discount.

The paper slipped from his hand, floated to the floor, and hit Buddy on the head. The dog jumped back, startled.

"Sorry, Buddy. It's just that I can't believe she didn't tell me." Fletch shook his head, remembering that she hadn't even told him about the promotion when it first happened. Why would she withhold such great news?

He thought back to their discussion at the Shekinah Festival. She had seemed nervous, but he had taken it as humility over her promotion. He thought she was celebrating, but was she really just relieved that he was happy for her. . .because. . .her signature dish was veal, and she was afraid to tell him?

If she was afraid to tell him, then she thought he was going to boycott veal. She didn't trust him, thought he was still allowing Marshall to call the shots. Not only that, what kind of statement was she trying to make with her signature veal dish? Surely she could have made spinach ravioli her dish. Why the veal? This was disturbing news.

CHAPTER 30

Buddy's tail vigorously thumped the wood flooring of the doddy house porch as Fletch waited for Lil to answer her doorbell. When the door cracked open, it was secured by a safety chain that Jake had added when Katy and Lil first moved into the doddy house.

"Fletch! Hi!"

He waited as she rattled the latch free. Buddy rushed in before Fletch could grab him.

"Uh-oh!"

"Buddy!" Fletch called sternly, embarrassed at the dog's poor manners. The basset obediently returned and gazed up at him.

"Sorry about that. I was going to ask if we could come in first. . . . I . . ."

"It's fine. Buddy just surprised me. He won't hurt Slinky?"

"That's why I brought him. I thought we should introduce them while Slinky's still a kitten. Buddy will accept Slinky because this is not his territory, but if we wait too long, Slinky might not allow a dog in his domain." He gave her a grin. "And I'd hate to think a mere kitten was keeping us apart."

Lil nodded skeptically. "Come in. Slinky's in his bed."

Fletch followed Lil into the living room, where she gently lifted up the kitten into her arms. He was pleased to see the bond that had formed between them. "Where's Megan?"

"At her folks. She misses them. Goes home pretty often."

"That must make it lonely for you."

"Yes. But it's a small sacrifice. I'm relieved to have my own place." She looked at the kitten. "How do we do this?"

"Why don't you pet Buddy and show your acceptance of the dog. Try to keep Slinky out of Buddy's space, or he'll poke his nose up against him and provoke the kitten to scratch. I'll help by holding Buddy's collar."

Lil gave a nervous nod, then knelt. With one hand, she kept Slinky in her lap. The other she extended toward Buddy. He sniffed her hand and leaned into her, his tail wagging. "Good, doggie. You're so cute. I've missed you."

Meanwhile, Slinky squirmed, and Lil wasn't able to restrain the kitten.

Slinky pounced off Lil's lap, gave Buddy's face a swat, and sprang to the floor. Buddy backed up, startled but not aggressive. He placed his face on his front paws, eyeing Slinky from his side vision, while pretending to ignore the kitten.

Lil softly giggled.

"We should probably just let them go. If Buddy gets tired of Slinky, he'll growl, and then we can separate them for a while."

The kitten pounced, swatted the dog, and retreated. Buddy squirmed.

By now both Fletch and Lil had lowered themselves to the oval braided carpet. Fletch moved to get comfortable, resting his arm on a sofa cushion. "How's your job going?" he asked, giving her the opportunity to be open about her veal dish.

"First I have to tell you the good news. Matt's hoop barns are being delivered on Friday. He's so excited. They already poured the cement pads."

"That is great news." Things remained strained between them, but Fletch had talked to Matt at church. At that time, he hadn't had a delivery date yet. This information was vital to the plan he had mentioned to

Lil at the Shekinah Festival. With it, he hoped to win back her family's acceptance and approval.

She reached down to pet the kitten, which had pounced back into her lap. "Matt still needs to procure a contract with an integrator company, but he claims that will be easier done, now that he's getting the barns. He said the procedures are almost like starting up a new farm. And of course he still needs to get the hogs healthy again."

"Yes. He needs to practice isolation before the disease spreads, and the sooner the better," Fletch agreed. "I'm glad things are working out for your family. How's your mom?"

"She's doing so much better." He listened as Lil told him about their recent conversation. She seemed excited that her parents were communicating again. It made him wonder why Lil was not being open with him. Did she want to follow in her parents' footsteps?

His parents had always shared a special intimacy. He wanted that kind of relationship with Lil. When it came to marriage, he wouldn't settle for anything less. He'd been disappointed when Lil turned down his idea of visiting each other's churches. To him, it felt like she wasn't ready to commit to their relationship. As his dad had mentioned, if they weren't moving forward, they were moving backward.

"Lil, how's work? How's the new position going for you?"

Her eyes darted nervously to the animals, avoiding eye contact with him. "It's hard. Real hard."

"Why is that?"

She met his gaze. "Because I have to make all the decisions. Not only that, but we've made some menu changes, and the cooks aren't getting it right. I'm not comfortable critiquing them, but if we don't get it right, Camila will hold me responsible. It's intimidating to be in charge of a kitchen full of outsiders with more seniority. I'm not sure I like being the boss."

"They wouldn't have chosen you for the position if they didn't respect you. Giovanni and Camila are confident you are the best qualified. Instead of trying to please the other cooks or even your boss, you need to focus on the food. You're good at that. They will follow your lead."

"I suppose."

Buddy crowded Fletch, trying to avoid the playful kitten. Absently, he massaged Buddy under the muzzle. "It will get easier. Every job has its less-enjoyable aspects. Tell me about the new items on the menu."

"Oh, look." The kitten had suddenly quit playing and curled up next to Buddy's side. "Isn't that cute? I think they're going to get along fine."

"So we can be one big happy family, right?" He pointed at her and back at himself a few times, hoping to coax a smile out of her, hoping she wanted their relationship to turn into something permanent as much as he did.

"I hope so."

What was with this cautious, hesitant attitude? Normally Lil was out-front with everything. This was a facet of her personality that had drawn him to her. He wondered if it was her means of pulling away from him. Figuring one of them needed to be direct, he finally admitted, "I read the newspaper article about your signature dish."

Her eyes widened, and her face paled. "I'm sorry. I should have told you."

He waited for her to explain, but she didn't. "Why couldn't you talk to me about this?"

Her eyes held remorse. "I thought it would make things more complicated between us."

"Can you tell me why you chose a veal dish?"

"It was Camila's idea. I was going to get her to change it."

"Change it, because?"

Her voice grew exasperated. "Because Marshall asked you to boycott veal."

"You think I'm Marshall's puppet?"

"You didn't tell me what your intentions were. And now that Marshall has cancer. . ." Lil shrugged. "You'd already destroyed the video. I didn't want to put more pressure on you."

Her lack of confidence disappointed him.

Buddy yipped, and the kitten jumped up, frightened. Lil scooped it up and cuddled it. "Shh. Shh."

Fletch hardly understood the disappointment and anger rising up to overwhelm him. Sure he'd made a mistake. But it was heartbreaking that nobody saw his good intentions and acknowledged the sacrifices he was willing to make. He was tired of shouldering the blame for everything, being the one who had to apologize over and over again. Sorry she didn't trust him.

Lil had been retreating from his advances from the beginning. He was tired of it. "Look, Lil. I feel as though I'm the only one trying to make us happen. You don't trust me. You throw up your guard at every turn, as if I'm making you choose between your family and me. Your job and me. It's not like that. I'm all about winning them back. I won't quit until that happens. I'm about making you happy. But you're constantly pushing me away."

She pressed her lips into a tight line and made no argument to convince him otherwise. Fletch stood up. "I've got a lot going on in my life, too. I'm tired of being the only one who cares here. And tired of being the community scapegoat."

Lil scrambled to her feet. "But I do care. It's just that. . .things are confusing-crazy right now."

Fletch gentled his tone. "You're judging everything from the outside. Blaming the farm, your family, and even your church for your insecurities. Just be who you are. Either there's a place for me on the inside, or there isn't."

Lil angrily brushed cat hair from her skirt. "I can't believe you are preaching to me."

"Me either. I didn't come to do that. I better go. Come on, Buddy." Fletch made for the door, and Buddy slinked after him as if he knew they were both in trouble. All the way to the door, Fletch longed for her to beg him to stay, to tell him that she wanted him. But she didn't.

⌒৩

Lil blotted her eyes with a tissue, "Oh, Megan, I'm so glad you're home."

Megan hurried to the couch. "What's happened? What's wrong? Is it your mom?"

"No. Fletch and I got in a huge argument."

Moving onto the couch next to her, Megan asked with concern, "About the veal?"

"Yes, and don't say you told me so. He saw our ad in the newspaper. He was angry that I hid it from him. Angry I didn't trust him." Lil sniffed. "He said he's tired of being the only one trying to make our relationship work. . .that I'm constantly pushing him away."

"Oh, wow."

"And he's right. He's done all the pursuing." She sniffed. "All I do is throw up red flags." She buried her face in the tissue.

Megan patted her back. "I'm sorry."

"I've never seen him so mad. When he left, he seemed bitter and hurt. I think he's giving up on us. I'm nothing but a thorn in his side, with my family and. . .everything else."

"Maybe this is for the best."

"What!" Lil blinked at Megan. "How can you say that?"

"Well, now you know what his limits are. I mean, it's time you decided if you want him or not. If you're willing to give it your all. If you love him."

"Of course I want him! Where have you been?"

Megan nodded with sympathy. "You're right. He has made all the moves. Now he needs encouragement from you. You'll have to pursue him."

"You're right. I haven't done my part. Our relationship seemed hopeless, and I was waiting for him to do all the changing, make everything right." Lil hiccupped.

"Let me make you some tea. If you're sure you want him, then I'll help you figure out how to win him back."

Lil gave a weak smile, clasping Slinky close. "Thanks." But the kitten squirmed and sprang to the floor, strutting off after Megan.

—☙—

In spite of their argument, Fletch was willing to give it one last try before he gave up on Lil. Winning back her family was paramount in winning her back. If his final plan failed, then he would concede and quit pursuing her and her family.

When Vic heard about Fletch's plan, he thought it was a great idea and offered to help him carry it through. So on the morning that the hoop barn was going up, they drove to the farm well before daylight. The farmers would be early at their chores, intent to make a long day of it. When they arrived, Vic's red Dodge pickup was conspicuous even in the dark, and Matt was the first one out of the barn.

In a nervous leap, Fletch jumped out of the cab.

"What's going on?" Matt asked.

"We know this is a big day for you. We came to help." He gestured to include Vic, who had now joined them.

Matt gave a crooked grin. "The thought's nice, but don't know how it will get received by the others."

Fletch clasped Matt's shoulder. "Please. Just put me to work."

About that time, Will came out of the barn. He strode to them and stopped beside Matt. "Hi, Vic. I thought I told you I didn't want *him* on my property."

"He's not here on my behalf. He's here on his own."

"Mr. Landis, I came to help you put up your hoop barns."

Fletch saw surprise flit across the older man's features, but he quickly hardened his expression. "Well, we don't need your kind of help."

Will's rejection was expected. In fact, Fletch had rehearsed his argument beforehand. "That may be true. I don't mean any disrespect, but I'm here to help, and that's that. If you throw me off your property, I'll crawl back on bloody nubs if I have to, because I *am* helping you today. Now it's going to be a long day, and the way I see it, you don't need to be wasting your time and energy arguing."

Will grunted, turned away, and stalked back into the barn. Fletch hurried after him, with Matt and Vic close at his heels. Inside, it was apparent that Hank and Stephen had gotten a quick rundown of the situation.

Hank looked angry. "Now you see here, Stauffer. We don't want your help."

"I understand. But I'm staying. I need to help."

Stephen turned to his brothers. "What are we going to do?"

"Why can't he help?" Matt heaved a feed bag over his shoulder. "We all know we could use the extra hands. Vic is volunteering, too. It's rude not to accept some neighborly help."

Fletch chewed the side of his cheek, disliking but knowing the best way to proceed with the stubborn bunch was to grovel again and make it real good this time. "It was despicable of me to take pictures of your sick animals. I'm not going to give you any excuses for it." By now they knew the reason. "I'm not naturally a backstabbing jerk. Usually, I'm honest and dependable. What I did was wrong. I'm sorry for betraying your trust and Vic's."

Vic quickly added, "I have to vouch for his good character. He's proved himself since the incident. He really wants to make amends. He needs to help you."

"That's because he wants to date Lil," Hank said distastefully.

"I like your sister, but that's not why I'm here. If I had misrepresented myself to any other farmer and had the opportunity to make amends, I would. It's the Christian thing to do."

Will studied Fletch. "I believe him. Sometimes, we just need to forgive." He offered Fletch a handshake.

Fletch gripped Will's hand as if it was his only lifeline. Fletch figured that whatever was happening between the farmer and his wife must have softened the older man's heart. Fletch determined not to disappoint him but to stick with the work until the last hour or until he was dead, whichever came first.

"He can stay," Hank relented. "But he's not fooling me."

Fletch gave Hank a smile. "Thanks for the chance." But Hank didn't respond. Stephen turned his back and moved to the watering trough. Fletch hadn't expected a homecoming like the one for the prodigal son. He was heartened enough that Hank permitted him to stay.

"While we finish choring, you can go haul a stack of lumber to the barn sites. I'll show you where." Matt led them out of the barn and shined a flashlight in the direction of two new cement pads that would go at either end of the two new barns. The lumber company had dumped the lumber just off the circle drive.

Once Matt had left them and returned to the barn, Fletch grabbed two two-by-fours and threw them over his shoulder. Vic only took one because he had the flashlight and he wasn't trying to impress anybody or earn anybody's forgiveness. By daybreak, the lumber was laid out in smaller stacks in two large, rectangular areas where the barns would be erected.

Over the years of his practice, the veterinarian had acquired a complete set of tools. Taking care of livestock got him into all kinds of situations. Fletch had borrowed a tool belt and a hammer, even though he didn't know anything about carpentry. The first order of business was installing treated posts and tongue and groove to make a four-foot exterior bearing wall.

Once Jake arrived, Fletch felt like he had another ally. Jake schooled him so that he was soon swinging his hammer along with the others, who mostly ignored him. It grated his pride when Hank affirmed the vet and didn't acknowledge Fletch's work.

By nine o'clock, a small crane arrived, and the steel tubular arches were secured to the ground posts and sidewalls. After that, the men climbed up to secure the polypropylene tarps. Fletch wasn't much for heights, so instead of following Jake, he stayed below and did groundwork.

Around noon, Fletch had just raised his arm to swing the hammer, when Lil walked up behind him.

"Hi, Fletch."

His reaction was a moment of hesitation, for he wanted to apologize to her yet needed to disregard her so that Hank didn't throw him off the farm. The second of hesitation broke his concentration and brought the hammer down hard on his thumb.

"Ouch!" He jumped back, tossing the hammer to the ground. He cradled his injured hand with all thoughts of Lil driven out by the explosion of pain. The first thing he focused on beyond the pain was a snicker. He looked over to see Hank's amusement. The second thing he heard was Lil calling everyone in to lunch. He didn't look at her. He couldn't.

Up at the house, several long tables were set up outside. Katy and the Landis women served huge platters of ham, potato salad, and baked beans. Fletch waited in line and washed up at an outdoor faucet, his thumb throbbing in waves of pain. He filled a plate and sat between Matt and Jake.

It was only the second meal Fletch had shared with the Landis family. He noticed with as much amusement as he could muster that Stephen, who sat on the other side of Matt, checked the lid of his saltshaker before using it.

Fletch rose to fill his glass from the water jug and returned to find his chair was missing. How did Matt have the energy to pull jokes? Fletch was tired, thirsty, and hungry, and his thumb felt as though it had an electrical current pulsating through it. It was enough to make a man cranky. And he was, but he tamped down his temper, reminding himself that he had a mission to perform.

With a great deal of self-control, he set his glass down by his plate. He slanted a warning brow at Matt and spied his chair folded up against a tree where several of the sisters-in-law had congregated.

He strode after the chair and tipped his cap to the girls, feeling embarrassed as their giggles followed him back to the table. He unfolded the chair and sat, and looked cautiously at his food to make sure everything was still in order. It seemed to be. He took a swig of his water. Beside him Matt began talking to Stephen. Fletch relaxed.

His stomach growled, and he brought the thick sandwich of ham and swiss cheese to his watering mouth and bit down into the delicious *hot, hot, hot, and more hot.* He jumped up. His chair crashed to the ground. Fletch wheeled from the table and spit. Came back for his water and washed down the fire.

Meanwhile Matt cracked up at his expense. In fact, all the Landis men seemed tickled pink. Fletch glared at Matt. It was obvious now that Hank wasn't the only unforgiving brother. He felt like jerking the young farmer out of his chair by the neck of his "Hog Heaven" T-shirt. But that's what they were all hoping to see, expecting. Provoking.

Just then Lil stepped in between Matt and Stephen with a water pitcher. She reached out and gave Matt's hat a push. He grabbed it before it fell into his food. Fletch didn't need Lil fighting his battle. He rose and went to whisper in Rose's ear. She gave a smiling nod and soon returned with a pitcher of his own water. Fletch carried it back to his seat.

The brothers snickered.

Fletch snapped his chair open and seated himself. Then he began the slow and painful process of finishing every bite of his Tabasco-seasoned sandwich, rinsing every couple of bites with another glass of water.

"At least you won't get dehydrated," Matt joked. His brothers laughed, but Will seemed to look at him with a new respect.

Once the attention was off him, he glanced toward the women again. Lil gave him a smile, then quickly diverted her gaze to talk to Katy. Well, Rome wasn't built in a day.

But to Fletch, it felt like it. Once they got the barn erected, there was the work of hauling bedding to the new structures. Fletch got the worst jobs, and by late afternoon it wasn't only his thumb that throbbed, but every muscle ached and groaned for relief.

Vic left around midafternoon, taking Fletch's only mode of transportation. But Fletch didn't want the brothers to see him as a quitter, so he remained behind. He figured he could hitch a ride with Matt after the evening choring. Fletch didn't know if he would be able to raise himself out of bed the next day, but he didn't regret his decision to show the Landis men he was sorry for his mistake.

It was an experience like none other to watch the barn go up and to feel the satisfaction of knowing that the hoop barn had been his idea. Whether Matt ever realized it or not, they had done the right thing. The hoop barns would help the Landis family fight their way out of debt, if that was possible. And now Fletch's conscience was clear.

He had given them the hoop barn idea and helped them erect the barns. He had erased the video so nobody had received false information about their farm or farming methods. He had given them hours of free veterinary service before they kicked him off the farm. And he had permitted them to belittle him, even make him the object of their jokes.

He'd done his part, and now it was up to the Landis family to accept or reject him. He didn't know Hank and Stephen that well, but he liked Matt, and he respected Will. Because he'd been praying for Rose, he already felt a bond there.

As for Lil, well, he loved her of course, but he didn't know if that was enough. He didn't know if she would use their recent argument as a chance to run in the other direction, or if she would be willing to try again. Either way, he wanted her family to succeed. He was more than happy he had done what he could do make that happen.

The men didn't quit to eat supper until after dark. Chores still waited. Fletch washed up, planning to eat another meal with them and help chore. But Matt stuck his head into the kitchen and asked his mom to make him and Fletch a sandwich for the road.

"I'll take you home now. We can eat on the way."

Fletch, who hadn't even asked him for a ride yet, started to protest. "Are you sure? I'm prepared to stay." He dried his hands on the towel and turned to find Hank staring at him.

"You've done your share," the older, darker son replied. "You don't have to stay till the last chore is done and crawl yourself home on bloody nubs." A smile formed on the corner of Hank's mouth. "We're not that callous."

Even though it was what Fletch had hoped for, now that Hank was actually softening toward him, it felt nothing short of miraculous.

"You didn't have to come today. It took guts to face us like you did and stick with us all day. You and I are good now. Thanks. Your help was appreciated."

"That. . .means a lot to me." Fletch offered his hand, and Hank clasped it. Stephen followed suit.

Will folded the hand towel. "We shouldn't have doubted you. You're welcome here anytime."

Fletch couldn't help but notice that nothing was mentioned about Lil, and she had disappeared. But later he guessed she must have sneaked out the front door, because when he reached Matt's truck, she was waiting for them.

"I need to talk to you."

Matt sighed. "I've got to get back and do chores." Her brother strode around to the other side of the truck and got inside. He turned on the truck and its headlights.

Her lip trembled in the dim light, and Fletch wondered if she was going to break up with him.

"I just wanted to say that. . .well, everything you said the other night was true. I'm sorry. . . ."

For the life of him, exhausted as he was and staring into her distressed eyes, Fletch couldn't remember a thing he had told her. Worse, he couldn't tell if she was trying to break up or trying to apologize.

He knew Matt was antsy inside the truck. "Could you give me a hint? Are you trying to break up here or are you trying to make up?"

"Don't make it so hard. I'm apologizing."

"Then I'm accepting. But I'm too tired to make much sense tonight."

"I know. I'd better go before I'm missed."

Fletch squeezed her hand, then flinched from the pain.

"Thanks for helping my family."

He watched her hurry back toward the house, climbing wearily into the cab.

Matt shook his head. "You just don't know when to quit, do you?"

"It would seem so."

CHAPTER 31

Fletch threw his gloves in the trash, then strode into the clinic's waiting room to call in the next client. "Who's next?"

A couple stood, but he didn't see any pet, and he quickly glanced up, expecting to hear a request for a prescription.

Frank Stauffer grinned at him, at eye level, now. He was still larger than Fletch, broader across the shoulders, and not quite as slim at the waist. The fiftyish eyes sparkled with amusement, but he didn't say anything or move a muscle to advance. Fletch's mother clutched her husband's arm. She was still blond and trim and modestly dressed. Her lips trembled. Tears rolled down her cheeks.

"Mom!" Fletch hurried forward and scooped her into his embrace. She cried and repeated his name over and over. Then she cupped his face with her hands and looked up at him. "You look wonderful. So handsome and tall like your father. How I've missed you."

Fletch struggled to keep his composure. Next, he turned toward his father, instinctively straightening, allowing the other man to examine him. But Frank gripped him hard in the upper arms, and pain from his sore muscles shot through his body. He swallowed. And his dad swept him into a lung-constricting, bear hug.

They separated, and Fletch gasped, "What a surprise." He stared at them with disbelief. He'd never dreamed that they would really come to see him.

"Take these people to lunch or something. You are making a spectacle." Vic's teasing voice came down the hallway.

Fletch turned. "You sure? Two days off in a row?"

"Yes. It's not every day that a man's parents come all the way from Africa to visit. Take the rest of the day off."

Grateful, Fletch made the introductions and even included the farmer with the goat that had gotten its head stuck in the fence, who now stood next to Vic. "Thanks again."

Vic took the farmer and his goat into one of the back rooms, and Fletch turned back to his parents.

"It's too early for lunch. Would you like to go to my apartment?"

"Yes," his mother replied. "This is a very nice clinic. Your boss seems nice, too."

"Vic? We get along now," Fletch replied. "But that's a long story."

"We'll have time," his dad replied.

"Look, I forgot about the time change. Maybe you are hungry? Did you just arrive?"

"Let's pick up some pop at a drive-through and then go to your place," Frank suggested. "I can't get enough pop."

"Sure. How did you get here?"

"Taxi," his mother said. "The driver was so nice."

Fletch had forgotten that about his mom. To her, everybody was so nice. Truth was, everybody loved her, too.

Frank got in the front passenger seat, and Fletch, still reeling from the shock, moved as if he walked inside his own dream. He opened the back door of the Focus for his mom and hurried round to the driver's side.

He pulled into the street and looked in his rearview mirror. "There's a little place called the Eskimo Queen. I can get you some pop there."

"Oh, I'd like a cone, too," Mom piped up.

A pang from some long-forgotten memories shot through him. He'd forgotten what it was like to be out of the country for so long and then wanting to make up for all their deprivations.

Dad thumped the dashboard. "This baby sure has held up."

"Yes. And hopefully it will for a while longer. Till I graduate and get a job."

"Doesn't the vet pay you, dear?"

"Just enough to cover the basics, Mom."

"All that's needed," Dad added. "The Lord supplies."

His dad firmly believed that, which was probably why he hadn't flinched when finding out he could lose Marshall's support. They pulled into the fast-food place, and Fletch picked up the items that would satisfy his parents' cravings, refusing his dad's offer to pay.

"This is wonderful. Thanks, honey," his mom purred from the backseat. "But you didn't get anything, Fletch."

"I'm good." They drove in silence for several moments until he realized that in all the excitement, he'd forgotten Buddy. "I need to backtrack. I forgot my dog. I need to get him because sometimes Vic has to leave in a hurry."

"Oh, you have a dog? That's fine. We like looking around."

"I don't live far, anyways."

Once he'd gotten Buddy, he cracked open the back door. "You want him, Mom, or should I put him in the front with Dad?"

"I'll take him," she replied.

Buddy jumped up on the floorboards. As Fletch had suspected, the basset took to Mom like he did all females, and she seemed to like him, too, but moments later, he heard her admonish Buddy to keep away from her ice-cream cone. His heart ached to think that his parents had swept into his life to touch his heart and flirt with his emotions only to leave him again. For regardless of what his dad had said about quitting mission work, Fletch wouldn't allow himself to believe they would stay long. Africa was their life. He was sure they would never leave it.

Inside his apartment, he motioned for them to sit, at the same time sweeping up a pair of underwear, socks, and a T-shirt and tossing them into a clothesbasket in his closet. "Sorry about that."

"Bachelors." His mom smiled. "Do you have any girlfriends?"

Fletch sat on the edge of his bed, allowing his parents to have the two chairs at the table. He didn't want to talk about himself, especially something so personal as his love life, but he didn't want to disappoint his mother's concerned curiosity. He'd never been able to figure out how she remained so upbeat and sweet, given their exposure to hardships, and the difficulty of living with Dad.

"I think so."

Dad found that amusing. "If you're in a state of confusion, then you're probably in love. Oh wonderful, hopeless love."

"Now Frank, let the boy speak for himself."

Dad deferred to Mom, probably wanting to watch Fletch squirm.

Fletch figured that if he started at the beginning, by the time he got to the end of his story, he might have figured out how to explain Lil. "Last summer I met a Conservative Mennonite girl. Her name is Lil." He saw his parents' surprise and continued, "She's a feisty little thing, not your typical. . . . Well, I never knew another Conservative girl. Anyway, we've been dating, but there've been some outside problems, so it's not been smooth sailing."

Dad slapped his knee. "What did I tell you?"

"Problems with her family?" Mom gently probed.

"Yes." Fletch got up to refill Buddy's water dish. "Actually the video I told you about, Dad? It was her farm. Her dad and brothers took a disliking to me after that." He rubbed his shoulder as he went back to the edge of his bed. "I'm still sore from spending all day Friday helping them erect two hoop barns. Figured I needed to make amends."

"Did you?" she asked.

"Yes. But there's still the issue of whose church we'll attend." He sighed. "And my uncertain future, her career. . ."

"Career?" Dad asked.

"She's head chef at a reputable restaurant, and she's very into it."

"Oh, a wonderful cook. Lucky boy." That was his mom again, looking on the bright side. "Can we meet her?"

"Well sure. How long are you going to be here? Do you have a place to stay? I can sleep on the floor if you need a place."

"Thanks, son. We'd be happy to take you up on that. Long as your boss doesn't mind."

Fletch couldn't believe they actually intended to move in with him, but then he realized that's what always happened with them. How many times had they stayed with friends, moving from place to place? "You saw for yourself that Vic was happy to see you."

"Tell him he doesn't have to pay us, too," Dad joked.

"It will be so wonderful to catch up, won't it?" Mom added.

"Yes. It's good to have you."

"It feels so right," she added. "But of course we'll find a place of our own as soon as we find some work."

"You're going to spend your entire furlough here?" Fletch asked tentatively.

The straw in Dad's super-sized drink hit air, and he set his cup aside. "I thought I explained that over the phone. We aren't going back to Africa."

Fletch's heart flopped like a bass in a net. "I thought you were. . . just dreaming."

"No dear," Mom tried to explain. "We grew restless there. It was as if God was prompting us to come home. To get to know you again. And then God supplied the mission with a young, eager couple to re- place us."

Home? Get to know him? Ohio wasn't their real home, but Fletch let out a sputtering laugh. "Well then, welcome to Plain City, Ohio."

⸻

That evening, Fletch grilled hamburgers while Dad watched, cola in one hand, the other scratching the basset. Inside, Mom was cooking potatoes in the microwave.

When he had apologized for not having a real kitchen, she cheerfully replied, "I've cooked with less."

He supposed that was why they didn't think his studio apartment was too small for the three of them. When a text message came through on his phone, he was happy for the diversion, even though it was from Marcus. Until he read the message: DAD'S IN TOWN. HE WANTS TO TAKE US TO DINNER TOMORROW NIGHT.

Fletch released a sarcastic laugh. "You aren't going to believe this. I just got a text from Marcus. Marshall's in town. He wants to take me to dinner tomorrow night."

"I want to see him. See if we can all go."

Fletch nodded and replied:

GREAT. MY PARENTS ARE HERE, STAYING WITH ME.
BRING THEM ALONG. BE HERE AROUND SIX?
CAN WE JUST MEET AT THE RESTAURANT?

Fletch flipped the burgers and added cheese, waiting for a reply. Finally Marcus sent him the name of a restaurant.

"This should be interesting," Dad remarked.

"He's mad at me, you know."

"Marshall should be worrying about his soul."

"He's such a nice man."

Fletch started. Mom stood on the tiny patio with them. She moved quiet as a mouse. He'd forgotten that, too.

"Invite your Lil to come. The potatoes are done."

Lil. He'd forgotten all about her. She probably wondered why he hadn't stopped in to talk after her apology. He'd go over after church— that is, if he could get a moment away from his parents.

CHAPTER 32

Lil blinked back tears and tried hard to remember why she had wanted to become a head chef, for there wasn't any glory in having to apologize to a customer for finding a hair in his meal. Why, he'd stared at her head as if it had been hers! Before that, there had been a commotion in the hostess area. A young man had been handing out flyers and boycotting her veal. She wondered if it was one of the volunteers from the shelter. Surely Ashley wouldn't do that to her. Or would they? To get revenge on Fletch?

And Fletch. . .she hadn't heard from him since the day he helped with the hoop barns. He had admitted he was too tired to think. Now he was probably wishing he had broken up with her on the spot, maybe that was even what he had been trying to do. The very thought made pain flash through her heart.

"Miss Landis! Lily!"

She swiped her arm across her eyes and wheeled about. "Yes?"

"Thomas burned his hand in a grease fire. Should he drive himself to the hospital?"

With a gasp of disbelief, she clattered through the kitchen to his station, pushing through the huddling cooks. "Move, please. Let me see."

Thomas held his arms out, and Lil felt sick to her stomach to see the large patches of reddened, blistering skin. "Elaine! You take him."

Quickly washing her hands and pulling on some gloves, Lil intended to take over both their places. She saw that the fire had been put out, but the work area needed to be cleaned. With a sinking heart, she realized she couldn't do everything. Tearing off her gloves, again, she went to the house phone and tried to recruit some workers because it was Saturday, their busiest night.

By the end of the evening, Lil's nerves were completely frazzled. Her legs hurt and her feet burned. At least Elaine had returned with a good report on Thomas. When the last customer departed and everything was finally put back in order, she called Camila to report the injury. The Italian matron told Lil she needed to keep all her tomatoes on the counter before they were all swimming in sauce. Because tomato sauce wasn't made for drowning people but for the taste buds, and did she understand that? Or did she need to come to the restaurant and explain it to her?

Lillian apologized and promised it wouldn't happen again. But she had wanted to shout, "Now I know why Giovanni went to Italy!"

~⌒~

On Sunday afternoon while Fletch's parents enjoyed a siesta, he went to the doddy house. To his pleased surprise, Lil came to the door.

"Hi. Would you like to go for a walk? Sometimes I can think better when I'm doing something."

"Will swinging work?"

He thought about the cottonwood tree at the Landis farm. About their first kiss. "You have a swing here?"

"Yep." She led him around to the back of the doddy house. A swing wide enough for two was suspended from a spreading oak tree.

"I didn't know this was back here. M'Lil, first." He gave a mock bow, gesturing for her to be seated.

"That's because Megan's dad just put it up yesterday. You should have dated her when you had the chance. Her parents are supportive, and she doesn't have a dozen stubborn brothers."

He settled in next to her. "Megan's a nice girl"—he heard his mother's voice horning in on his date—"but it was you I wanted to date."

Lil glanced up at him and smiled. "Are you saying you still want to?"

"I'd like nothing more."

"Me, too. I'm sorry that I pushed you away."

He took her hand. "You'll try to trust me?"

She nodded. "Yes."

"Thank you." She looked so lost and vulnerable, and he longed to kiss away her misgivings. But if he did that, he'd forget all the important things he wanted her to know about him.

"I believe I've made amends with your family. Do you feel like I have?"

"Oh yes. Everyone's forgiven you. You've helped them, and the offense is all in the past now."

"Good. I know we still don't agree on which church we'll attend and that serving the Lord is important to both of us. You're just getting settled in your career, and I don't even know if I'm staying in Plain City. But"—he saw her brows crease with worry and continued—"we'll get to those things, if you still want to date me after you've met my parents."

Her face lit up with surprise. "They're here?"

"The three of us are squeezed into my studio apartment."

Her hand flew out of his, and she grasped his sore arm. "When did they come? How long will they stay? When can I meet them? What if they don't like me?"

"Whoa, whoa. Lily? You want to meet them?"

"Yes, but what if they think I'm too plain for you?"

Fletch chuckled. "That's the least of our worries. They'll adore you. But it's not going to be the most conducive atmosphere for a first meeting."

He saw her growing confusion and anxiety. "I'm trying to trust you."

"Marshall's also in town. He's taking me and my parents to dinner tonight, and my mom insists you come, too. You can refuse if it's too much."

"She insisted? Why? Is she worried I won't be right for you?"

"No. She's excited to meet you."

Lil fidgeted with her skirt. "What time?"

"Six." Fletch glanced at his watch. "It's 3:30 now. I can come pick you up on our way to the restaurant, or else you can come with me when I leave, which would give you some time to meet my parents before we meet Marshall. I'll let you decide."

"Oh." Lil sucked in her bottom lip and glanced at the oak's canopy. "I think either would work. What do you think would be best?"

"I'd like you to come back with me now."

"All right!" she said, jumping up.

Fletch reached out and caught her by the arm. "Not now! I just got here. And we have some making up to do."

She tilted her face. "I thought we just did that."

"You're right, we did." He gave her his most persuasive smile. "But I thought we might work on our tradition." Slowly he pulled her closer.

"I don't know what you mean," she teased.

"I think your meeting my parents calls for a good-luck kiss."

"Or two, if I recall."

He'd just pulled her into his lap, when Megan called, "There you two are. My dad's here to put sealer on the swing."

Lil fairly flew out of his arms, and he felt his own cheeks sting as he rose to meet Megan's dad for the first time. Fletch wondered if Lil really knew Megan's parents at all, because Mr. Weaver didn't seem all that friendly or lenient. And then he remembered Lil saying that he was an elder at their church.

CHAPTER 33

And so a monkey was the culprit after all," Bonnie exclaimed.

Lil's eyes widened as she followed the graceful movements of the amazing woman wearing a flowered shirtdress. "And if I could have caught that miscreant, at that moment, he would have landed in the stewpot. After that, Frank fixed the window, and the creature never ventured inside again."

Bonnie's story captured Lil's imagination as much as the floor's old-world Saltillo tile and the bright blue-and-orange tiles that graced the walls around them with painted images of birds and flowers. The Mexican restaurant's huge potted plants easily swept Lil into the jungle mood.

"Oh, it was Bonnie's scream that scared it away, but she softened over the years. She even fed an orphan vervet two years ago."

"Yes. I suppose I did. But enough talk about us. Lil, I hear you love to cook?"

"Never tried monkey stew, but I have ventured out a bit from the traditional Mennonite fare."

"I like that." Frank sent Fletch a look that Lil translated as positive. But the atmosphere changed immensely when moments later,

Marshall, Marcus, and Ashley joined them. The other girl was dressed in tight black slacks and a glittery beaded top that once might have made Lil feel plain. But oddly, she didn't feel any barriers between them. She greeted her with enthusiasm.

Fletch jumped to his feet to greet Marshall. By their emotional embrace, Lil could see that whatever their differences, the reunion touched them both.

Marshall also greeted Fletch's parents warmly. Next, he came to Lil's chair with a tight smile. "And this must be the girl."

The words could have been meant for a compliment, implying she was special, but the way he said *the* made it seem like just the opposite. Lil interpreted it as "the girl who interfered with my plans for you."

She glanced at Fletch and saw a flicker of pain cross his eyes, but he didn't respond as if he had been offended. "Yes, Lillian Landis. May I introduce my special friend, Marshall Lewis."

"I've never met anyone from Texas before. I wish I had a poem or something for you to read. I love listening to your voice."

"He could read us the menu," Frank suggested, causing everyone to laugh.

"And ya have an accent as well. What is it?"

"Dutch, I suppose. My grandparents spoke a form of German that our people refer to as Dutch."

He glanced at her covering. "I see. Charmed to meet ya."

When everyone was seated, Fletch gave her hand a squeeze from under the table.

Lil quietly sized up the situation. Marshall, who was footing the bill, had called the group together and was the man in charge. Frank, who had a commanding presence, seemed the most at ease. Conversation lulled in an almost awkward silence as they looked over the menu, which Marshall chose not to read to the others.

After the orders were taken, bowls of chips and salsa appeared.

With the lively background music, Lil couldn't catch all of the conversation, but she had just raised her water to her lips when she clearly heard, "I guess ya'll know about my absurd situation?"

Peering over the rim of her glass, she saw that Marshall had directed his gaze at Frank.

"It is tragic. I suppose it's those nasty cigars."

Lil choked, and quickly brought her napkin to cover her mouth.

"That's the spirit. I hate when ya'll gush over me. Just wanted to get it out in the open and over with. Now we can enjoy ourselves."

Lil dipped a chip in the small bowl of salsa she was sharing with Fletch, who at best looked dismayed.

"It is wonderful to see ya'll again." Marshall was talking to Fletch's parents. "But it is for Fletch's sake that I called this little rendezvous." He tapped a chip with a ringed finger, then brought it to his mouth. She got a flash of his watch, its face encircled in clear jewels, and Lil guessed that they were real diamonds.

"For me?" Fletch asked.

"Yes, I know we've been playing a little cat and mouse lately, but let's just say I have a new perspective. Cancer does that. I want to offer ya a real job."

Lil joined the others in staring at Fletch. She saw his jaw clench and knew that he was bracing himself for yet another of Marshall's schemes.

"You've already done more for our family than we can ever repay. Perhaps we've. . .I've leaned too heavily on your generosity. I need to learn to. . .make my own way."

"Of course. Ya want to prove your manhood. Maturity includes the ability to recognize opportunities. Life-changing opportunities."

Lil clasped her hands in her lap, her face on fire in embarrassment for Fletch. How could he have been so enamored and under the spell of this condescending man? If not for Fletch's parents and Marshall's cancer, she might not have been able to hold her tongue.

Beside her, Fletch said, "I'm listening."

"I'm going to set ya up at the shelter. The shelter of your choice. If you're not happy at the Plain City Shelter here with my Marcus, there's the farm in Indiana. I believe we need a full-time veterinarian on staff." He waved a flash of diamonds. "Take your time to decide." He ran a warning gaze over Lil, and it sent a chill down her spine. She jutted her chin and met his disdainful gaze, but beneath the table, she twisted her napkin.

"It's a generous offer."

And it was, because Fletch had told her that getting started wasn't easy.

"But the shelter is not my cause."

Lil felt relief flood over her. She'd never felt as attracted to Fletch as she did at that moment.

"I'll probably take an internship after I graduate. I'm sure the school will have some recommendations."

"I find your rejection quite disrespectful."

"Now wait a minute," Frank interrupted. "You don't own my son."

Marshall set down his water glass so forcefully that it spilled onto the table. "I've been more of a father to him than ya have."

"Gentlemen," Bonnie said, "please, calm yourselves."

"And lower your voices," Marcus added. "People are staring."

"Let them stare! I'll buy this restaurant," Marshall cursed. "See if I care about gawkers!"

Lil's family may have had their share of arguments around the kitchen table, but they never had made themselves a public spectacle.

Marshall glared at Frank. "I've a mind to withdraw my support."

Frank replied calmly, "Marshall, that is not the important thing here. Nor any of your charitable causes, commendable as your life has been in that area and appreciative as I am for your support over the years. But now is the time for you to search your soul. You don't have time for anything less."

"I don't want to hear ya'll—"Marshall suddenly coughed and lost his voice. The southerner slumped, took several deep wheezing breaths.

"Dad?"

"This isn't finished," he gasped, standing up. He clenched his fists, then turned abruptly and left the dining room.

Marcus slapped a couple of large bills on the table and hurried after his dad.

"Sorry, everybody," Ashley mumbled, then scurried to catch up with the Lewis men.

They could hear Marshall coughing as he left the restaurant.

"He's a changed man," Bonnie gasped. "I don't even recognize him."

Fletch turned to Lil. "He wasn't like this before."

"Are you sure you just never crossed his purposes before?"

"No, he and Frank have had a few differences," Bonnie explained. "It must be the cancer."

"He's a desperate man," Frank observed. "He's worked hard to buy his way into heaven. And he's afraid he hasn't done enough."

After Marshall left, everyone was subdued. Frank made an attempt to praise his son for holding his ground, but Fletch simply withdrew. And when he dropped Lil back off at the doddy house, he was still restless, as if the argument was working on him.

They stood on the doddy house porch while Lil looked for her keys.

"Sorry for a terrible evening."

"Almost made me feel at home."

"Hardly."

"I like your parents, but your dad isn't the way I had him pictured." Fletch gave a bitter laugh. "How's that?"

"I expected a missionary to be gentle, but he's so bold."

She saw Fletch flinch and wished she'd kept her observation to herself. He didn't need more ammunition against his father.

"Domineering. And I need to get him out of my house before he drives me crazy."

"Your mom is sweet."

"Yes, but she's spunky. She has to be to live with him."

"Are you worried about Marshall?"

"Of course I am," he snapped. "The man's dying. He's trying to tie up loose ends, and we picked a fight with him. He's always been there for me. Now when he needs me. . .I'm rejecting him."

"It was almost like he came trying to pick a fight."

Fletch narrowed his eyes. "We told you, he's changed. That's the whole point. He's struggling right now. What if that whole scene was a struggle of wills. And the only reason my dad came was to win?"

"Win what?"

"Me. You heard what Marshall told him. That he was more of a father than my dad had ever been."

"Well if he came to win you back, then that's a good thing, isn't it?

That he realizes he made a mistake and—"

"Not to win my affection. Just to win out over Marshall."

"Oh, Fletch. I don't know, I—"

"I don't expect you to understand any of this. Look. I need some time to sort through all this. I need to go. I'll be in touch."

"In touch?" Lil felt her stomach knot with confusion and dread. "Fletch, what are you saying?"

"Don't try to put words in my mouth."

"I'm not."

"Good." He reached up and touched her chin, stared into her eyes, but she felt like his soul was miles away, perhaps back at the restaurant or even traveling out to the shelter where Marshall was staying. Would he go out to see him once he left her? Or would he go back to his apartment to his sleeping bag on the floor?

His caress on her chin was a far cry from the good-luck kiss he had promised earlier in the day, the one Megan's dad had spoiled for them. She nodded, leaned her cheek into his hand, hoping he would understand her need. But he pulled away and strode silently to his car.

Lil sank to the stoop in despair, silent tears rolling down her cheeks. Just when she'd decided to give her all to this relationship, he'd pulled away. She wondered if this was how miserable he'd been feeling when she was the one dragging her feet. But then she remembered the promise she had made him. *I trust you, Fletch Stauffer. You may not believe in yourself right now, but I do.*

She gazed up at the expanse of glittering September stars and realized that she hadn't spoken to God for a while. She dipped her face in the crook of her arms and apologized to the One who had formed both their souls. Marshall's face popped into her mind, and she wanted to squirm out of praying for the man whose cold eyes had warned her to stay away from Fletch. Or were they daring her to pray for him?

⁓

"You didn't have to wait up." Fletch patted Buddy on the head and put his car keys on a small hook.

"This is close quarters, dear. We are rather in this all together," Mom replied. "We've been sitting on the patio. But it got chilly so I made us some decaf coffee. Would you like a cup?"

"Sure."

Fletch slipped to the floor, careful not to spill his coffee, and leaned his back against his bed.

"That's a lot of sighing going on down there," she said from her seat at the table.

"It just feels like we've used Marshall for his money, and now that he needs us to walk with him, we're tossing him aside."

"If that were the case," Dad replied, "we would be staying all the more in his good graces in hopes of getting something out of his will. A friend tells the truth, even when it hurts."

"But does it have to be so harsh?" Fletch asked, which really was a major issue he had with his dad.

"I was proud of your firmness with Marshall."

"He called it disrespect."

"No, you weren't disrespectful, dear. It's just that Marshall wanted you to accept so badly that he lashed out. And Frank, put some sugar in your coffee beans."

"So you both think I came across too strong."

"He could be the apostle Paul's twin," Mom observed.

Dad ignored her comment. "What I told him, about searching his soul? That goes for you, too, son."

"What's that supposed to mean?"

"I sense restlessness in you."

Not until you came.

"Just make sure you're following your calling, not man's."

"Marshall was there for me when I didn't know what classes to take. He pointed out my natural gifts and talents when I didn't think I had any."

"There's more than one reason your mother calls me the apostle Paul. When I was young, I resisted God's call. I was a rebel. My dad forced me into a box so I fled. I'd turned my back on God altogether until I was in a motorcycle accident and fell in love with my nurse. But she wouldn't have anything to do with me. That's when I looked inside.

Tried to figure out why."

He chuckled. "And there it was all the time, the call to adventure. Only not motorcycles, but Africa. I guess that's why I never tried to interfere with your life. I didn't want to push you to rebel, like my dad did me." Sadly, Dad swirled the shallow contents of his cup. "I guess I gave you too long of a leash. And I certainly didn't expect a stranger to step in and do what I tried not to do."

"I guess the leash was so long I didn't realize it existed. I felt alone in a big world. Bigger than most kids'. I didn't have a backyard to play in. I had a jungle. You know?"

Mom stared into her cup.

"Just don't make the same mistake I did," Dad replied, "and run from your calling just because your father didn't do his job right."

"And. . ." Mom shot Dad a stern look.

"And. . . God's been nudging me to come to you. I didn't know why until I got here. But now I understand. I need your forgiveness for how I've treated you."

Fletch hadn't hoped for affection from the man who never showed him the acceptance he craved. But when it came, it deeply moved him. It carried something divine in it that couldn't be denied. He was ready to forgive. Ready to find healing. He went to his dad. Opened his arms.

Dad gripped him in an ironlike embrace.

Fletch whispered, "I forgive you."

"I love you," Dad said, releasing him and clapping his shoulders.

There was more shoulder clapping and bear hugs and manly sniffles, and finally Fletch realized that some of them were feminine, too. He went to his mom and gently embraced her.

"Love you, Mom."

When they'd finished, Fletch sank back to the floor, clasping his bent knees and swiping his arm across his eyes. "Thanks for coming home."

"Well!" Mom exclaimed. "Tomorrow is job hunting. Won't that be fun!" And with that, they all fell to laughing and yawning and getting their beds in order.

But Fletch couldn't fall asleep. First of all, Dad snored. Secondly, if

God had blessed him by healing the rift he'd always felt toward his dad, then maybe he needed to take what his dad had told him to heart. The part about searching his soul and hearing his calling.

Had he ever really done that, or had he just assumed Marshall's guidance was right for him? He had never questioned Marshall until lately. Had he been rejecting his dad, or had he been rejecting God's calling? He plumped his pillow and turned to his side. And what about Lil? Would she be patient while he sorted through this? She was a girl who'd always known what she wanted. What would she think of his uncertainty?

CHAPTER 34

Lil blew her bangs out of her eyes, not wanting to reposition her bobby pins, because then she'd have to wash her hands again. The pins were no good, too loose. She might as well toss them in the trash. She was going over her supply list one final time because yesterday they'd run low on mozzarella cheese and had to skimp.

"Hi, Lil." Megan now had the run of the restaurant, being given the VIP treatment every time she popped over from nearby Char Air.

Lil looked up. "Is it one o'clock already?"

"Yep. I just have five minutes though, because I have to run some errands for the boss."

Lil glanced up, forever searching her friend's expression at the mention of her good-looking, off-limits boss. But Megan had become good at concealing her feelings about him.

Megan sniffed with pleasure. "Got a doggie bag for me?"

Lil yelled over her shoulder, "Elaine! Bag some spaghetti for me?"

"What time will you be home tonight?"

"I'll be late. Fletch came over last night and invited me to go to dinner at his boss's."

Megan made an ugly face. "Another dinner? The last one had you in a funk for over a week."

"I know. But Vic's never asked him before. And Fletch wants to talk to me about something. I'm thinking it must be something good. He wouldn't take me to his boss's to break up with me, right?"

Megan leaned on the counter. "He's not going to break up. He loves you."

"It's rocky right now. You know that."

Elaine brought the doggie bag, and Megan thanked her. "He's probably going to apologize for his behavior the last couple of weeks. Sorry. I've gotta go."

Lil had just started concentrating on her list again when she heard the hostess take a reservation for a large party of Ranco customers. The back room would have to be prepared. She was going to have to hustle to make her date.

⎯ ᴄᴐ

Lil felt dazzled from the moment she stepped into the softly lit foyer of the Fullers' two-story, track home and handed her coat to Britt. The other woman wore a jean skirt that skimmed her knees and a pink sweater set. She had silver hoop earrings that flashed in and out of her dark bob. Soft, side-swept bangs fringed expressive brown eyes. She still carried some of her baby fat from her last child, but it softened her in a pleasing way, as did her generous smile. "Come into the kitchen. I have some appetizers. If we don't get to them soon, the kids will."

They moved past a magazine-worthy living room and stepped into a tiled, open area that served as kitchen, breakfast nook, and family room. Vic motioned Fletch to a sectional where he was watching a sports game on the television.

Fletch squeezed Lil's hand, and she whispered, "Go ahead. I'm fine."

Britt called to her husband, "Vic! Why don't you turn the TV off?"

"Oh." The thin, redheaded vet shot Lil a contrite expression and reached for the remote. "Sorry."

"You don't have to do that on my account," Lil said. "But thanks for the offer."

"You sure?" he asked, looking to his wife for validation.

Britt shrugged, and Vic returned the remote to the side table.

"Can I help with anything?"

"No, just pull up a barstool. Only, I can't believe I'm cooking for you. Vic told me you're head chef at Volo Italiano."

Lil shifted in the stool. "Where I was on my feet all day. But then, I suppose you were, too."

Taking the sour cream container from the refrigerator, Britt replied, "Not all day. I shuffled the boys off to school, did two loads of laundry, and some dinner preparations. But before I had to pick them up again, I watched my favorite reality show. I tape it and treat myself each—I'm sorry." She dropped the sour cream lid on the counter and shook her head. "I'm as bad as Vic. Watching television isn't all we do. I mean—"

"Please," Lil interrupted. "I'm in your home. I understand that most people watch television. In fact, a lot of restaurants have them, too. Although the church I attend doesn't allow them, I've broken the rules a few times."

Britt added the sour cream to her stroganoff, turned off the burner, and stirred the sauce until it was blended. She whispered, "Don't tell the kids, but I've been known to bend a few, too."

"Oops. Sorry," Lil said, looking to see if any of the boys had overheard their conversation, but Fletch was showing them how to build a truck with their plastic building blocks.

Lil took a bite of the cracker appetizers, swallowed, and ventured, "Can I ask you a personal question?"

"Of course."

"How do you get your bangs to do that? Mine are about that length, and all they ever do is fall in my eyes."

Britt carried her skillet to the counter with a stack of plates, glancing at Lil's hair. "I can help you with that. After dinner, I'll get out my straight iron."

Lil moved to hand her plates as Britt served up their dinner. "You can do that with a straight iron?"

"Yep. I can finish here if you want to call the guys."

Lil strolled across the sparkling tile to the family room and placed a hand on Fletch's shoulder. "Britt wants us to come eat."

Vic flicked off his show and gathered up his boys. Lil was glad Britt was keeping it casual, the adults dining at the kitchen table while the boys ate at the kitchen island.

Vic cleared his throat. "Fletch, you want to pray?"

"Wait, boys," Britt told her sons, who had already started eating.

Lil bit back a smile as the youngsters' forks clanged onto the granite countertop. Fletch took her hand.

"Lord, I thank You for this home and for providing me with such a generous employer. Bless Britt for making this meal, and bless the boys in all they do. I thank You for this food. Amen."

"That was nice," Britt said. "But you do realize that since you two got involved in my husband's life, our world has turned topsy-turvy."

Fletch's fork stopped halfway to his mouth. "Just for the record, it was really Lil who wrecked your car."

Lil grimaced. "Sorry about that. It was how we met."

"Tell us what really happened that day, Lil," Vic urged.

When the story had been told, the couple agreed with Fletch that it was Lil's fault, after all. But the dinner turned out to be nothing like the meal with Marshall. This one was warm and personal, and Lil felt as though she'd made friends with Vic and Britt.

On the ride home, Fletch reached across the console and touched her hand. "I like your hair."

She gave her bangs a puff. "These? Thanks. Britt has a knack. She's pretty and sweet. But I was kind of surprised that she doesn't work. She really had her house in order."

"She's a stay-at-home mom."

Lil watched the moonlit trees moving past her window. "In the Conservative Church, we don't even use that expression. It's taken for granted. It's just what women do."

"Not all of them," Fletch observed.

Lil ignored his reference to her own career. "Britt seems to be a good mother. I mean, it would be better if she took the boys to church, but. . .I liked her."

"Vic claims she's great with the boys. He just wishes she didn't like to spend money."

Lil laughed. "Ugh, money. I don't even have time to spend mine anymore."

Fletch fell into a contemplative mood until they reached the doddy house. "Can we sit in the car and talk?"

When he had picked her up that evening, he had given her a quick apology about being in a bad mood the last time they were together. She assumed that was their talk. Now, her apprehension returned. "Sure."

He turned to face her. "Let me start by telling you that my dad and I worked some things out, and things are better between us. But he said some things that got me to thinking. He asked me if I was running from God's calling."

"Isn't your veterinary career your calling?"

"I thought so, but I've been praying, and now I see there's more to it. I don't know how to tell you—I know that your career is important to you, and I don't know how this will affect our relationship."

"What is it?" she asked nervously.

"You know how I've always vowed that I would never go into missionary work?"

Lil felt her heart sinking into despair. She blurted out, "You want to be a missionary?"

Fletch sighed. Became stone still.

"I mean, is that it?" Lil urged, seeing she'd frustrated him.

"I was afraid that would be your response. I had hoped you'd be willing to at least consider. . ." His voice faltered.

"It's just that I didn't see this coming. It's out of the blue. Are your parents going back to Africa? Are you going with them?"

"No. But there's a program at OSU. It's available for veterinary students. They go to other countries to treat and train others regarding the care of their farm animals. It's called Christian Veterinary Mission. I want to check it out. Try to understand. All this time I thought I was rejecting my dad. Now I wonder if I was rejecting God's calling. I need to find out."

"I don't know what to say. This is so unexpected." Lil shook her head and stared straight ahead, unable to meet his gaze given the way he was breaking her heart.

"Lily," he pleaded. "Look at me."

She turned, fighting back tears of resentment that he would come into her life and make her fall for him. He had persuaded her to trust him. Just when she was willing to give their relationship her all, he got restless on her. And now he wanted to run off and find himself doing missionary work. As if their church predicament wasn't bad enough.

"Lil?"

At his request, she stared into his pleading brown eyes, knowing that she would never recover from loving him. "What?"

"I want you to know I love you."

She shook her head. "Why would you tell me that now?"

"Because I'm asking you to wait."

"What?"

"A little while. Give me time to talk to my professor and find out more. Time to pray. I need to spend time with my dad. If God wants us together, He's going to make a way for us. Right now, if I asked you to marry me, I wouldn't even know what I was offering you."

"Have you heard me asking for a marriage proposal?" Why couldn't they just go on dating. Let things work out?

"Isn't that where we're headed?"

She bit her lip to keep from saying something that would ruin all her chances with him. "If you love me at all, will you wait and pray? For us?"

"Let me get this straight. We're not exactly breaking up, just taking a break? And am I supposed to be trusting you during this little interval?"

"I think it would be better if we both trusted God right now."

"Whew!" She puffed her bangs again. That clarified things.

─૭─

Furious, Lil slammed the door and marched through the doddy house. "Megan!"

Peeking over the arm of the sofa and looking at her with one eye, for the other was covered with a waterfall of hair, Megan replied, "What?"

Lil sank to the sofa.

Megan snatched up her legs to keep them from getting crushed.

Lil tossed Megan's Christian novel onto the coffee table.

"You just lost my page." Megan ran a hand up the side of her face, further ruffling her hair. "You crying?"

"I just got dumped."

"He didn't!"

"He's dumping me to become a missionary."

Megan suddenly perked up. "What? Did he ask you to go with him? Did you even give it any thought?"

Lil's mouth flopped open. "I shouldn't have expected you to understand. And no, he didn't ask me." She stopped, thought back to make sure that he hadn't. She was unsure. "He wants me to wait for him while he figures out his future. Later, if I fit into his plans, he might be back. I don't think he's willing to make compromises anymore. He's taking charge. He's changing."

"That all sounds pretty iffy," Megan said with disappointment.

"I didn't see this coming. I thought our last hurdle was deciding which church to attend."

Megan wrapped an arm around Lil. "I'm so sorry. I don't suppose there're any Italian restaurants in Africa?" But then her friend turned thoughtful. "Well we don't know that for a fact, do we?"

"It's not about me. I'm not the barrier. I don't even like my stupid job."

Her face twisting in horrific disbelief, Megan blinked. "You don't?"

"It's not as glamorous as I thought it would be. It's glorified slavery. The higher up you go, the harder the work."

"Really?"

"Trust me. Tonight when we were at Britt and Vic's, I envied her for her little homemaking life."

"Has your face been too close to the gas burner all day?"

"I've been trying to tell you. And Fletch, too. Except, I haven't seen him that much lately. And nobody's listening. Maybe I need to do like he's doing and go find myself."

"That's kinda scary, because you always knew what you wanted."

"I thought I knew what I wanted." Slinky rubbed against Lil's ankles. She swept the purring kitten up against her cheek then settled him on her lap.

"Let's back up. Fletch wants to find himself?"

"Yes, but he didn't put it that way. He said we needed to pray. He told me not to trust him, but to trust God."

Megan tilted her head thoughtfully. "There's nothing wrong with that advice. For any of us."

Lil gave Megan a sideways glance. "Your boss isn't bothering you, is he?"

"No, but something's bothering him, and of course, that affects me, but I do like my job. I'm sorry you don't."

Lil felt suddenly weary. It felt like they were talking in circles, and it had already been such a trying day for her. There had been too many trying days in a row. She was exhausted. "Thanks for being here for me. I don't know what I'd do without you."

CHAPTER 35

Rolling the kinks out of his shoulders, Fletch climbed out of Vic's pickup and followed the vet into the clinic. Successive nights of camping out in a sleeping bag on the floor of his apartment was taking its toll. Make that half a sleeping bag. Buddy assumed the floor pallet was an invitation for him. The dog's dead weight wouldn't budge. His breath wasn't that appealing either.

He opened the clinic's back door for the guilty party to use the dog walk. When he went back inside, Vic asked him to go fetch an extra cage from the truck.

Fletch stepped back outside, and a swirl of brown leaves skittered across his red sneakers and down the sidewalk.

"It only takes one hard freeze. Soon they'll all be dead. All gone."

He halted. Turned. "Marshall?"

The older man raised a gloved hand. "I came to apologize. Your dad was right. I've been manipulating ya, and that was wrong." He sighed deeply and cleared his throat. "I didn't do it on purpose. There's so little time, and in my mind I thought I knew what would be best for everybody. But I can't make the world a perfect place."

"I understand. Earth's far from perfect. Or fair. It hurt, bad, to hear about your cancer. But there are survivors."

"I won't be one of them. The most we can do is slow it down." He squatted and picked up a leaf. Crumbled it. Scattered it on the sidewalk. "It's only a matter of time."

There was no changing that, Fletch thought glumly.

The southerner stood. "On the bright side, I'm taking your dad to lunch tomorrow."

Giving Marshall a wry smile, Fletch said, "Now that's a scary thought." Although Marshall's anger had dissipated and he was releasing his control over Fletch, this still wasn't the friend that Fletch had known all his life. This was a grieving man.

He was thrilled Marshall was having lunch with his dad. But after the scene at the restaurant, the image that shot in his mind—of Frank and Marshall chatting together—was that of a pile of leaves and a match.

"I'm going to give him one shot to preach to me."

"You are?" Fletch had to chuckle now. "I mean, that's great." God did have a sense of humor to orchestrate this—Marshall's most important moment on earth. But after all those years of Marshall supporting Dad's ministry, it was the perfect plan. Fletch's admiration for both men grew considerably. For his dad, because he'd been tough but said just the right thing to set Marshall thinking. For Marshall, because he wasn't bowing to his pride.

And if God could set Marshall's mind at peace, then Fletch should be able to trust Him with his own future.

Marshall reached into his coat pocket and pulled out an envelope. "Ya know how I like to give gifts?"

"Oh no, Marshall. Please don't—"

"It's for Lily. I think I offended her."

Join the club, Fletch thought, remembering how she flew out of his car in a tiff on their last date. He took the paper that Marshall offered. "What's this?"

"It's a phone number of a Mexican restaurant chain that will give the Landis family a contract if they agree to certain organic methods."

Shaking his head, Fletch stared at the paper. "I don't know how to thank you. It's too much."

"I think Lily's perfect for you. She was delightful, by the way. Makes me think of my Barbara. She passed long ago. Now she was a fine Christian woman."

"I wish I could have met her." He would give the information to Matt. His friend was supporting him in his decision to take a break from Lil. To figure out what he really wanted to do with his future. A lump formed in his throat at Marshall's generosity. "Lil's friend Megan loves her job."

"Good. Good."

Fletch stepped forward. "Thank you for everything. You've been such a blessing in my life."

Marshall studied him with a smile.

After this, they would drift apart. They both knew it. Marshall would draw strength from Marcus. Fletch and his dad would enjoy the relationship they had never known. "I really needed you."

"Our friendship was no accident."

Fletch thought they must both be thinking about the next day's lunch.

"Are ya on your way—" Marshall's words cut off with a sudden cough.

"No. Vic sent me to fetch something off his truck." He watched the man wheeze and fight for control of his breathing.

When he was able to speak, Marshall said, "Well, stop by the shelter if ya have time. I'm headed home on Friday."

"Thanks." Neither Fletch nor Vic had been at the shelter in days. Fletch felt as though his time there was finished. But he did want to see Marshall again, hoped to see how the lunch went. "I'll try."

—⚘—

It was embarrassing that Lil hadn't been to Katy's new house yet. She and Jake had dropped by the doddy house a few times since the move, but the weeks had flown by with new jobs and everybody settling in. One October Saturday, however, Katy invited Lil and Megan for tea. Lil made some oatmeal raisin cookies and Megan took a stack of Christian novels she wanted to share.

DIANNE CHRISTNER

They walked up the pristine, perennial-lined sidewalk that led to the front door. Lil rang the doorbell. "This is nice."

Megan shifted her novels to the other arm. "I like the gray siding. It's one of my favorites."

Katy opened the door and pulled them inside. "I've missed you."

"Yeah, but you've got the chump to keep you company," Lil teased.

"He's off playing basketball with Chad. I usually go along, but today I needed to see my friends."

Katy gave them a quick tour of the house. Though small, it had high ceilings and three bedrooms. One of them was made into Jake's home office. The other one remained empty. When Lil stepped into the kitchen, she froze. "Granite countertops?"

"They came with the house. You know it was a model, so they had it fixed up nice." Katy filled the teapot with water and turned on the burner. She was all smiles. "I have to admit, it's really fun to clean our new home."

Lil unwrapped the plastic that covered the cookies and set them on the table. "We have played musical chairs. I never pictured it would be like this. I always thought we'd all three live together."

"We don't have to live together to be best friends. Where do you want these books?"

Katy took them to the living room and returned just as the teakettle whistled. She served them their chamomile along with Lil's cookies. She'd been sporting a smile ever since they arrived. At first Lil thought it was just the joy of showing them her home, but now her friend's smile deepened, spread across her face, and lit up her eyes.

"I have something to tell you both. Aside from Jake, you're the first to know."

A sweet inkling blossomed inside Lil. "Yes?"

"We're going to have a baby."

Megan and Lil squealed, jumping up to hug Katy.

"This is wonderful. How do you feel?"

"I'm not even sick. Just a little tired."

"When's it due? What does Jake say?"

"The baby is due the end of April. Will you help me prepare the nursery?"

"Of course!" Lil touched Katy's arm, thinking about the empty bedroom. "We'll give you a shower, too."

"That would be nice. Maybe after Christmas."

"Perfect."

"Are you going to keep working?" Megan asked.

"Probably until the baby comes. Then I guess we'll see how it goes. If I do, I'm sure I won't work as much."

"I imagine the chump's excited?"

"He's been wonderful, doting on me. But we've only known a few days. I suppose that will wear off soon."

Lil clasped her cup with both hands. "Your baby will be born right after Michelle's. Maybe they'll play together."

"I hope so." Katy talked happily about her baby, and they emptied the teapot.

Lil hadn't known there were so many things to say about an unborn child, but Katy already seemed to be well informed. She'd picked up some library books on the subject.

Katy gave a happy sigh. "Enough about me. What's going on in your lives?"

Lil crossed her legs and swung her foot in tiny circles. "I haven't heard anything from Fletch since he asked me to wait for him. But Matt says he's still in town. That's something. Matt doesn't really want to talk about Fletch. He feels like he's squealing on his friend."

Megan went to refill her cup, but the pot was empty. "I see his point, but the brother–sister bond should be stronger."

"It's frustrating."

Katy refilled the teapot and set it on the stove. During the second pot of tea, Lil told them about her frustrations at work. When she was finished, she glanced at Megan. "Tell Katy what you found out yesterday."

Megan turned pink. "My boss is getting back together with his wife. It's a good thing. He is taking an extended leave of absence. In the meantime, his brother is taking his place. He worked in the field before."

"How will this affect you?" Katy asked. "Should we make a third pot for you?"

"I'll tell you the story, Katy. But please, no more tea."

—⟨⟩

The baby's due in April. Jake is wonderful, doting on me. Lil remembered their earlier conversation. The words kept swirling in her mind, long after she and Megan left Katy's home.

Why wasn't she happier? Sure, she'd done the garbanzo dance at the time, but now she felt bereft. Lil glided slowly on the swing, remembering the Sunday when Fletch sat next to her, swinging and talking optimistically about their relationship. She sighed. That was before he realized he wasn't happy with his life. She bit her lower lip, wondering if he had felt as miserable as she now did.

She wasn't even happy with her job. It wasn't the hard work—she'd never been afraid of work. It just didn't fulfill her like she had hoped.

Her Bible lay open on her lap. She had been fighting against Fletch's request to trust God with their relationship. Instead, she'd pleaded with God to bring Fletch back to her.

She gazed up at the canopy of brittle oak leaves and followed the trail of one to the ground. Her hopes and dreams were like those leaves. *Lord, what are You trying to tell me? Have I been following the wrong dream all along? Fletch claims he had. Have I, too?*

She stared at her Bible. Everything had pivoted around her goals for so long she didn't know how else to live. Then her eyes fell upon a passage she had never read or heard before. She glanced at the header and thought grimly, *I'm in the book of Job. How fitting, for of all Bible characters, Job's life was one of affliction.*

Starting at Job 8:12, she read a few verses: "Whilst it is yet in his greenness, and not cut down, it withereth before any other herb. So are the paths of all that forget God; and the hypocrite's hope shall perish: whose hope shall be cut off, and whose trust shall be a spider's web. He shall lean upon his house, but it shall not stand: he shall hold it fast, but it shall not endure."

Lil gasped. She understood what the writer meant. Without God, her dreams were fragile and unable to hold up to life's pressures. Like a spider's web. Like brittle leaves. Her motives had been full of selfish ambition, always yearning for the spotlight. Just like those circus performers so long ago. Her dreams were never about God's will. She was supposed to give the glory to God, but she'd fought all these years to claim it for herself.

She began to pant, *Oh no. Oh no.*

She'd been chasing something that was as foolish as a circus performer using a spider's web for a net. "Foolish, foolish, foolish," she gasped. She'd been just like her mom.

I'm so sorry, Lord. So ashamed. She put her face in her hands and cried out to God in waves of repentance until she had laid out all the ugliness. All her selfish whims and desires. Even rejecting the farm, hating it when it had been God's gift to provide for her family. It had been a generational gift. A gift that had given her a pleasant childhood. Living on the farm, she had been able to enjoy nature, good food, and animals. He'd given her many friends and a loving family who stuck together no matter how much they disagreed.

I'm so sorry. I admit I'm caught in a sticky spider's web. What now, Lord? Can You change my heart? I need firm ground for my feet and clear direction because I haven't learned how to hear Your voice or appreciate Your gifts.

⁓ஃ

Two weeks passed. Peace settled over Lil. She still held the same job, but she went to work with a renewed bounce in her step. She was naturally a bouncy-step-type person, but she'd discovered the source of joy. It came from a continual, silent conversation with God. Telling Him her thoughts. Listening for those impressions He placed in her heart. Making Him a part of her day.

She couldn't disregard a strong yearning for Fletch and wished she didn't have to wait, that she could find out what was on his mind.

She hoped someday she would get the chance to tell Fletch how she'd changed. If she got another chance with him, she would be open to consider all the options for their future. She couldn't picture herself as a missionary, and every time she tried to, she was impressed not to worry, to just trust God.

She spent her evenings searching scripture and allowing God's powerful words to penetrate her spirit. Her resentment toward the rules and regulations of the church disappeared when her studies revealed the reasons behind them.

She'd had a long talk with her mom about the situation and discovered they were at similar places in their lives. It was heartening to think she didn't have to wait forty years but could learn it now alongside her mom.

The goals no longer seemed as important as the journey itself.

CHAPTER 36

One day in early November, Lil stood in the vestibule speaking to Brother Troyer. "So I've been thinking about the spider web analogy in Job, and. . ." Brother Troyer's gaze went spacey as if trying to recall her particular analogy, and he gave her a patient nod. "You know how spiders' webs are all sticky and gross and once you get them on you, you can't get them off?" His mouth twitched on the left. "And sometimes they're so invisible you don't see them and walk right into them. Other times they're beautiful and useful to the spider, too. I mean without them, spiders wouldn't eat, and I suppose spiders are good for something or God wouldn't have created them. Anyway, I'm thinking of. . .say, television. Do you think it's like that?"

Brother Troyer coughed. "Yes, I can see the similarities, but what is the question, exactly?"

In the many discussions they'd had since Lil had been reading her Bible and praying, she sometimes thought the preacher could be so dense. She opened her mouth to go at it from a different angle but snapped it closed again when every muscle in her body tensed. For somebody much more interesting than Brother Troyer had just stepped through the church doors and hesitated in the foyer.

Fletch? He looked taller, more wonderful. His jean-clad legs were planted purposefully, and somewhere beneath that button-down dress shirt was a heart that had surely stolen hers. His gaze swept over his surroundings. His hand went up to smooth his wind-tousled hair. It had been so long since she'd seen him that she'd forgotten how much the sight of him could send her heart racing and turn her brain to mush. And then his soft brown gaze rested on her.

"I. . ." Lil couldn't remember what she and the preacher had been speaking about. "Excuse me." She took a few steps toward Fletch and stopped.

Why was he here? To break up for good? To confess his love? She swallowed. Was she ready to accept his decision, or should she scram out the back door? She couldn't move. He started toward her. And when he was so close she could have reached up and brushed his hair in place, he stopped. "Hi. I'd hoped you hadn't forgotten me."

Lil gave a nervous little laugh. "If I had, my memory is jogged now."

"I came, Lily, to make my offer."

Her heart did the complete somersault. "Here? Now?"

Then he smiled. "I thought it was the perfect place. If you're willing, I'd like to be your guest this morning. See what your church is like. Do you think they'll kick me out?"

She glanced down and couldn't believe he'd worn his red tennis shoes. It was as if he had done it on purpose, because they didn't even match his shirt. She looked back at him with confusion.

He shrugged and gave her a disarming, yet boyish smile. "If they'll accept me, they need to know who I am. That's not to say I won't change."

Her congregation already knew all about him. There were no secrets in this church. She nodded, wet her lips. The service was ready to begin, and they were the last ones in the vestibule. She wanted to tell him how she'd changed and pour out her heart about how she'd found God, but she was curious about his offer.

"Mmm, you mentioned an offer?"

"Another reason I wore these shoes. To barter. I'll give up my shoes or whatever else you or your elders require if you'll let me pursue that mission opportunity I told you about. I went to some of their campus meetings. They have lots of short trips to other countries. I could go on those for now, and after I have my own practice and we have children"— he grinned mischievously—"there are other ways that veterinarians can support the work without actually traveling."

"Children? I think your plan skips an important step."

"No, I didn't forget it. It's all I can think about. But let me finish my offer. In return, I'd let you pursue your career."

"You're staying in Plain City?"

"If you'll have me. Vic has offered me a job. I know what I want, Lil. I want you. I've already talked to your father. He gave me permission to date you with intentions toward marriage. Will you give me another chance?"

Lil reached up to touch his cheek. "Yes, I will. But I have one condition."

"All right."

"You'll let me visit your church, too. And I have so much to tell you."

"I'd like to kiss you right now, but I think that will have to wait until after the service."

"I'm going to claim that kiss today. But right now you'd better hold my hand real tight or I'm going to embarrass both of us by doing the garbanzo dance down the aisle."

⁓

Flowers were strewn down the center aisle of Fletch's church, ribbons tied on the oak pews. After months of preparations, the day to unite their dreams and lives had finally arrived. Outside the church, dogwoods were making a showy splash of white and pink. May brought newness to Plain City and to Lil's heart.

She examined herself in the mirror, still surprised every time she saw her reflection since Britt had taken her to a hairstylist. Lil had gotten her bangs professionally trimmed and her hair styled to wear straight just below her shoulders. She'd wanted something easy to care for when she went with Fletch on his upcoming mission trip to Vinces, Ecuador.

Michelle helped her position her veil, a traditional style that hung long down her back.

"Mommy, when I grow up, can I wear a covering like that?" little Tate asked. She held her yellow flower girl skirt out, posing in front of the mirror.

"When you're older, we'll see."

Lil's elegant dress was a slim, A-line style. Beaded lace adorned the bust and sleeves and ruched charmeuse accented her waist. She'd doubled her sit-up regimen. The plain satin skirt had a scallope lace hem.

Megan popped her head into the dressing room. "Katy's feeding the baby; then Marie will take little Jacob, and Katy will join us."

"Perfect."

Megan fluttered over her, tugging here and moving there. "You look beautiful." Together, they had shopped to find the perfect combination of elegant and modest. Not only in her wedding dress, but in her new wardrobe items.

No longer did Lil feel plain and restricted, but her clothes reflected her heart, modest in cut and cheery in color. She and Megan had grown close over the months they had shared the doddy house. There had been a time when Megan seemed sad, and Lil knew it had something to do with falling for a man she couldn't have, but Megan had found her peace. The experience had given her an even lovelier spirit than before.

Dressed in a yellow bridesmaid dress, Megan reflected Lil's joy. Her friend had been eager to move home again so the doddy house would become a honeymoon shack for the second time.

Lil clutched Megan's hand. "I'm nervous. I need to see him."

"You will soon enough."

Katy opened the door and stepped into the room with Lil's mom, who carried Michelle's baby boy. "Jake said Fletch is ready. But you'll never guess what your brothers did to him."

"Oh no," Lil groaned.

"They changed his real tux jacket out for one that was two sizes too small."

"Oh, that's going to ruin the wedding!"

"No. They had the right size, too. They just wanted to see Fletch squirm."

Mom handed the baby to Michelle. "I'm sure Matt was the genius behind it. But I have a surprise for him."

"You do?" Lil asked.

"I was thinking a squirt of hot sauce on his cake would be the perfect payback."

Lil giggled, relieved her mom's sense of humor had returned. "The cake is so lovely." She took her mom's hand. "Thank you for everything. You've taught me so much."

Mom squeezed her hand. "Now stop, or we'll have to cry. Anyway, the church is filled. I'm going to go ahead and get seated. Your dad is waiting in the foyer."

Lil found him there, and together they watched Lil's bridesmaids take their turns walking up the aisle. "I'm so happy," she told him.

He patted her hand. "It all turned out good."

Remembering that morning so long ago when her dad had first confided that the farm was in trouble, she knew his words held plenty of meaning. They expressed happiness over the farm's financial breakthrough. Matt had signed the contract with the Mexican restaurant chain, and the herd's disease was on the decline. But her dad also referred to the way the family had accepted Fletch and then agreed with Lil's decision to attend a different church. The family was united and stronger than ever for working through their differences.

"It's time, honey."

Lil gripped Dad's arm and floated down the aisle toward the blond groom in a perfect-fitting black tuxedo. Ever since their accidental meeting, he was all she had wanted in a man. His looks and charm first attracted her, but she'd fallen in love with his gentle strength.

Fletch's sister, Erica, all the way in from Canada, sat at the piano and played the bridal procession. At rehearsal, Fletch had helped her position the piano bench just right so that she could reach across her pregnant belly. And Lil loved the French accent of Erica's husband.

Her groom's gaze, so full of reassurance and a dash of daring, drew her toward the altar where they would exchange their vows before

God, family, and friends.

When at last the preacher said, "I pronounce you husband and wife; you may kiss your bride," Lil melted into her groom's embrace.

"For luck for the rest of our lives," he whispered.

"And love!" she added breathlessly.

His sister started the music again, and together they swept down the aisle. About halfway, Lil couldn't resist a few steps of the garbanzo dance. Laughing, Fletch clasped his hand around her waist and rushed her out of the sanctuary.

In the lobby, he drew her close for a real marriage kiss. She closed her eyes and cherished her husband's eager embrace. Afterward, she looked into his tender gaze, so glad that she had dared to let go of old dreams and embrace something new.

At their reception, each person they greeted reinforced the Lord's blessings along their journey. There was Giovanni waving them over to meet his wife and baby.

"This. . .eh. . .reminds us of our own wedding. In Italy. What can I say? It is spring and love is in the air."

Lil asked if she could hold the little one. "Here," Giovanni's wife placed a cloth over Lil's shoulder. "You must protect your pretty dress." But she beamed to share her little one. "We are happy to be back in the States. Thank you for giving Giovanni his job back."

"I was happy to fill in for him," Lil replied, giving the baby a final kiss and returning her to her mama. She had never felt as relieved as when Giovanni returned and reapplied for a cooking position.

She smiled at Giovanni. "Remember your promise to give me time off when Fletch has his mission trips."

"You already have the time off for your honeymoon. Eh! You are so demanding of Giovanni."

Next, Fletch shook hands with Vic, and Britt hugged Lil. "Come for dinner when you get back from your honeymoon. I want to hear everything."

"All right. But after that, it'll be my turn to cook."

—⌒—

Fletch and Lil paused in the vestibule before they made a dash for the limousine Marshall had insisted on renting. Marshall's remission had been the only wedding gift Fletch had desired from his longtime friend.

Outside the doors, two long lines had formed, and they were to make a pass through the middle. It wouldn't have been so bad if Lil's brothers didn't form one long, intimidating stretch of that line. His parents were first, clutching birdseed Dad had supplied from his job at the discount pet store. Mom had spent the winter editing her journals into a devotional for publication with a Christian publishing house. She was encouraging Lil to get started on her cookbook.

"Why are we waiting, Fletch? Are you getting cold feet?"

Fletch smiled at his adorable bride. "Not on your life. It's not that I don't want to get to the limo or start our new life together, but did you notice that long row of Landis men?"

"I'll protect you," she teased, grabbing up her gown's hem in readiness. "Anyway, you might as well get used to it."

"You're right about that." Fletch loosened his necktie. "Ready. Set. Go!"

Laughing, they ran through the line, spitting birdseed and making it without incident to the limo. The driver opened the door and waited until they were inside. Fletch wanted to steal another kiss, but Lil was waving madly at their family and friends.

The chauffer started the engine. When he did, the car came alive. Really alive! Turn signals blinked, lights glared, window wipers swished, and the radio blared. Every accessory had been turned on.

They burst into laughter as the chauffer struggled to get everything back in order.

"How did they manage that?" Fletch asked.

"I saw Hank talking to the driver."

"Ah, the diversion tactic."

As the limo eased into the street and left the church behind, they relaxed into the plush seating.

Lil squeezed his hand. "That was amazing."

"You're amazing. I have a gift for you." Fletch leaned forward and reached under the seat. He placed the gift box on her satin skirt.

She bit her bottom lip. "But I don't have anything for you."

He touched those lips. "Oh, but you do, and I can't wait to—"

She gave him a playful shove. "Shush. The driver might hear us."

"He can't. The sliding window is closed."

She gingerly untied the ribbons. The box had a lid, and she removed it. "For me?" Grinning, she pulled out a pair of red tennis shoes, almost a perfect match for the ones he owned. Those had become a commonplace sight in the Landis mudroom over the past couple of months. "I love them!" Then she noticed what he had attached to one of the shoestrings. "What's this?"

Fletch helped her remove it then held the golden circle between his fingers. "It's your wedding band." He knew that Conservative Mennonites didn't wear rings. Some people in the church they now attended did. He watched her eyes soften. "You don't have to wear it, but I wanted you to have one. I didn't want to offend anyone who might be attending the wedding."

"That's so thoughtful."

"I hope it's not too plain." He searched her expression hopefully.

"How could it be plain? When it belongs to you?"

THREE BEAN SALAD

¾ cup red wine vinegar
¾ cup sugar
¾ cup vegetable oil
Dash dry mustard
½ teaspoon dried tarragon
1½ teaspoons dried cilantro
1 (16 ounce) can green beans, drained
1 (16 ounce) can garbanzo beans, drained
1 (16 ounce) can kidney beans, rinsed and drained
1 red onion, diced
1 red bell pepper, chopped

In small saucepan or microwave heat vinegar, sugar, oil, and seasonings until sugar dissolves. Pour over remaining ingredients. Stir and chill.

LIL'S SUMMER CHILI

1 pound ground pork
1 onion, diced
1 green bell pepper, chopped
2 teaspoons chili powder
2 cloves garlic, pressed
1 teaspoon pepper
5 cups diced tomatoes
2 (16 ounce) cans kidney beans (or any other kind)
½ cup water
¼ cup chopped cilantro
1 cup corn

Brown pork, onion, and pepper together. Drain off fat. Mix in all other ingredients and simmer for at least a half hour. May serve cold.

Zucchini Relish

10 cups chopped, unpeeled zucchini
4 cups chopped onions
5 tablespoons salt
2¼ cups cider vinegar
5 cups sugar
½ teaspoon pepper

2 teaspoons celery seed
¾ tablespoon nutmeg
¾ tablespoon turmeric
1 tablespoon dry mustard
1 tablespoon cornstarch
1 green bell pepper, chopped
1 red bell pepper, chopped

Mix together zucchini, onions, and salt, and let stand overnight. Rinse and drain.

Place vinegar and sugar in large pot. Stir in pepper, celery seed, nutmeg, turmeric, dry mustard, and cornstarch. Bring to boil. Remove from heat and add drained zucchini mixture and peppers. Return to heat and simmer, uncovered, stirring occasionally for 30 minutes. Pour into canning jars. Cover with lids and rings according to manufacturer's instructions. Process in hot water bath according to recommendations of local extension service.

Chocolate Zucchini Cake

2 cups flour
1 cup sugar
¾ cup unsweetened cocoa powder
2 teaspoons baking soda
1 teaspoon baking powder
½ teaspoon salt
1 teaspoon cinnamon

4 eggs
¾ cup vegetable oil
¾ cup applesauce
3 cups grated zucchini
½ cup walnuts, chopped
½ cup chocolate chips

Preheat oven to 350 degrees. Grease and flour a 9 x 13 oblong pan.

In large bowl, mix together dry ingredients. Stir in eggs, oil, and applesauce. Mix well. Fold in zucchini, walnuts, and chocolate chips. Pour into baking pan. Bake 50 to 60 minutes. Frost with favorite frosting or dust with powdered sugar.

Veal and Spinach Ravioli

1½ pounds veal
1 onion, diced
3 cloves garlic
2 tablespoons butter
1 teaspoon salt
½ teaspoon pepper
1 cup dry white wine (ginger ale can be substituted)
1½ cups beef broth
6 ounces Parmesan cheese, grated
2 eggs
4 ounces fresh spinach, chopped
40 pasta squares
1 egg white

Grind veal, onion, and garlic. Brown in butter. Add seasonings and wine. Sauté until dry. Add beef broth and simmer until dry. Cool. Add Parmesan, eggs, and spinach. Mix well. Coat pasta squares with egg white, fill and fold. Seal. Boil ravioli for 7 minutes. Serve with Lil's special sauce.

Lil's Special Sauce

½ cup mushrooms
6 tablespoons butter
4 cloves garlic, pressed
1 cup grated Parmesan cheese
1 teaspoon basil
2 cups heavy cream or to taste

Sauté mushrooms in butter. Add garlic, cheese, and basil. Blend until heated. Stir in cream.

Herb Chart

Basil: Meat, pesto, salads, soups, stews, tomato dishes
Bay leaves: Meats, sauces, soups, stews, vegetables
Borage: Salads
Catnip: Tea
Chervil: Fish, salads, sauces, soups, stuffing
Chives: Appetizers, cream soups, eggs, garnish, salads
Coriander: Confections, salads, Asian foods
Dill: Bread, fish, salads, sauces, vegetables
Marjoram: Fish, poultry, soups, stews, stuffing, vegetables
Mint: Beverages, desserts, fish, sauces, soups
Oregano: Fish, Italian dishes, meats, sauces, soups, vegetables
Parsley: Garnishes, sauces, soups, stews
Rosemary: Casseroles, fish, salads, soups, vegetables
Sage: Fish, meat, poultry, soups, stuffing
Savory: Poultry, meat, salads, sauces, soups, stuffing, vegetables
Tarragon: Eggs, meats, poultry, salads, sauces, tomatoes
Thyme: Fish, meats, poultry, stews, stuffing, tomato dishes

About the Author

Dianne Christner enjoys the beauty of her desert surroundings in Phoenix, Arizona, where life sizzles when temperatures soar above 100 degrees. She and husband Jim have two married children and five grandchildren. Before writing, Dianne worked in office management, in admissions and as a teacher's assistant in a Christian school, and owned an exercise salon in Scottsdale, Arizona.

Her first book was published in 1994, and she now writes full-time. She has published several historical fiction titles and writes contemporary fiction based on her experience in the Mennonite church. Her husband was raised on a farm in Plain City, Ohio, in a Conservative Mennonite church. Dianne was raised in an urban Mennonite setting. They both have Amish ancestors and friends and family in various sects of the Mennonite church. Now Dianne and Jim attend a nondenominational church.

You may find information about her other books at www.diannechristner.net where she keeps a blog about the Mennonite lifestyle.